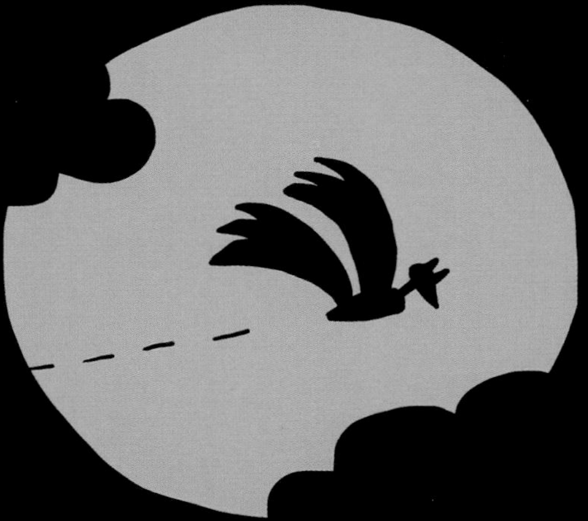

PUBLISHED BY TOP SHELF PRODUCTIONS, PO BOX 1282, MARIETTA, GA 30061-1282, USA. PUBLISHERS: BRETT WARNOCK AND CHRIS STAROS.

CHECK US OUT ONLINE AT:

TOPSHELFCOMIX.COM AND JESS-SMILEY.COM

1. CHILDREN'S BOOKS 2. VAMPIRES/HALLOWEEN
3. GRAPHIC NOVELS ISBN: 978-1-60309-88-9

FIRST PRINTING, OCTOBER 2012. PRINTED IN CHINA.

FOR MIKELLE,
NOAH and EVELYN

UPSIDE DOWN
A VAMPIRE TALE

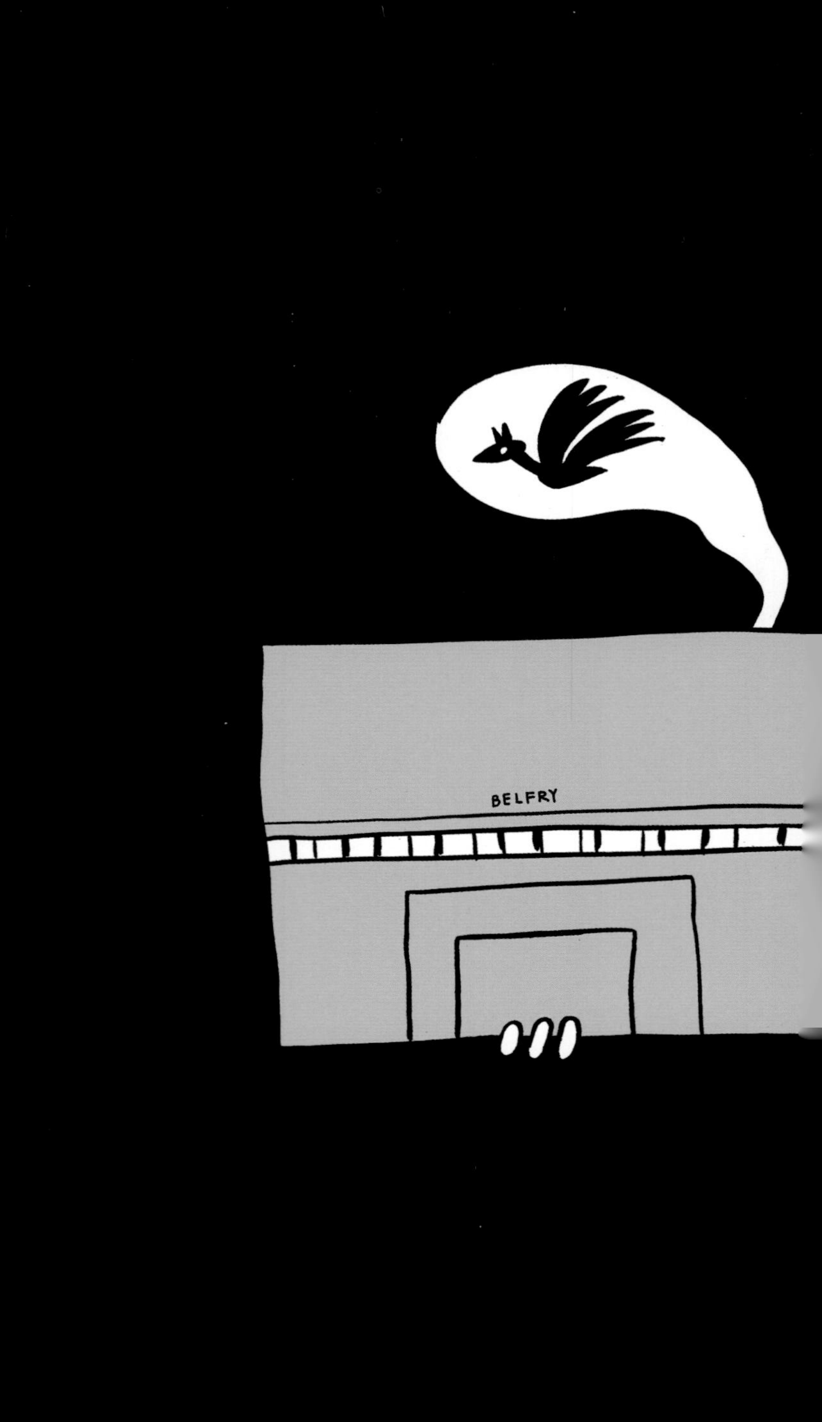
BELFRY

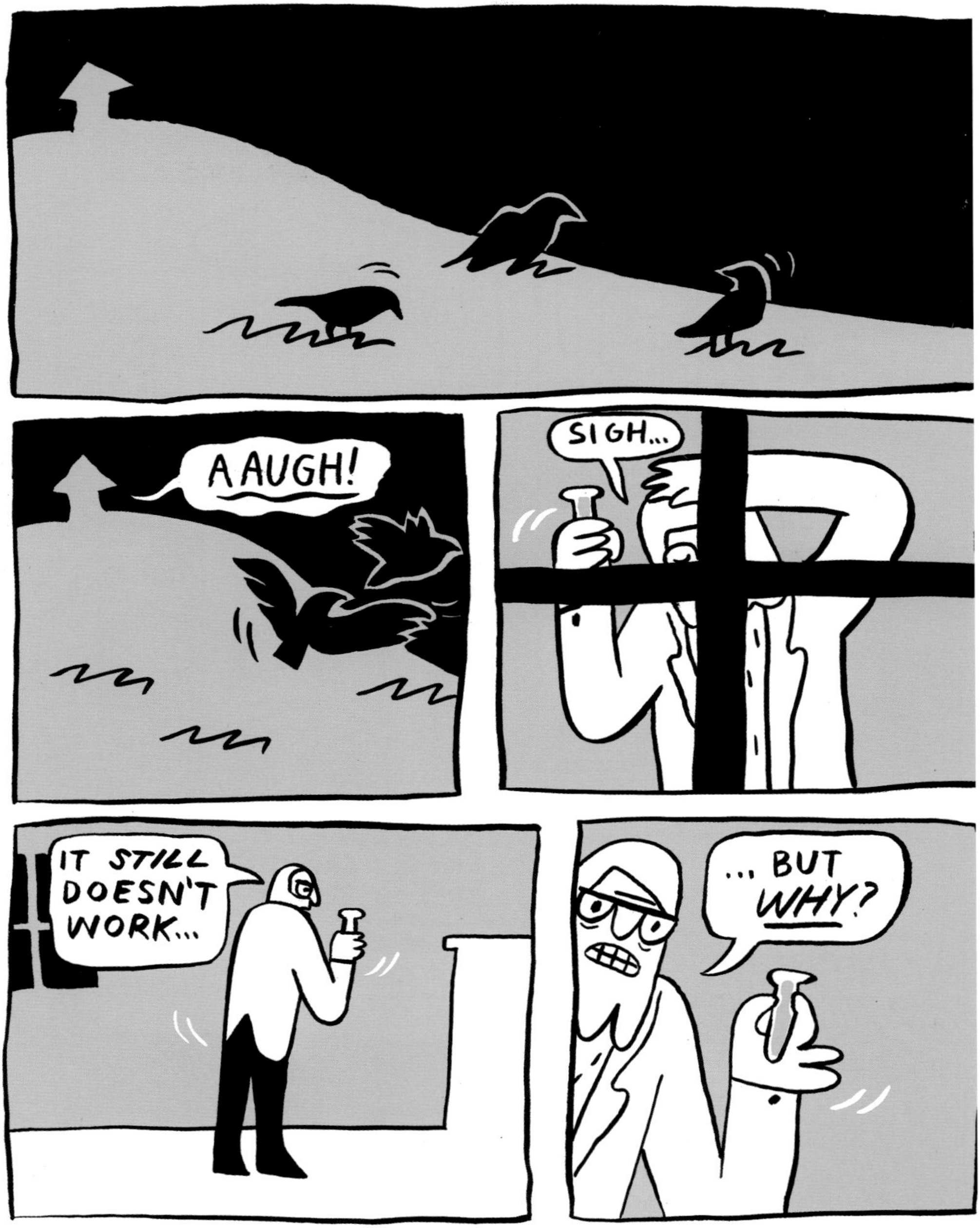
AAUGH!
SIGH...
IT STILL DOESN'T WORK...
... BUT WHY?

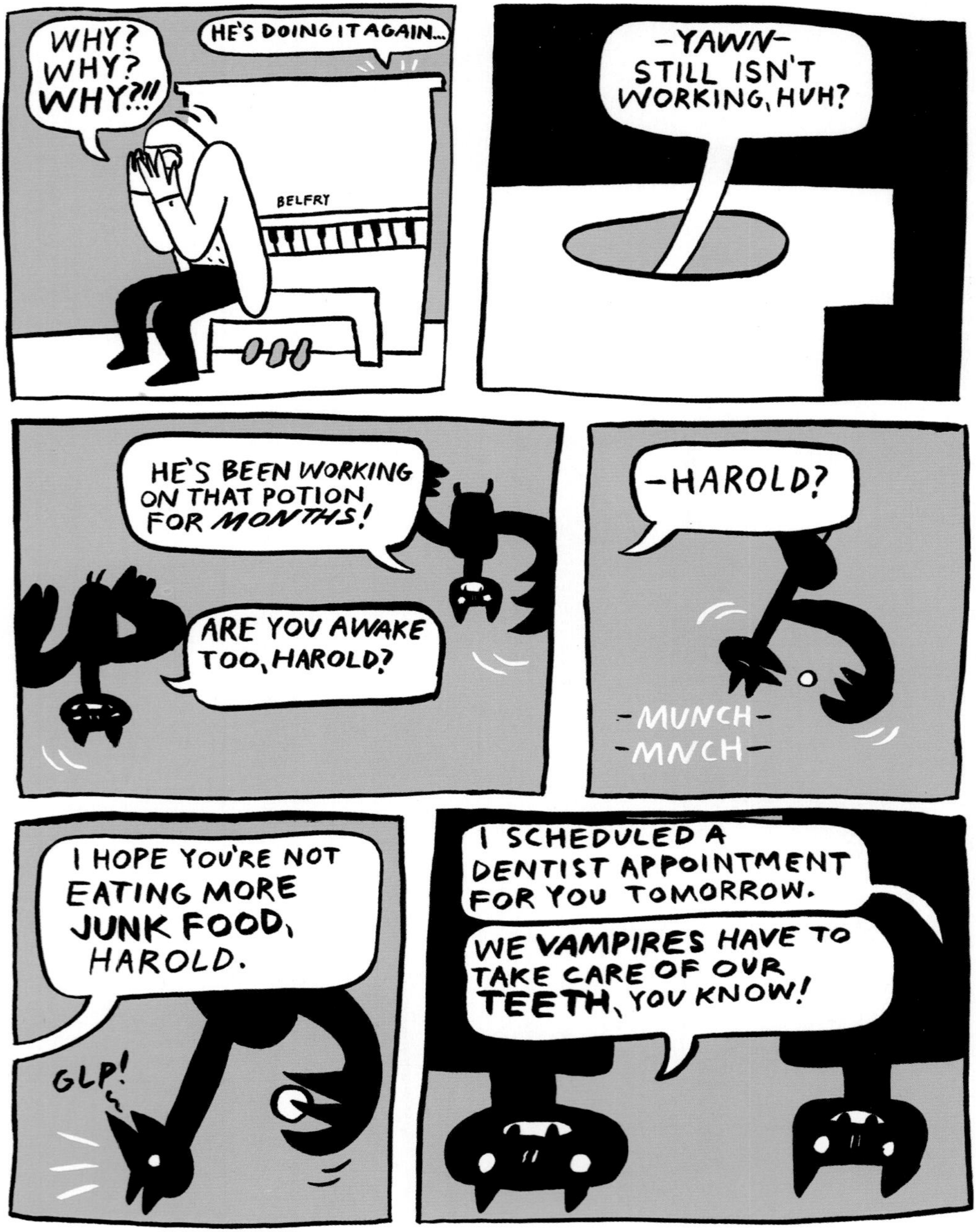
WHY? WHY? WHY?!!
HE'S DOING IT AGAIN...
BELFRY
-YAWN- STILL ISN'T WORKING, HUH?
HE'S BEEN WORKING ON THAT POTION FOR MONTHS!
ARE YOU AWAKE TOO, HAROLD?
-HAROLD?
-MUNCH-
-MNCH-
I HOPE YOU'RE NOT EATING MORE JUNK FOOD, HAROLD.
GLP!
I SCHEDULED A DENTIST APPOINTMENT FOR YOU TOMORROW.
WE VAMPIRES HAVE TO TAKE CARE OF OUR TEETH, YOU KNOW!

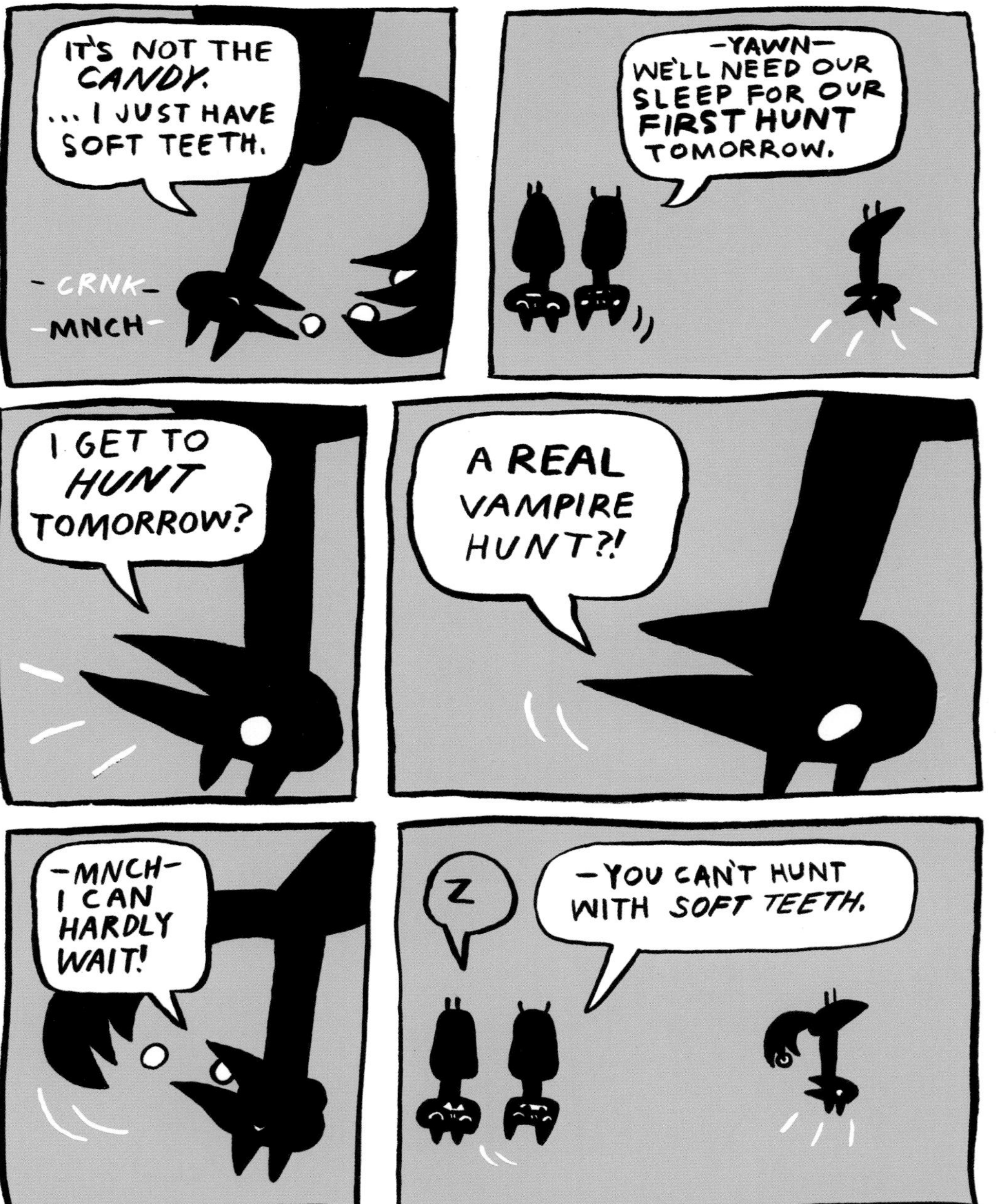
IT'S NOT THE CANDY.
... I JUST HAVE SOFT TEETH.
-CRNK-
-MNCH-
-YAWN- WE'LL NEED OUR SLEEP FOR OUR FIRST HUNT TOMORROW.
I GET TO HUNT TOMORROW?
A REAL VAMPIRE HUNT?!
-MNCH- I CAN HARDLY WAIT!
Z
-YOU CAN'T HUNT WITH SOFT TEETH.

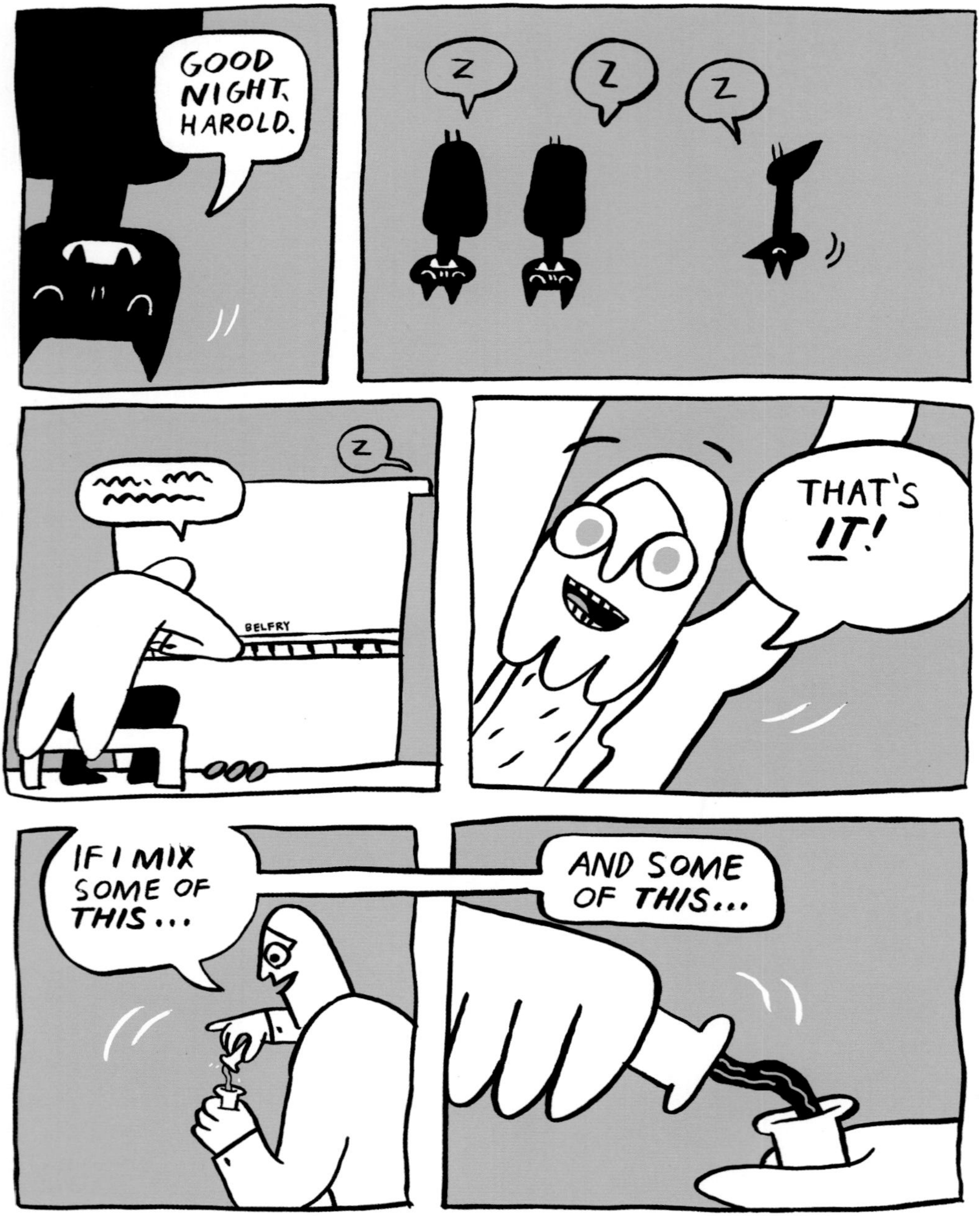
GOOD NIGHT, HAROLD.
Z
Z
Z
Z
BELFRY
THAT'S IT!
IF I MIX SOME OF THIS...
AND SOME OF THIS...

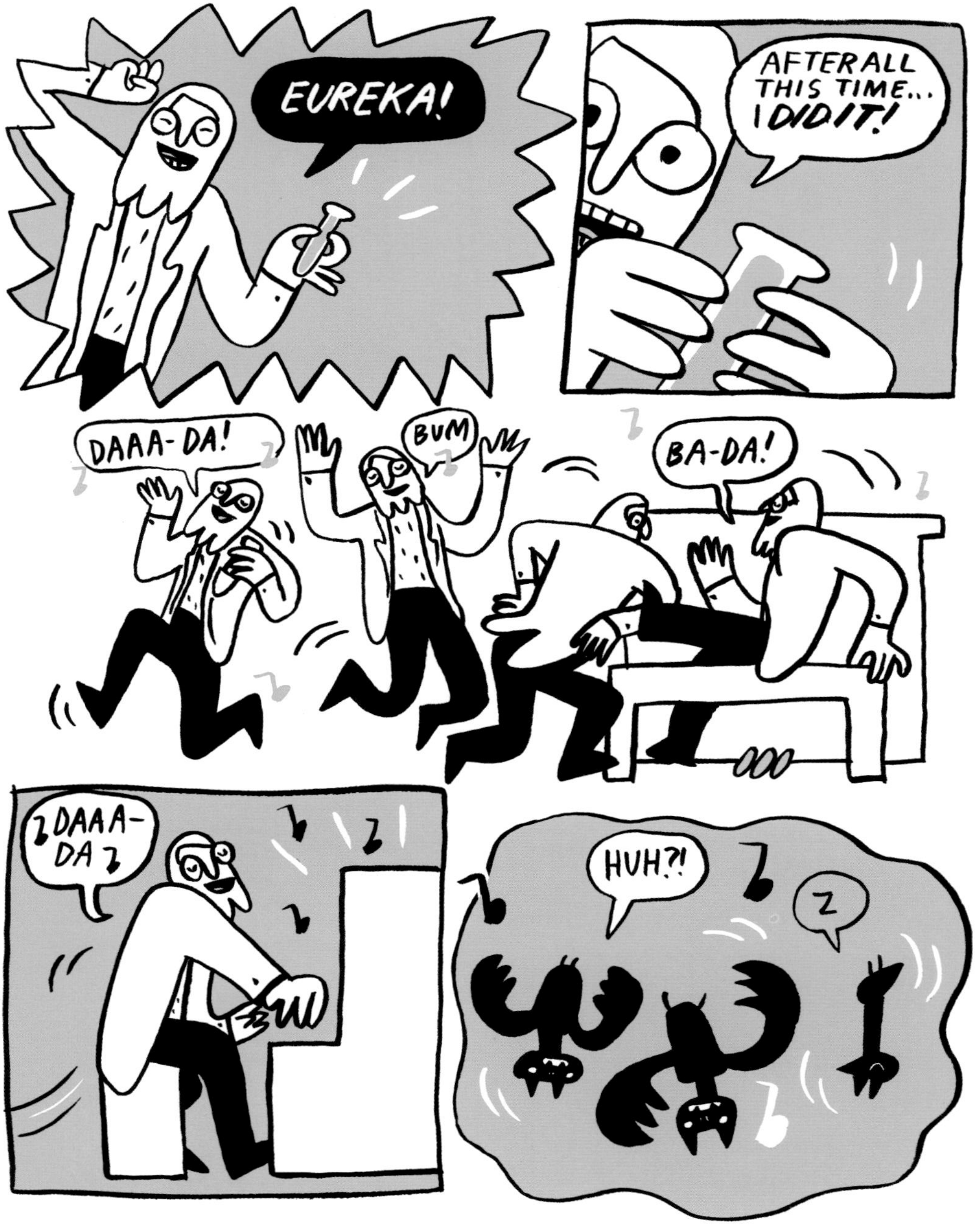
EUREKA!
AFTERALL THIS TIME... I DID IT!
DAAA-DA!
BUM
BA-DA!
DAAA-DA
HUH?!
Z

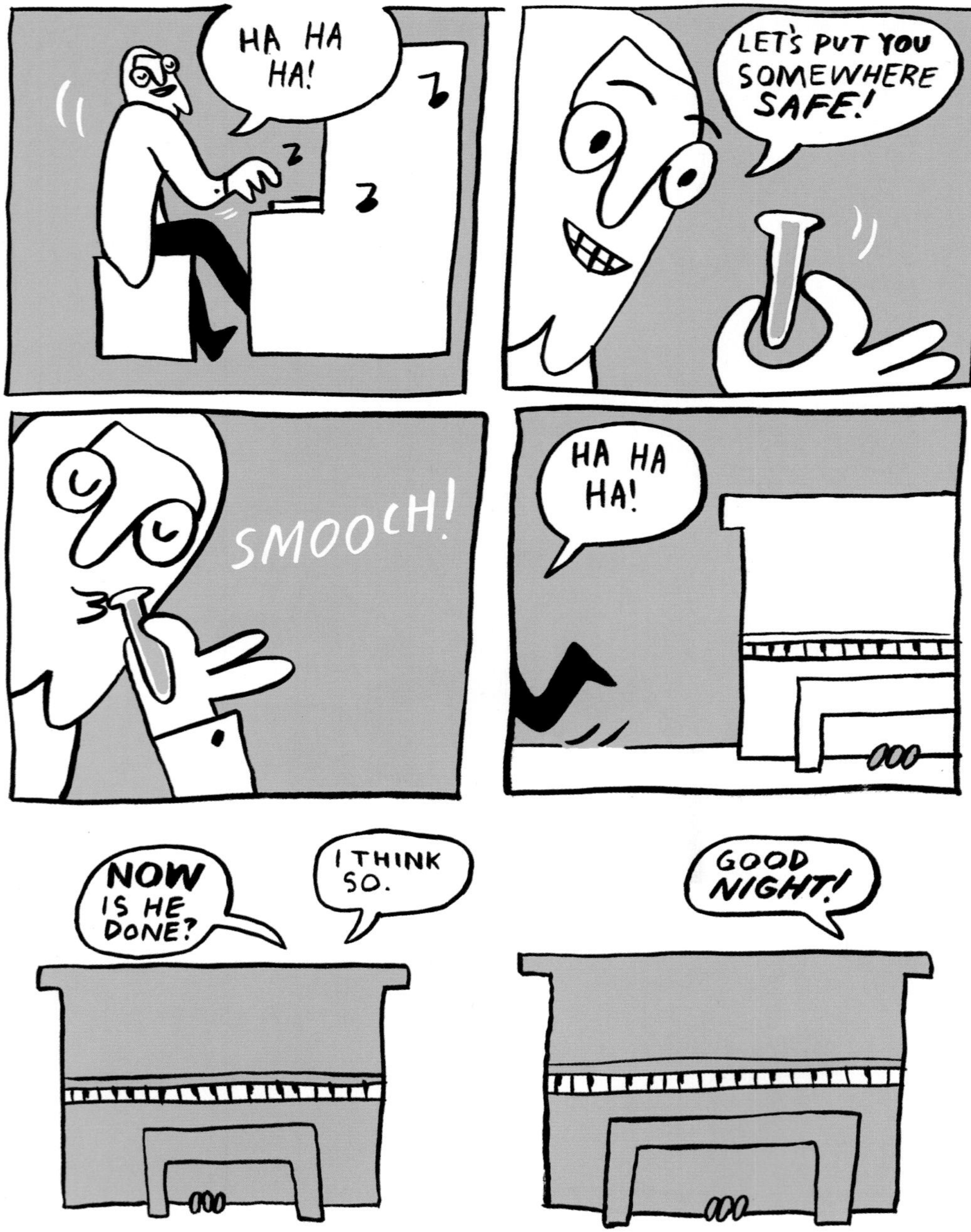
HA HA HA!
LET'S PUT YOU SOMEWHERE SAFE!
SMOOCH!
HA HA HA!
NOW IS HE DONE?
I THINK SO.
GOOD NIGHT!

UPSIDE DOWN

A VAMPIRE TALE

BY JESS SMART SMILEY

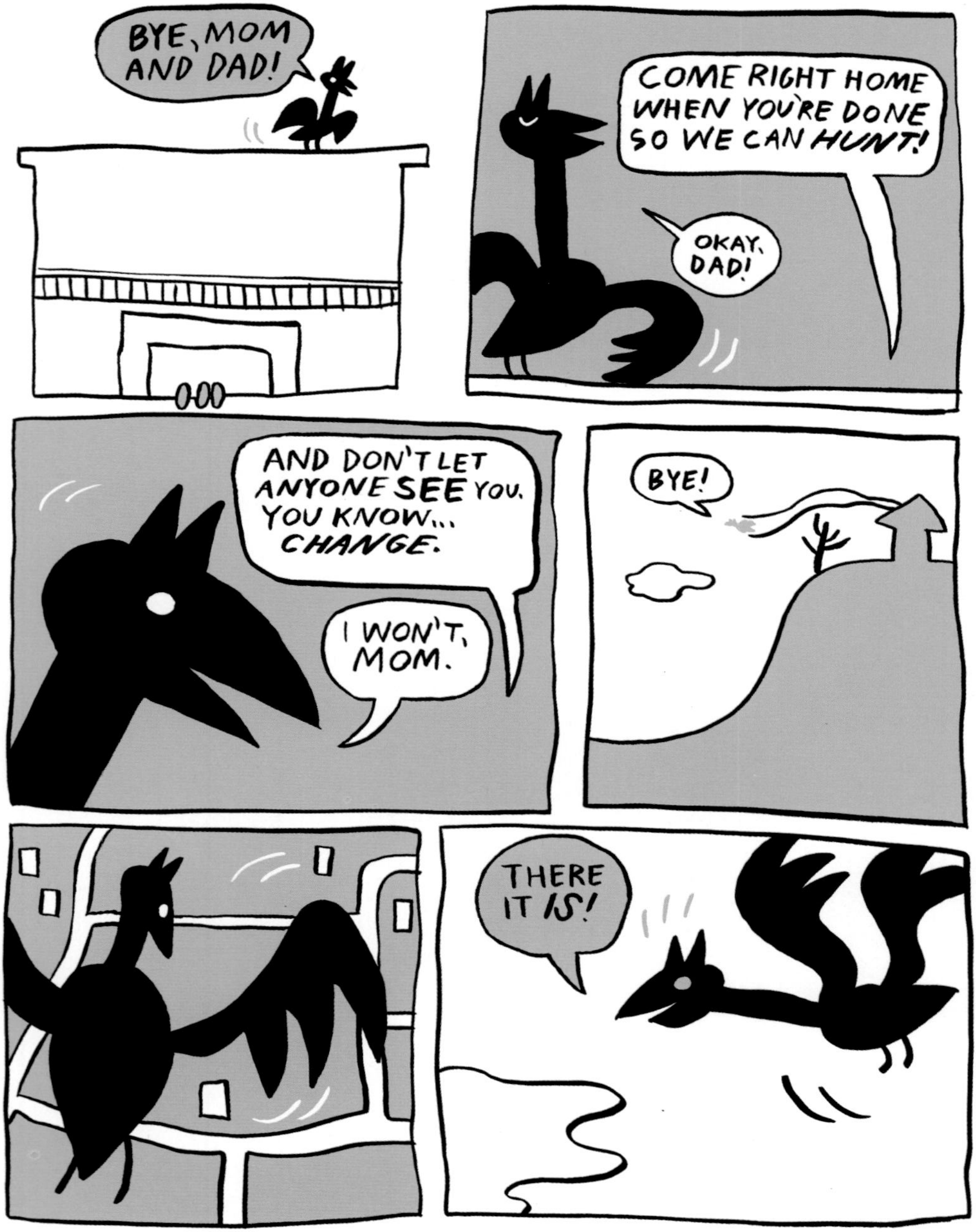
BYE, MOM AND DAD!
COME RIGHT HOME WHEN YOU'RE DONE SO WE CAN HUNT!
OKAY, DAD!
AND DON'T LET ANYONE SEE YOU. YOU KNOW... CHANGE.
I WON'T, MOM.
BYE!
THERE IT IS!

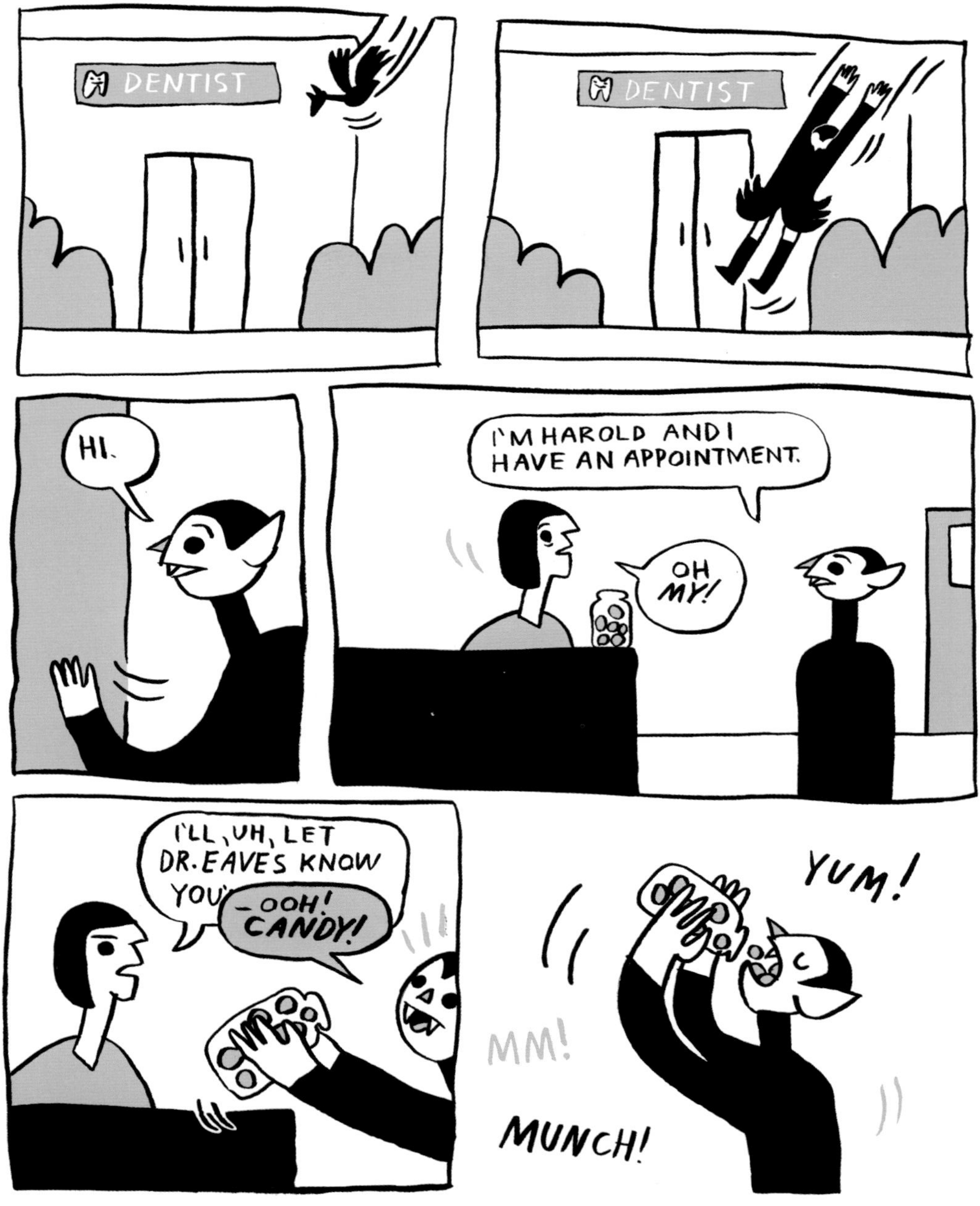
DENTIST
DENTIST
HI.
I'M HAROLD AND I HAVE AN APPOINTMENT.
OH MY!
I'LL, UH, LET DR. EAVES KNOW YOU'
–OOH! CANDY!
YUM!
MM!
MUNCH!

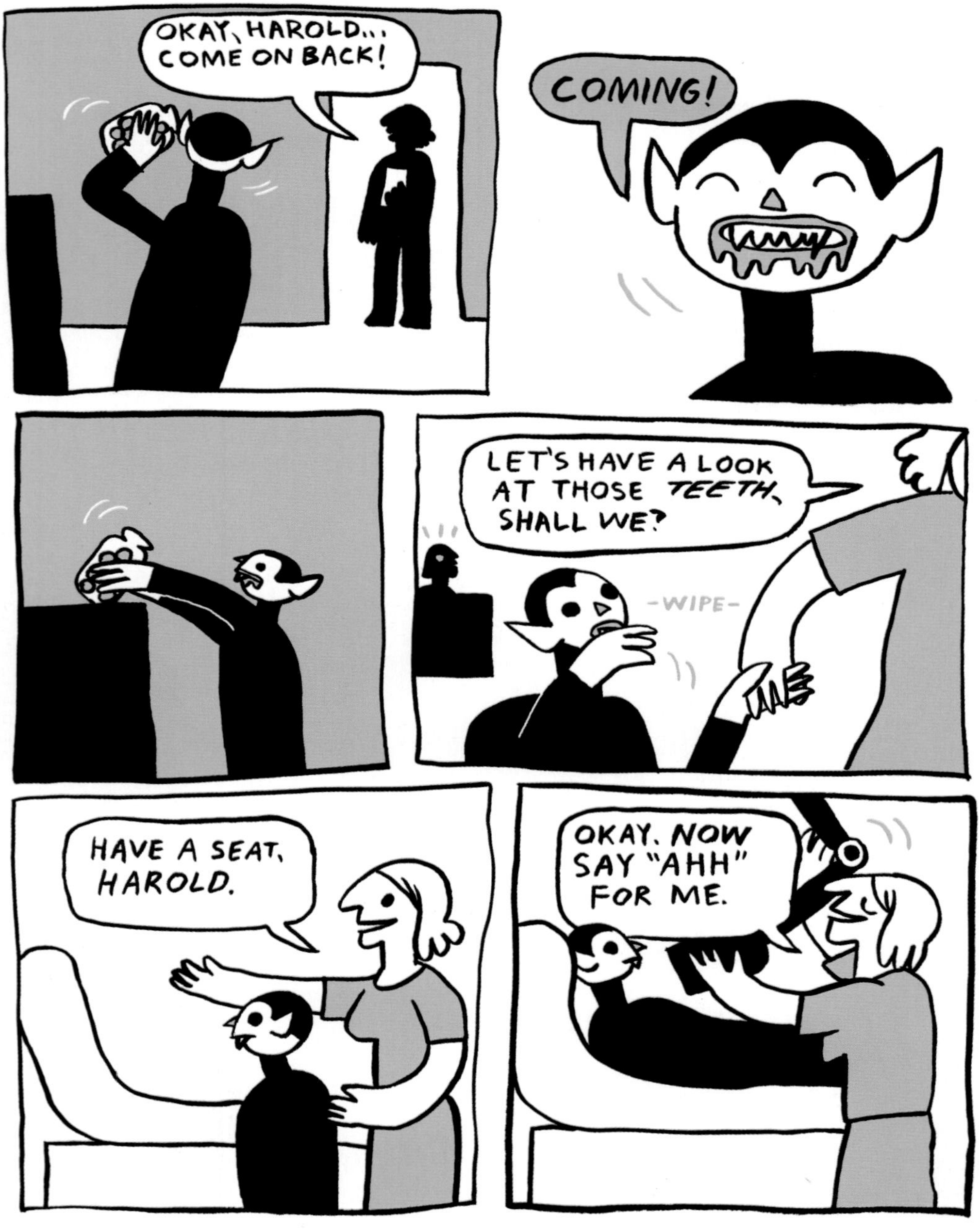
OKAY, HAROLD...
COME ON BACK!
COMING!
LET'S HAVE A LOOK AT THOSE *TEETH*, SHALL WE?
-WIPE-
HAVE A SEAT, HAROLD.
OKAY. *NOW* SAY "AHH" FOR ME.

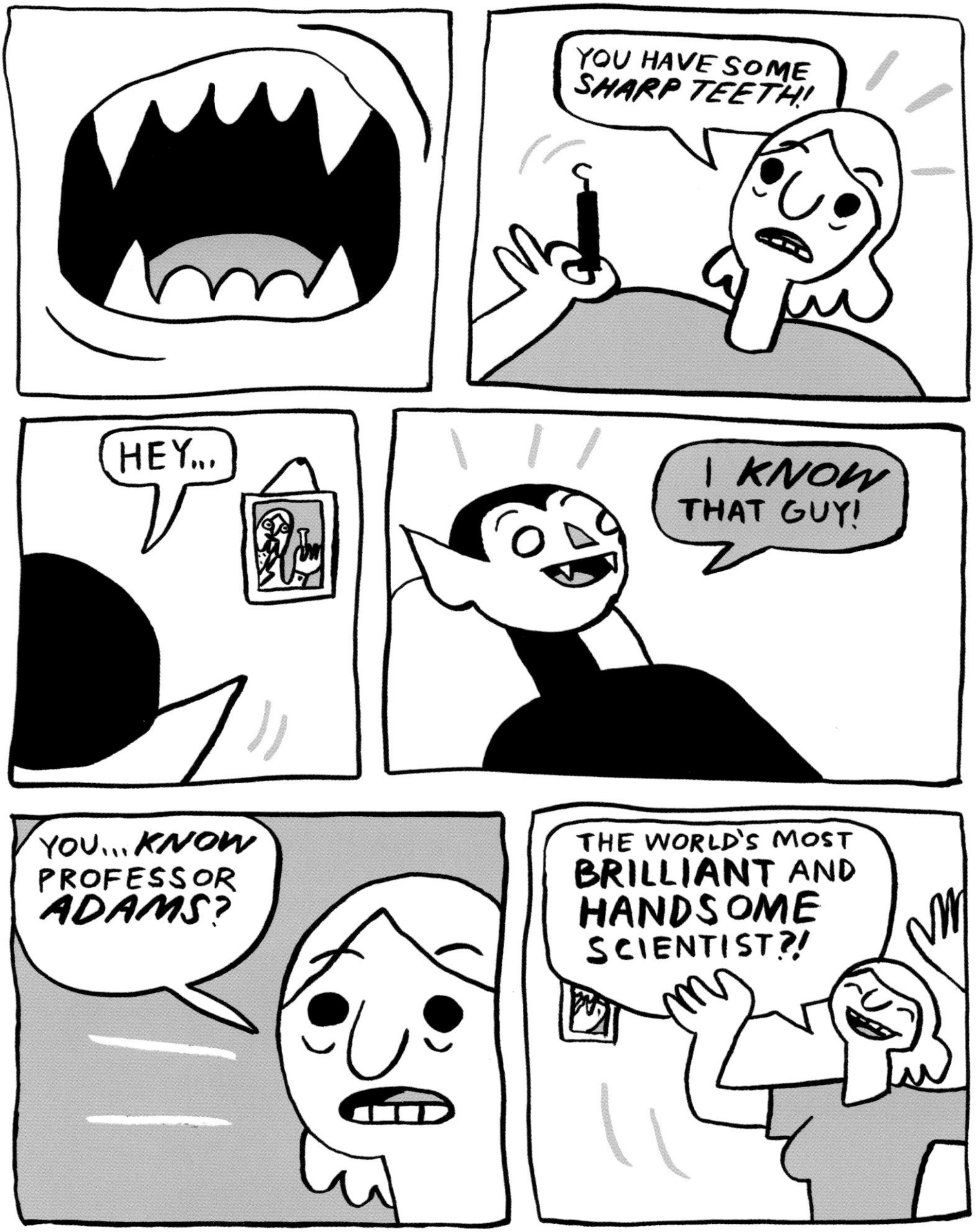
YOU HAVE SOME SHARP TEETH!
HEY...
I KNOW THAT GUY!
YOU... KNOW PROFESSOR ADAMS?
THE WORLD'S MOST BRILLIANT AND HANDSOME SCIENTIST?!

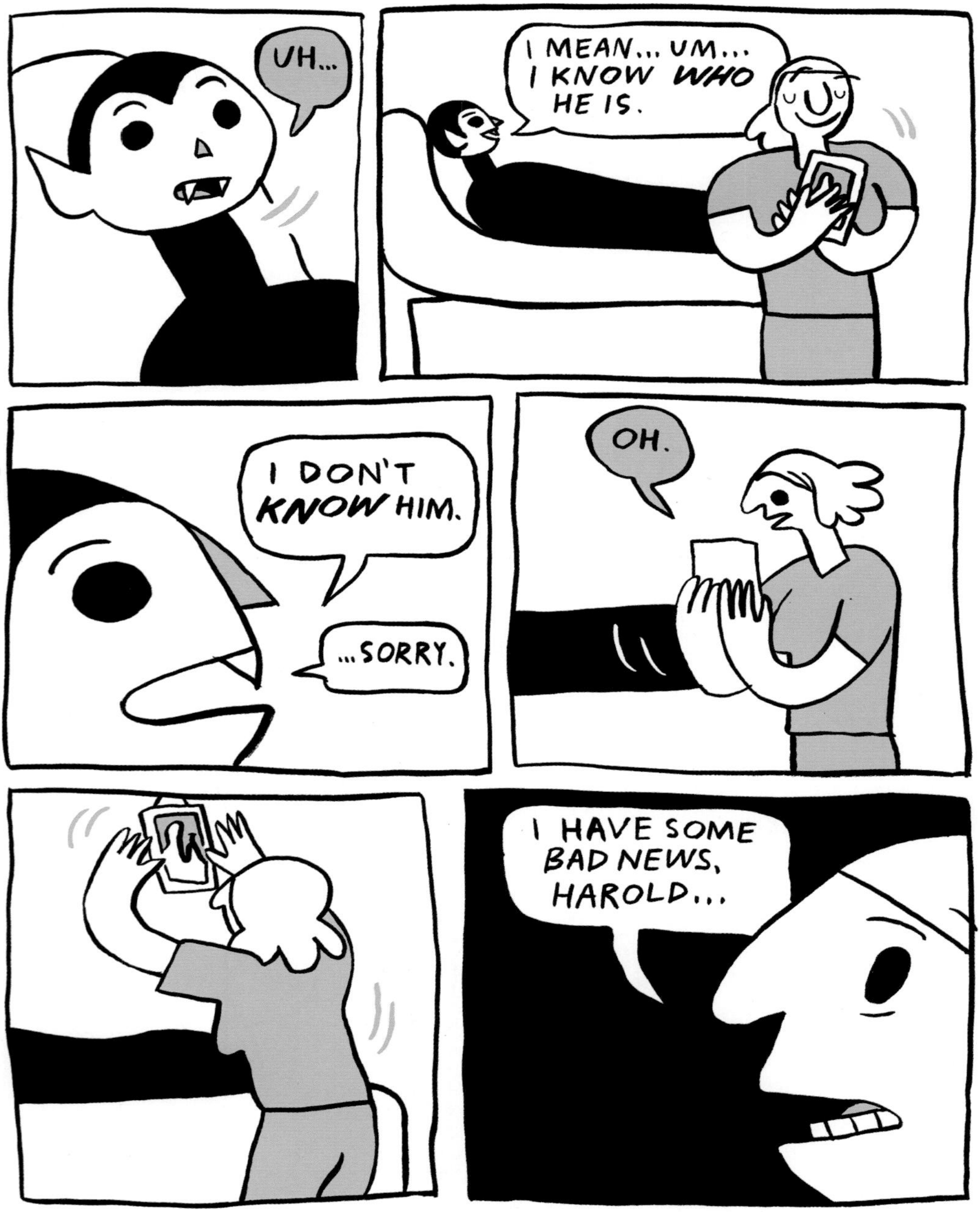
UH...
I MEAN... UM... I KNOW WHO HE IS.
I DON'T KNOW HIM.
...SORRY.
OH.
I HAVE SOME BAD NEWS, HAROLD...

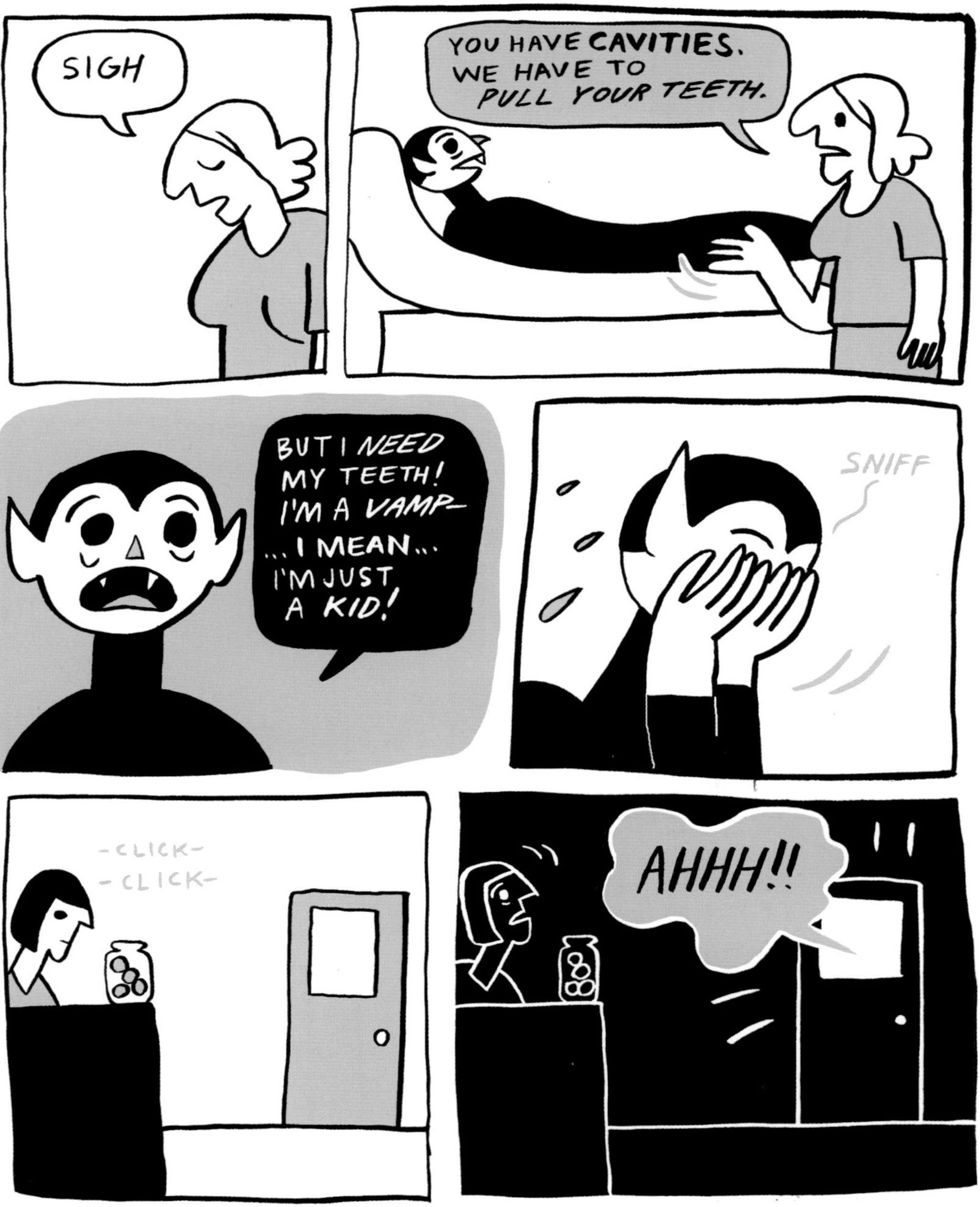
SIGH
YOU HAVE CAVITIES. WE HAVE TO PULL YOUR TEETH.
BUT I NEED MY TEETH! I'M A VAMP- ...I MEAN... I'M JUST A KID!
SNIFF
-CLICK-
-CLICK-
AHHH!!

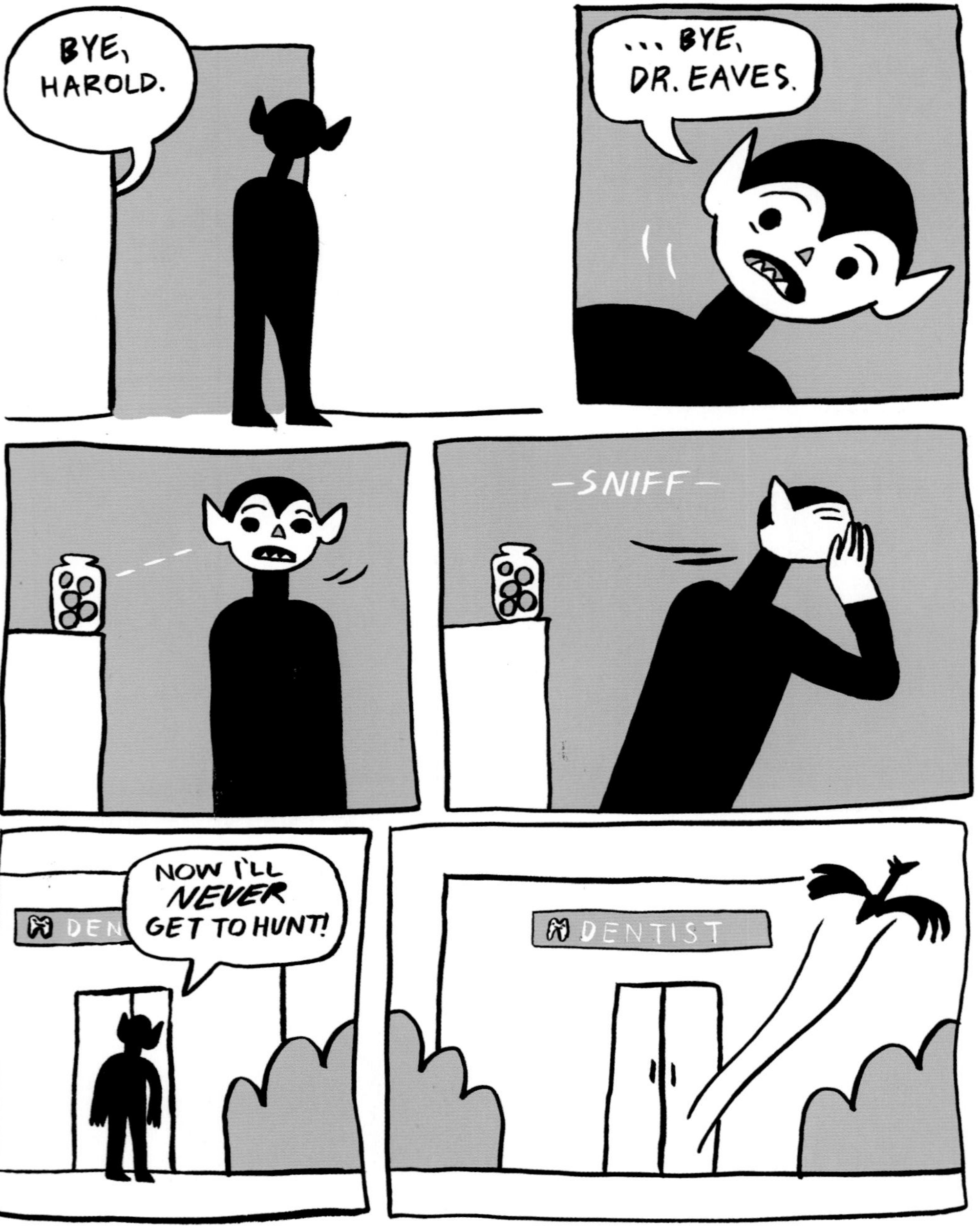
BYE, HAROLD.
... BYE, DR. EAVES.
-SNIFF-
DENTIST
NOW I'LL NEVER GET TO HUNT!
DENTIST

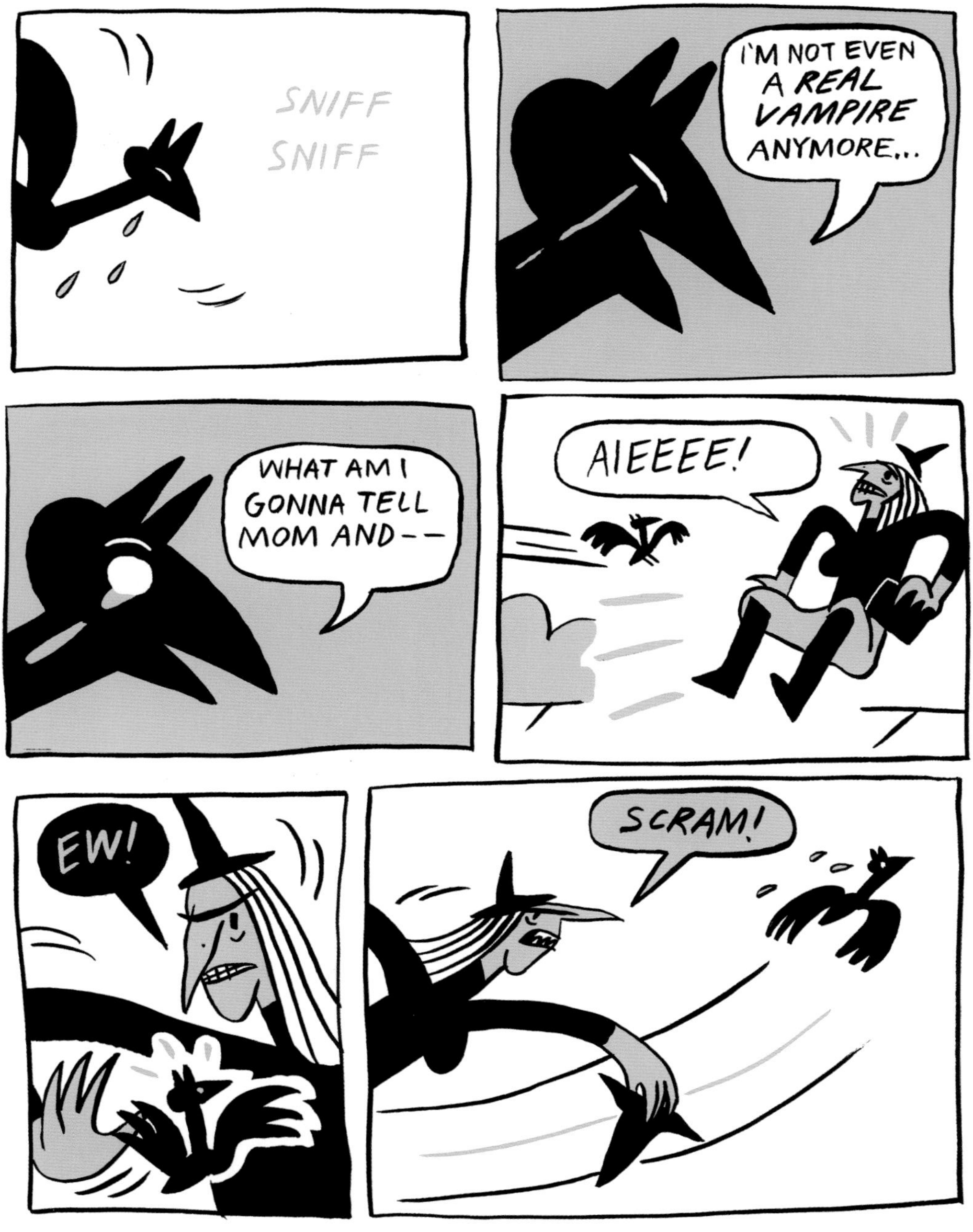
SNIFF
SNIFF
I'M NOT EVEN A REAL VAMPIRE ANYMORE...
WHAT AM I GONNA TELL MOM AND--
AIEEEE!
EW!
SCRAM!

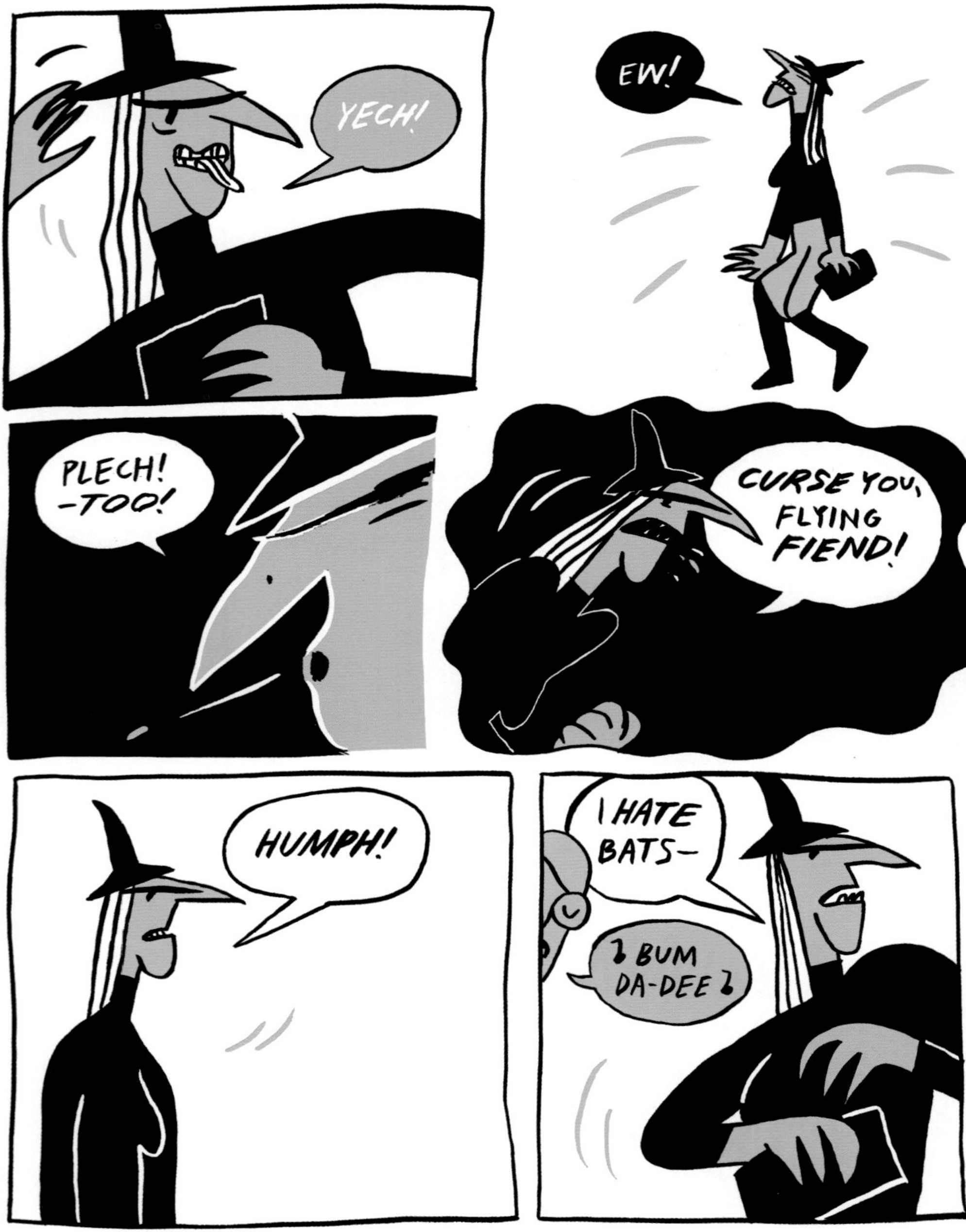
YECH!
EW!
PLECH! -TOO!
CURSE YOU, FLYING FIEND!
HUMPH!
I HATE BATS—
BUM DA-DEE

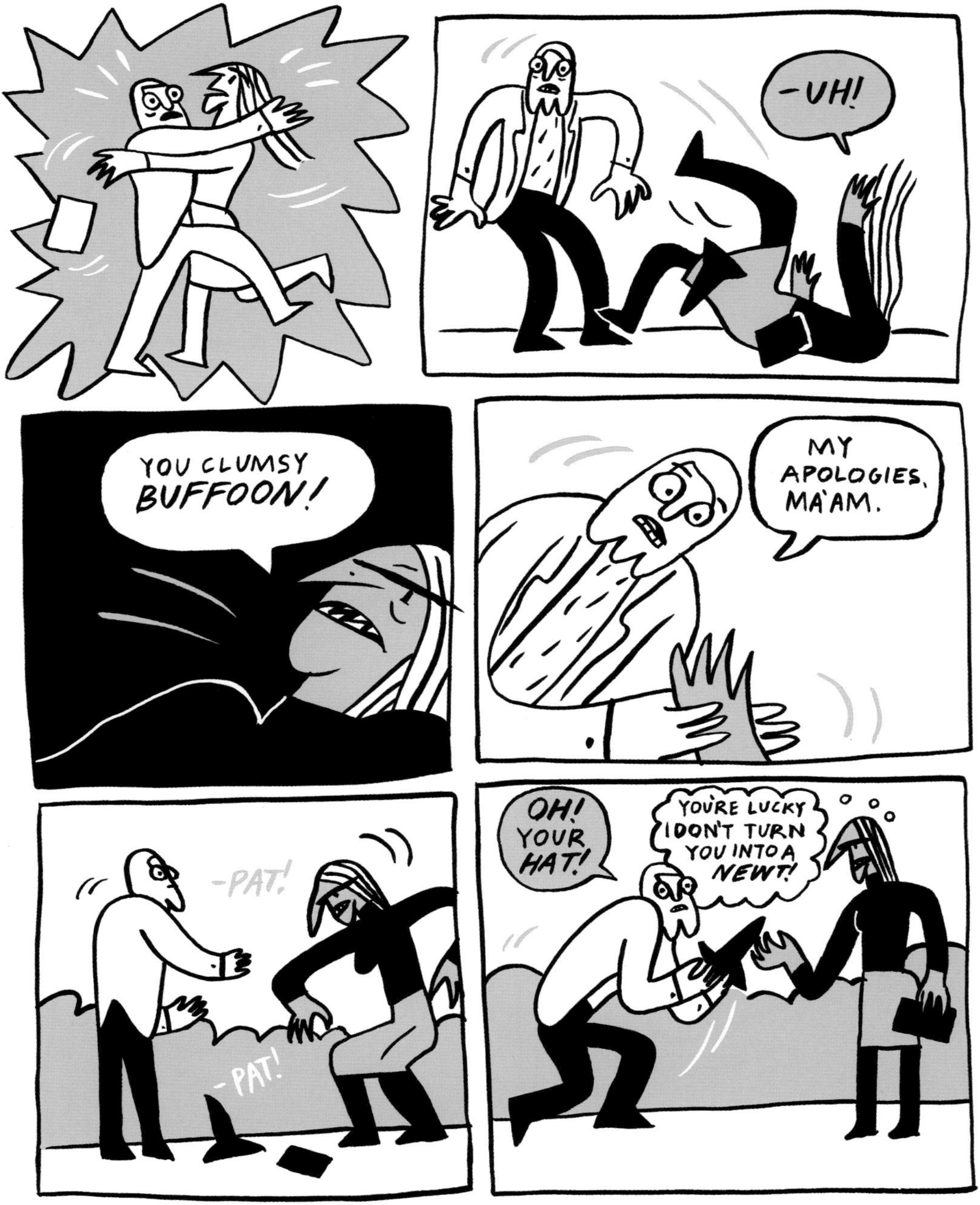
-UH!
YOU CLUMSY BUFFOON!
MY APOLOGIES, MA'AM.
-PAT!
-PAT!
OH! YOUR HAT!
YOU'RE LUCKY I DON'T TURN YOU INTO A NEWT!

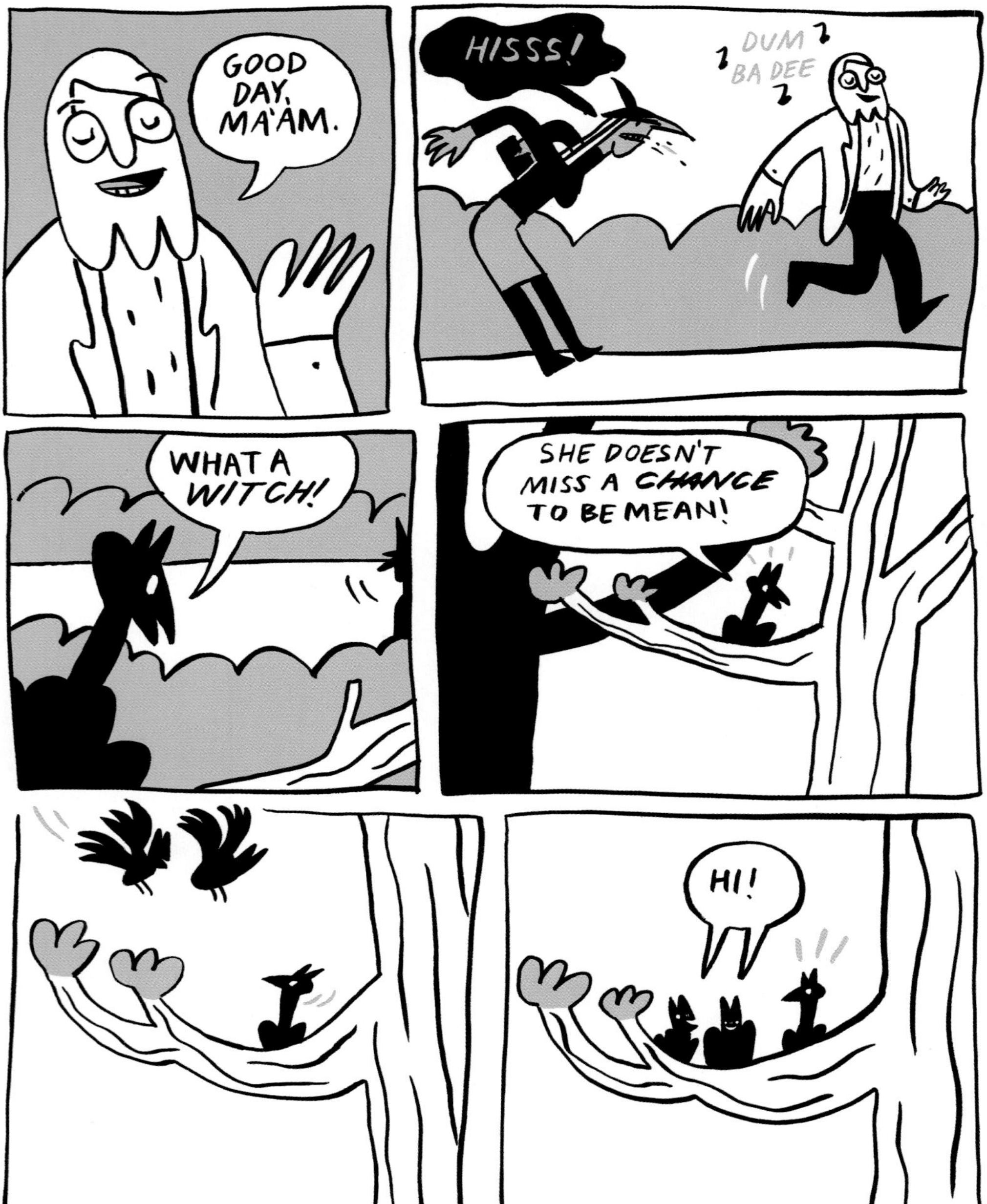
GOOD DAY, MA'AM.
HISSS!
DUM BA DEE
WHAT A WITCH!
SHE DOESN'T MISS A CHANCE TO BE MEAN!
HI!

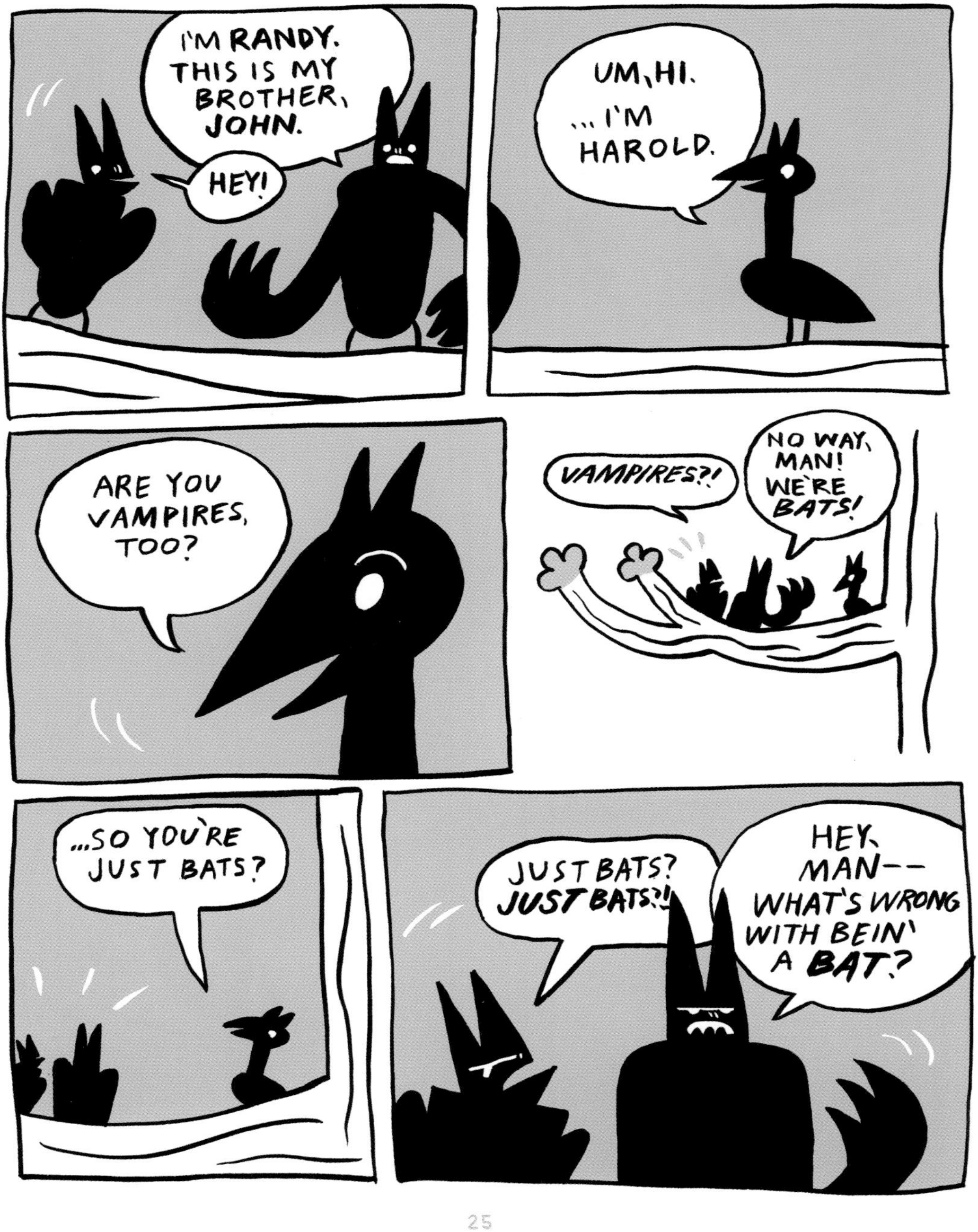
I'M RANDY. THIS IS MY BROTHER, JOHN.
HEY!
UM, HI. ...I'M HAROLD.
ARE YOU VAMPIRES, TOO?
VAMPIRES?!
NO WAY, MAN! WE'RE BATS!
...SO YOU'RE JUST BATS?
JUST BATS? JUST BATS?!
HEY, MAN-- WHAT'S WRONG WITH BEIN' A BAT?

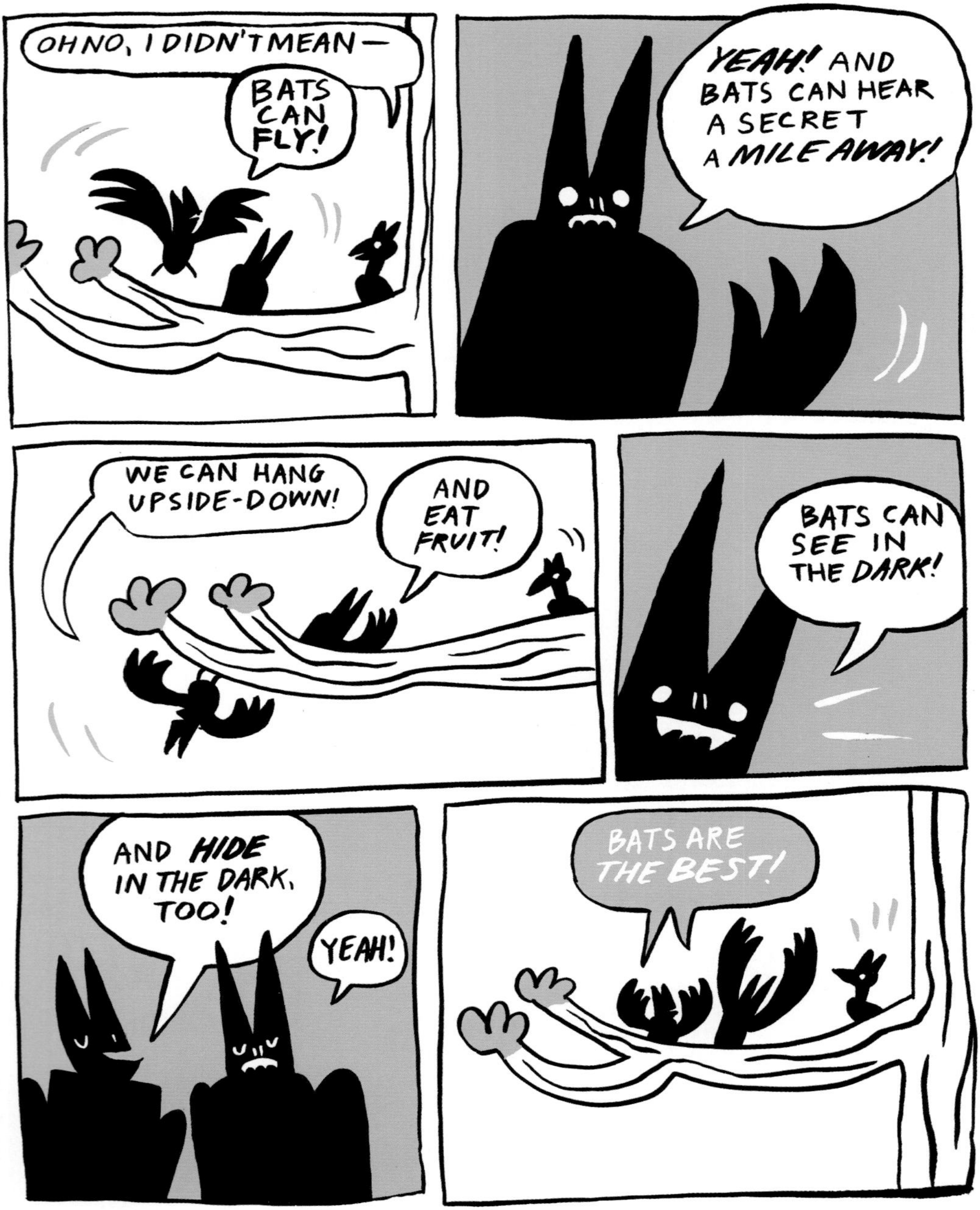
OH NO, I DIDN'T MEAN—
BATS CAN FLY!
YEAH! AND BATS CAN HEAR A SECRET A MILE AWAY!
WE CAN HANG UPSIDE-DOWN!
AND EAT FRUIT!
BATS CAN SEE IN THE DARK!
AND HIDE IN THE DARK, TOO!
YEAH!
BATS ARE THE BEST!

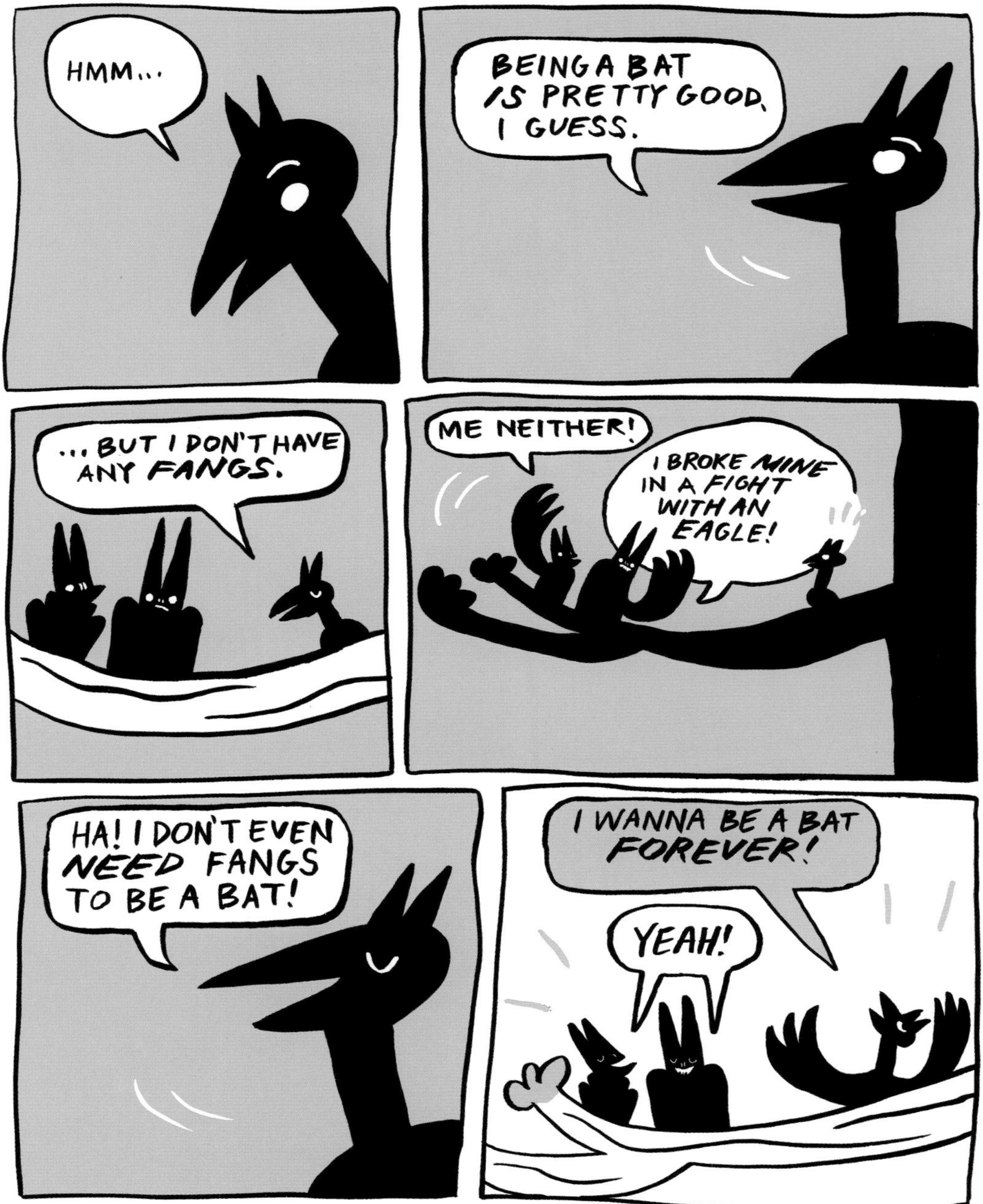
HMM...
BEING A BAT IS PRETTY GOOD, I GUESS.
... BUT I DON'T HAVE ANY FANGS.
ME NEITHER!
I BROKE MINE IN A FIGHT WITH AN EAGLE!
HA! I DON'T EVEN NEED FANGS TO BE A BAT!
I WANNA BE A BAT FOREVER!
YEAH!

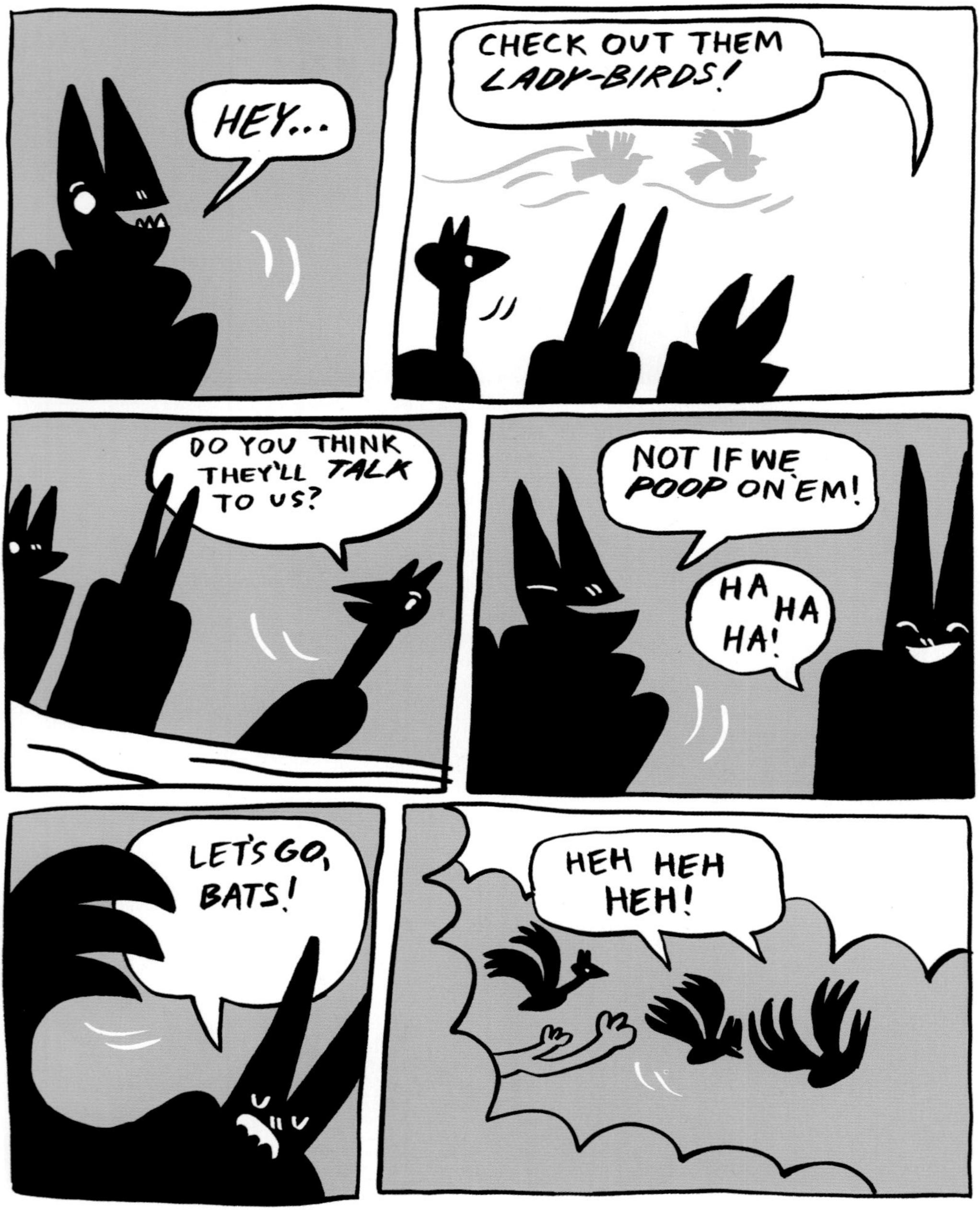
HEY...
CHECK OUT THEM LADY-BIRDS!
DO YOU THINK THEY'LL TALK TO US?
NOT IF WE POOP ON 'EM!
HA HA HA!
LET'S GO, BATS!
HEH HEH HEH!

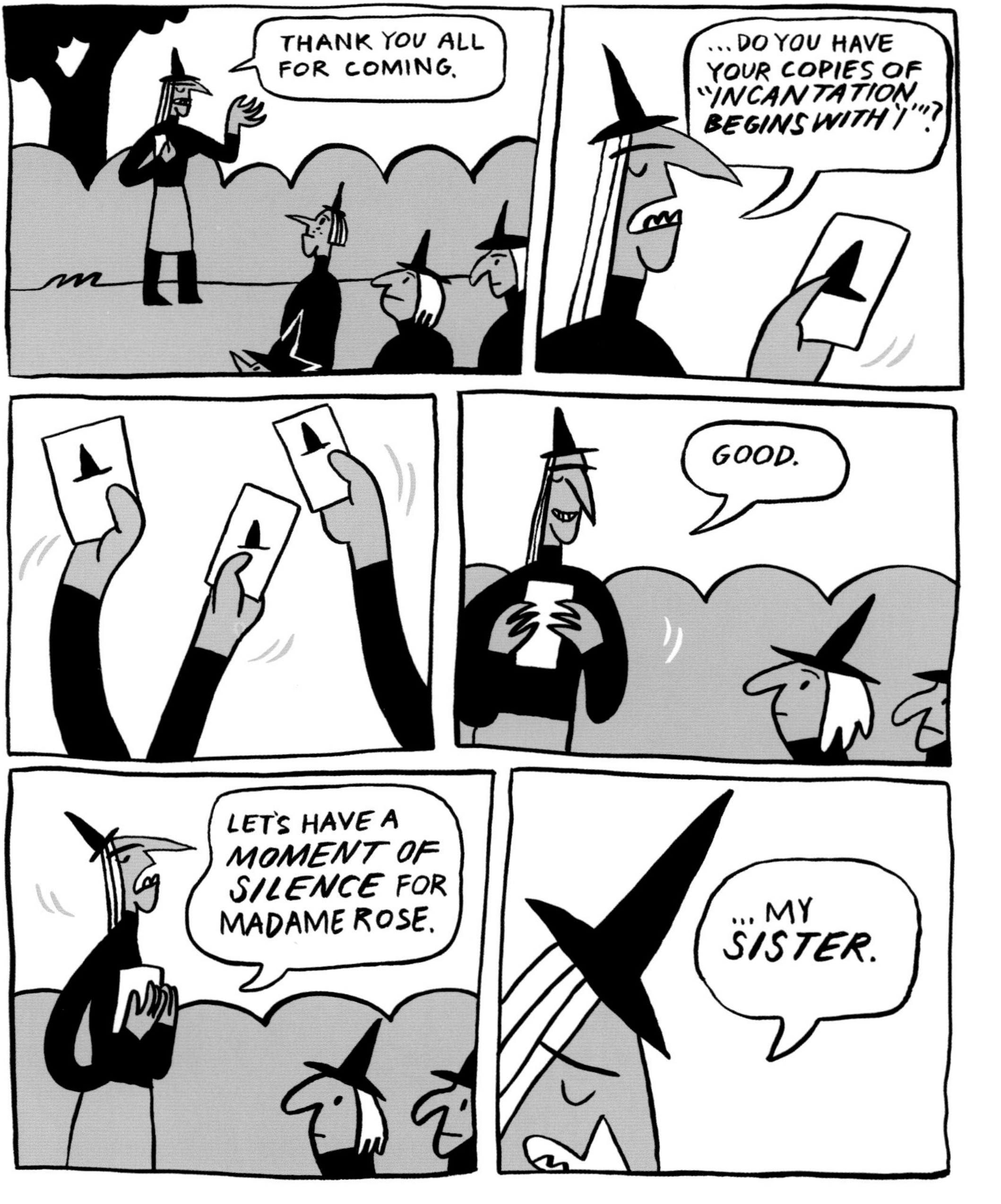
THANK YOU ALL FOR COMING.
...DO YOU HAVE YOUR COPIES OF "INCANTATION BEGINS WITH 'I'"?
GOOD.
LET'S HAVE A MOMENT OF SILENCE FOR MADAME ROSE.
...MY SISTER.

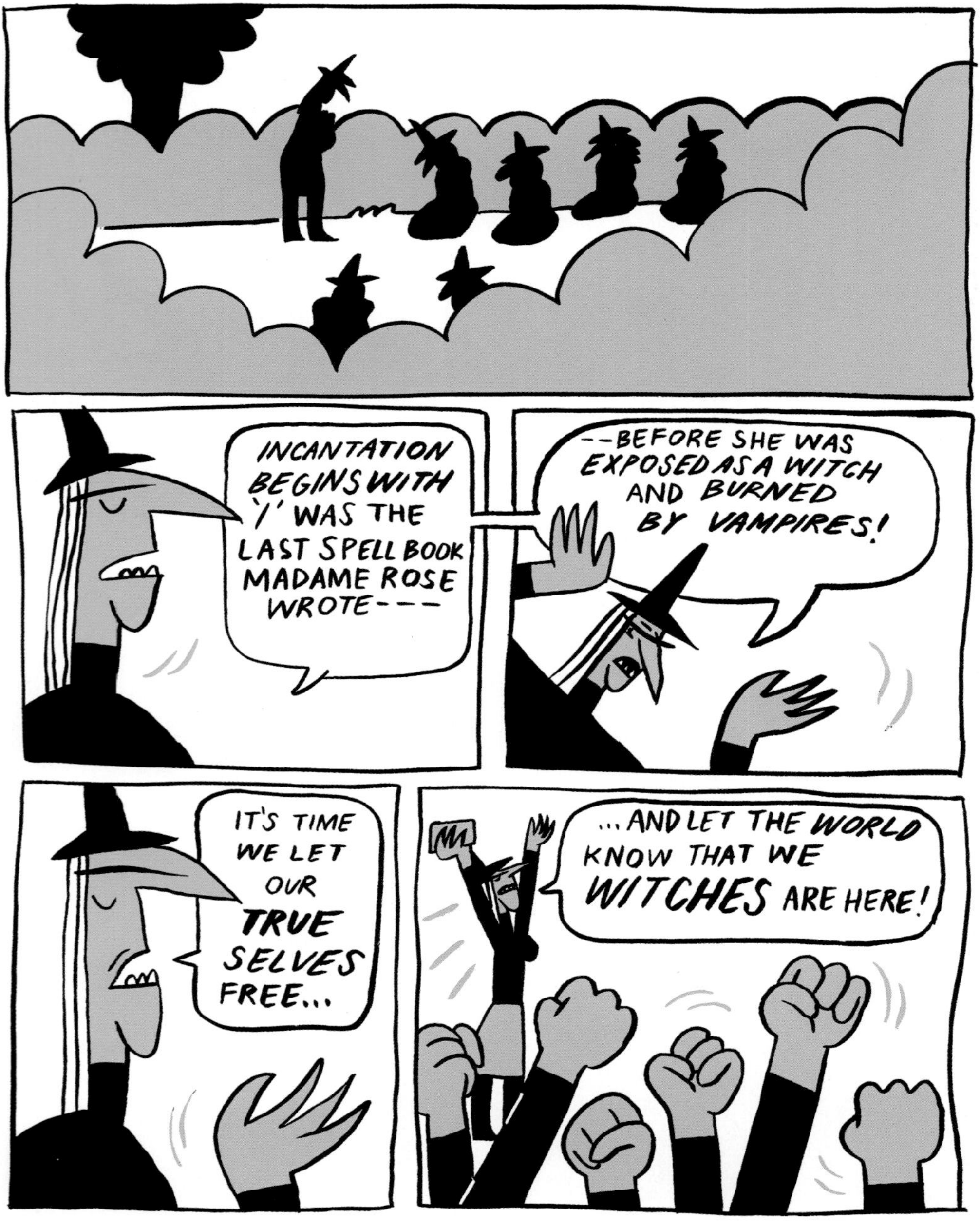
INCANTATION BEGINS WITH 'I' WAS THE LAST SPELL BOOK MADAME ROSE WROTE---
--BEFORE SHE WAS EXPOSED AS A WITCH AND BURNED BY VAMPIRES!
IT'S TIME WE LET OUR TRUE SELVES FREE...
...AND LET THE WORLD KNOW THAT WE WITCHES ARE HERE!

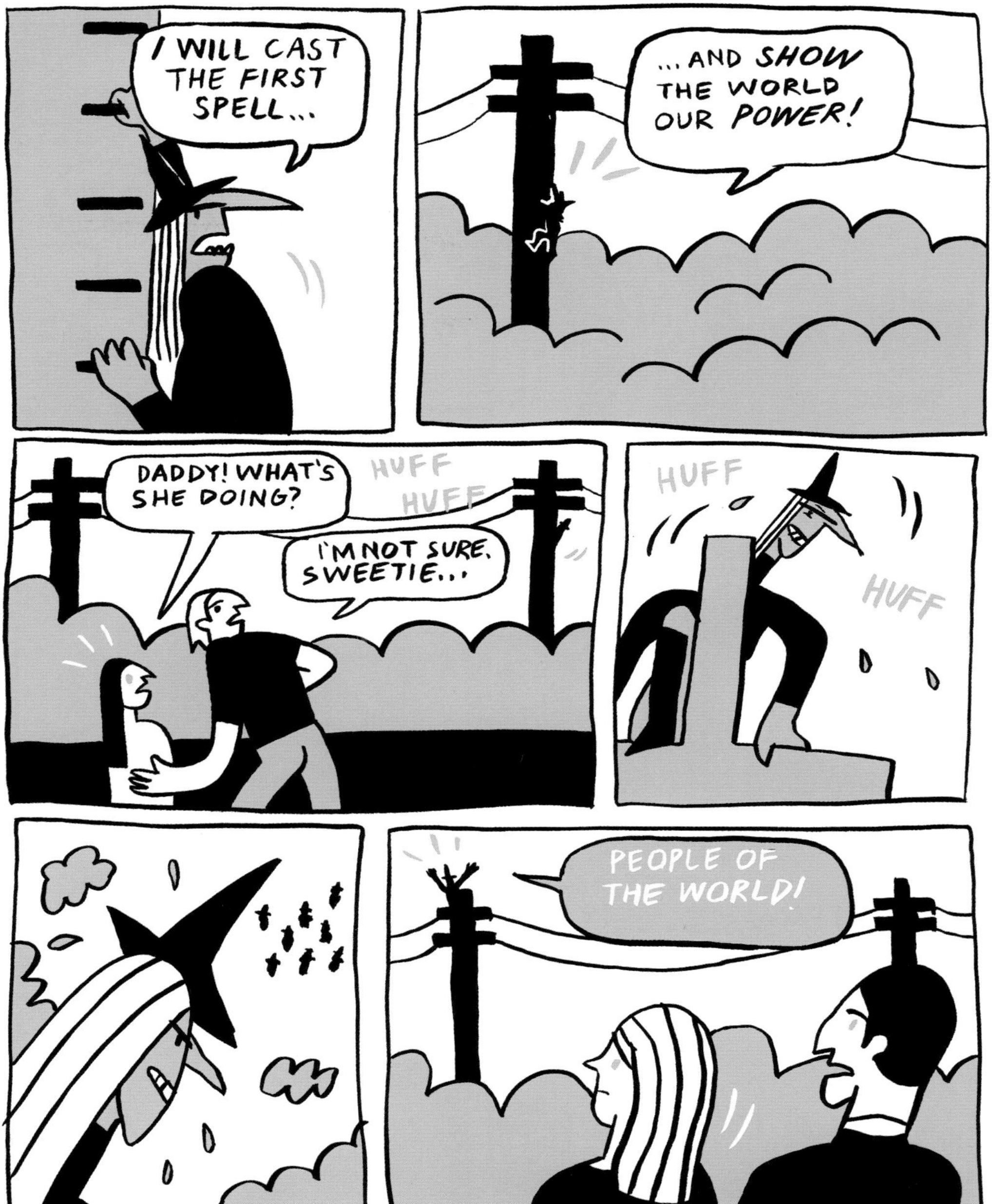
I WILL CAST THE FIRST SPELL...
...AND SHOW THE WORLD OUR POWER!
DADDY! WHAT'S SHE DOING?
HUFF HUFF
I'M NOT SURE, SWEETIE...
HUFF
HUFF
PEOPLE OF THE WORLD!

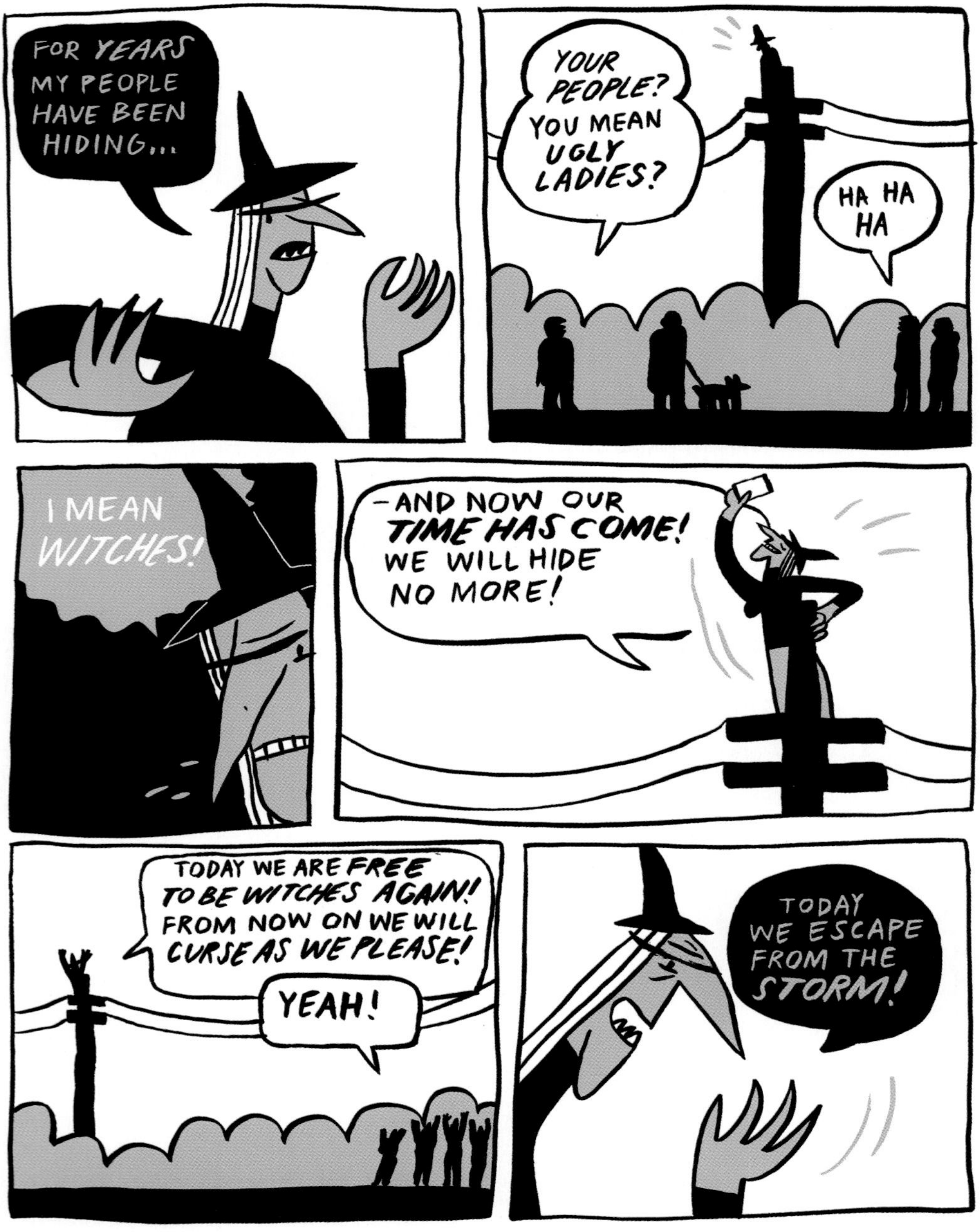
FOR YEARS MY PEOPLE HAVE BEEN HIDING...
YOUR PEOPLE? YOU MEAN UGLY LADIES?
HA HA HA
I MEAN WITCHES!
-AND NOW OUR TIME HAS COME! WE WILL HIDE NO MORE!
TODAY WE ARE FREE TO BE WITCHES AGAIN! FROM NOW ON WE WILL CURSE AS WE PLEASE!
YEAH!
TODAY WE ESCAPE FROM THE STORM!

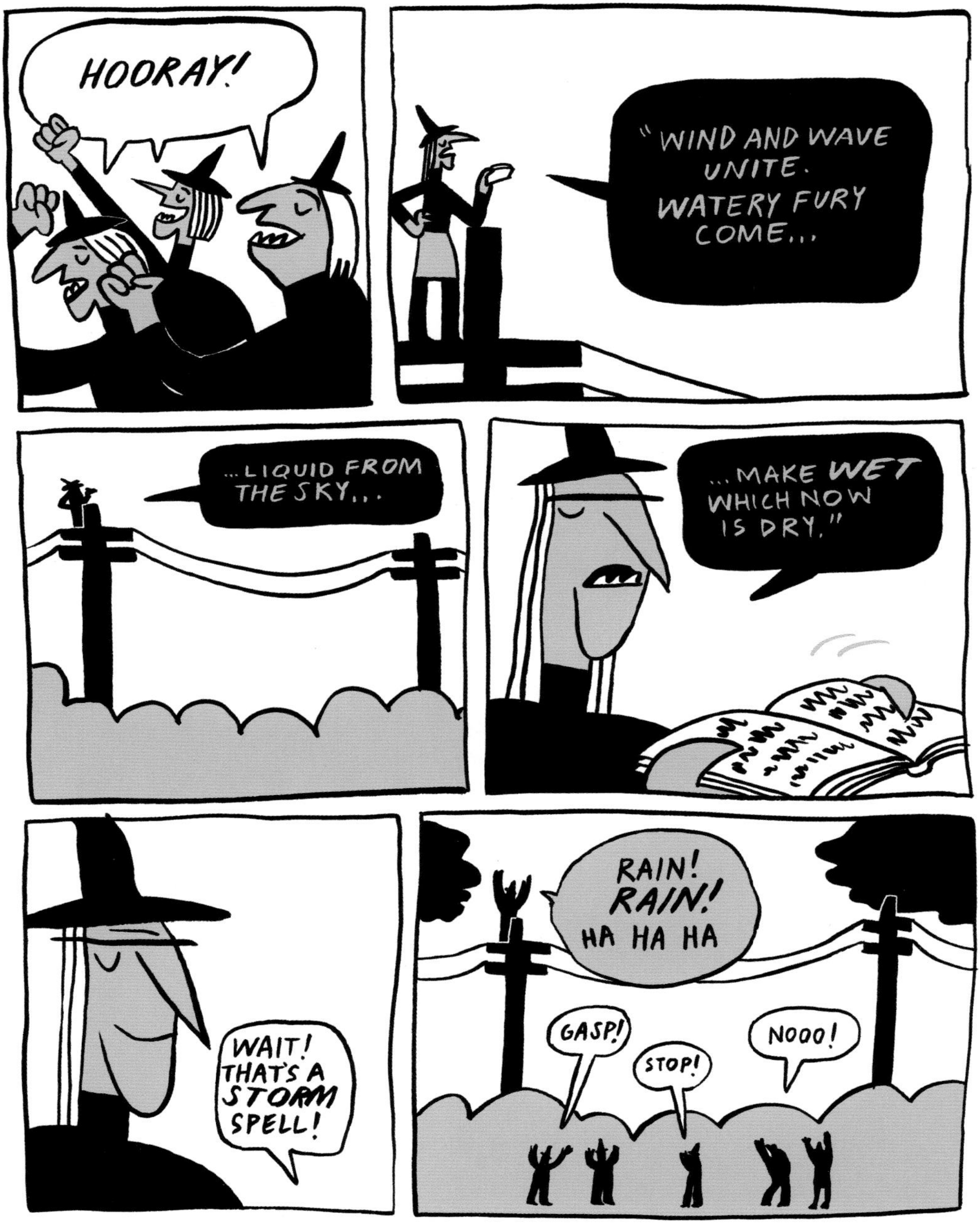
HOORAY!
"WIND AND WAVE UNITE. WATERY FURY COME...
...LIQUID FROM THE SKY...
...MAKE WET WHICH NOW IS DRY."
WAIT! THAT'S A STORM SPELL!
RAIN! RAIN! HA HA HA
GASP!
STOP!
NOOO!

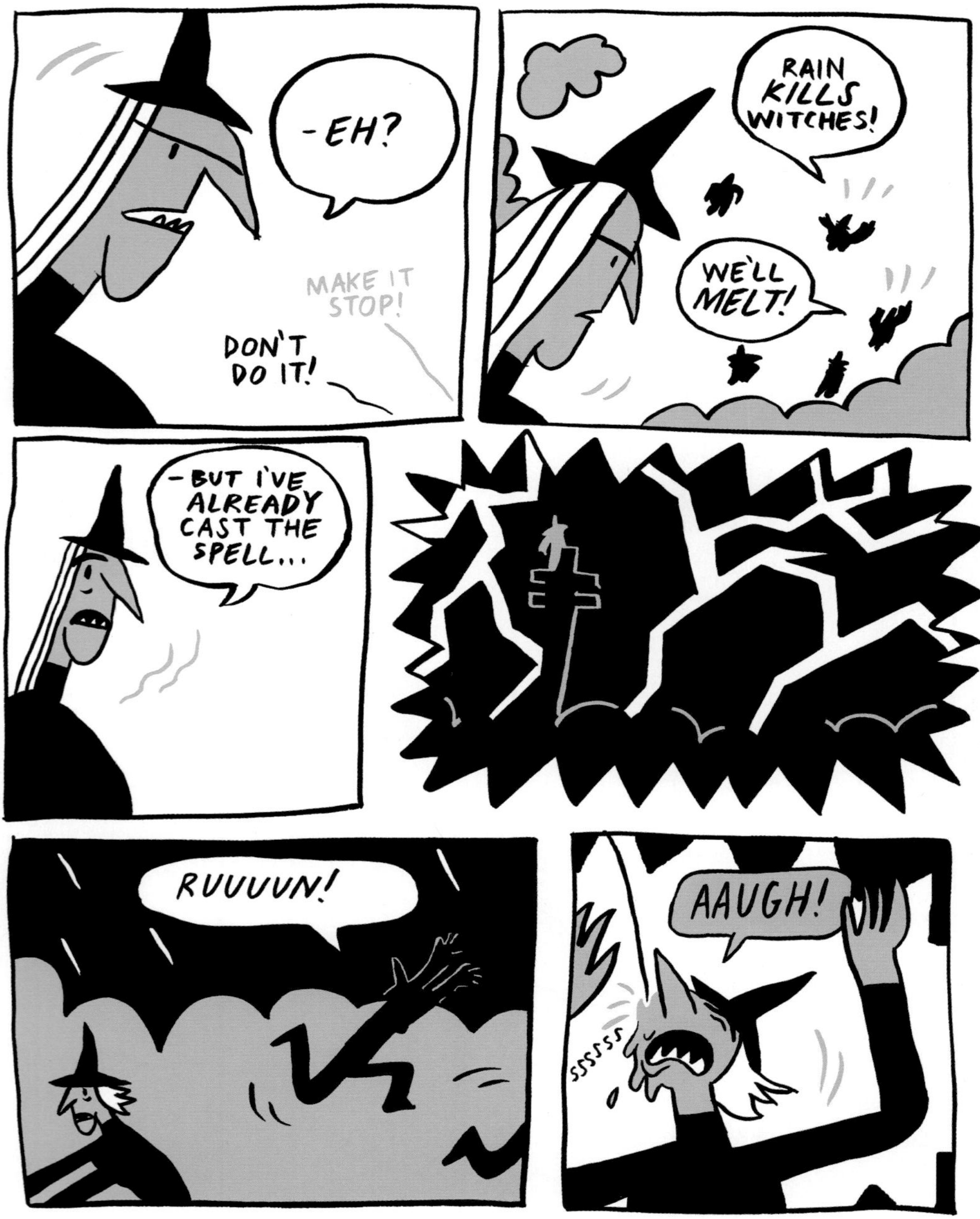
-EH?
MAKE IT STOP!
DON'T DO IT!
RAIN KILLS WITCHES!
WE'LL MELT!
-BUT I'VE ALREADY CAST THE SPELL...
RUUUUN!
AAUGH!
SSSSSS

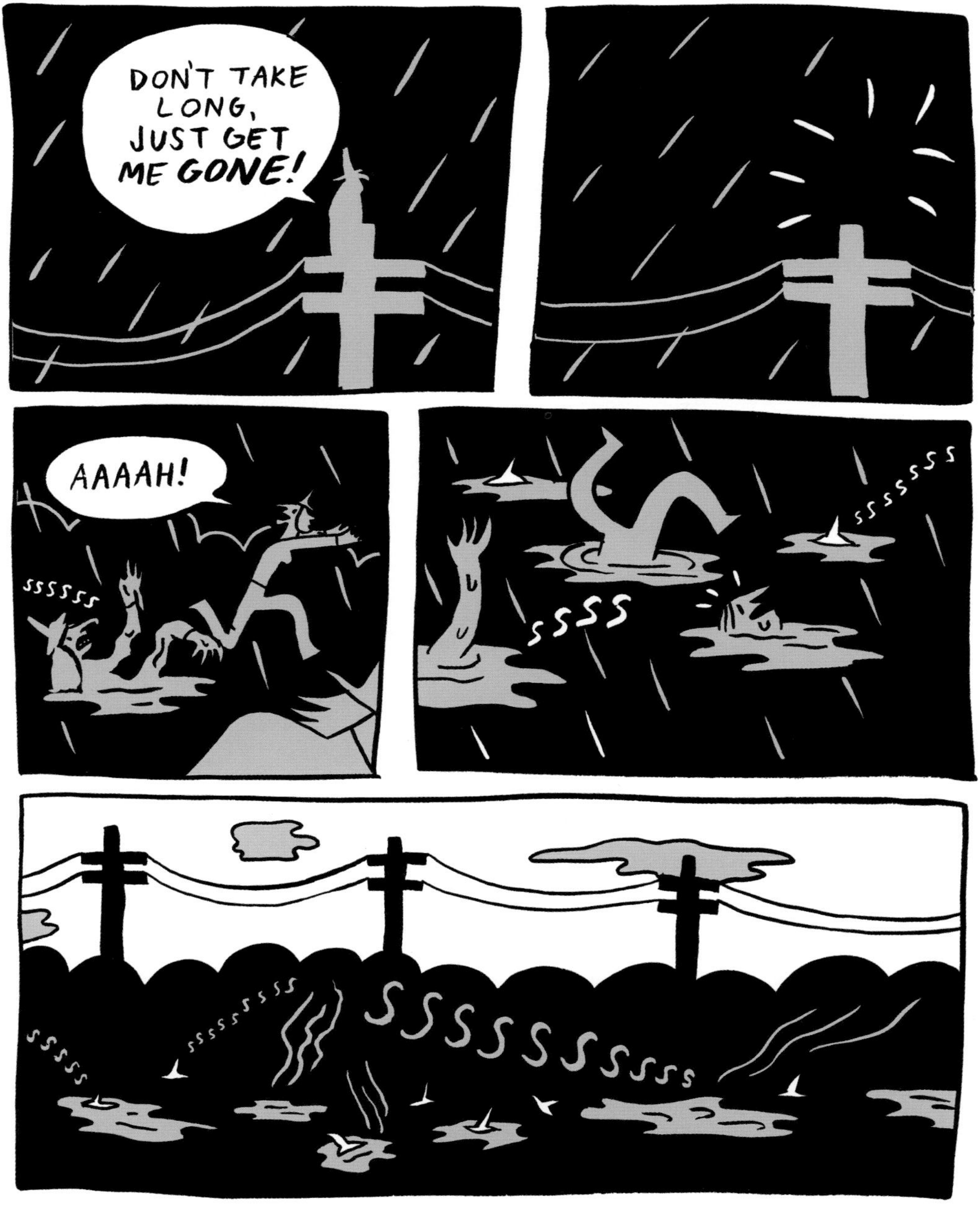
DON'T TAKE LONG, JUST GET ME GONE!
AAAAH!
SSSSSS
SSSS
SSSSSSS
SSSSS
SSSSSSSSS
SSSSSSSSSSSS

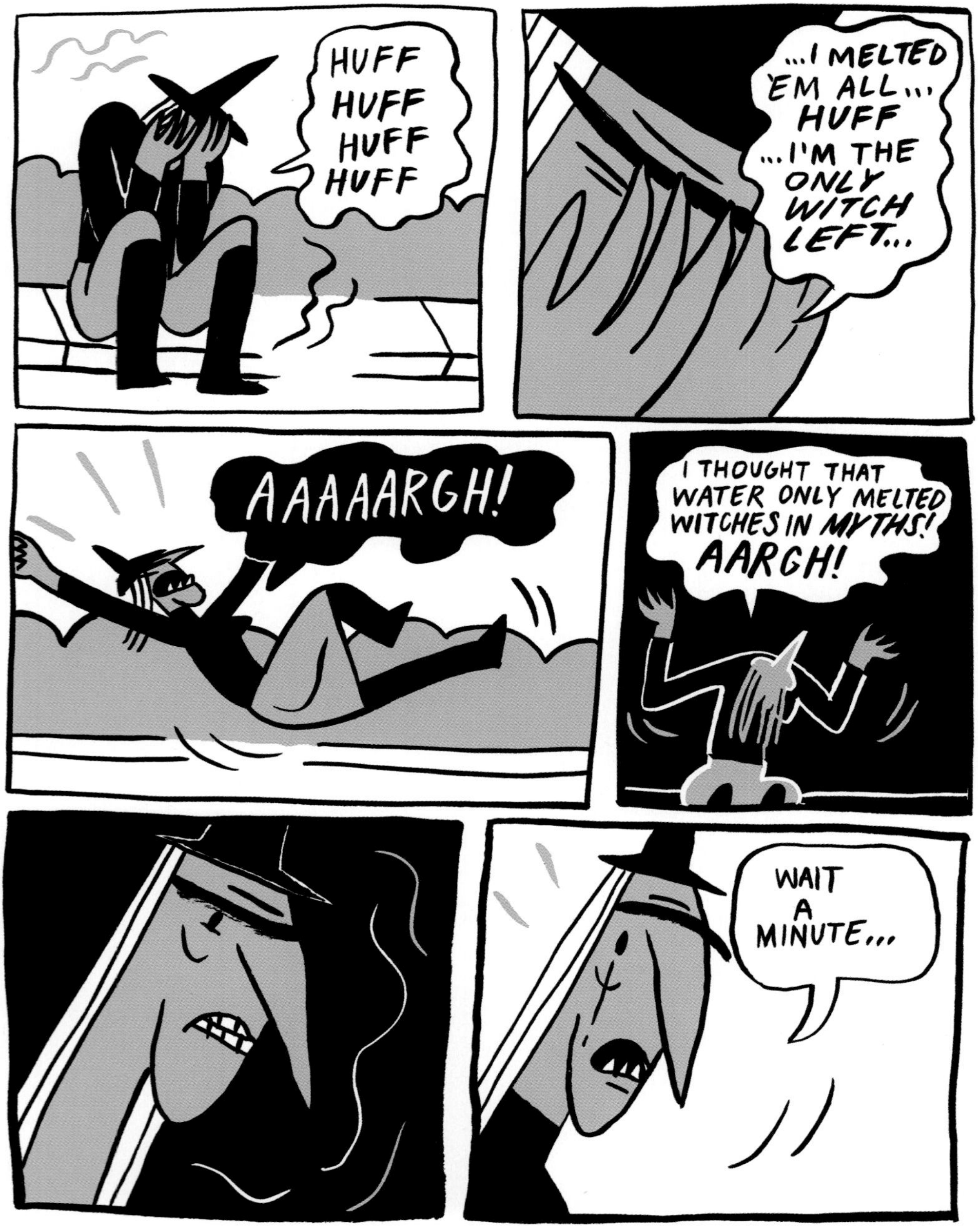
HUFF HUFF HUFF HUFF
...I MELTED 'EM ALL... HUFF ...I'M THE ONLY WITCH LEFT...
AAAAARGH!
I THOUGHT THAT WATER ONLY MELTED WITCHES IN MYTHS! AARGH!
WAIT A MINUTE...

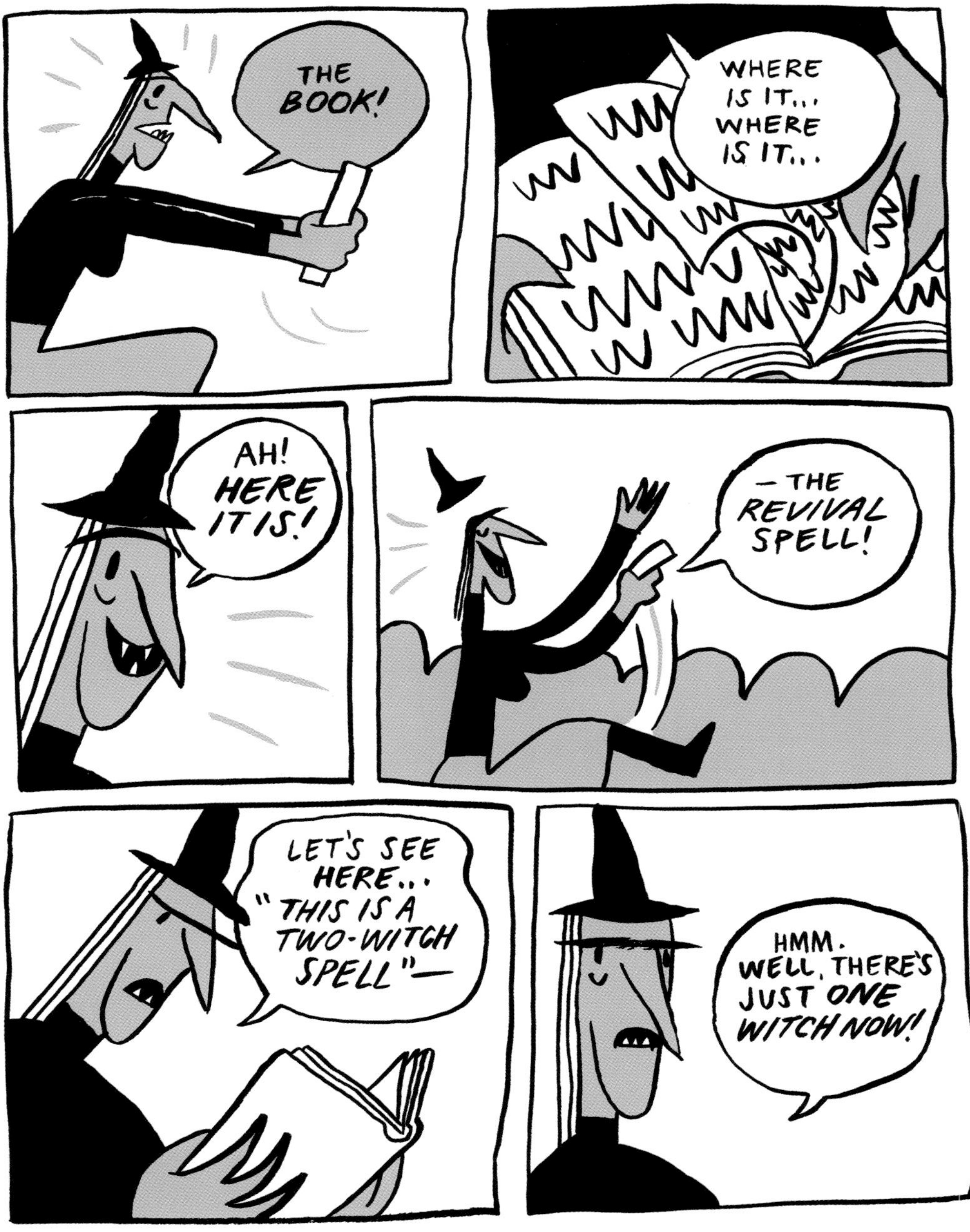
THE BOOK!
WHERE IS IT... WHERE IS IT...
AH! HERE IT IS!
—THE REVIVAL SPELL!
LET'S SEE HERE... "THIS IS A TWO-WITCH SPELL"—
HMM. WELL, THERE'S JUST ONE WITCH NOW!

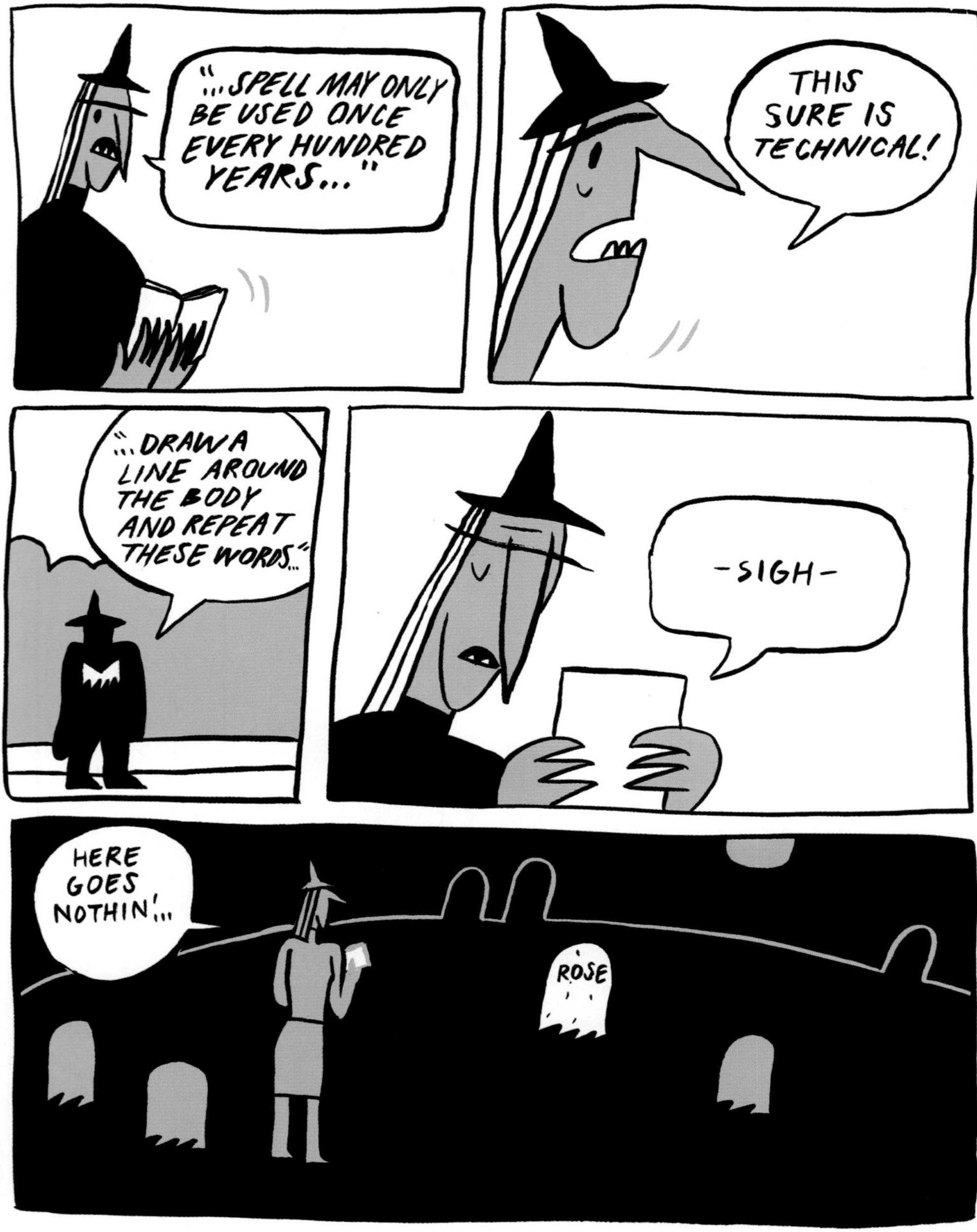
"...SPELL MAY ONLY BE USED ONCE EVERY HUNDRED YEARS..."
THIS SURE IS TECHNICAL!
"...DRAW A LINE AROUND THE BODY AND REPEAT THESE WORDS..."
-SIGH-
HERE GOES NOTHIN'...
ROSE

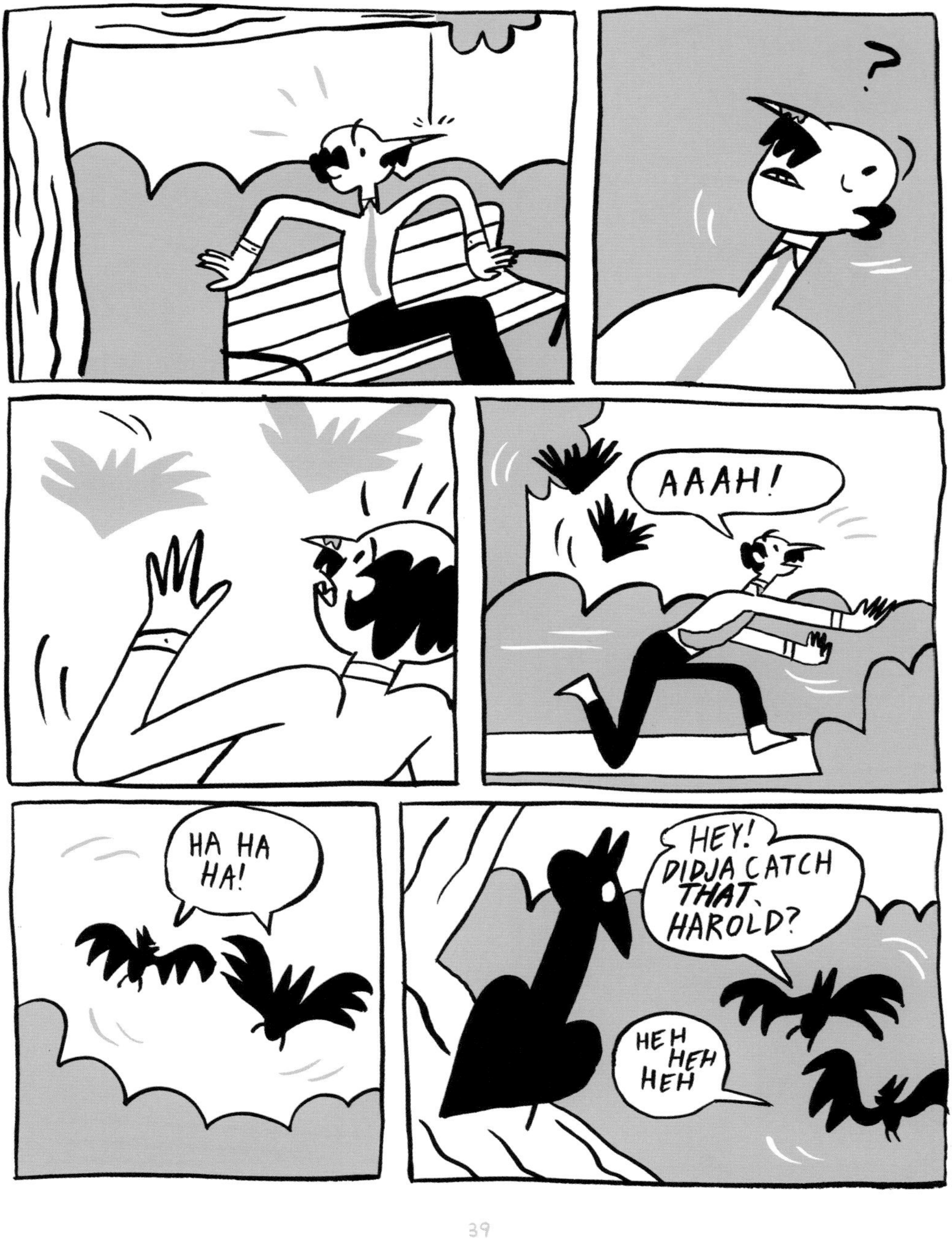
?
AAAH!
HA HA HA!
HEY! DIDJA CATCH *THAT*, HAROLD?
HEH HEH HEH

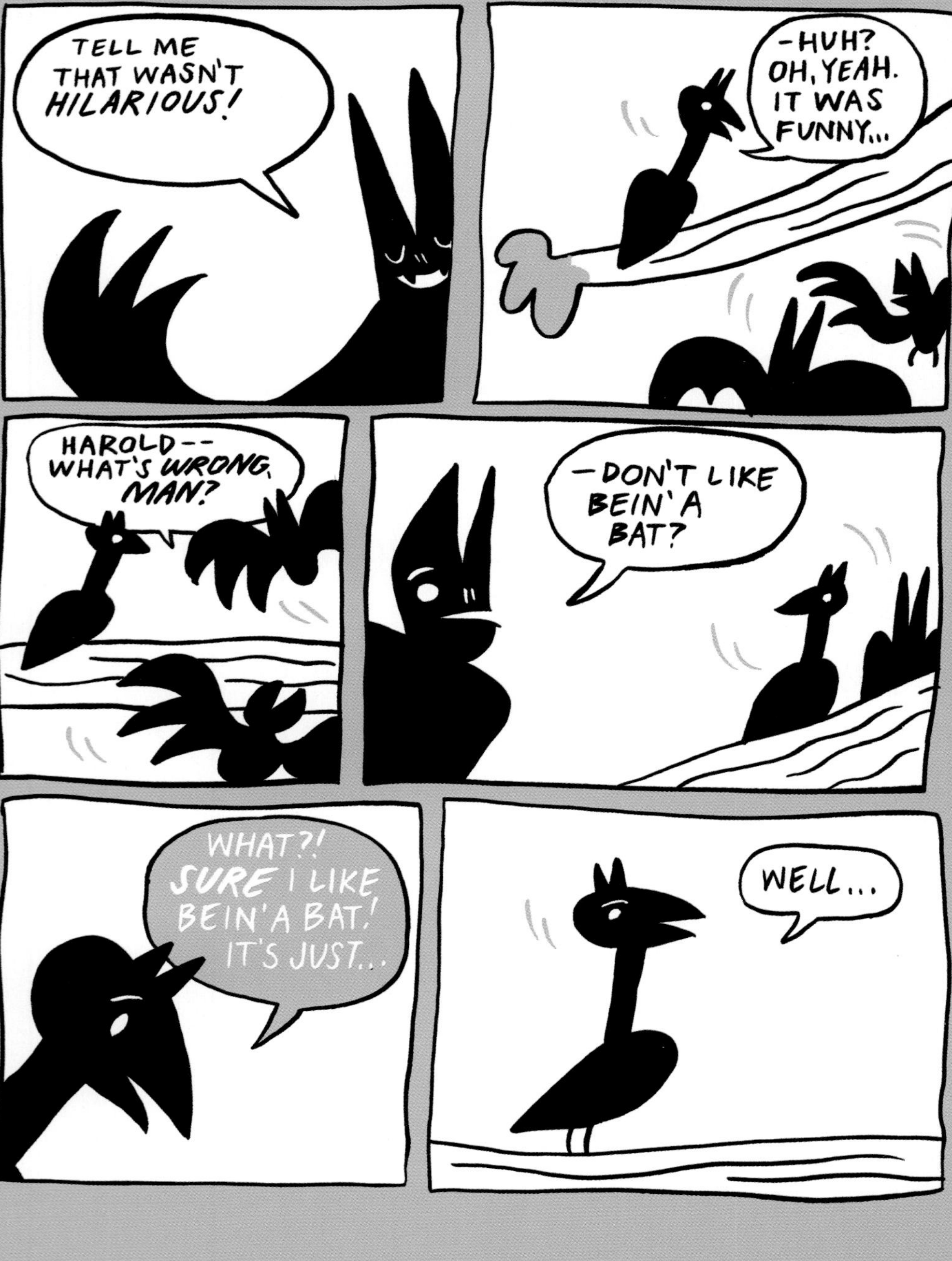
TELL ME THAT WASN'T *HILARIOUS!*
-HUH? OH, YEAH. IT WAS FUNNY...
HAROLD-- WHAT'S *WRONG*, *MAN?*
-DON'T LIKE BEIN' A BAT?
WHAT?! *SURE* I LIKE BEIN' A BAT! IT'S JUST...
WELL...

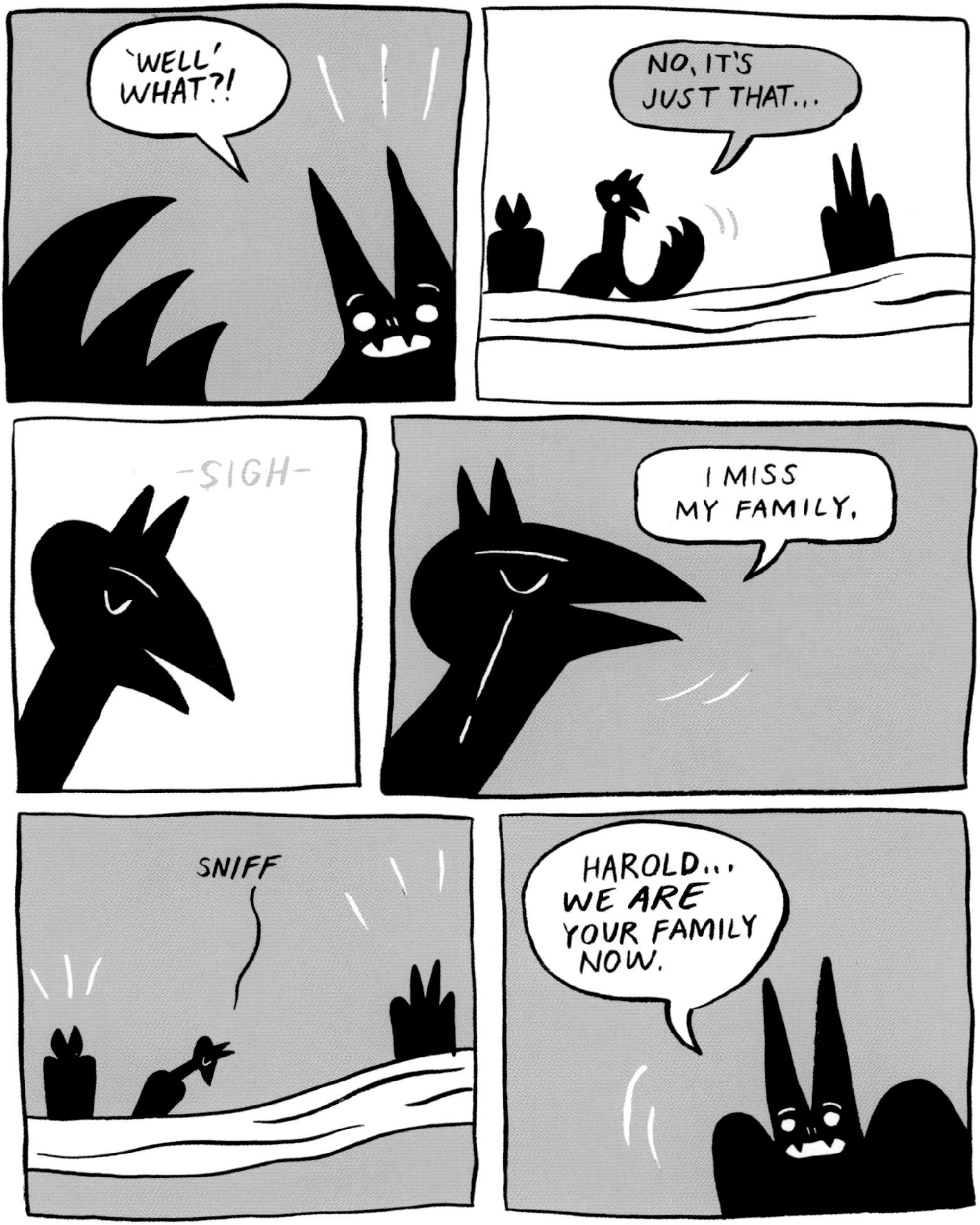
`WELL'
WHAT?!
NO, IT'S
JUST THAT...
-SIGH-
I MISS
MY FAMILY.
SNIFF
HAROLD...
WE ARE
YOUR FAMILY
NOW.

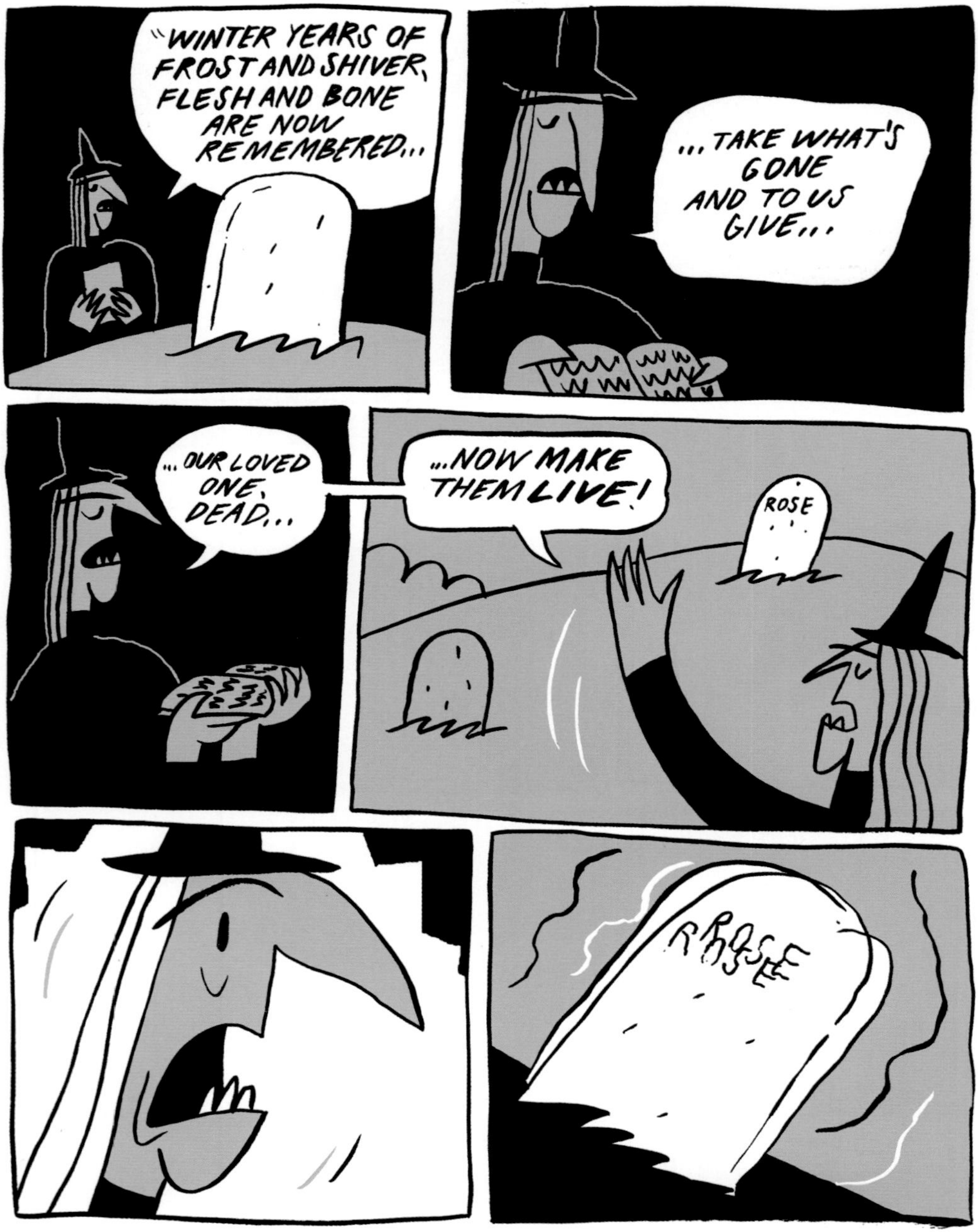
"WINTER YEARS OF FROST AND SHIVER, FLESH AND BONE ARE NOW REMEMBERED...
...TAKE WHAT'S GONE AND TO US GIVE...
...OUR LOVED ONE, DEAD...
...NOW MAKE THEM LIVE!
ROSE

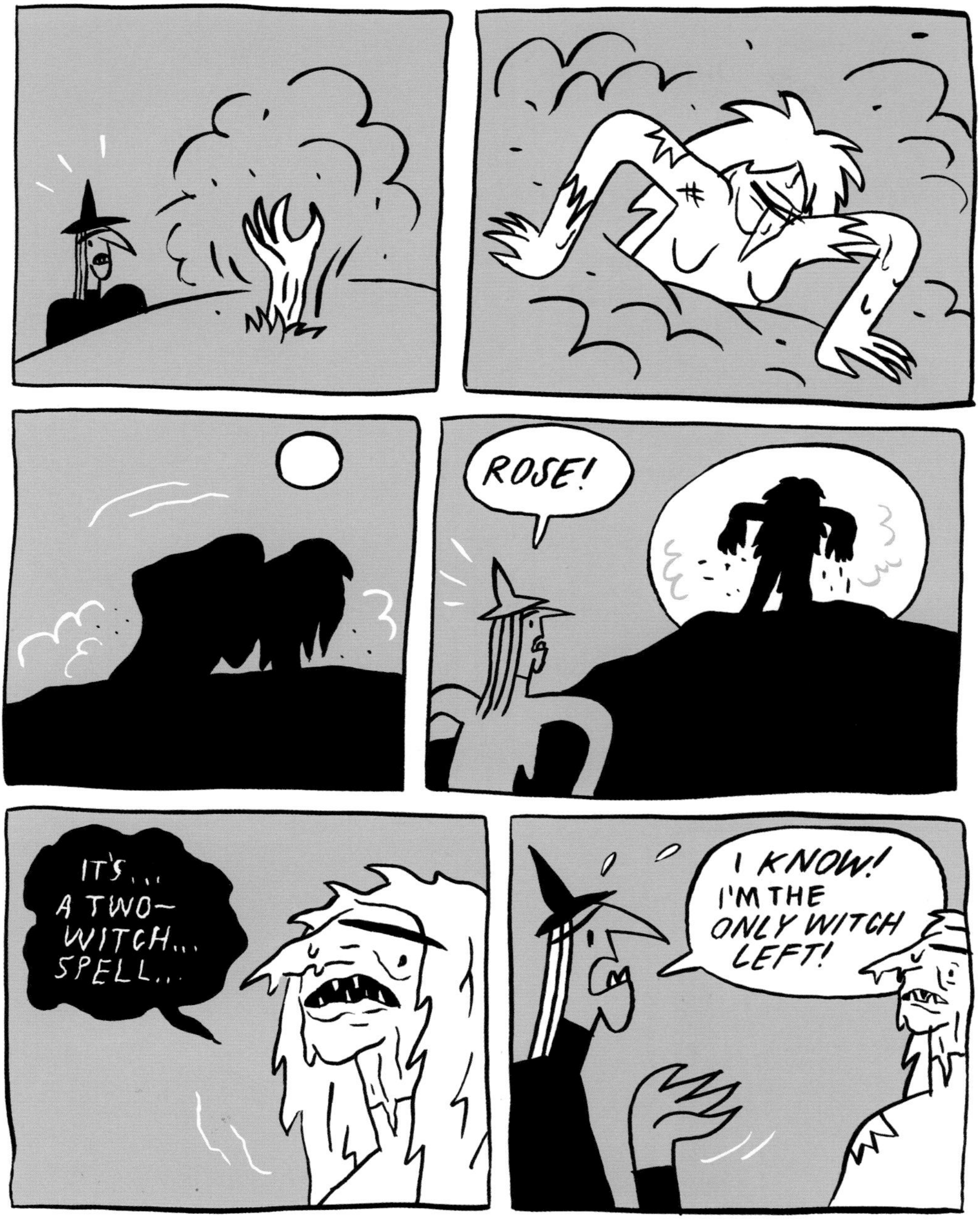
ROSE!
IT'S... A TWO-WITCH... SPELL...
I KNOW! I'M THE ONLY WITCH LEFT!

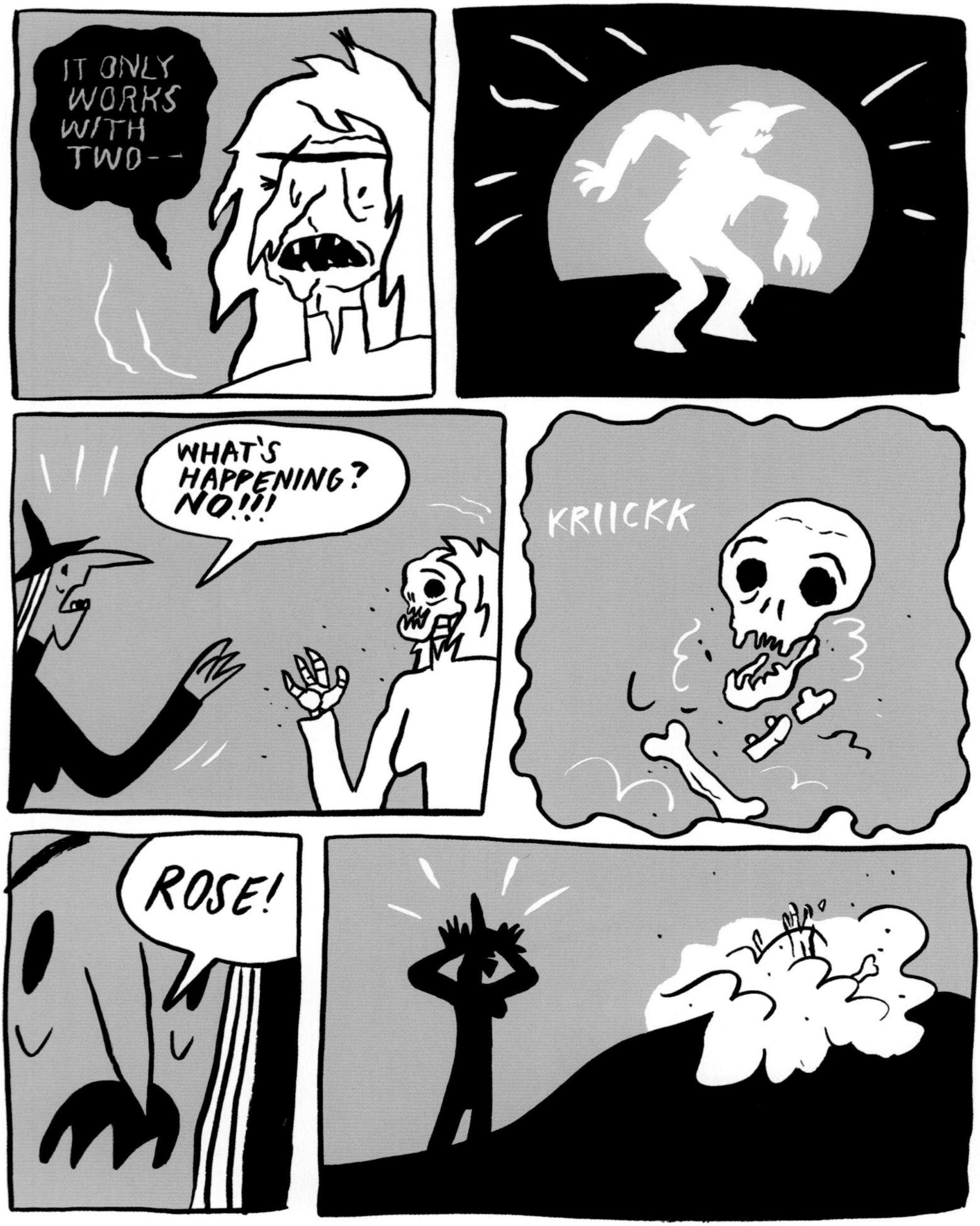
IT ONLY WORKS WITH TWO--
WHAT'S HAPPENING? NO!!!
KRIICKK
ROSE!

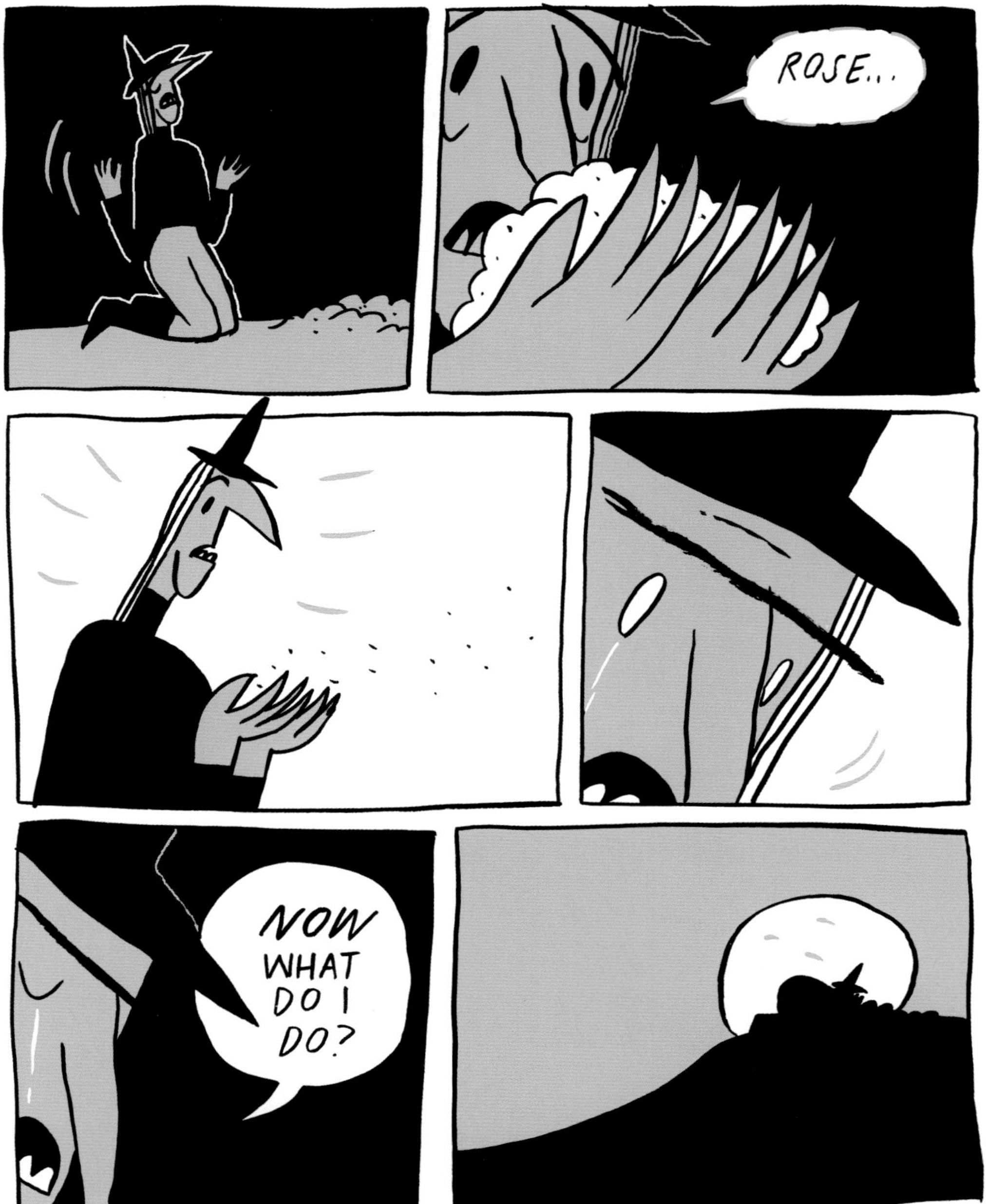
ROSE...
NOW WHAT DO I DO?

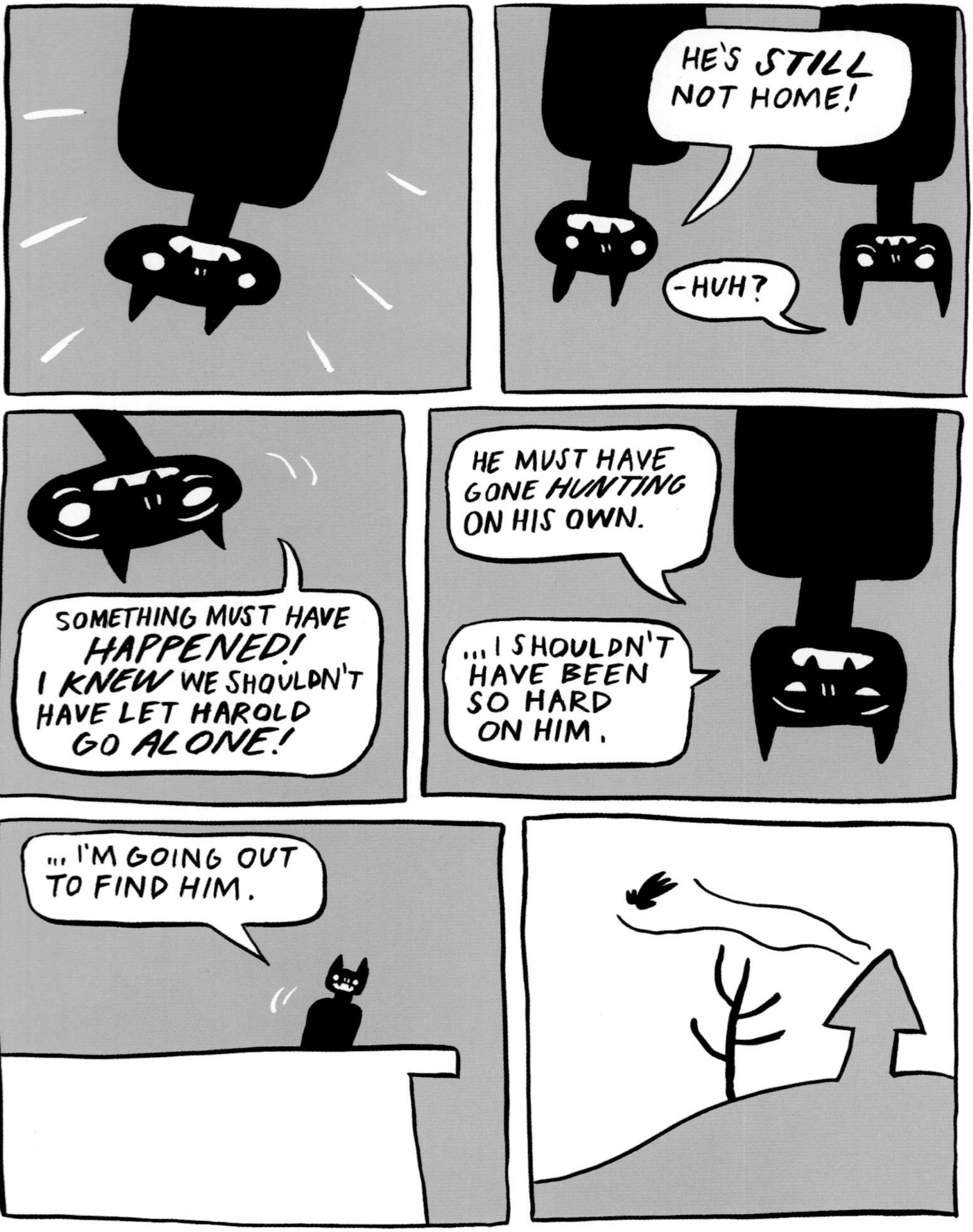
HE'S STILL NOT HOME!
-HUH?
SOMETHING MUST HAVE HAPPENED! I KNEW WE SHOULDN'T HAVE LET HAROLD GO ALONE!
HE MUST HAVE GONE HUNTING ON HIS OWN.
... I SHOULDN'T HAVE BEEN SO HARD ON HIM.
... I'M GOING OUT TO FIND HIM.

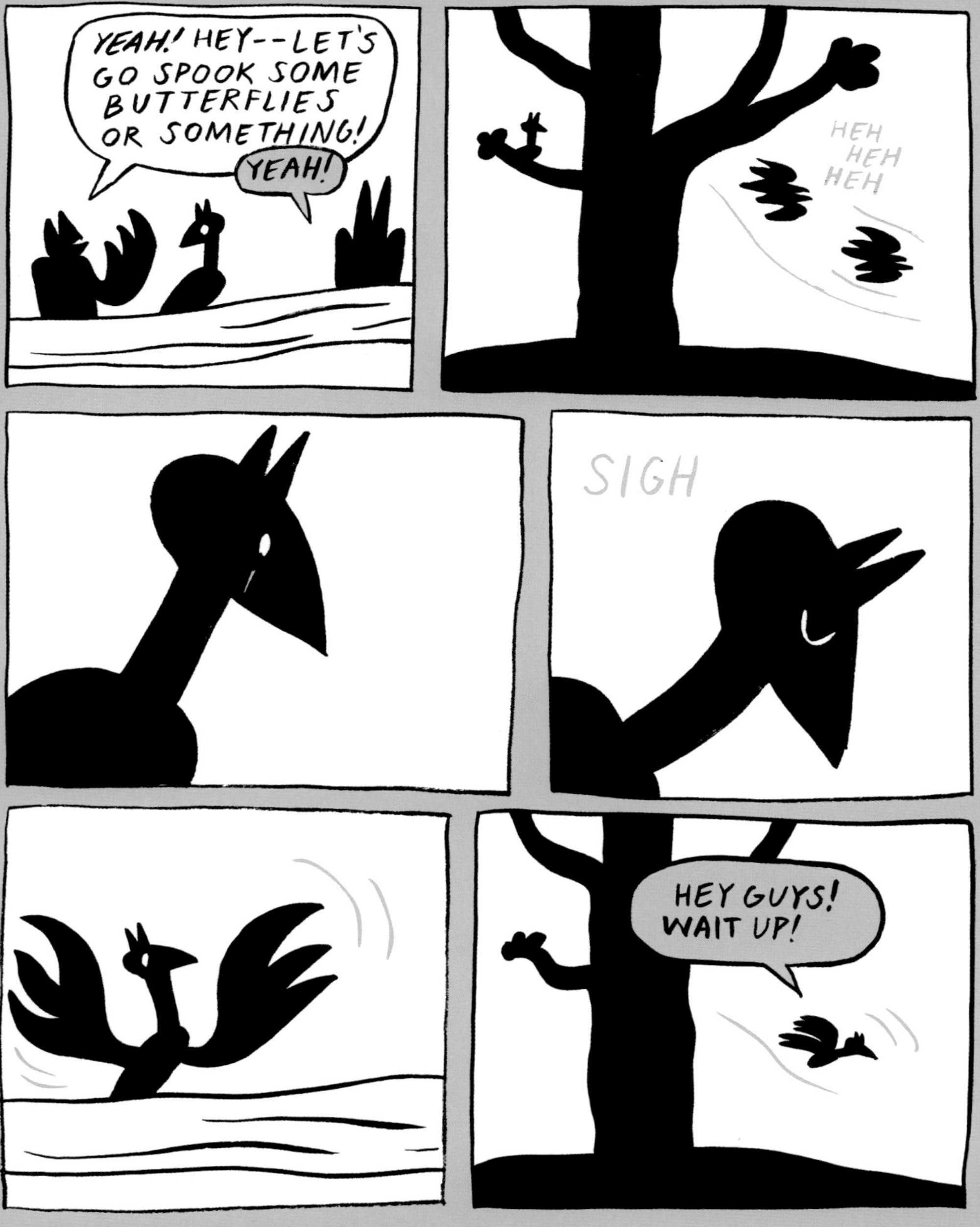
YEAH! HEY--LET'S GO SPOOK SOME BUTTERFLIES OR SOMETHING!
YEAH!
HEH HEH HEH
SIGH
HEY GUYS! WAIT UP!

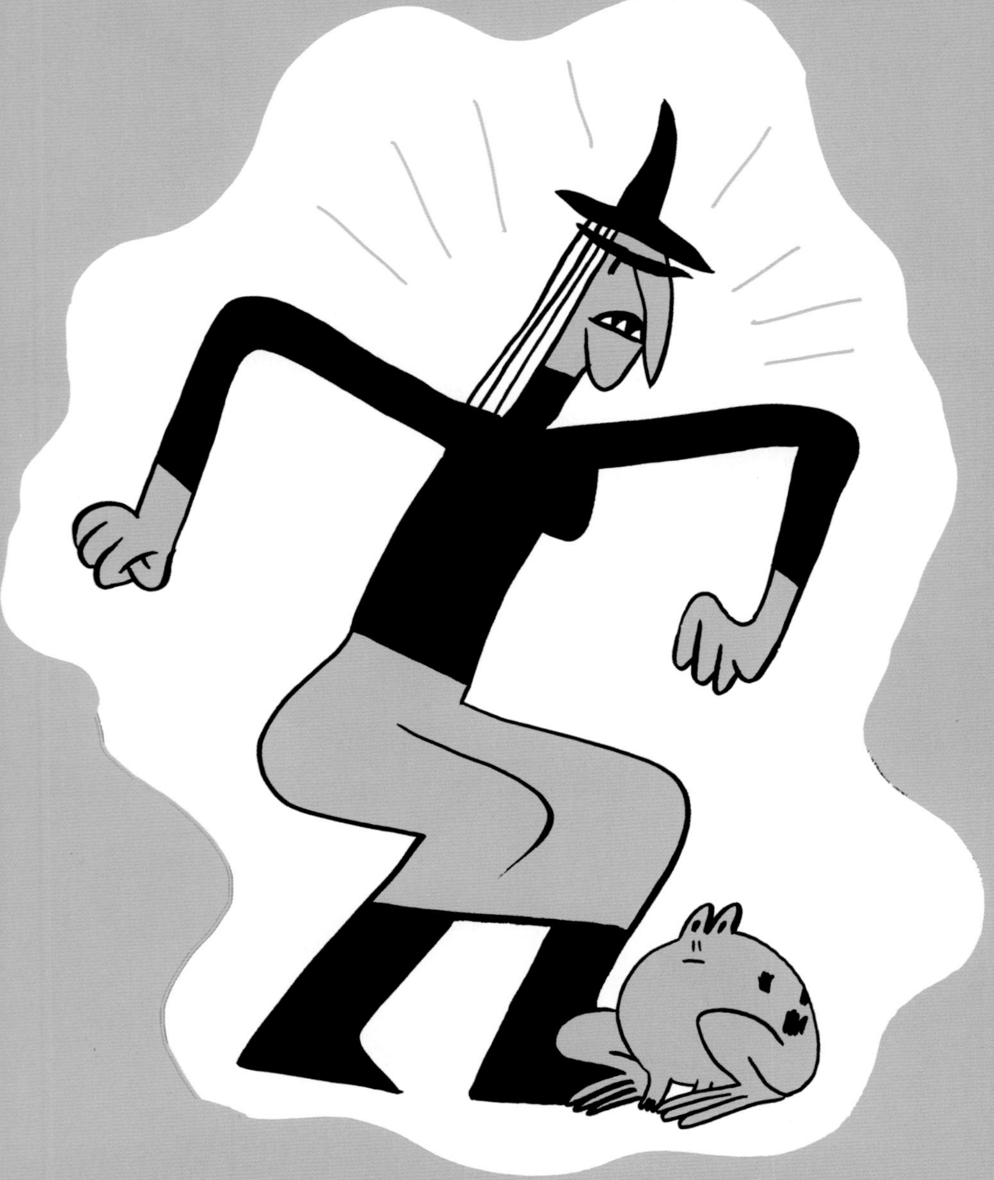

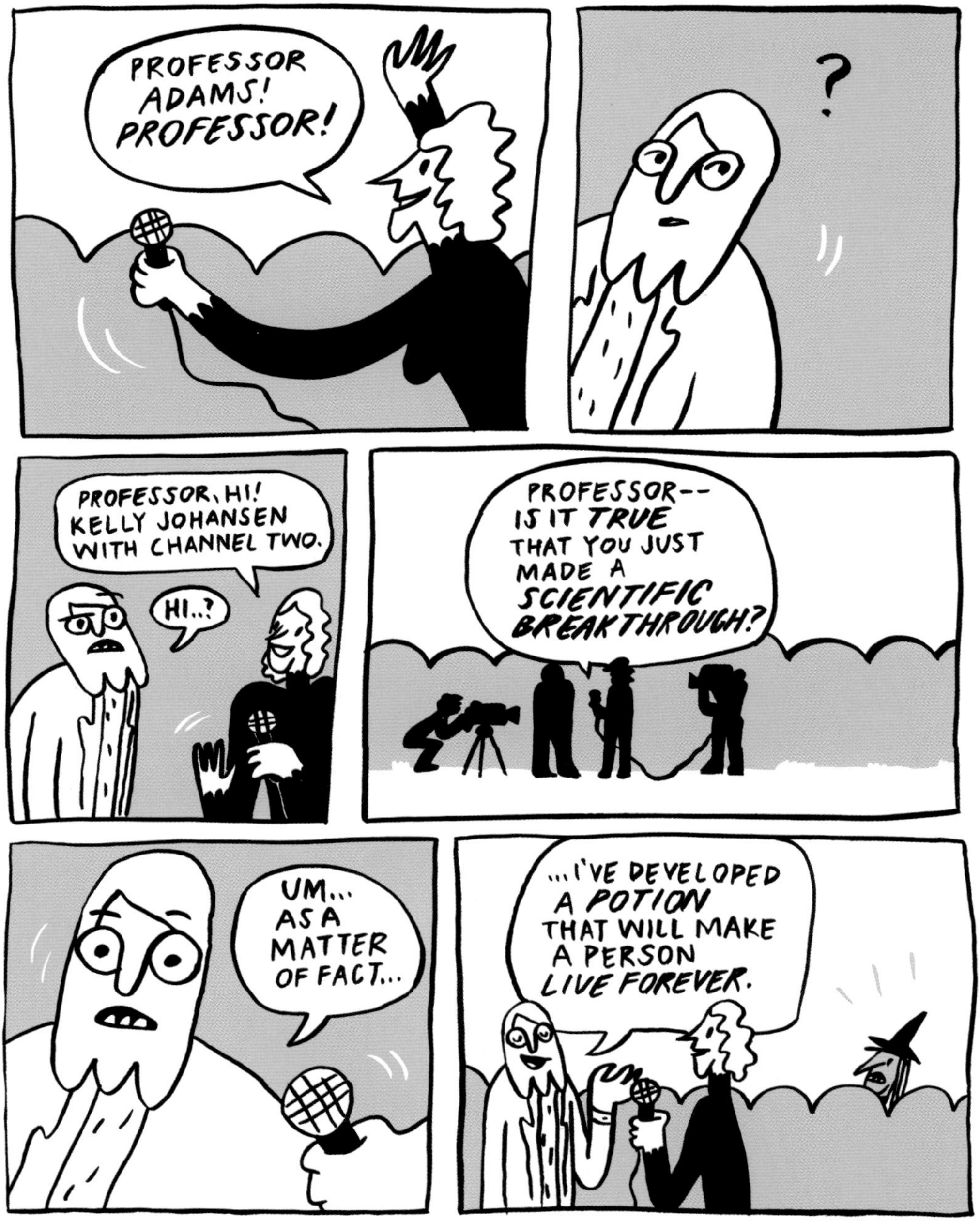
PROFESSOR ADAMS! PROFESSOR!
?
PROFESSOR, HI! KELLY JOHANSEN WITH CHANNEL TWO.
HI..?
PROFESSOR-- IS IT TRUE THAT YOU JUST MADE A SCIENTIFIC BREAKTHROUGH?
UM... AS A MATTER OF FACT...
...I'VE DEVELOPED A POTION THAT WILL MAKE A PERSON LIVE FOREVER.

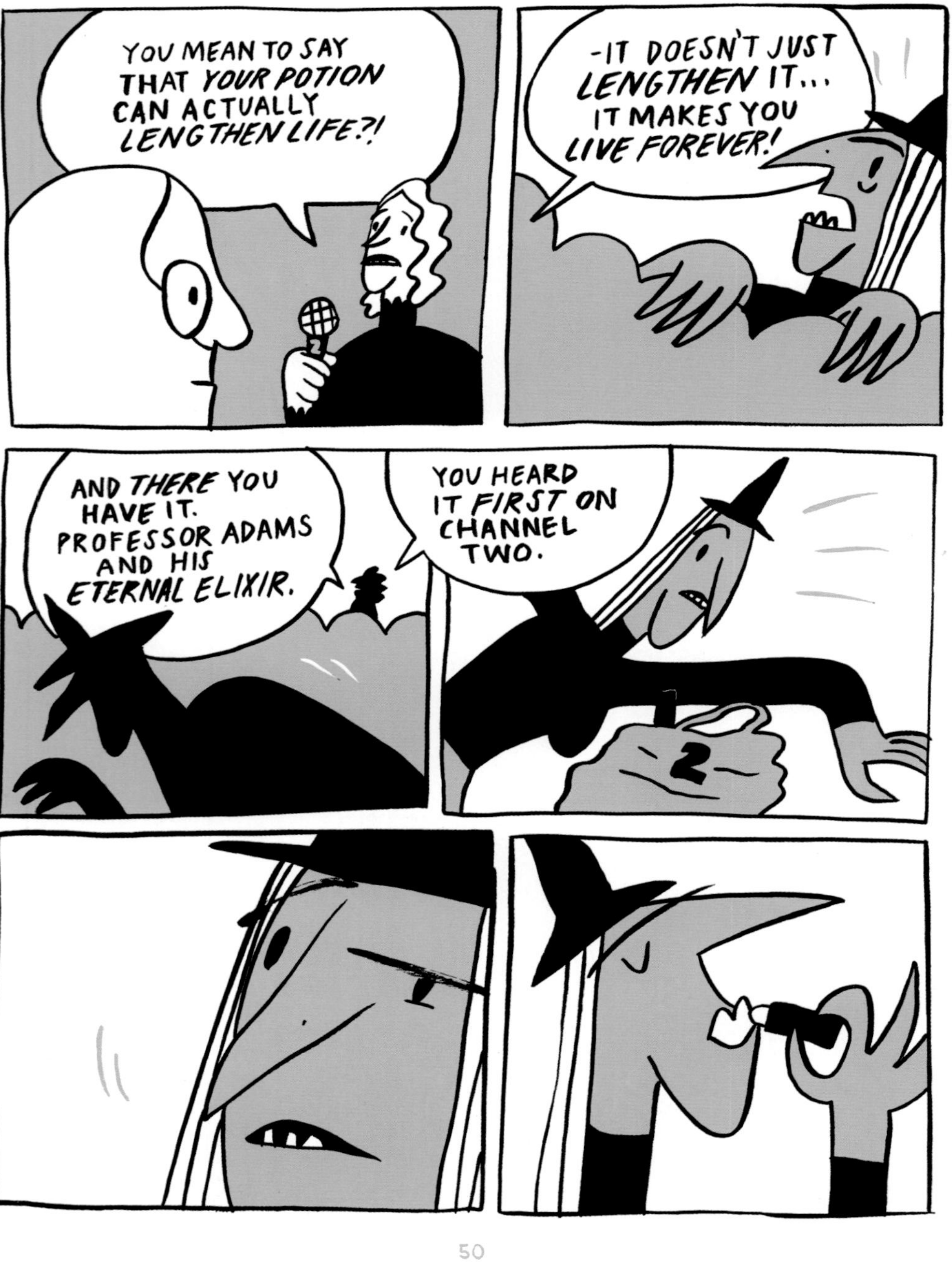
YOU MEAN TO SAY THAT YOUR POTION CAN ACTUALLY LENGTHEN LIFE?!
-IT DOESN'T JUST LENGTHEN IT... IT MAKES YOU LIVE FOREVER!
AND THERE YOU HAVE IT. PROFESSOR ADAMS AND HIS ETERNAL ELIXIR.
YOU HEARD IT FIRST ON CHANNEL TWO.

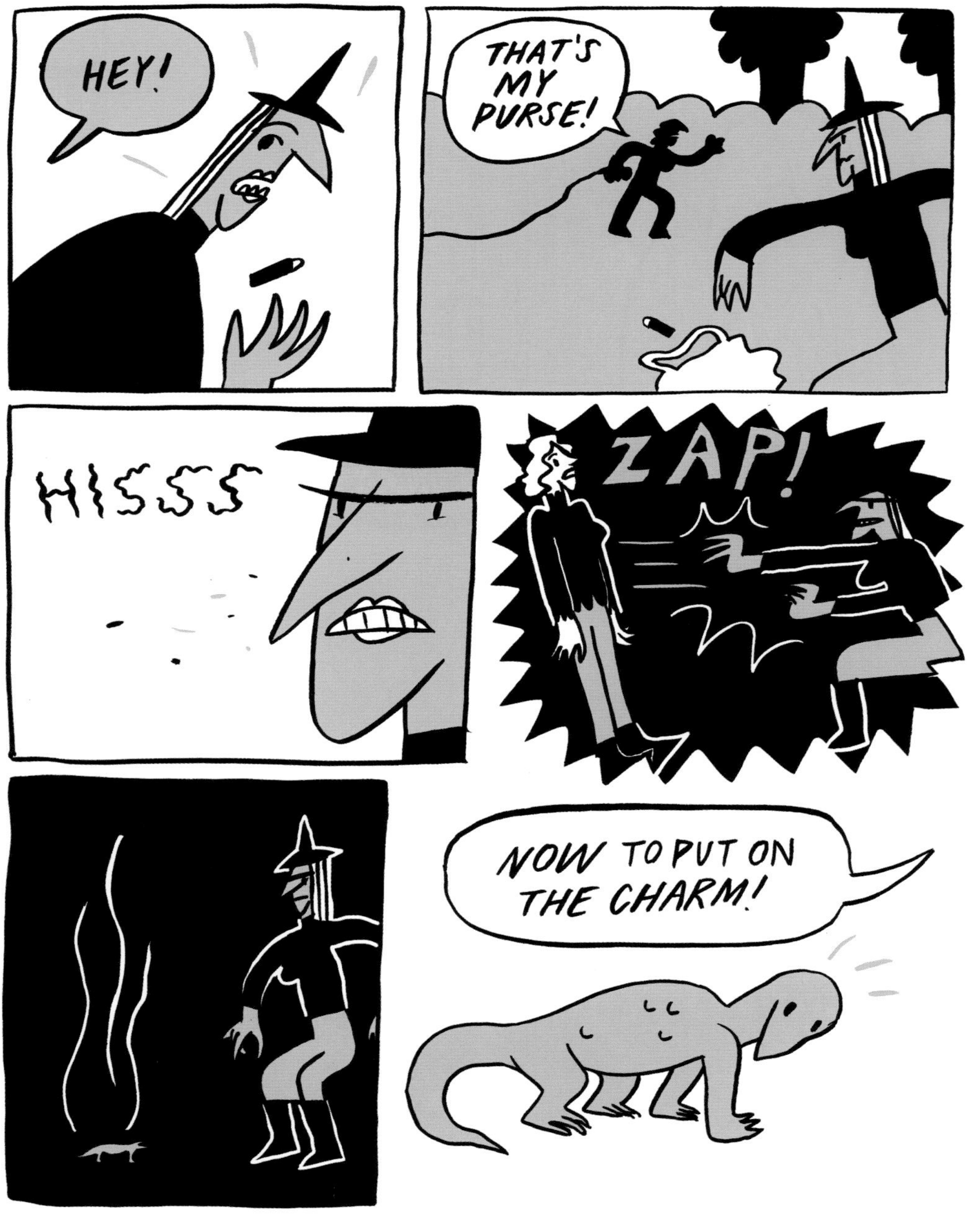
HEY!
THAT'S MY PURSE!
HISSS
ZAP!
NOW TO PUT ON THE CHARM!

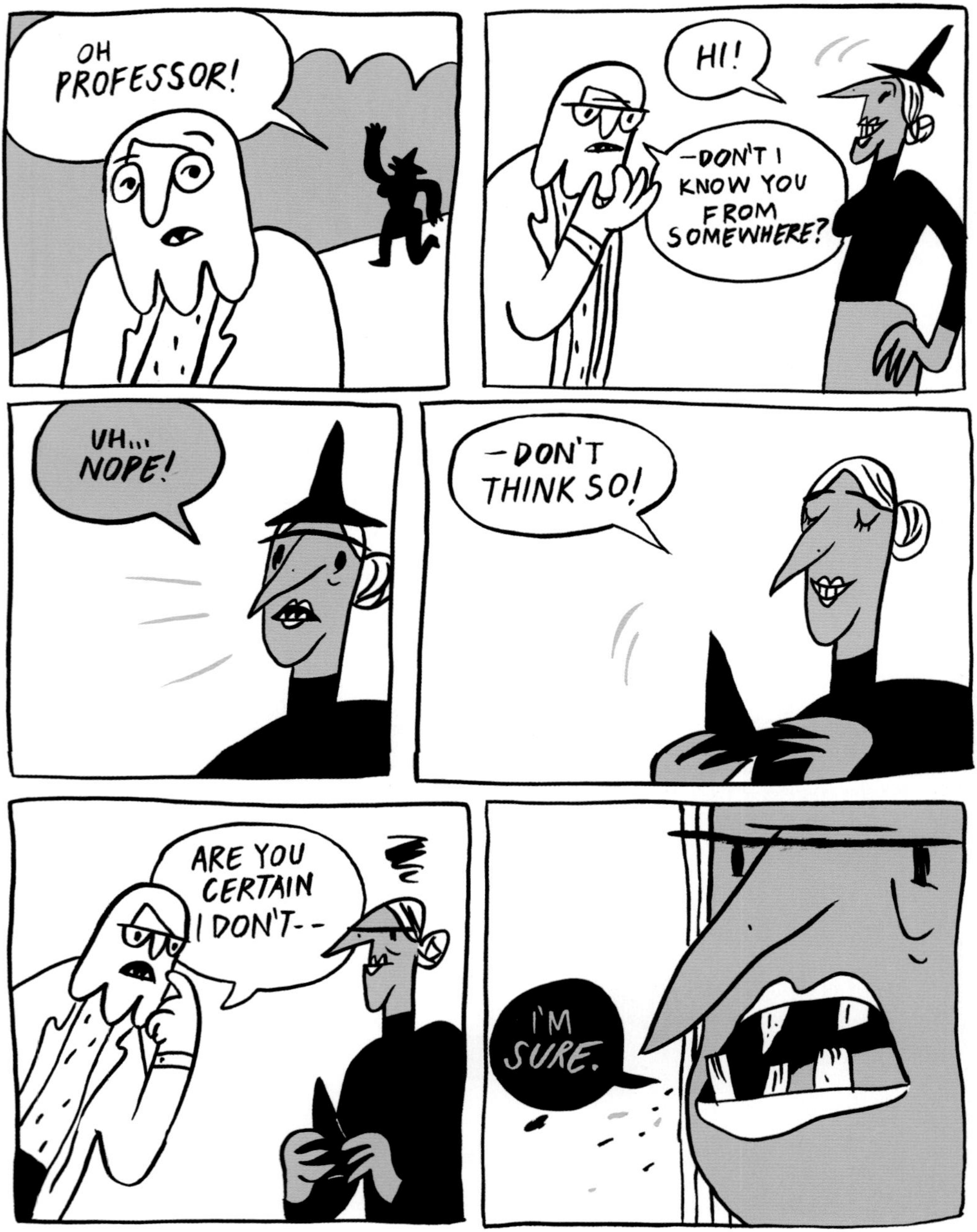
OH PROFESSOR!
HI!
-DON'T I KNOW YOU FROM SOMEWHERE?
UH... NOPE!
-DON'T THINK SO!
ARE YOU CERTAIN I DON'T--
I'M SURE.

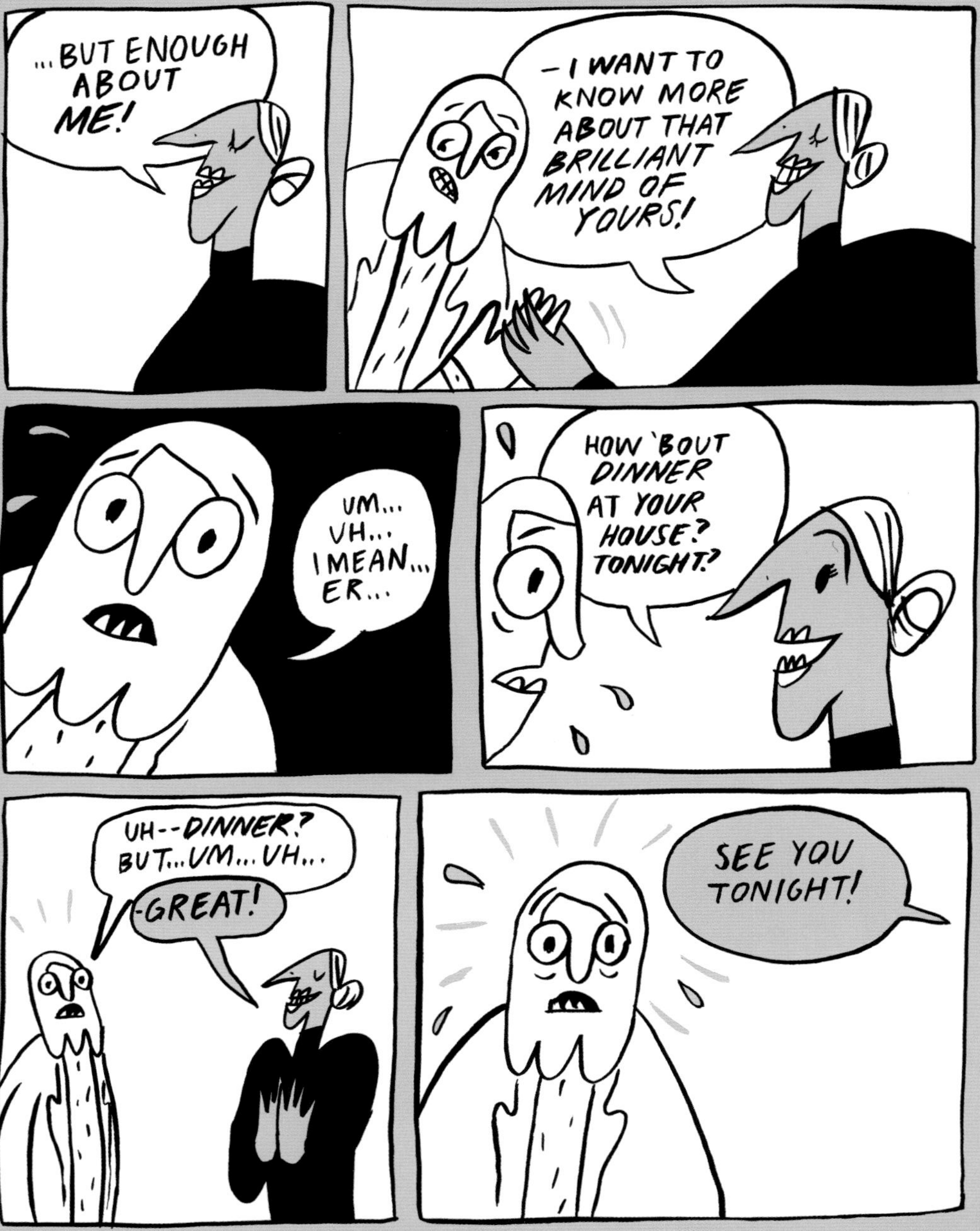
...BUT ENOUGH ABOUT *ME!*
-I WANT TO KNOW MORE ABOUT THAT BRILLIANT MIND OF YOURS!
UM... UH... I MEAN... ER...
HOW 'BOUT *DINNER* AT *YOUR HOUSE? TONIGHT?*
UH--*DINNER?* BUT...UM...UH...
-GREAT!
SEE YOU TONIGHT!

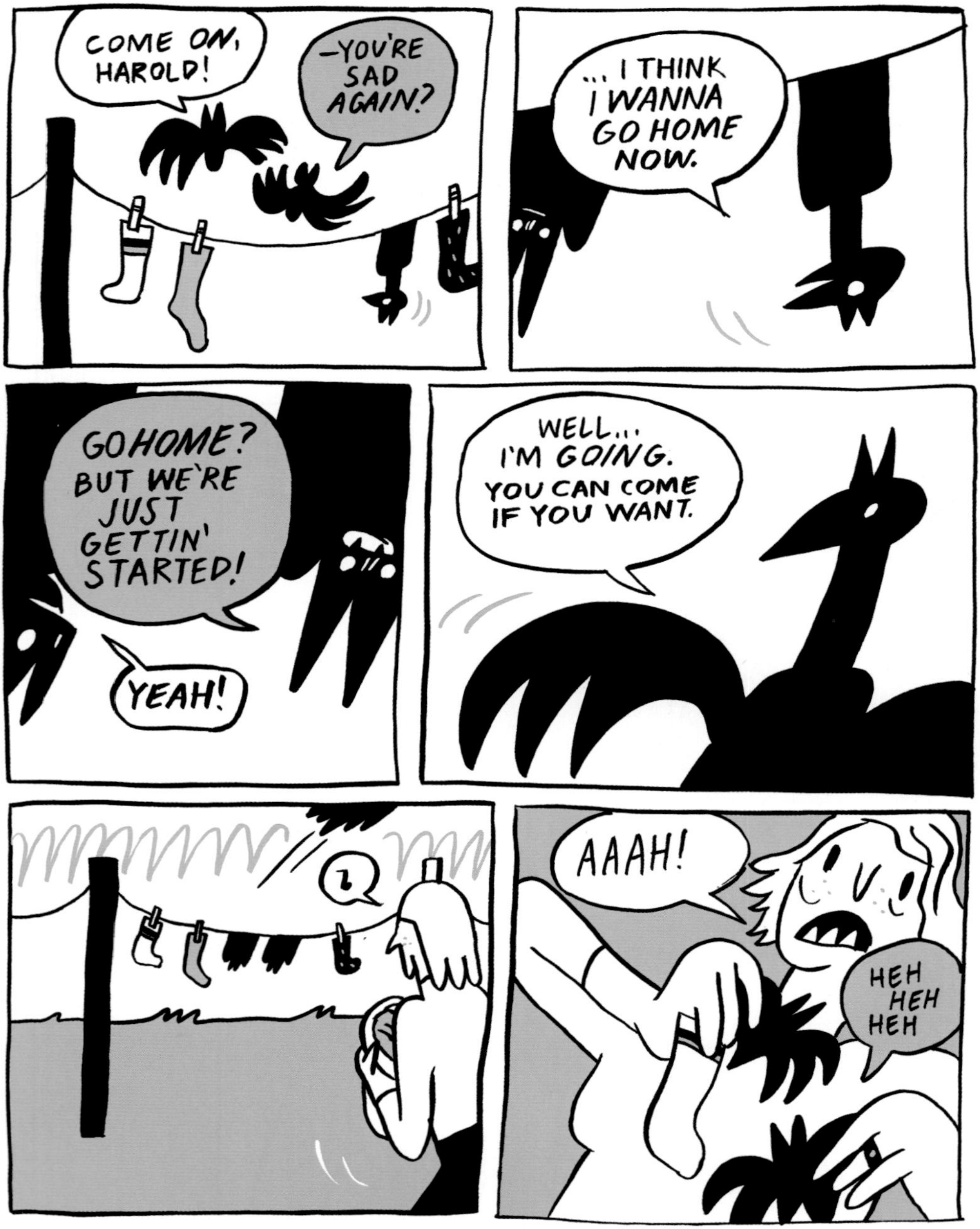
COME ON, HAROLD!
—YOU'RE SAD AGAIN?
... I THINK I WANNA GO HOME NOW.
GO HOME? BUT WE'RE JUST GETTIN' STARTED!
YEAH!
WELL... I'M GOING. YOU CAN COME IF YOU WANT.
?
AAAH!
HEH HEH HEH

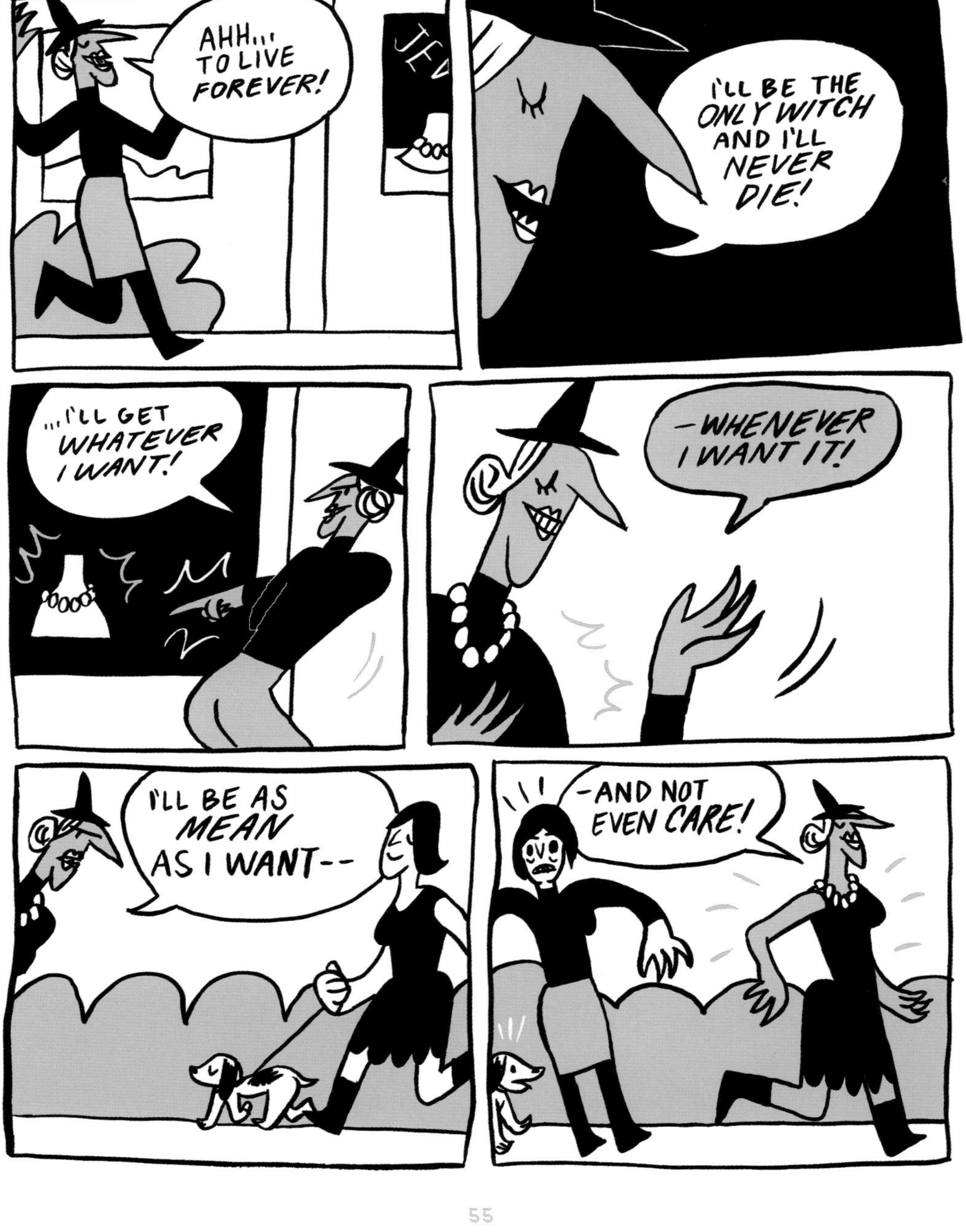
AHH... TO LIVE FOREVER!
I'LL BE THE ONLY WITCH AND I'LL NEVER DIE!
...I'LL GET WHATEVER I WANT!
-WHENEVER I WANT IT!
I'LL BE AS MEAN AS I WANT--
-AND NOT EVEN CARE!

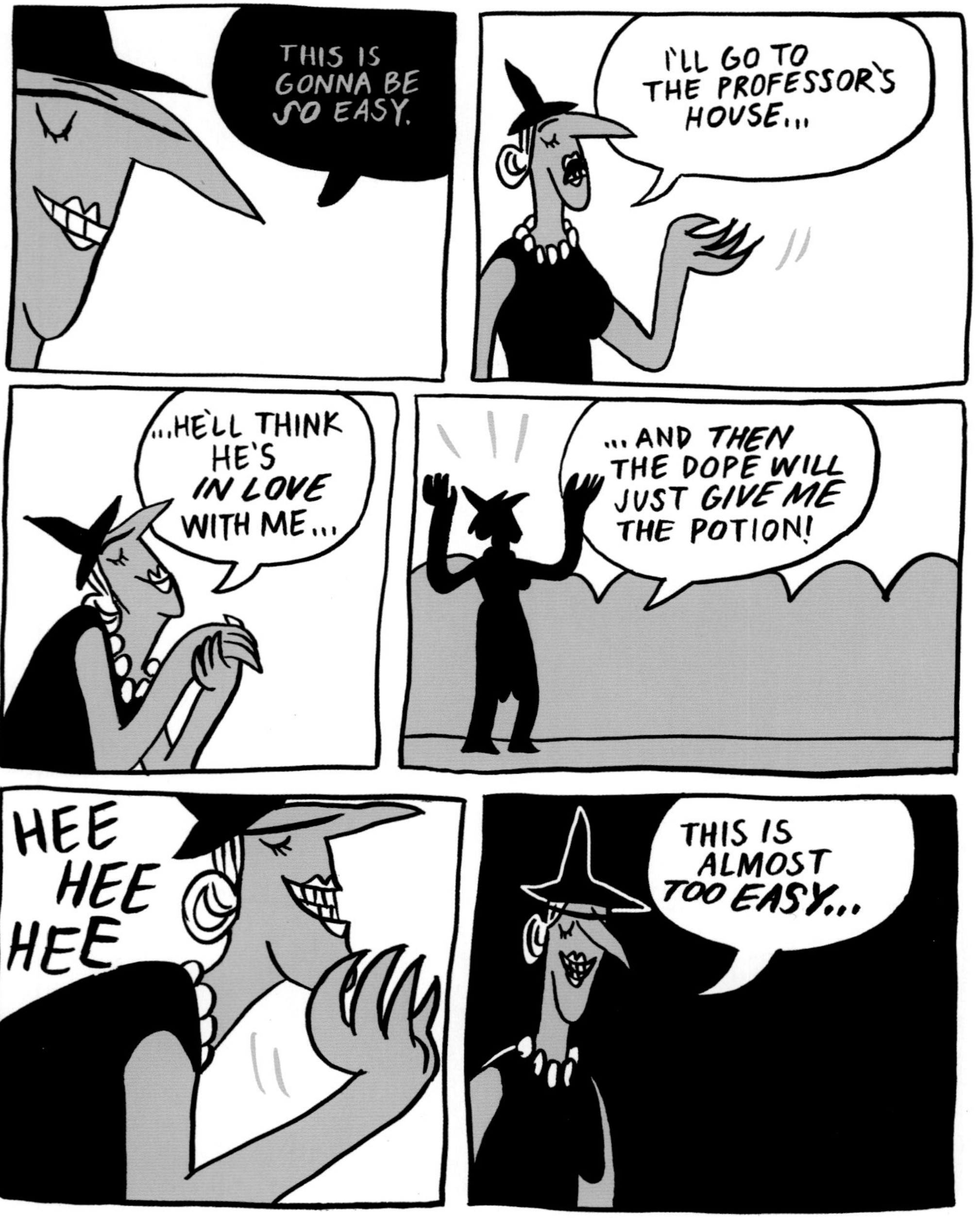
THIS IS GONNA BE SO EASY.
I'LL GO TO THE PROFESSOR'S HOUSE...
...HE'LL THINK HE'S IN LOVE WITH ME...
...AND THEN THE DOPE WILL JUST GIVE ME THE POTION!
HEE HEE HEE
THIS IS ALMOST TOO EASY...

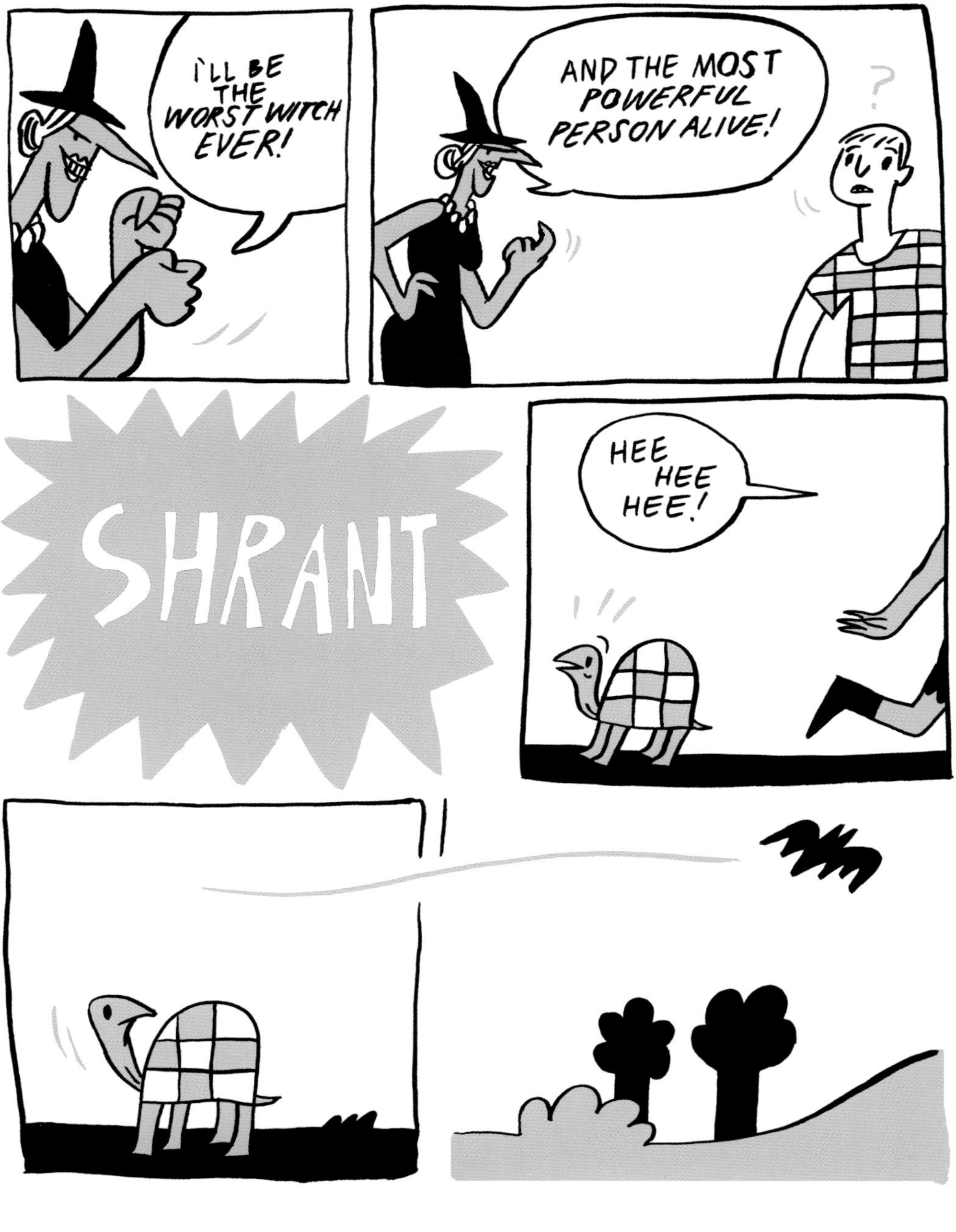
I'LL BE THE WORST WITCH EVER!
AND THE MOST POWERFUL PERSON ALIVE!
?
SHRANT
HEE HEE HEE!

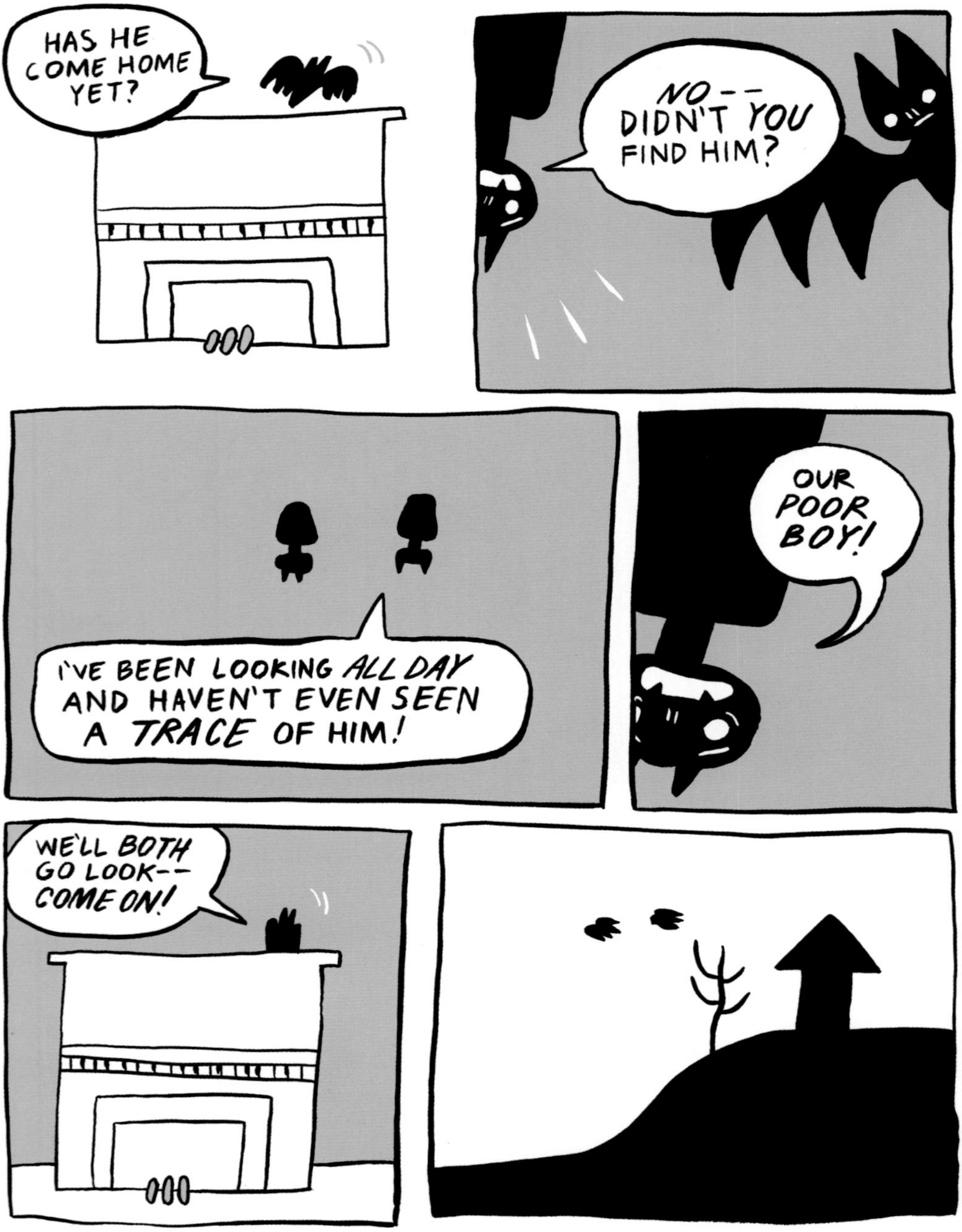
HAS HE COME HOME YET?
NO-- DIDN'T YOU FIND HIM?
I'VE BEEN LOOKING ALL DAY AND HAVEN'T EVEN SEEN A TRACE OF HIM!
OUR POOR BOY!
WE'LL BOTH GO LOOK-- COME ON!

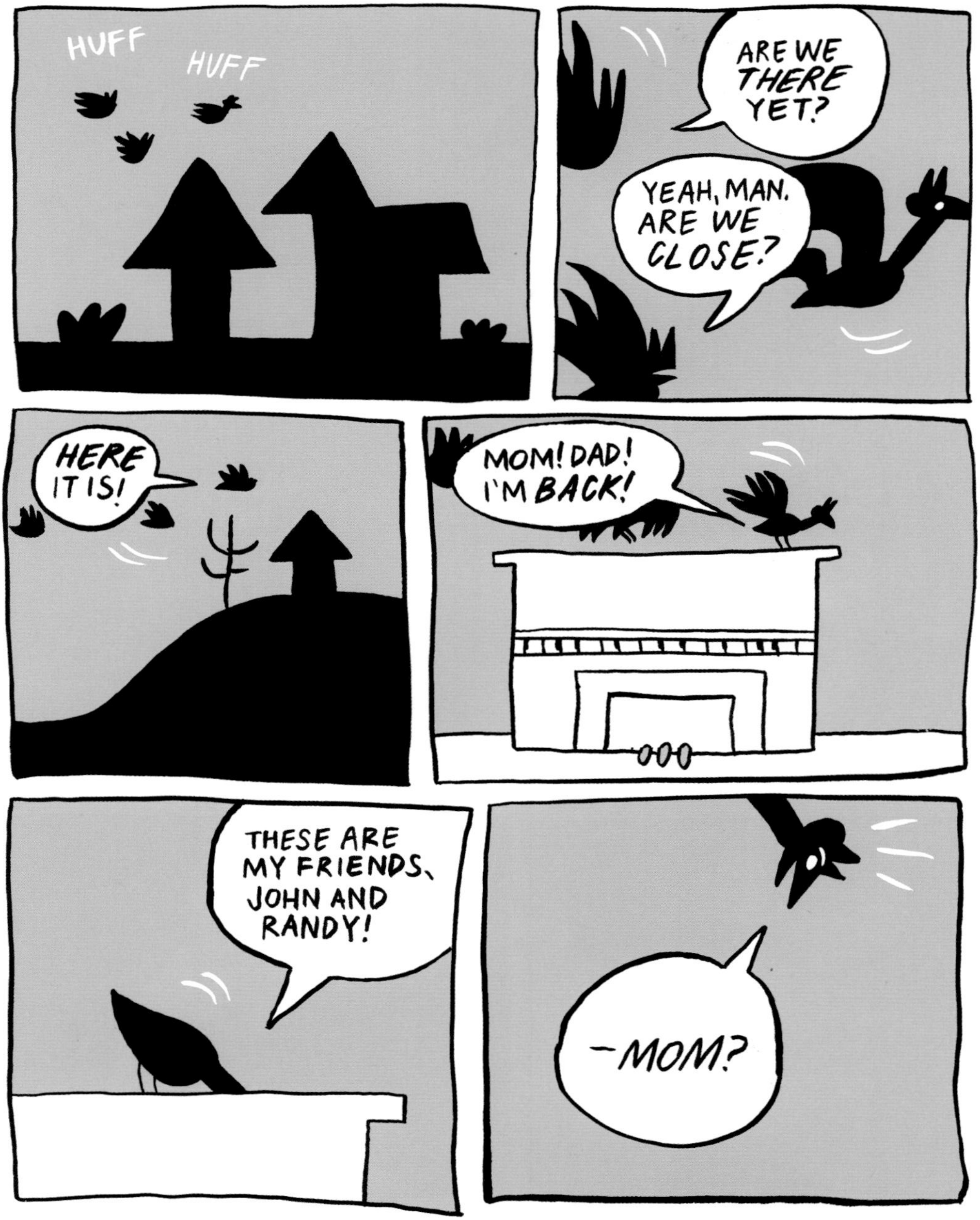
HUFF
HUFF
ARE WE THERE YET?
YEAH, MAN. ARE WE CLOSE?
HERE IT IS!
MOM! DAD! I'M BACK!
THESE ARE MY FRIENDS, JOHN AND RANDY!
—MOM?

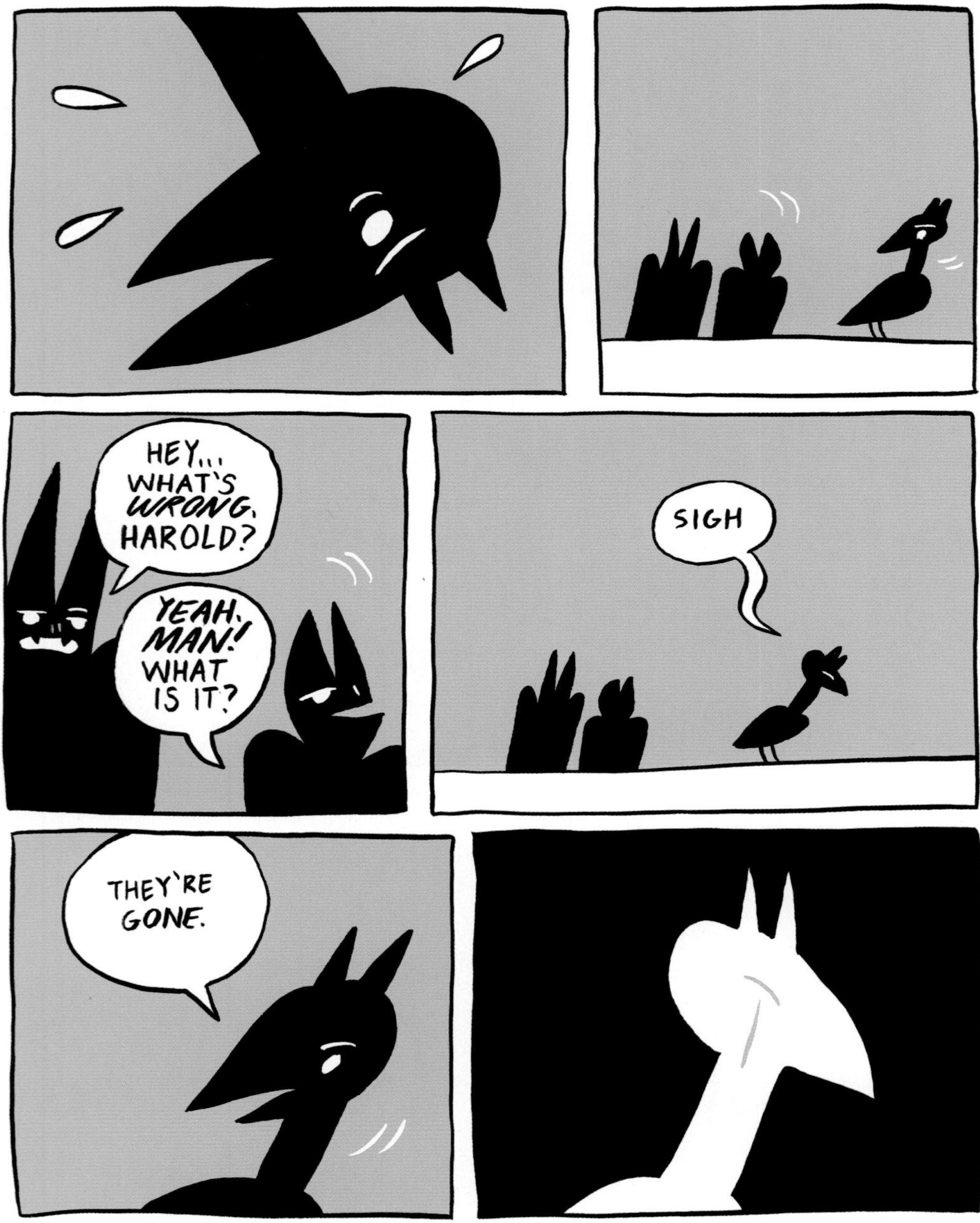
HEY... WHAT'S WRONG, HAROLD?
YEAH, MAN! WHAT IS IT?
SIGH
THEY'RE GONE.

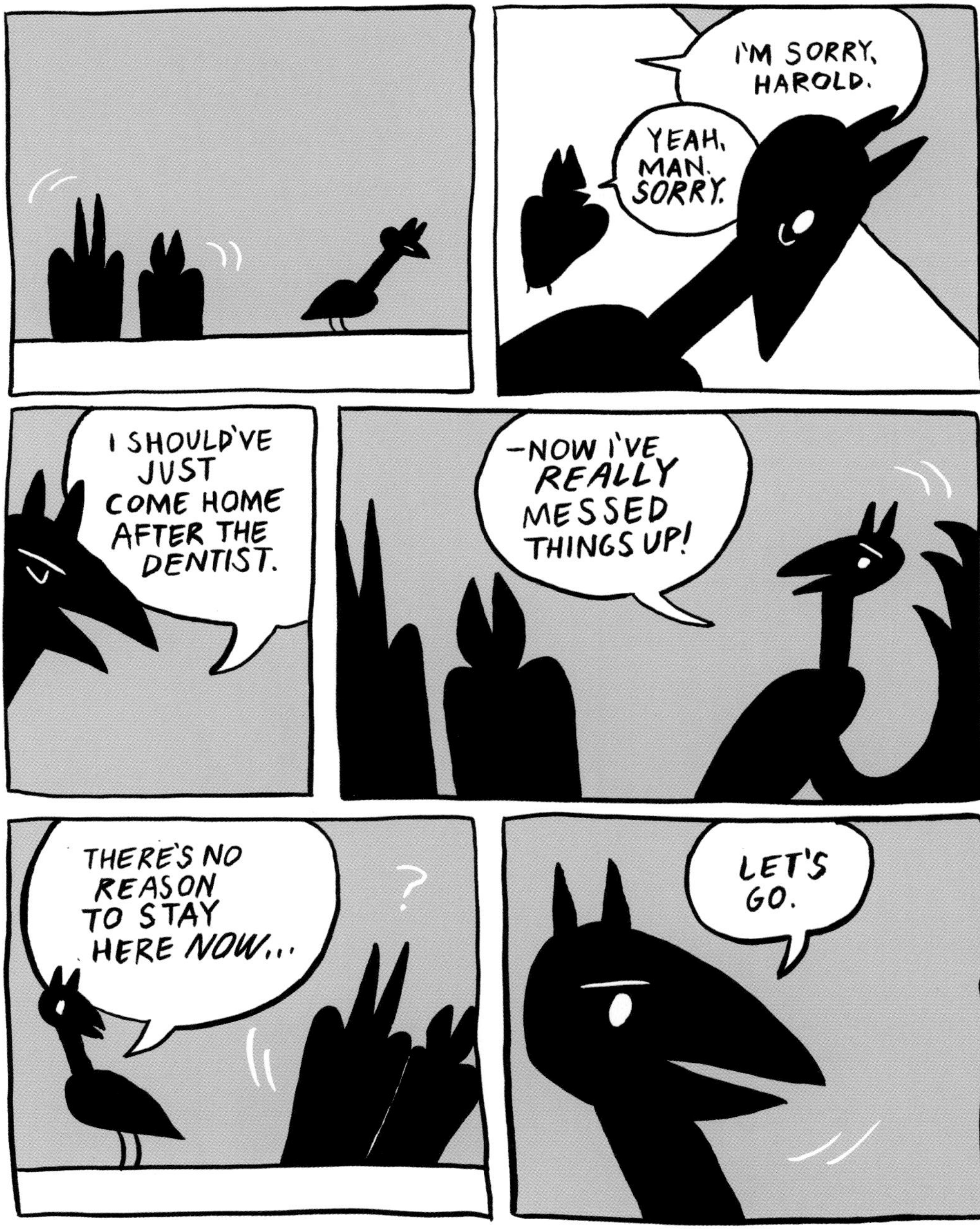
I'M SORRY, HAROLD.
YEAH, MAN. SORRY.
I SHOULD'VE JUST COME HOME AFTER THE DENTIST.
-NOW I'VE *REALLY* MESSED THINGS UP!
THERE'S NO REASON TO STAY HERE *NOW*...
?
LET'S GO.

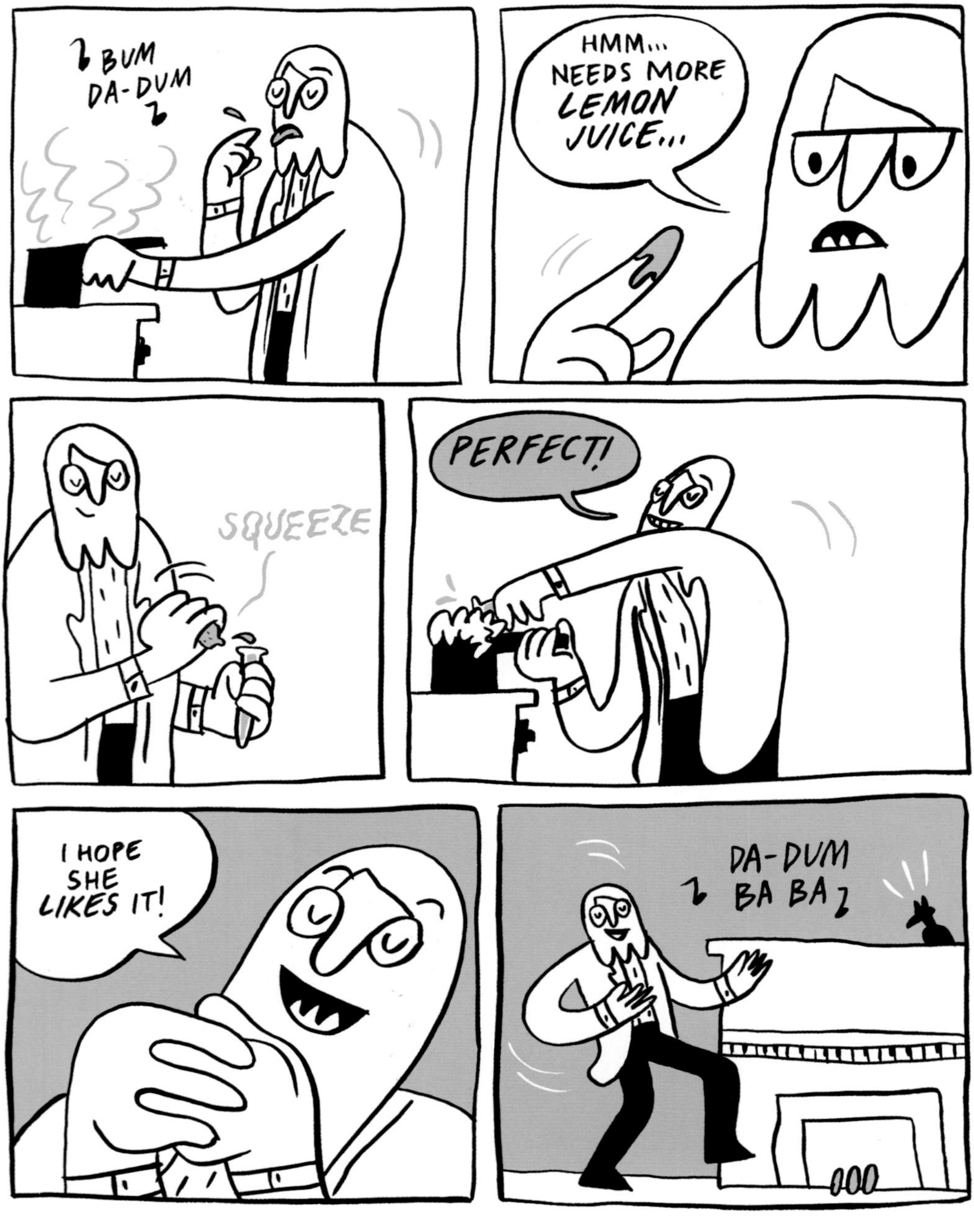
BUM DA-DUM
HMM... NEEDS MORE LEMON JUICE...
SQUEEZE
PERFECT!
I HOPE SHE LIKES IT!
DA-DUM BA BA

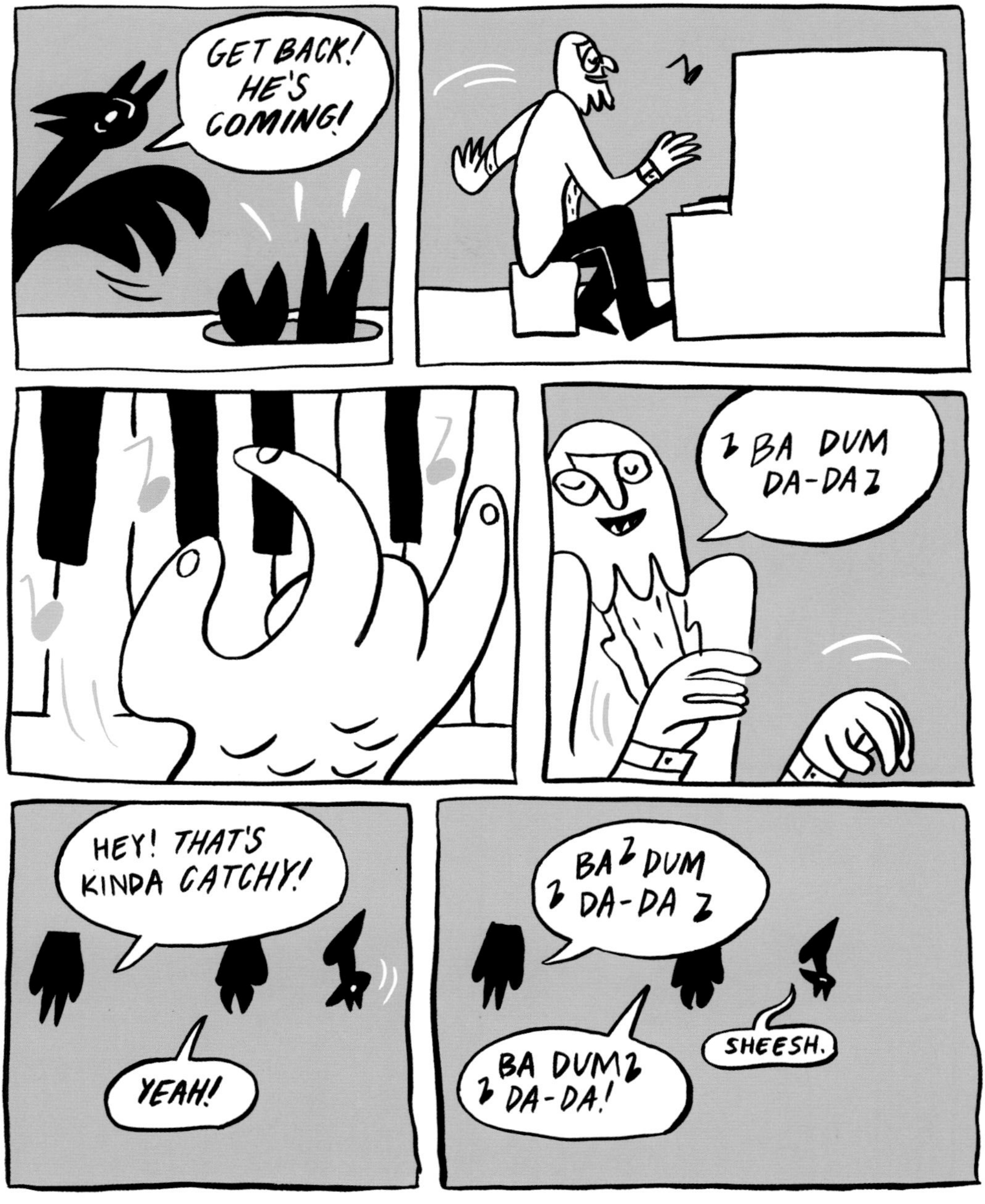
GET BACK! HE'S COMING!
BA DUM DA-DA
HEY! THAT'S KINDA CATCHY!
YEAH!
BA DUM DA-DA
BA DUM DA-DA!
SHEESH.

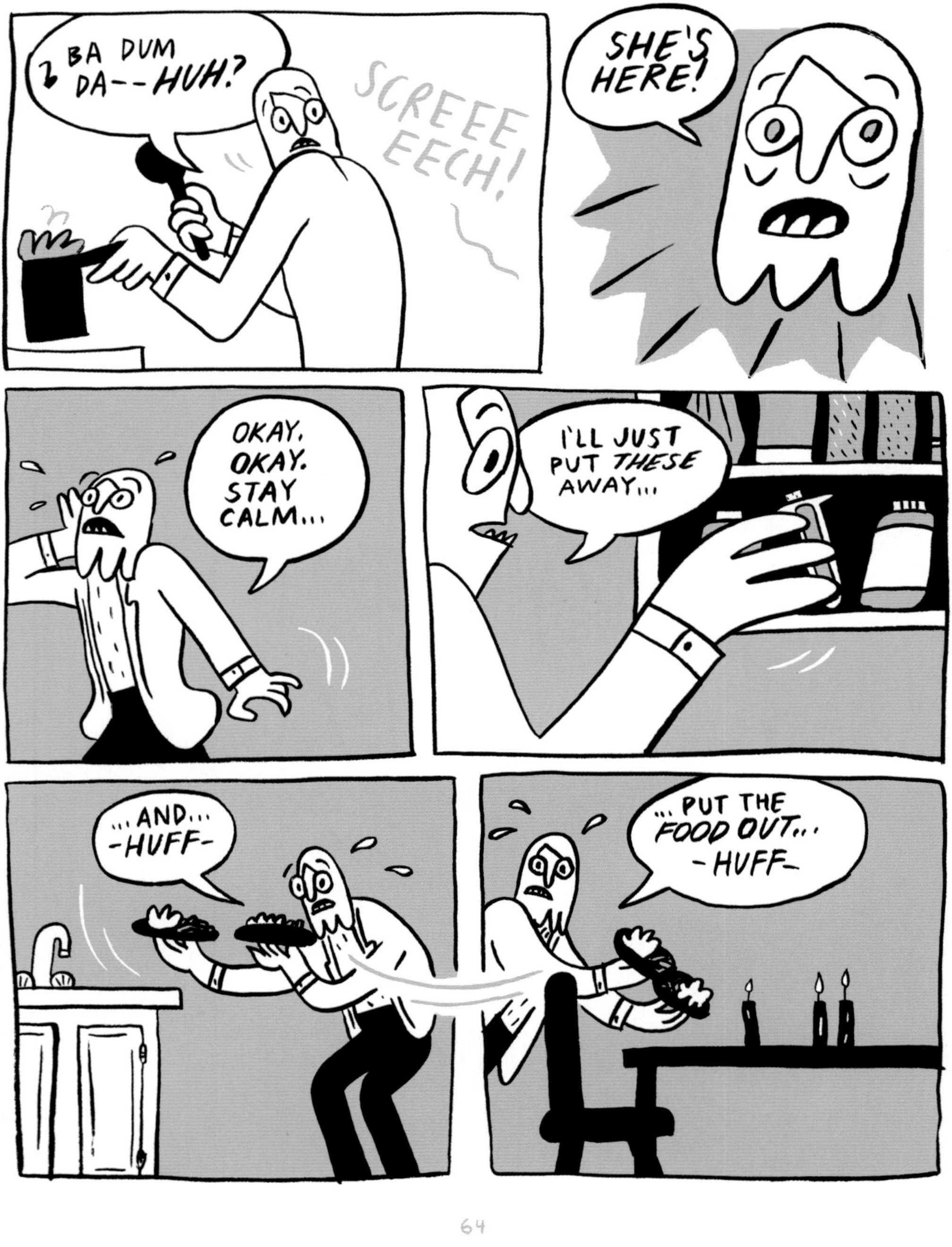
♪ BA DUM DA--HUH?
SCREEEEEECH!
SHE'S HERE!
OKAY. OKAY. STAY CALM...
I'LL JUST PUT THESE AWAY...
...AND... -HUFF-
...PUT THE FOOD OUT... -HUFF-

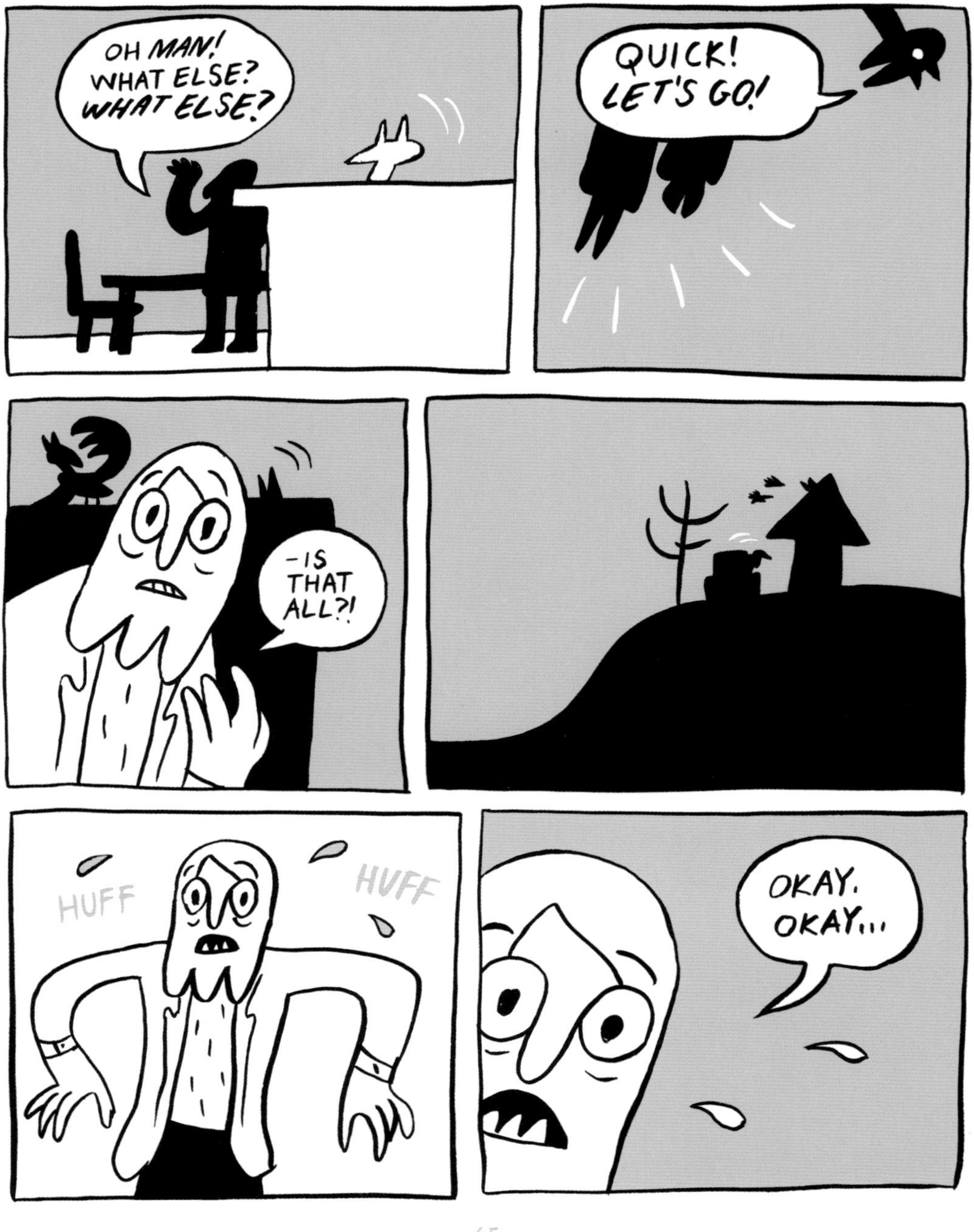
OH MAN! WHAT ELSE? WHAT ELSE?
QUICK! LET'S GO!
-IS THAT ALL?!
HUFF
HUFF
OKAY. OKAY...

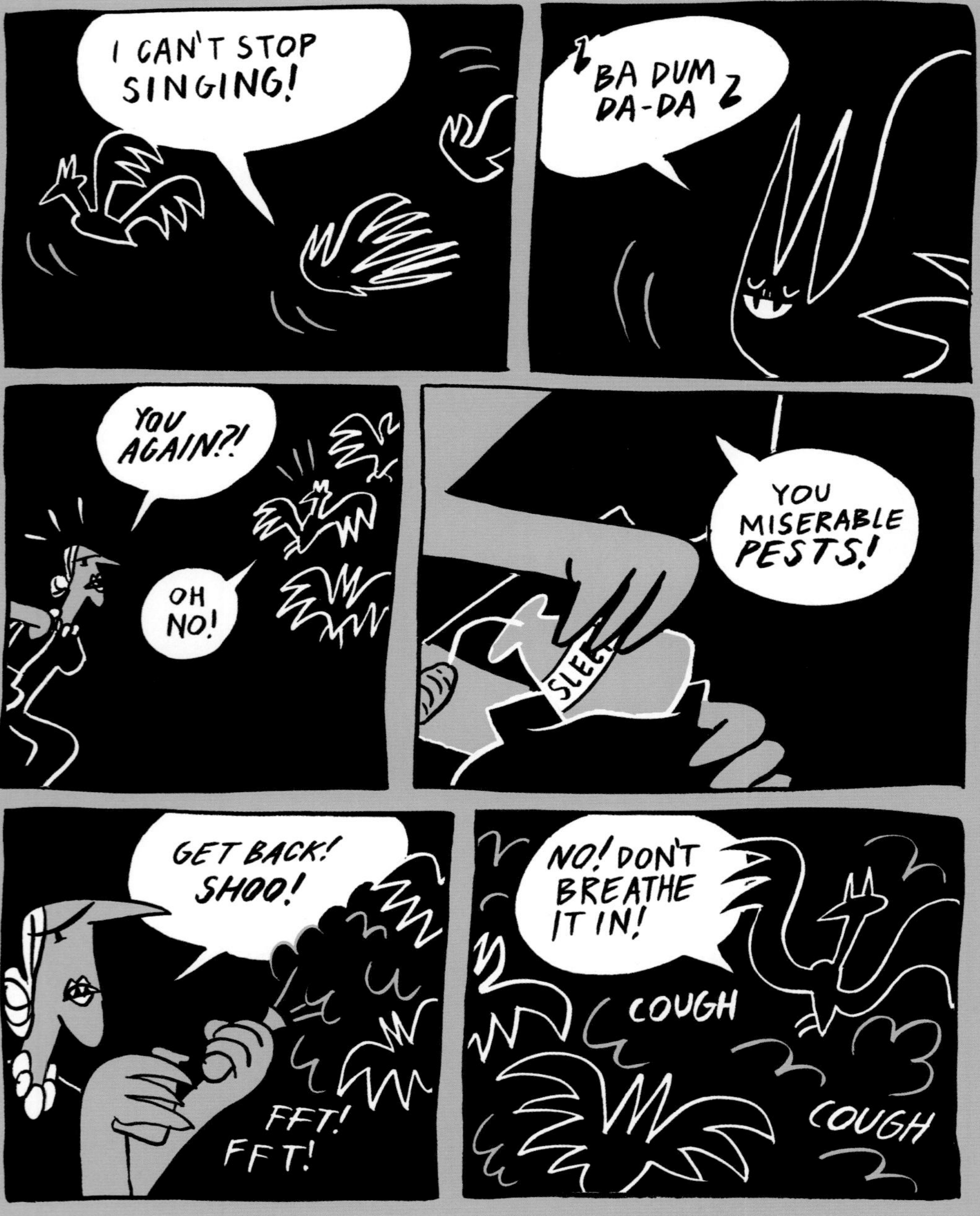
I CAN'T STOP SINGING!
BA DUM DA-DA
YOU AGAIN?!
OH NO!
YOU MISERABLE PESTS!
SLEE
GET BACK! SHOO!
FFT! FFT!
NO! DON'T BREATHE IT IN!
COUGH
COUGH

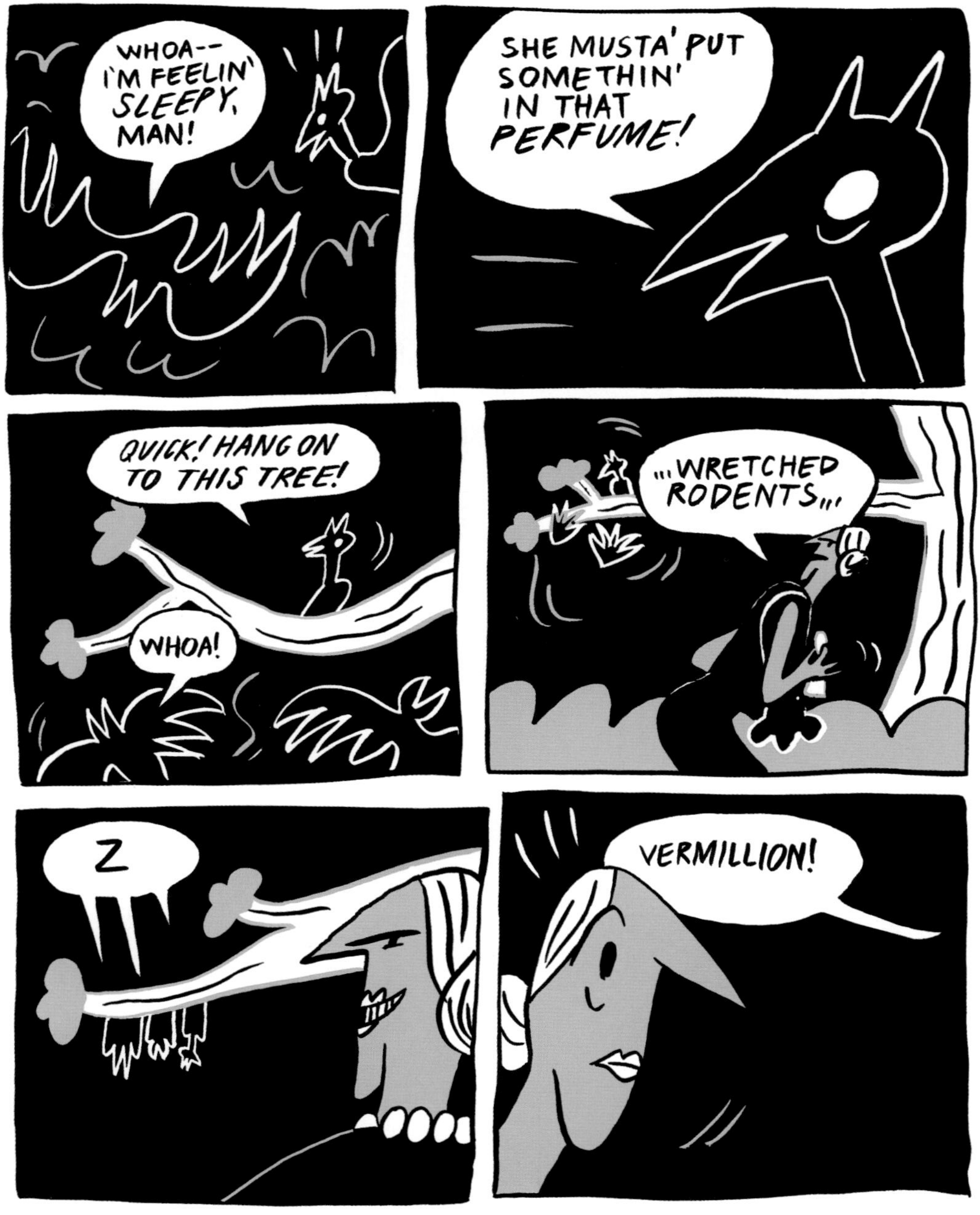
WHOA-- I'M FEELIN' SLEEPY, MAN!
SHE MUSTA' PUT SOMETHIN' IN THAT PERFUME!
QUICK! HANG ON TO THIS TREE!
WHOA!
...WRETCHED RODENTS...
Z
VERMILLION!

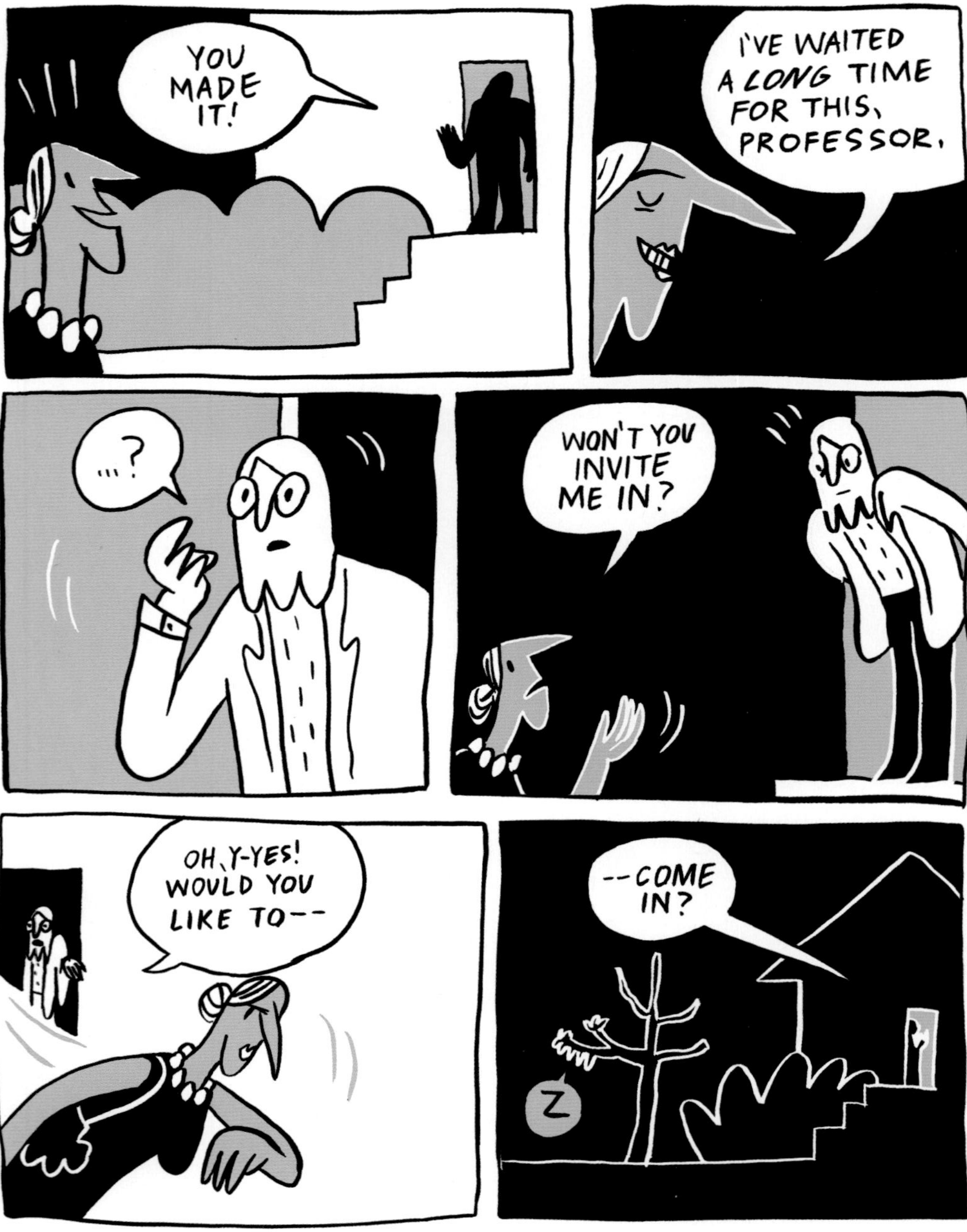
YOU MADE IT!
I'VE WAITED A *LONG* TIME FOR THIS, PROFESSOR.
...?
WON'T YOU INVITE ME IN?
OH, Y-YES! WOULD YOU LIKE TO--
--COME IN?
Z

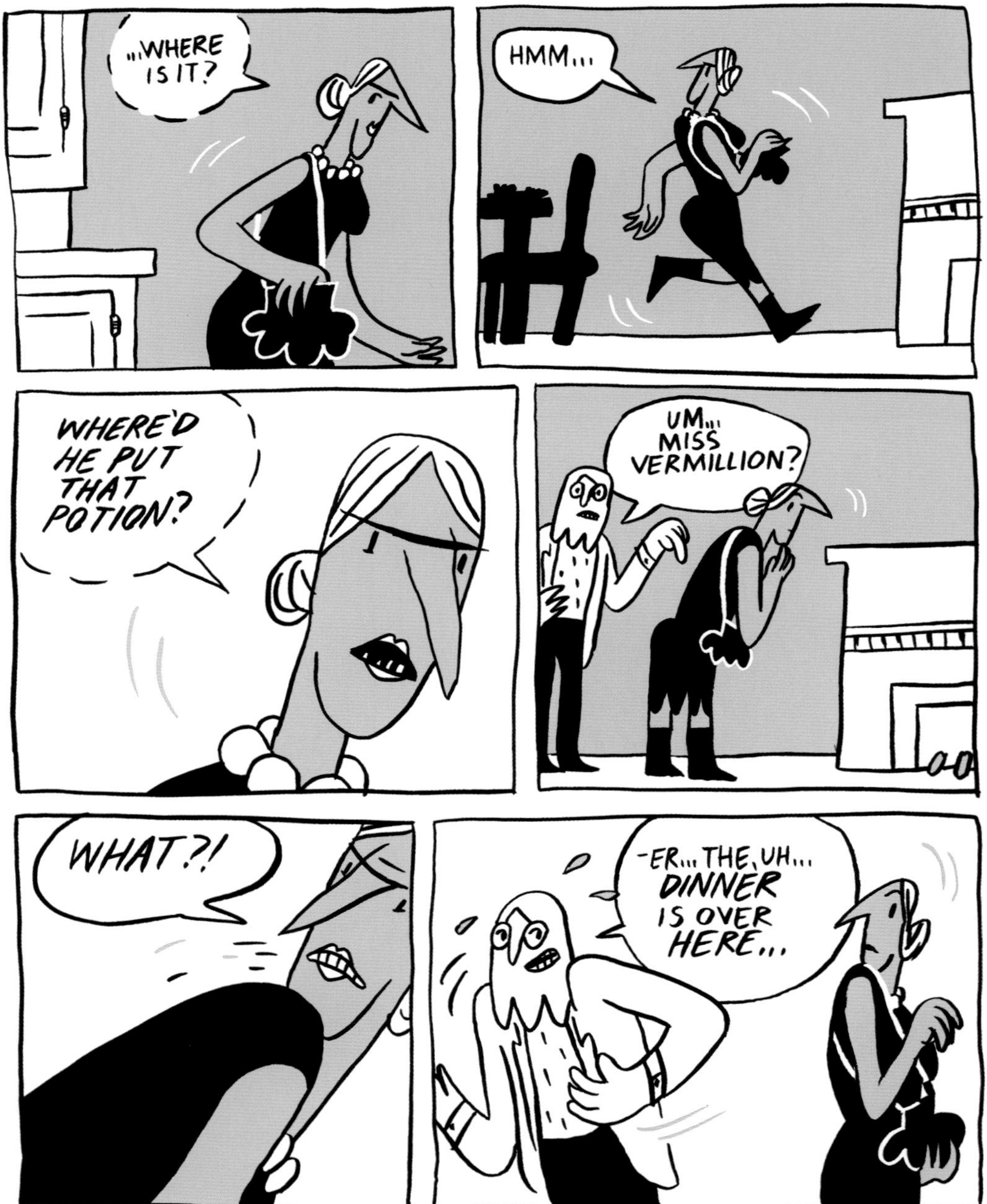
...WHERE IS IT?
HMM...
WHERE'D HE PUT THAT POTION?
UM... MISS VERMILLION?
WHAT?!
-ER... THE, UH... DINNER IS OVER HERE...

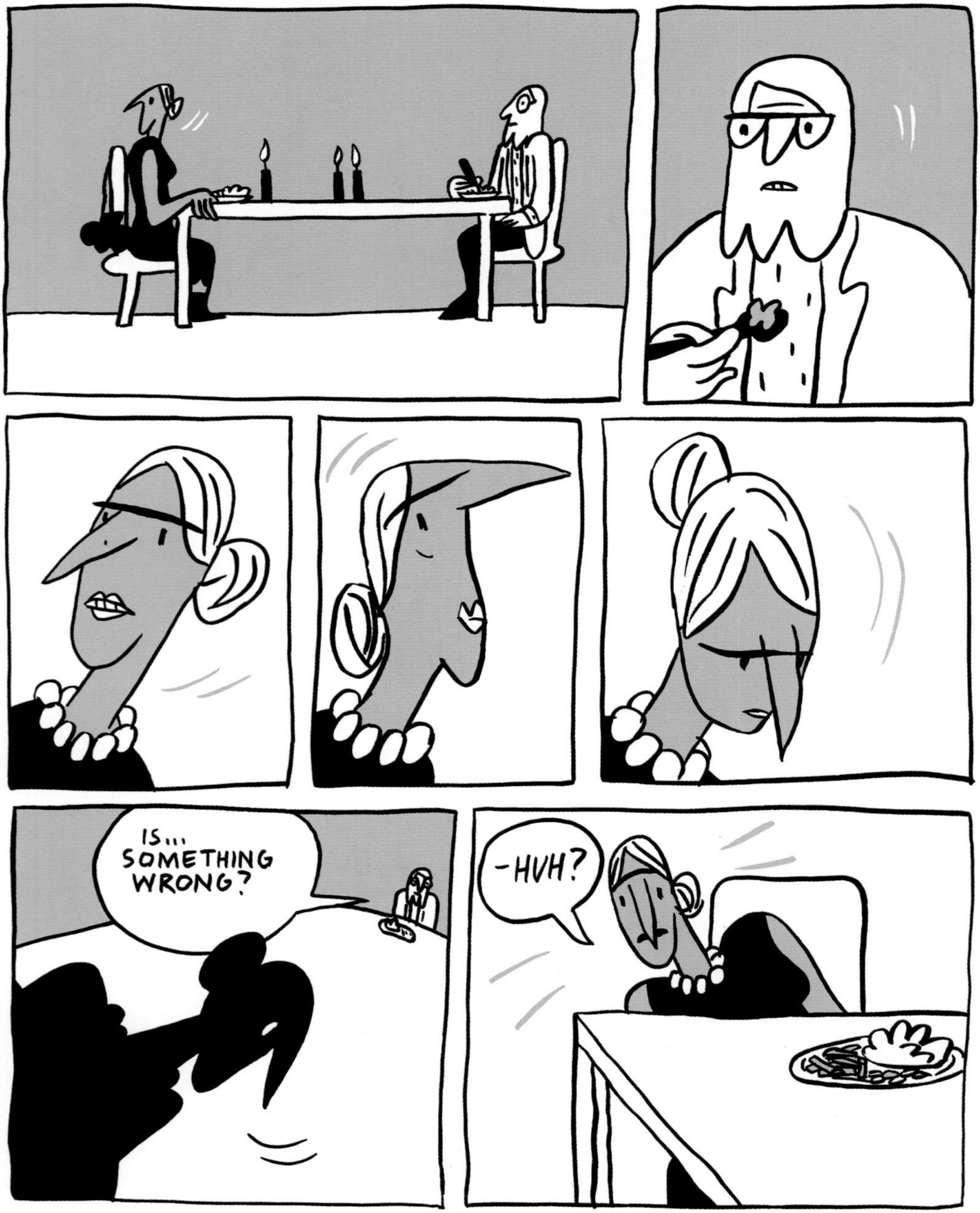
IS... SOMETHING WRONG?
-HUH?

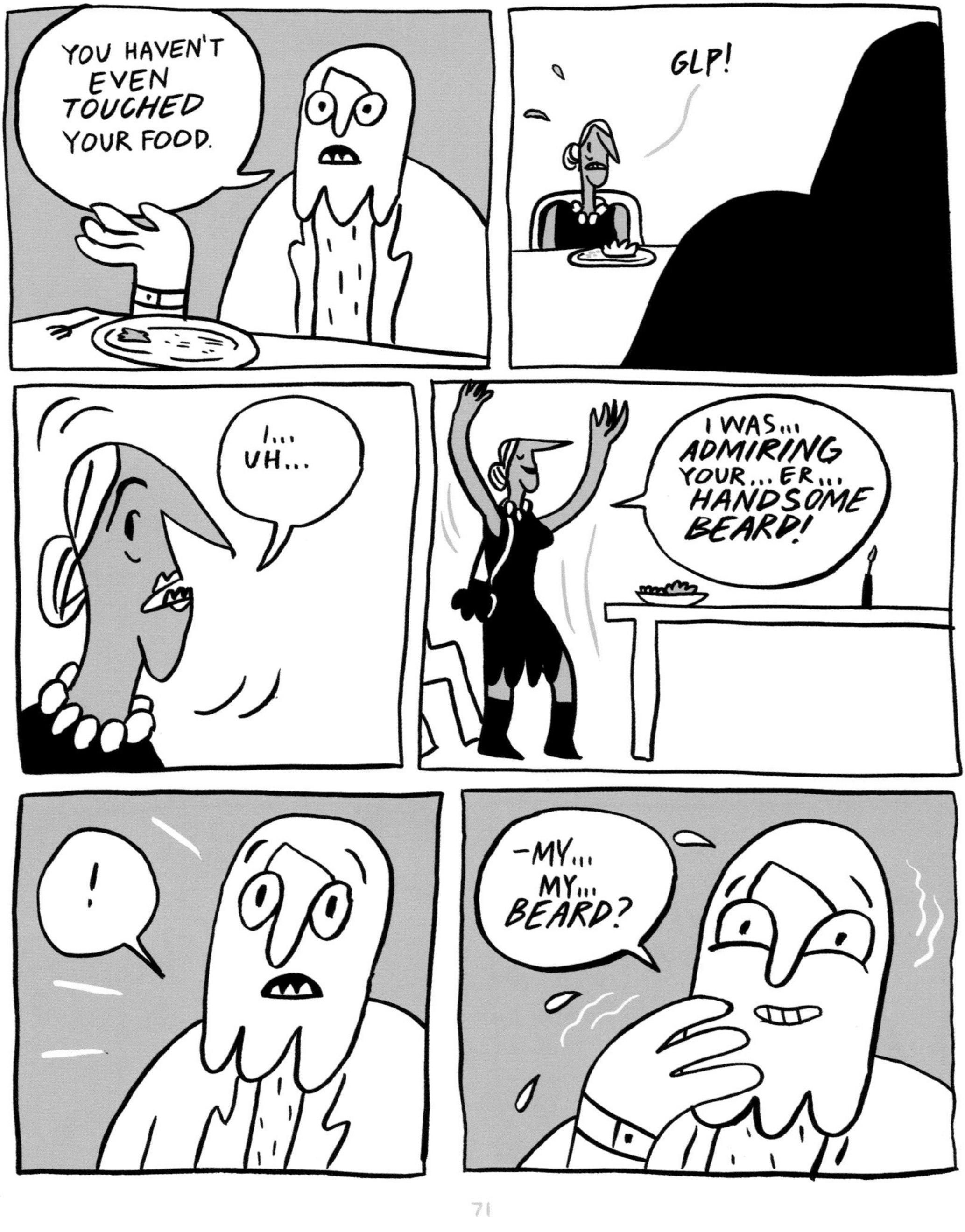
YOU HAVEN'T EVEN TOUCHED YOUR FOOD.
GLP!
I... UH...
I WAS... ADMIRING YOUR... ER... HANDSOME BEARD!
!
-MY... MY... BEARD?

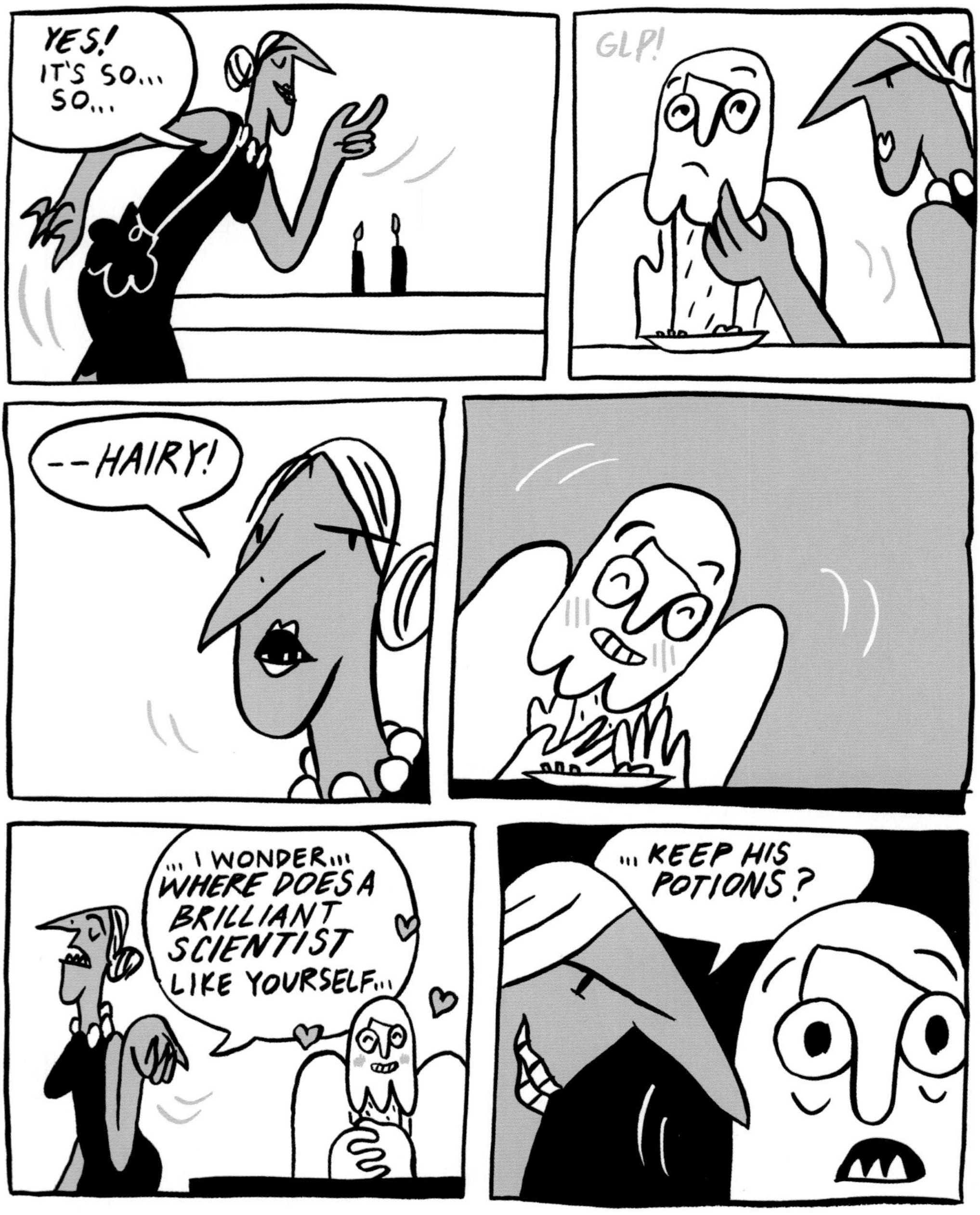
YES! IT'S SO... SO...
GLP!
--HAIRY!
... I WONDER... WHERE DOES A BRILLIANT SCIENTIST LIKE YOURSELF...
... KEEP HIS POTIONS?

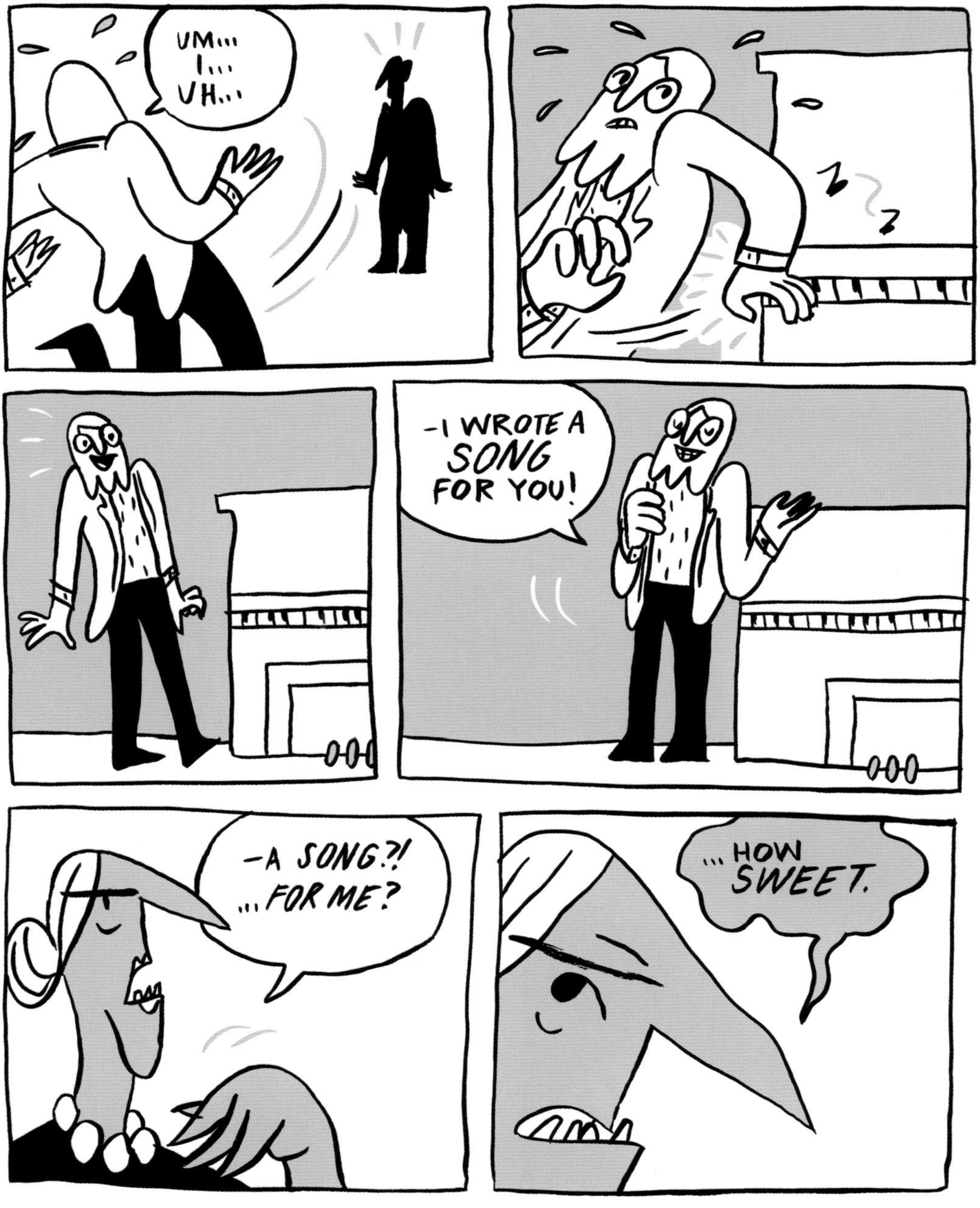
UM...
I...
UH...
-I WROTE A SONG FOR YOU!
-A SONG?! ...FOR ME?
...HOW SWEET.

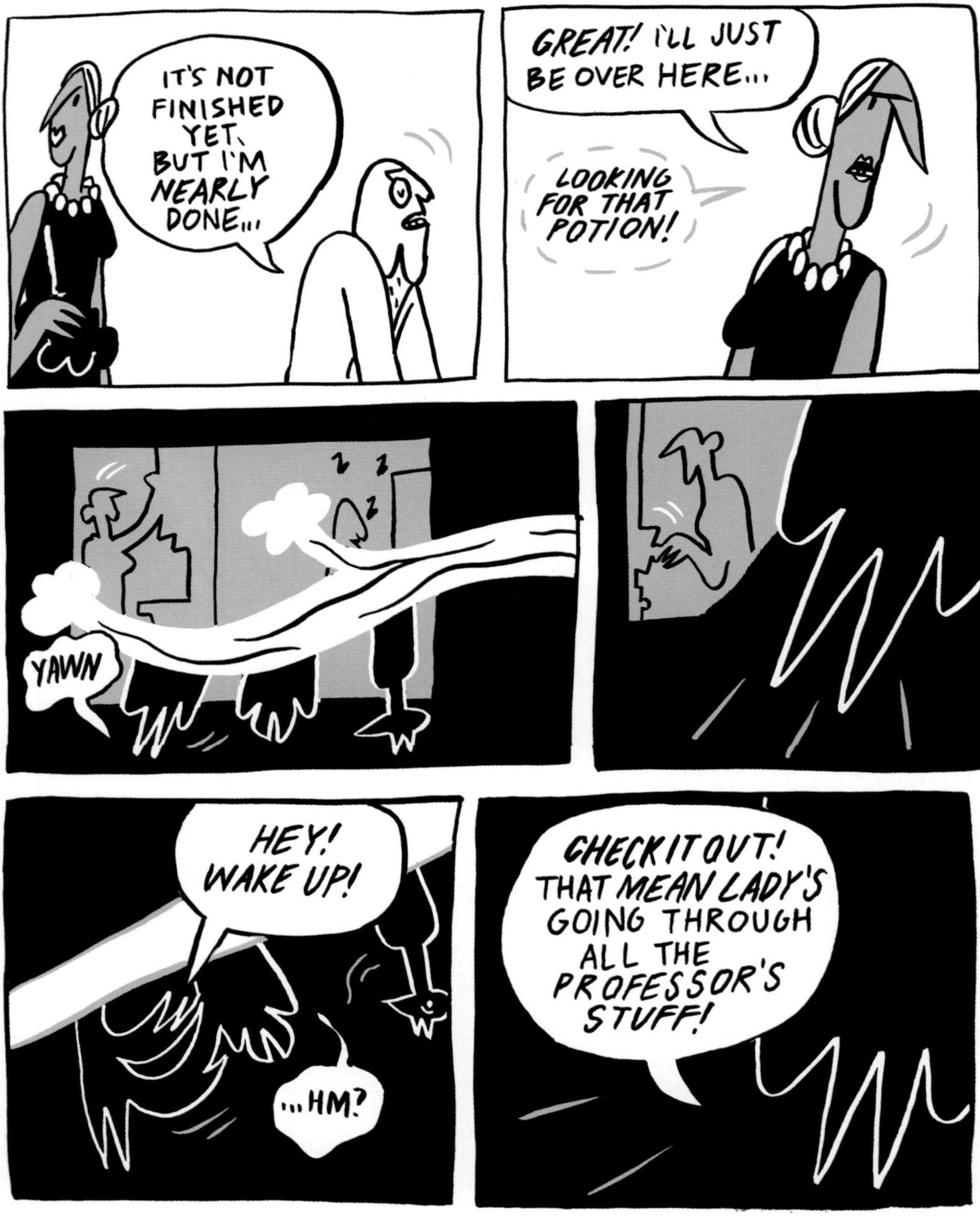
IT'S NOT FINISHED YET, BUT I'M NEARLY DONE...
GREAT! I'LL JUST BE OVER HERE...
LOOKING FOR THAT POTION!
YAWN
HEY! WAKE UP!
...HM?
CHECK IT OUT! THAT MEAN LADY'S GOING THROUGH ALL THE PROFESSOR'S STUFF!

BUT WHY IS SHE--
GOTCHA!
-THE POTION!
HEE HEE HEE
SHE JUST STOLE THE PROFESSOR'S POTION FOR ETERNAL LIFE!
-HE DOESN'T EVEN KNOW IT!

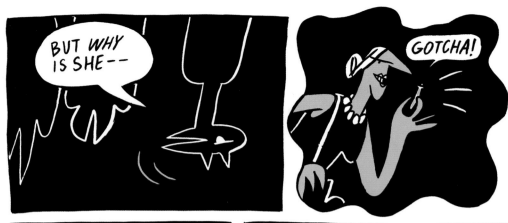

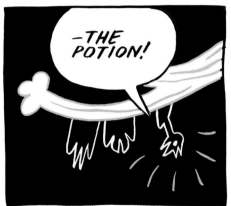

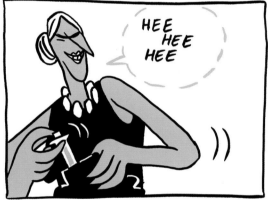

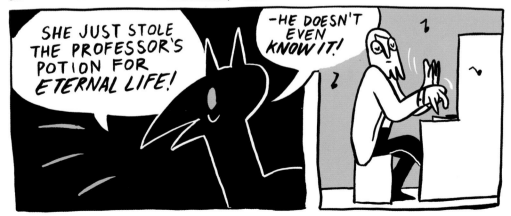

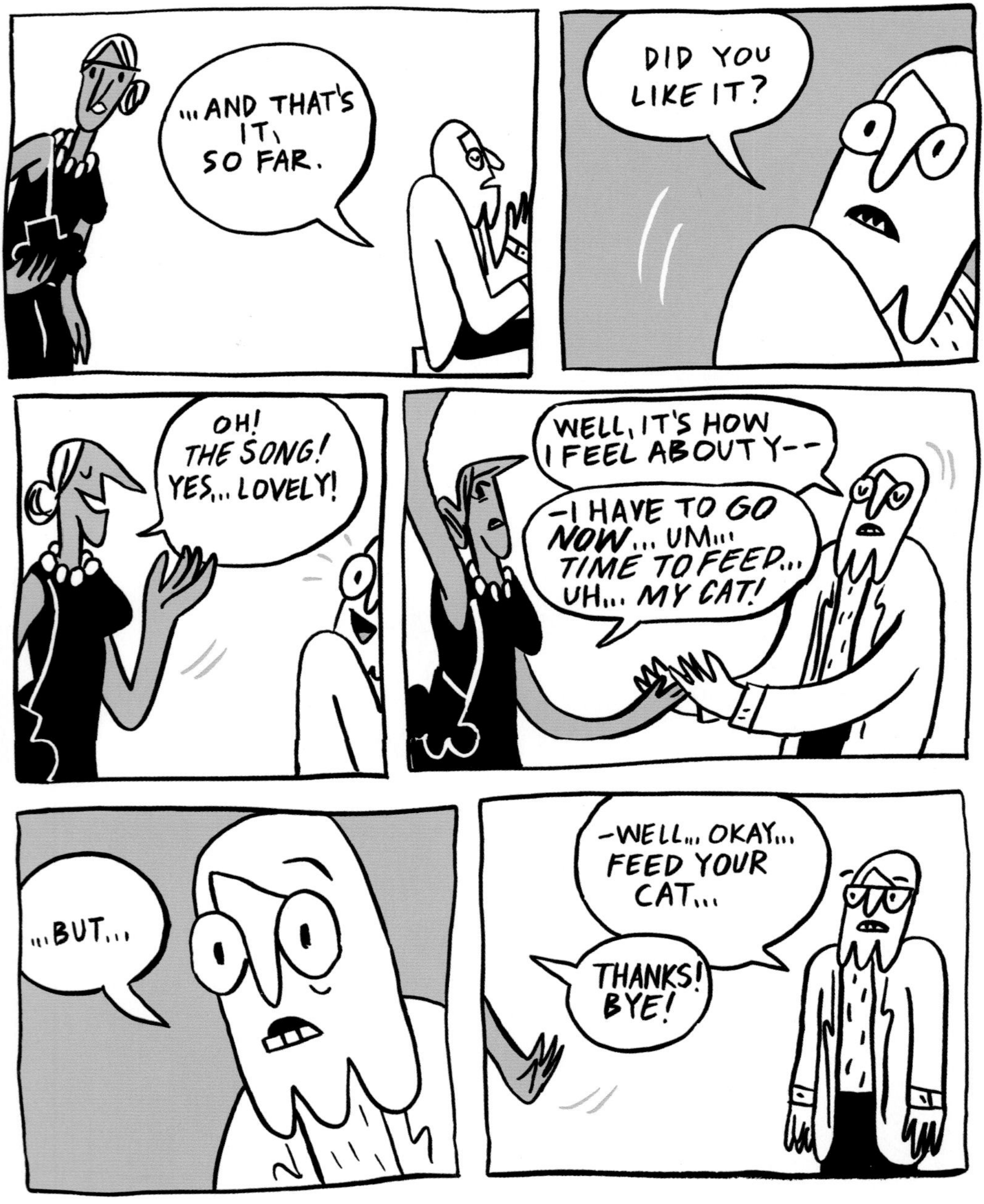
...AND THAT'S IT, SO FAR.
DID YOU LIKE IT?
OH! THE SONG! YES... LOVELY!
WELL, IT'S HOW I FEEL ABOUT Y--
-I HAVE TO GO NOW... UM... TIME TO FEED... UH... MY CAT!
...BUT...
-WELL... OKAY... FEED YOUR CAT...
THANKS! BYE!

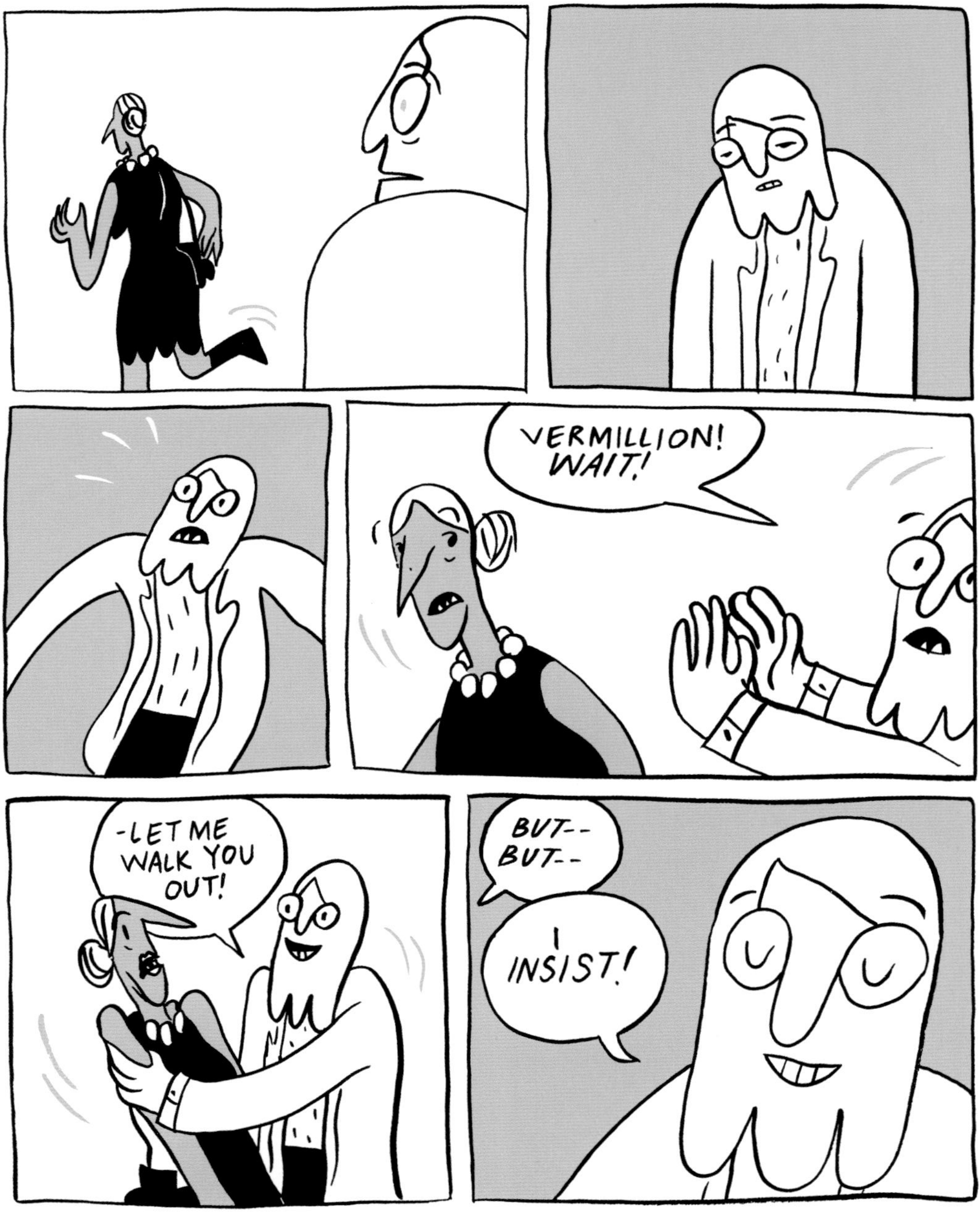
VERMILLION! WAIT!
-LET ME WALK YOU OUT!
BUT-- BUT--
I INSIST!

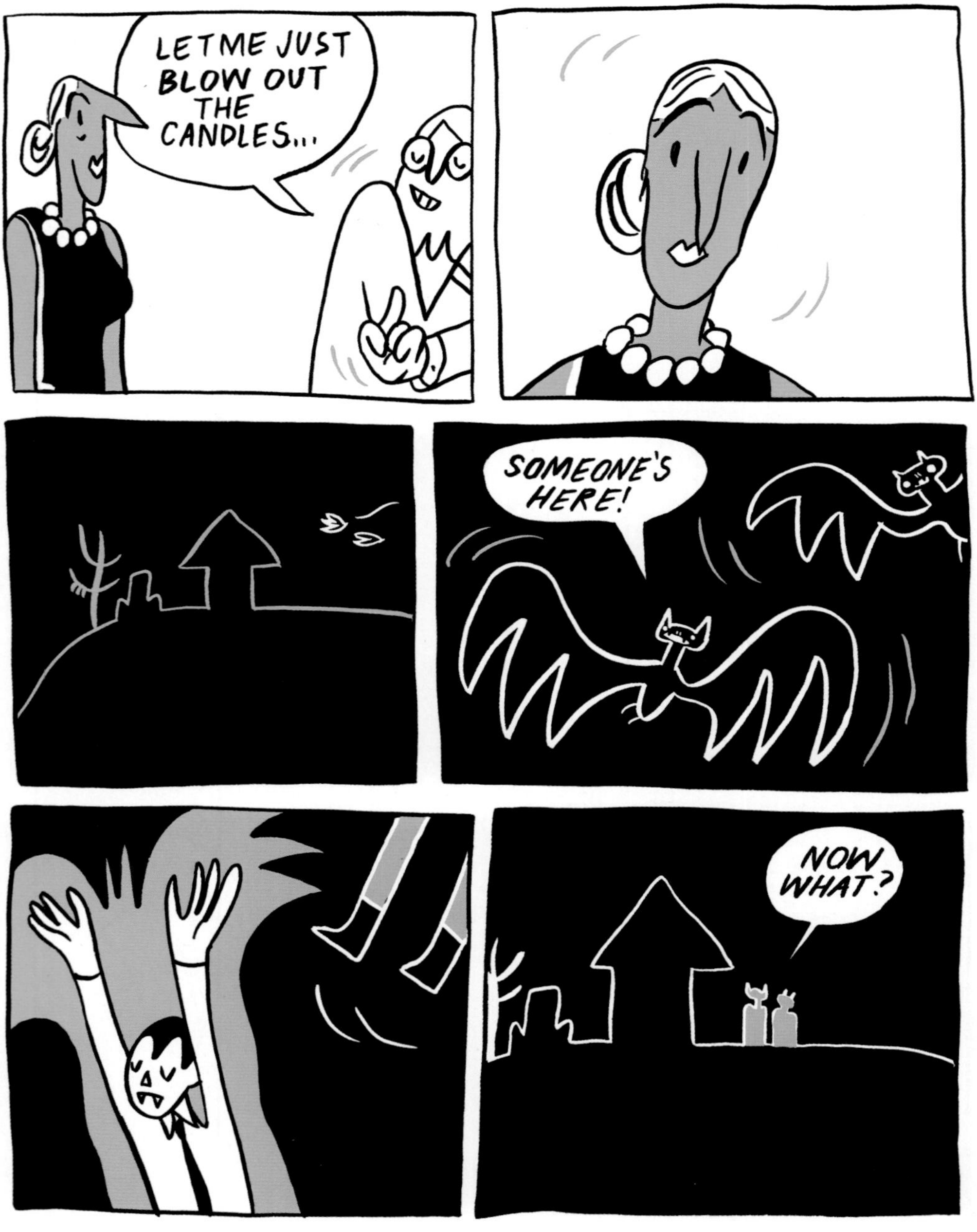
LET ME JUST BLOW OUT THE CANDLES...
SOMEONE'S HERE!
NOW WHAT?

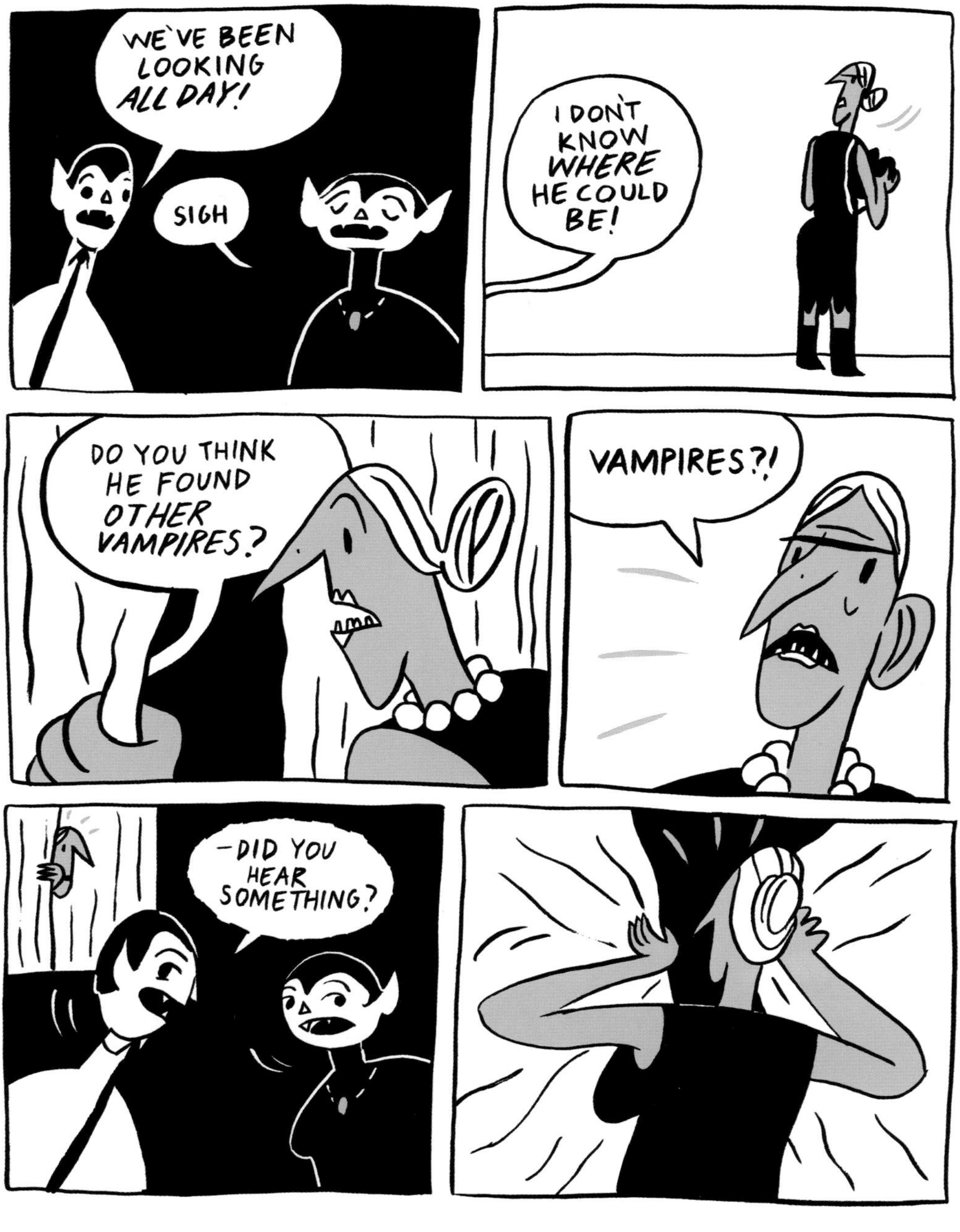
WE'VE BEEN LOOKING ALL DAY!
SIGH
I DON'T KNOW WHERE HE COULD BE!
DO YOU THINK HE FOUND OTHER VAMPIRES?
VAMPIRES?!
-DID YOU HEAR SOMETHING?

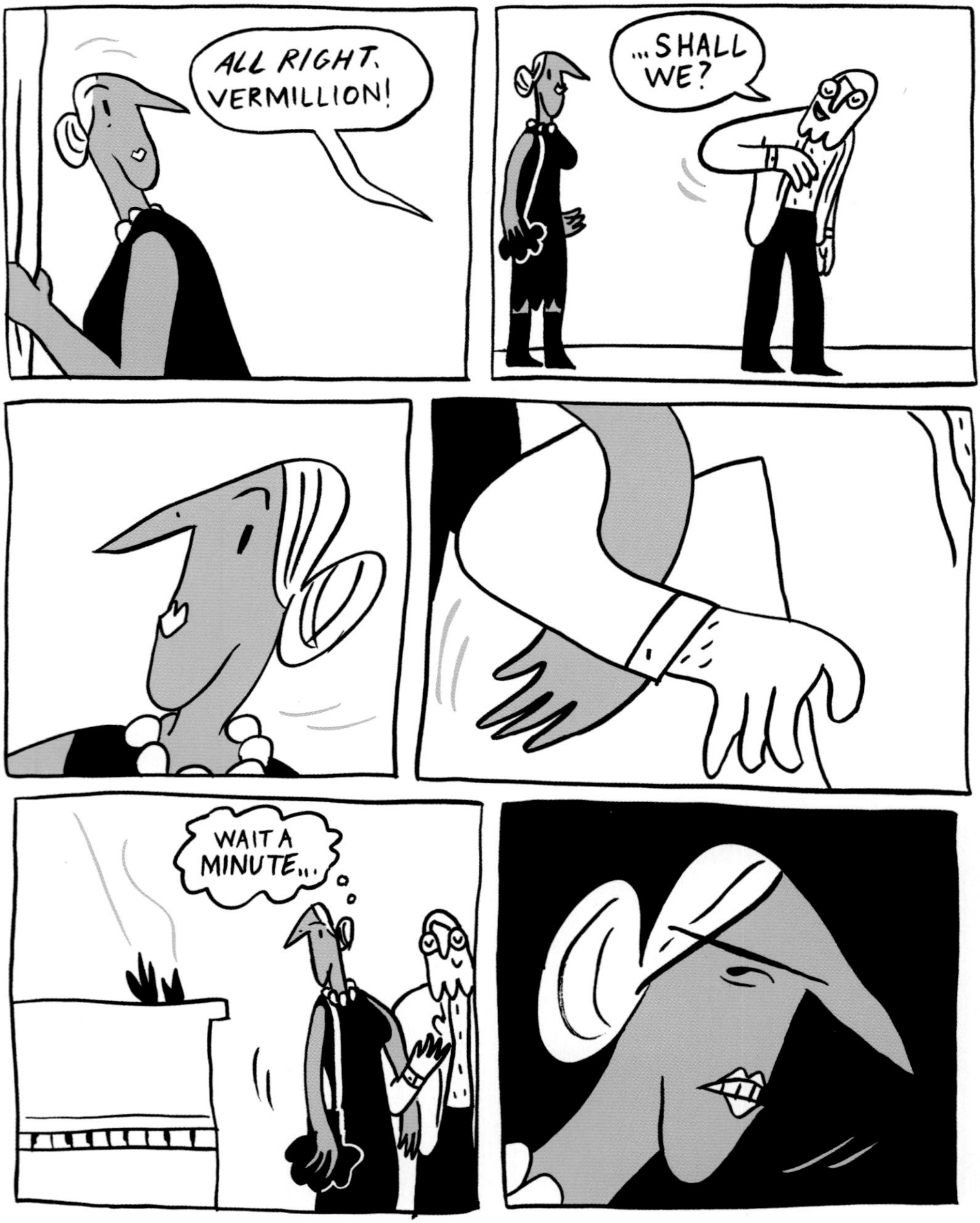
ALL RIGHT. VERMILLION!
...SHALL WE?
WAIT A MINUTE...

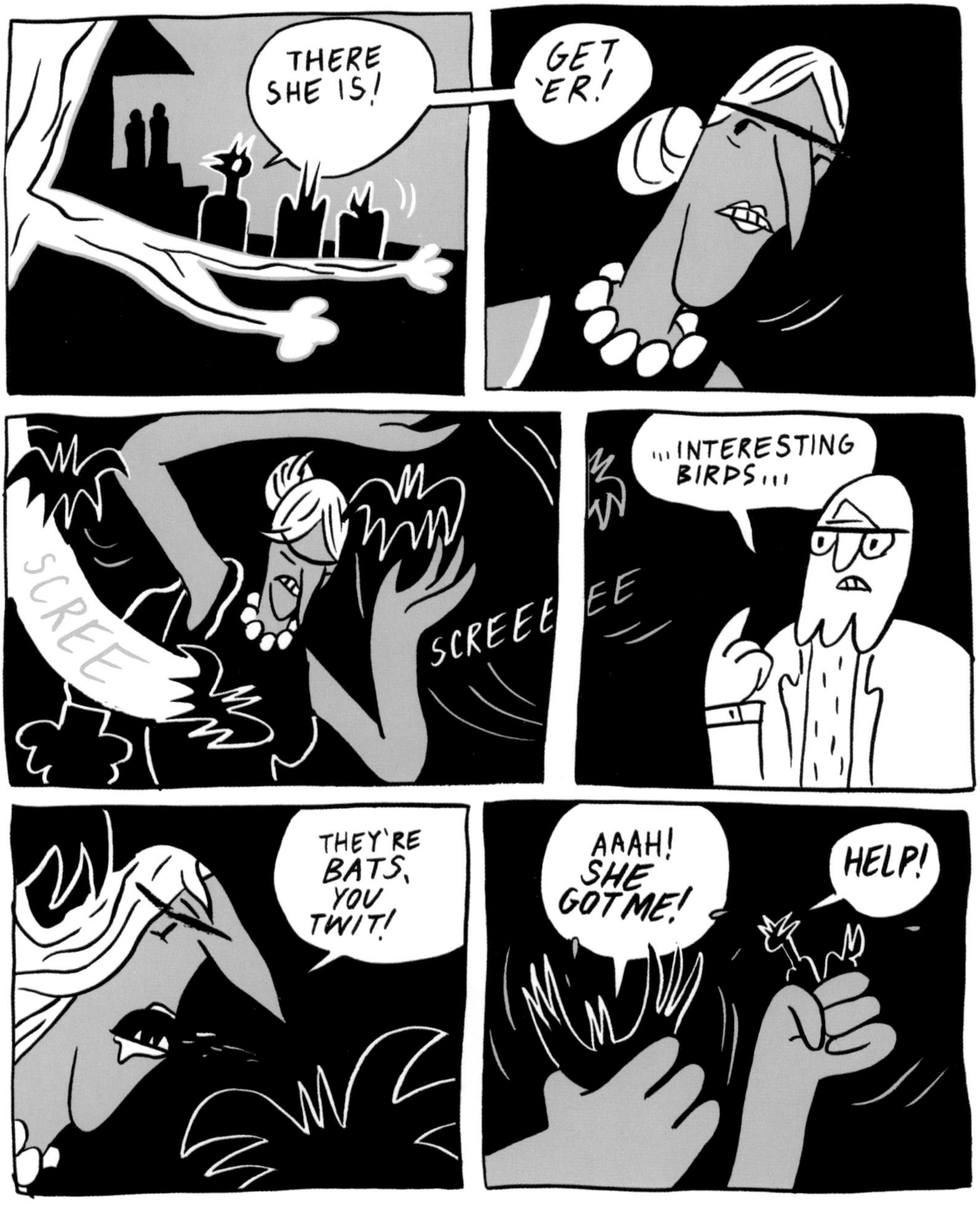
THERE SHE IS!
GET 'ER!
SCREE
SCREEEEEE
...INTERESTING BIRDS...
THEY'RE BATS, YOU TWIT!
AAAH! SHE GOT ME!
HELP!

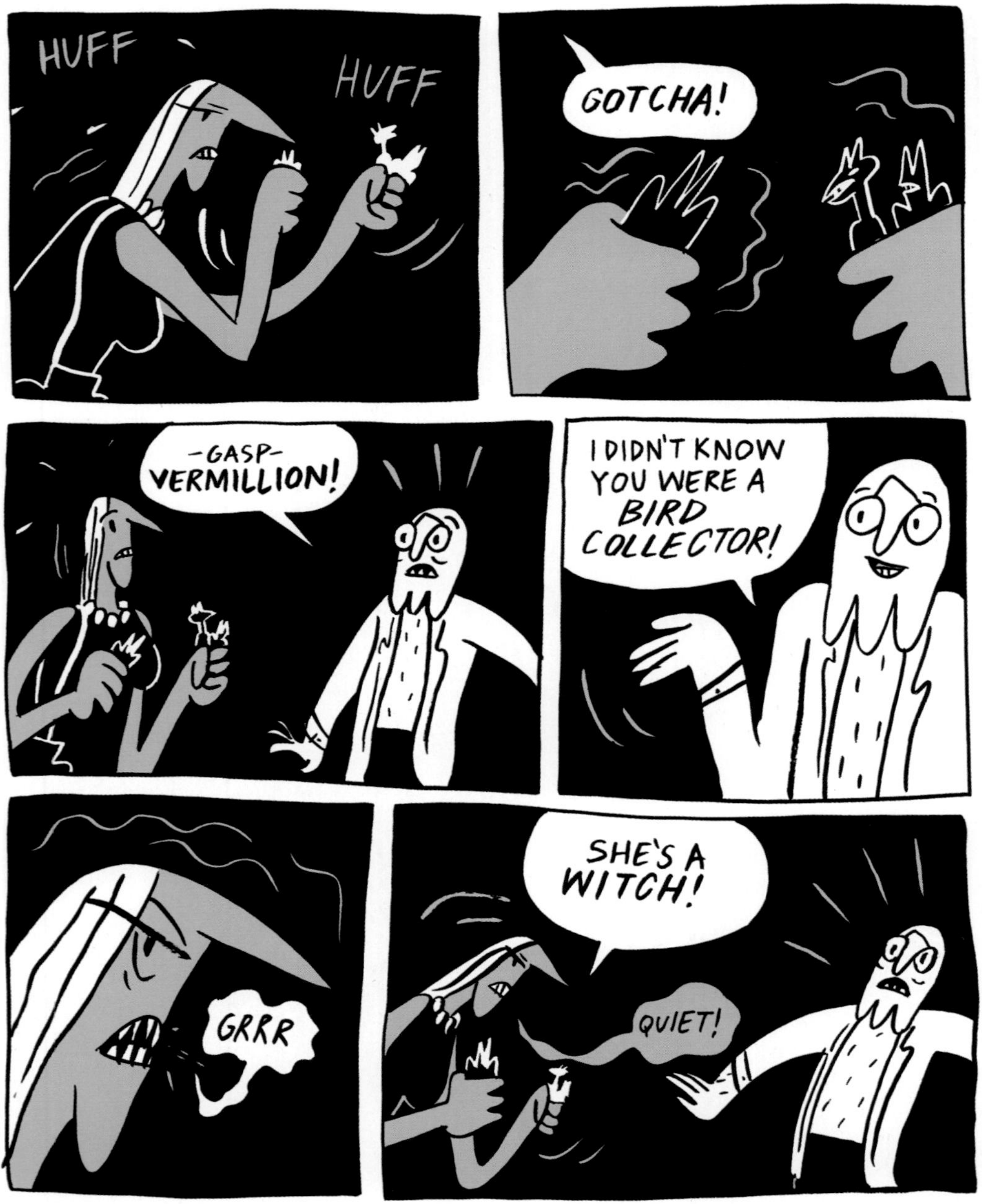
HUFF
HUFF
GOTCHA!
-GASP-
VERMILLION!
I DIDN'T KNOW YOU WERE A BIRD COLLECTOR!
GRRR
SHE'S A WITCH!
QUIET!

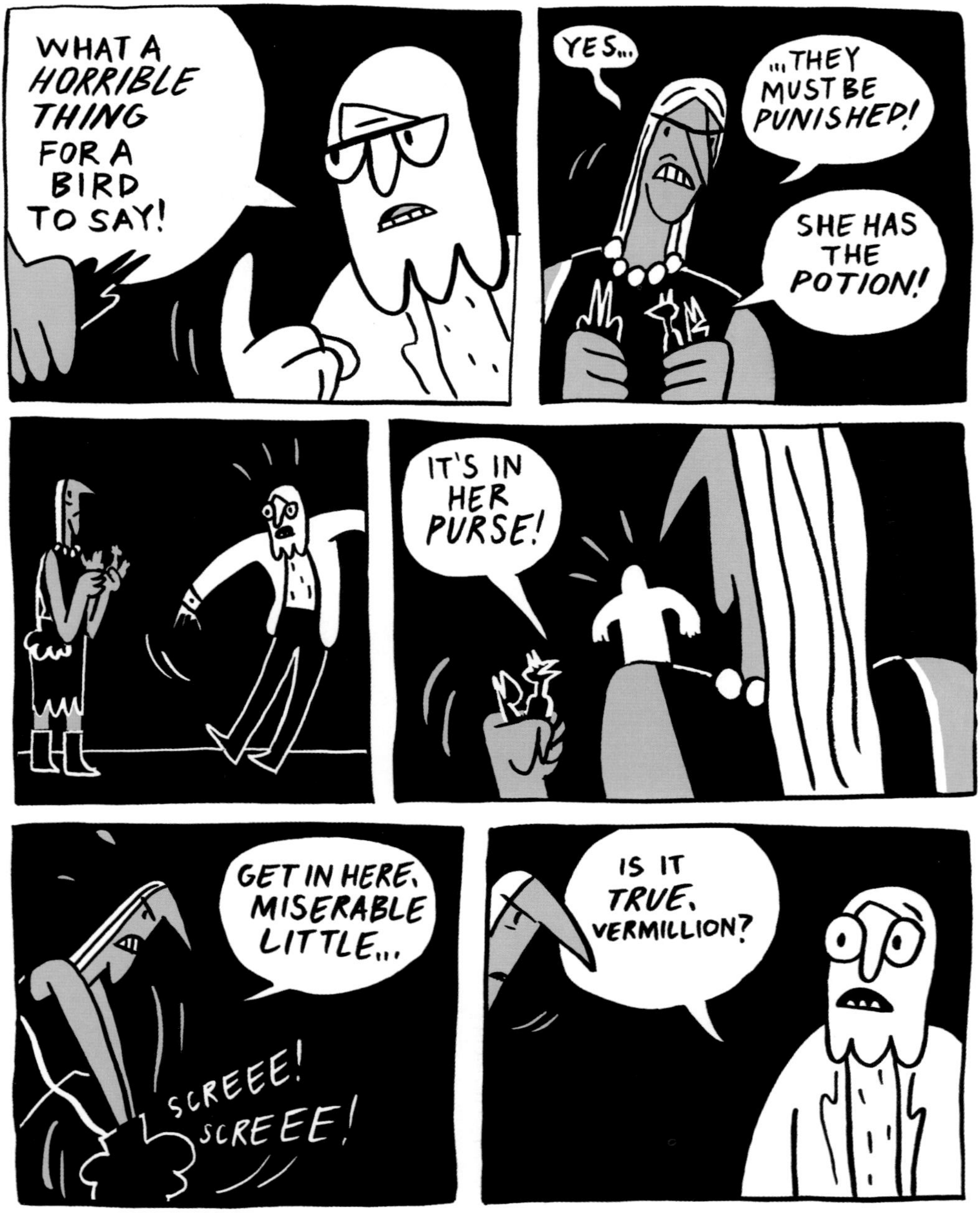
WHAT A *HORRIBLE THING* FOR A BIRD TO SAY!
YES...
...THEY MUST BE *PUNISHED!*
SHE HAS THE *POTION!*
IT'S IN HER *PURSE!*
GET IN HERE, MISERABLE LITTLE...
SCREEE! SCREEE!
IS IT *TRUE*, VERMILLION?

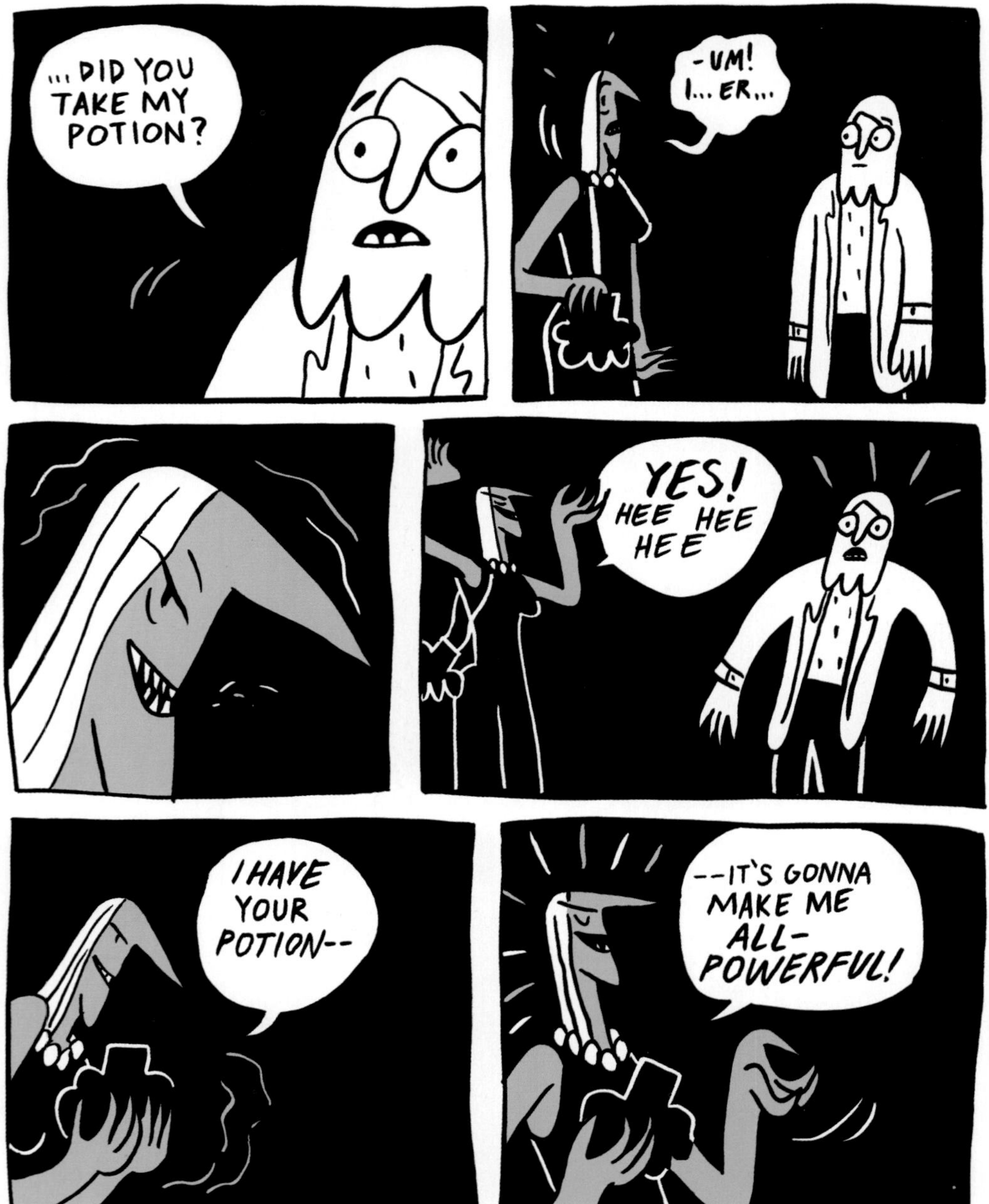
...DID YOU TAKE MY POTION?
-UM! I... ER...
YES! HEE HEE HEE
I HAVE YOUR POTION--
--IT'S GONNA MAKE ME ALL-POWERFUL!

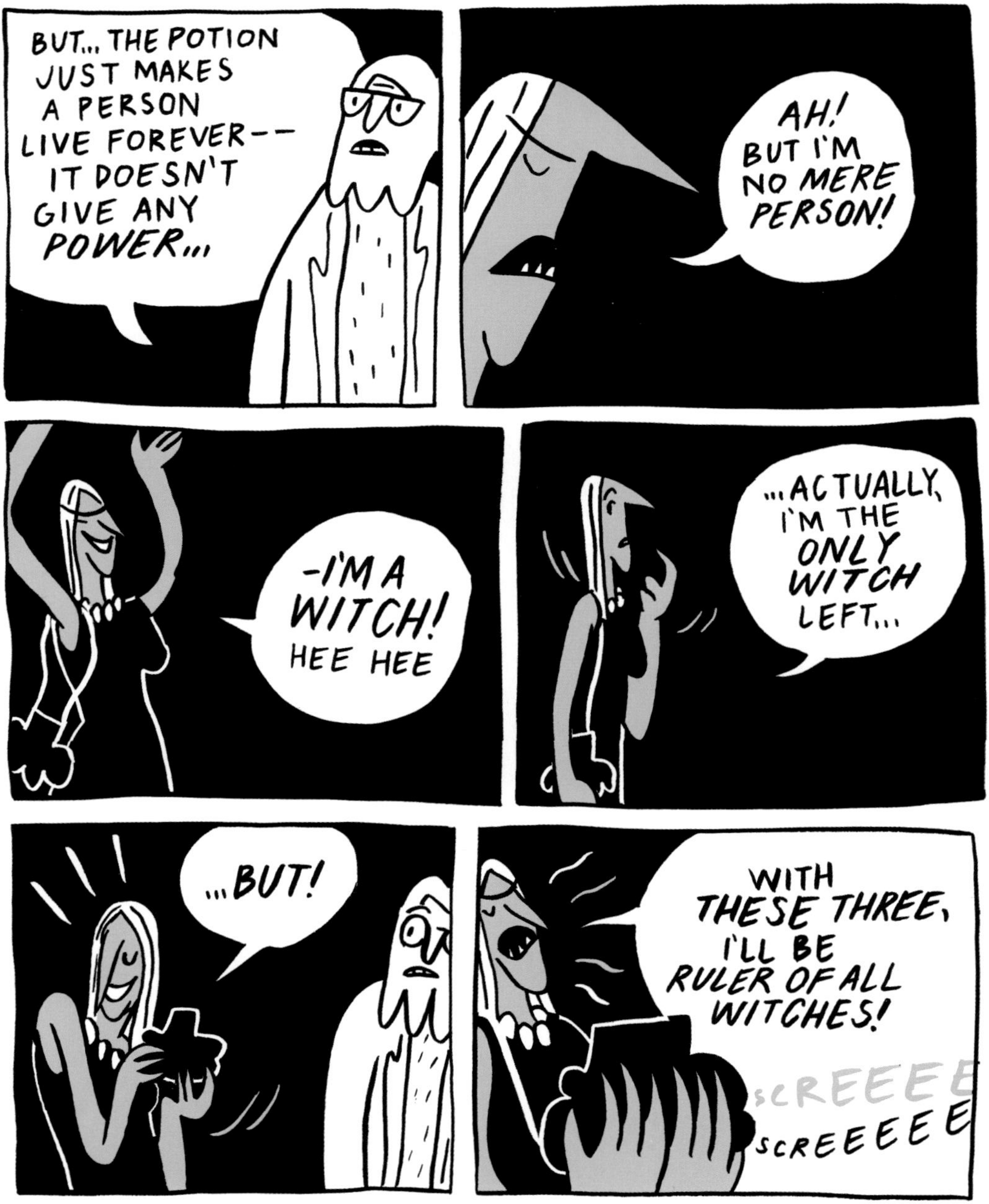

BUT... THE POTION JUST MAKES A PERSON LIVE FOREVER-- IT DOESN'T GIVE ANY *POWER...*
AH! BUT I'M NO *MERE PERSON!*
-I'M A *WITCH!* HEE HEE
...ACTUALLY, I'M THE *ONLY WITCH* LEFT...
...*BUT!*
WITH *THESE THREE,* I'LL BE *RULER OF ALL WITCHES!*
SCREEEEE
SCREEEEEE

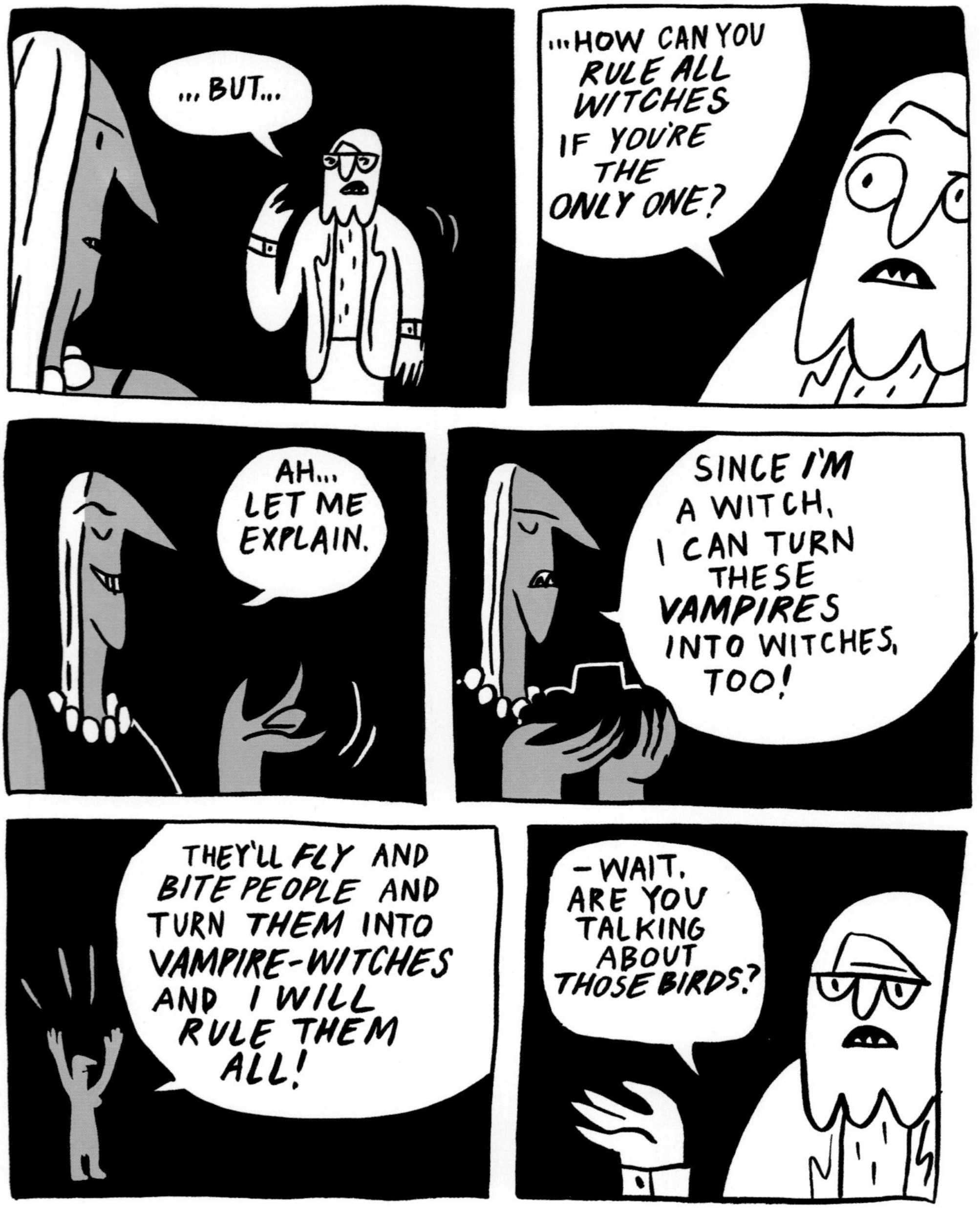
...BUT...
...HOW CAN YOU RULE ALL WITCHES IF YOU'RE THE ONLY ONE?
AH... LET ME EXPLAIN.
SINCE I'M A WITCH, I CAN TURN THESE VAMPIRES INTO WITCHES, TOO!
THEY'LL FLY AND BITE PEOPLE AND TURN THEM INTO VAMPIRE-WITCHES AND I WILL RULE THEM ALL!
-WAIT. ARE YOU TALKING ABOUT THOSE BIRDS?

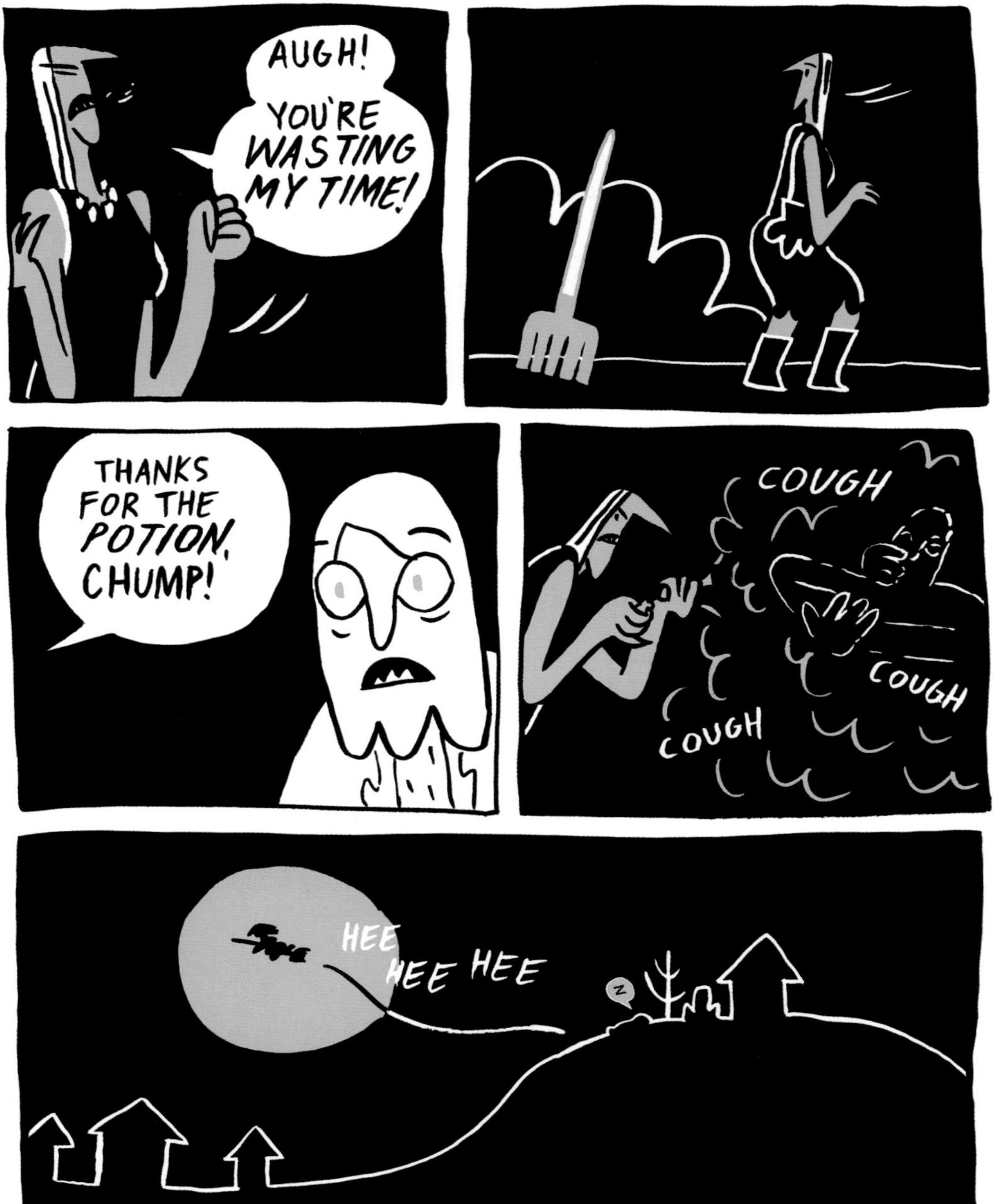
AUGH!
YOU'RE WASTING MY TIME!
THANKS FOR THE POTION, CHUMP!
COUGH
COUGH
COUGH
HEE HEE HEE
z

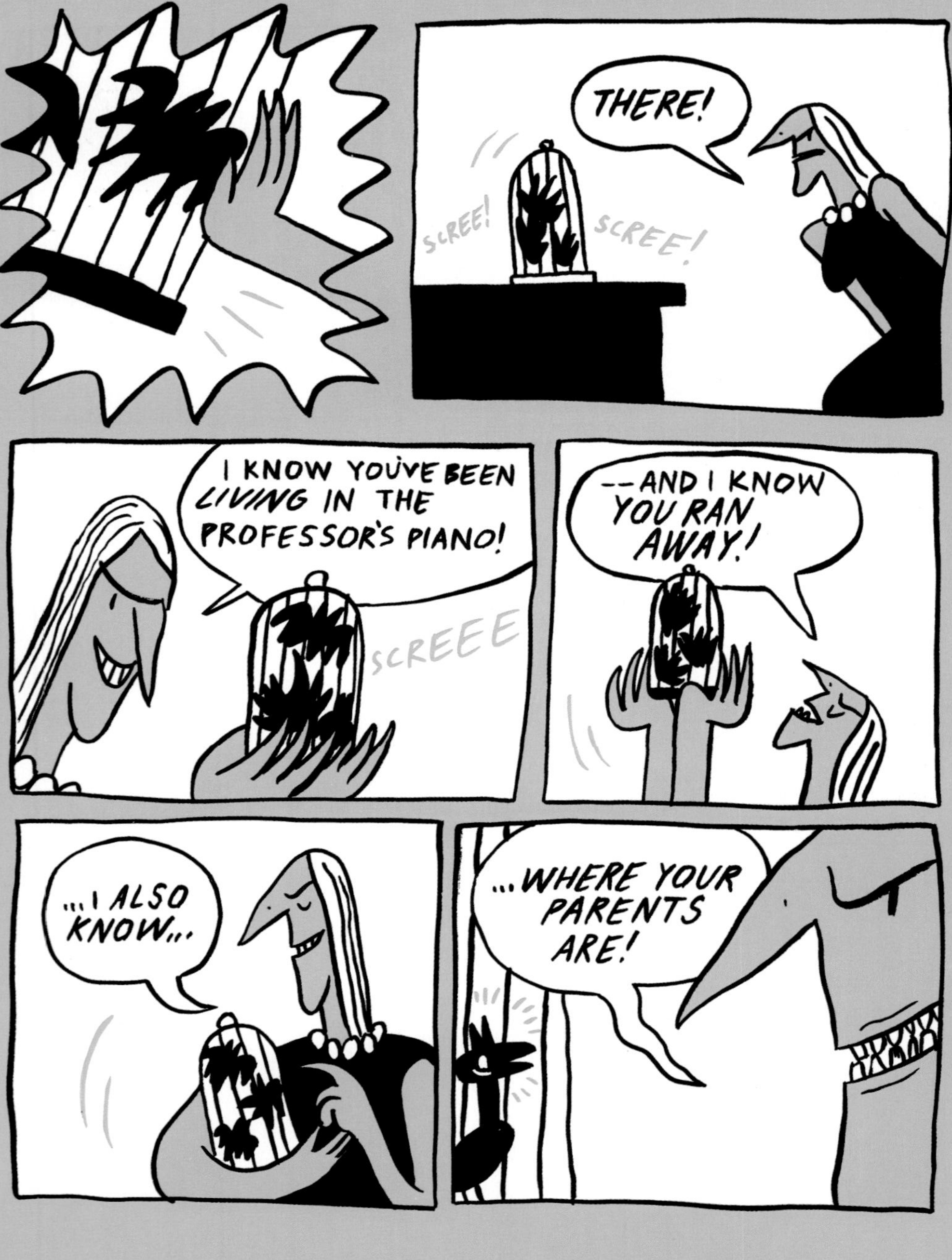
THERE!
SCREE!
SCREE!
I KNOW YOU'VE BEEN LIVING IN THE PROFESSOR'S PIANO!
SCREEEE
--AND I KNOW YOU RAN AWAY!
...I ALSO KNOW...
...WHERE YOUR PARENTS ARE!

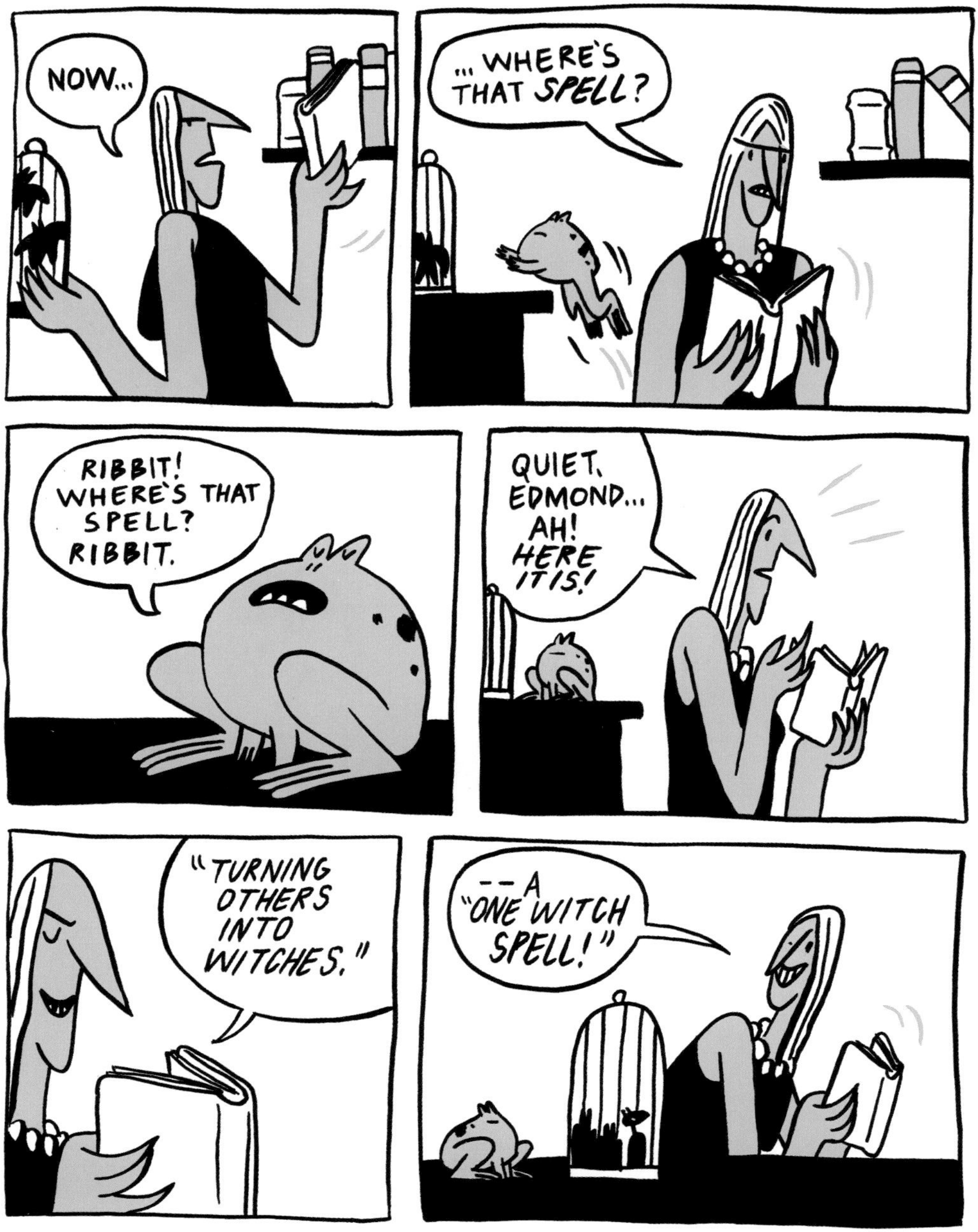
NOW...
... WHERE'S THAT SPELL?
RIBBIT! WHERE'S THAT SPELL? RIBBIT.
QUIET, EDMOND... AH! HERE IT IS!
"TURNING OTHERS INTO WITCHES."
-- A "ONE WITCH SPELL!"

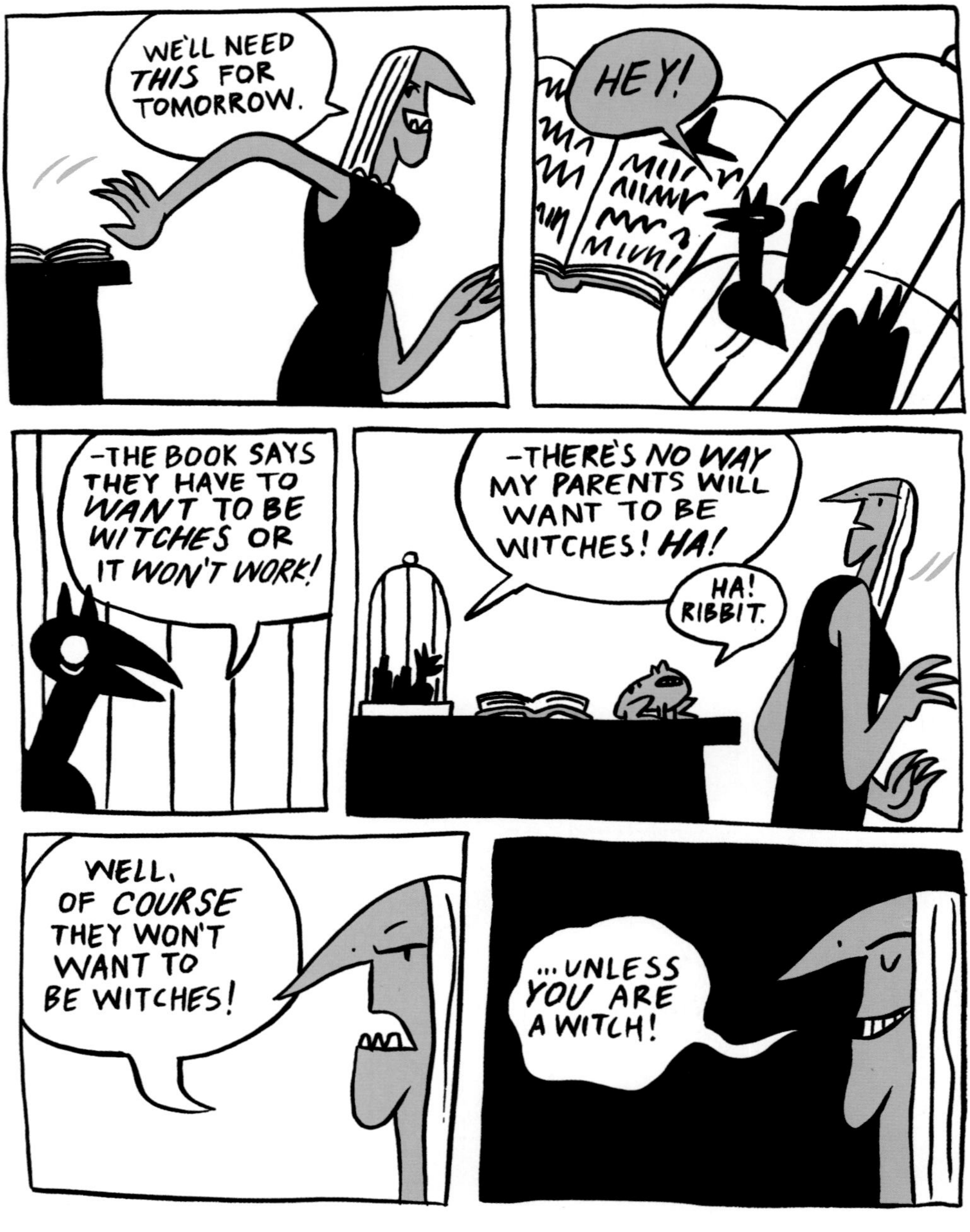
WE'LL NEED THIS FOR TOMORROW.
HEY!
-THE BOOK SAYS THEY HAVE TO WANT TO BE WITCHES OR IT WON'T WORK!
-THERE'S NO WAY MY PARENTS WILL WANT TO BE WITCHES! HA!
HA! RIBBIT.
WELL, OF COURSE THEY WON'T WANT TO BE WITCHES!
...UNLESS YOU ARE A WITCH!

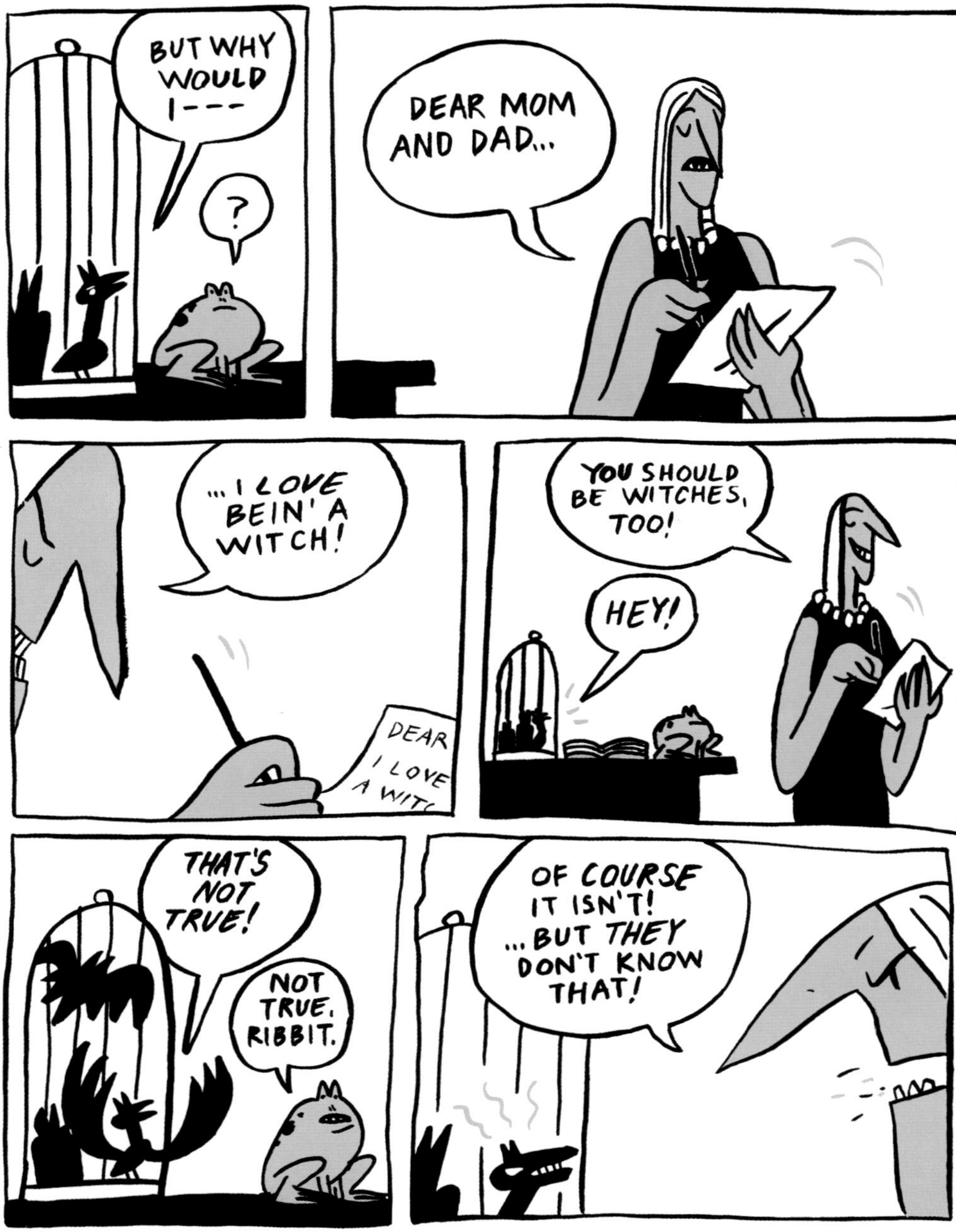
BUT WHY WOULD I---
?
DEAR MOM AND DAD...
...I LOVE BEIN' A WITCH!
DEAR
I LOVE
A WITC
YOU SHOULD BE WITCHES, TOO!
HEY!
THAT'S NOT TRUE!
NOT TRUE, RIBBIT.
OF COURSE IT ISN'T! ...BUT THEY DON'T KNOW THAT!

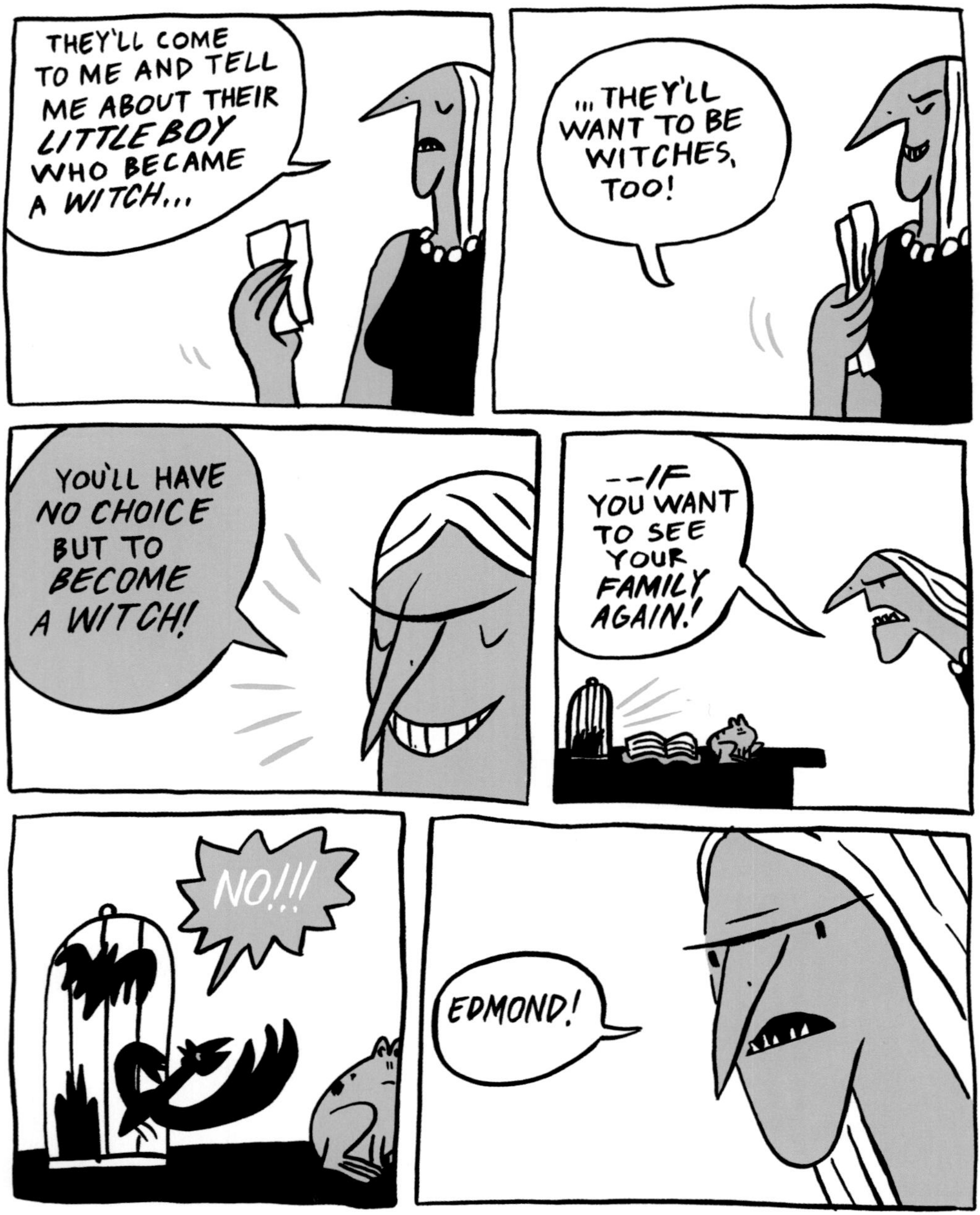
THEY'LL COME TO ME AND TELL ME ABOUT THEIR LITTLE BOY WHO BECAME A WITCH...
...THEY'LL WANT TO BE WITCHES, TOO!
YOU'LL HAVE NO CHOICE BUT TO BECOME A WITCH!
--IF YOU WANT TO SEE YOUR FAMILY AGAIN!
NO!!!
EDMOND!

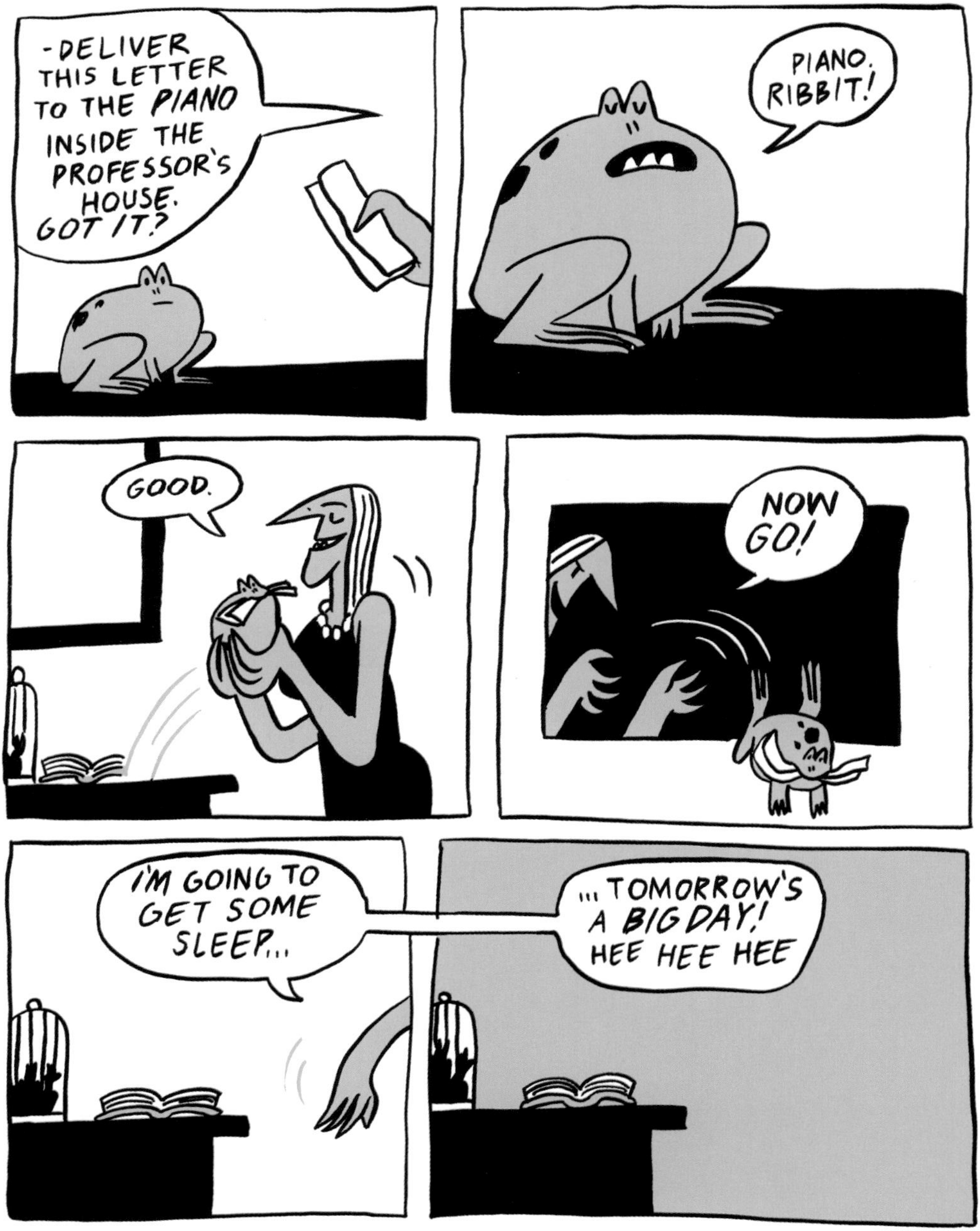
-DELIVER THIS LETTER TO THE PIANO INSIDE THE PROFESSOR'S HOUSE. GOT IT?
PIANO, RIBBIT!
GOOD.
NOW GO!
I'M GOING TO GET SOME SLEEP...
...TOMORROW'S A BIG DAY! HEE HEE HEE

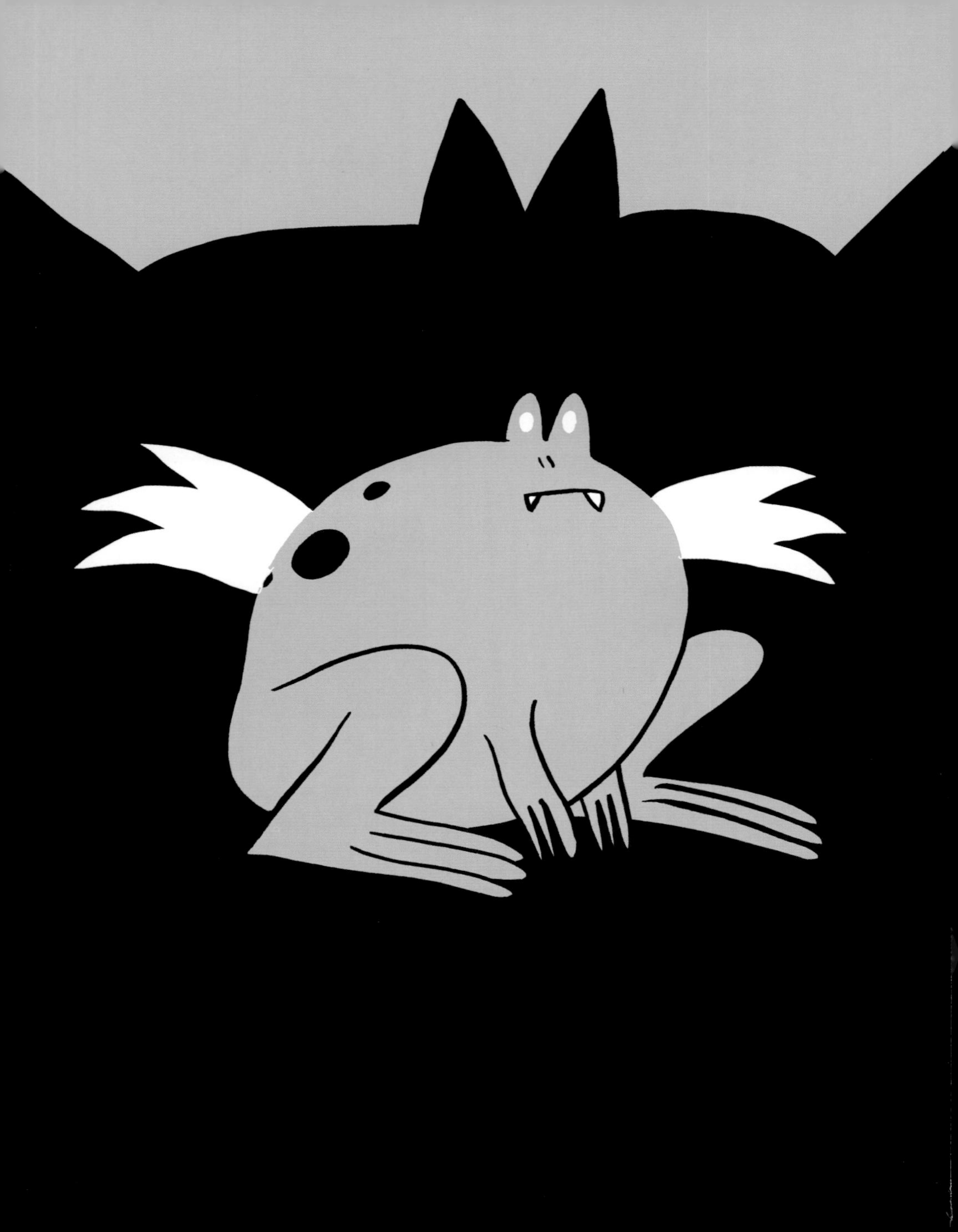

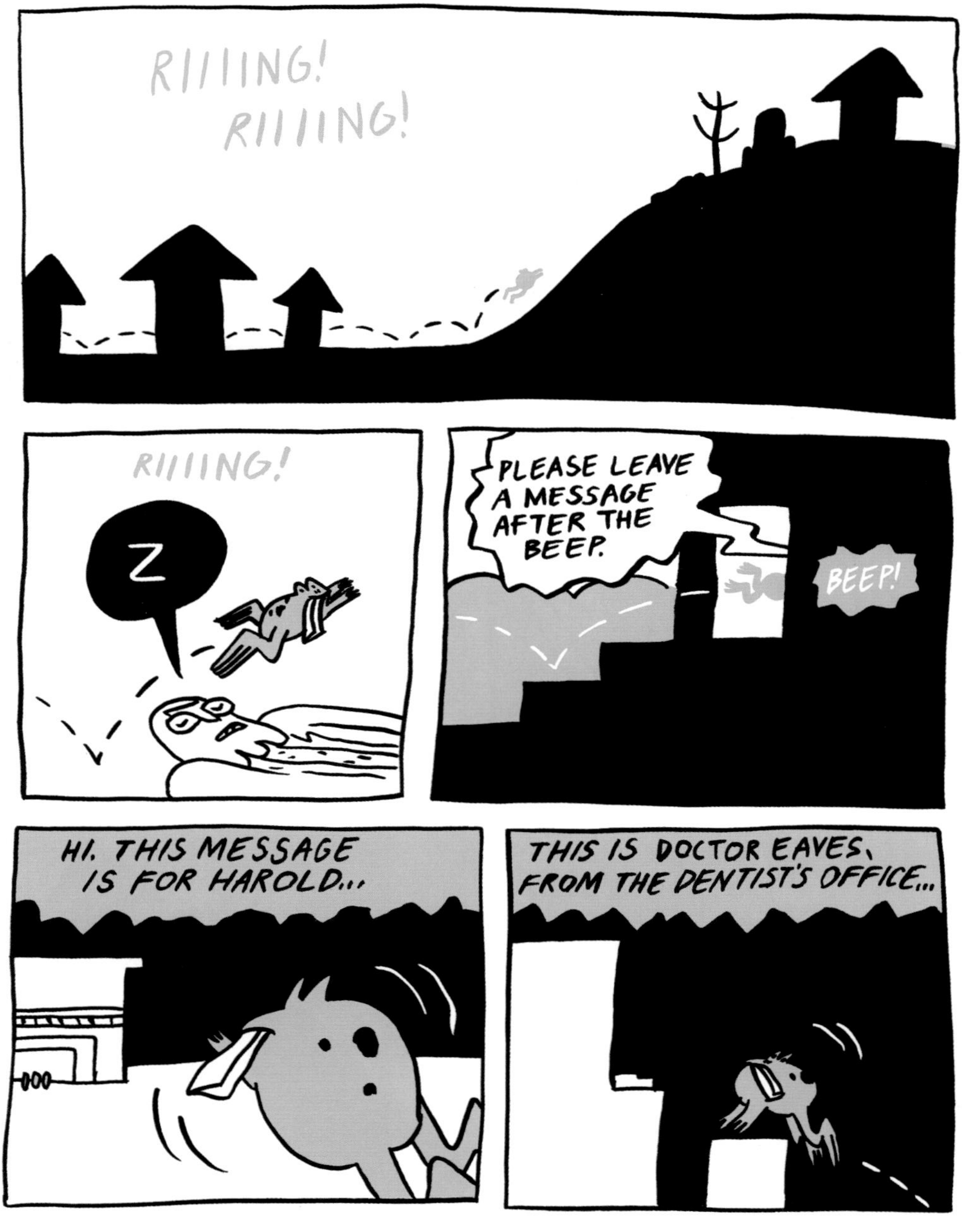
RIIIING!
RIIIING!
RIIIING!
Z
PLEASE LEAVE A MESSAGE AFTER THE BEEP.
BEEP!
HI. THIS MESSAGE IS FOR HAROLD...
THIS IS DOCTOR EAVES, FROM THE DENTIST'S OFFICE...

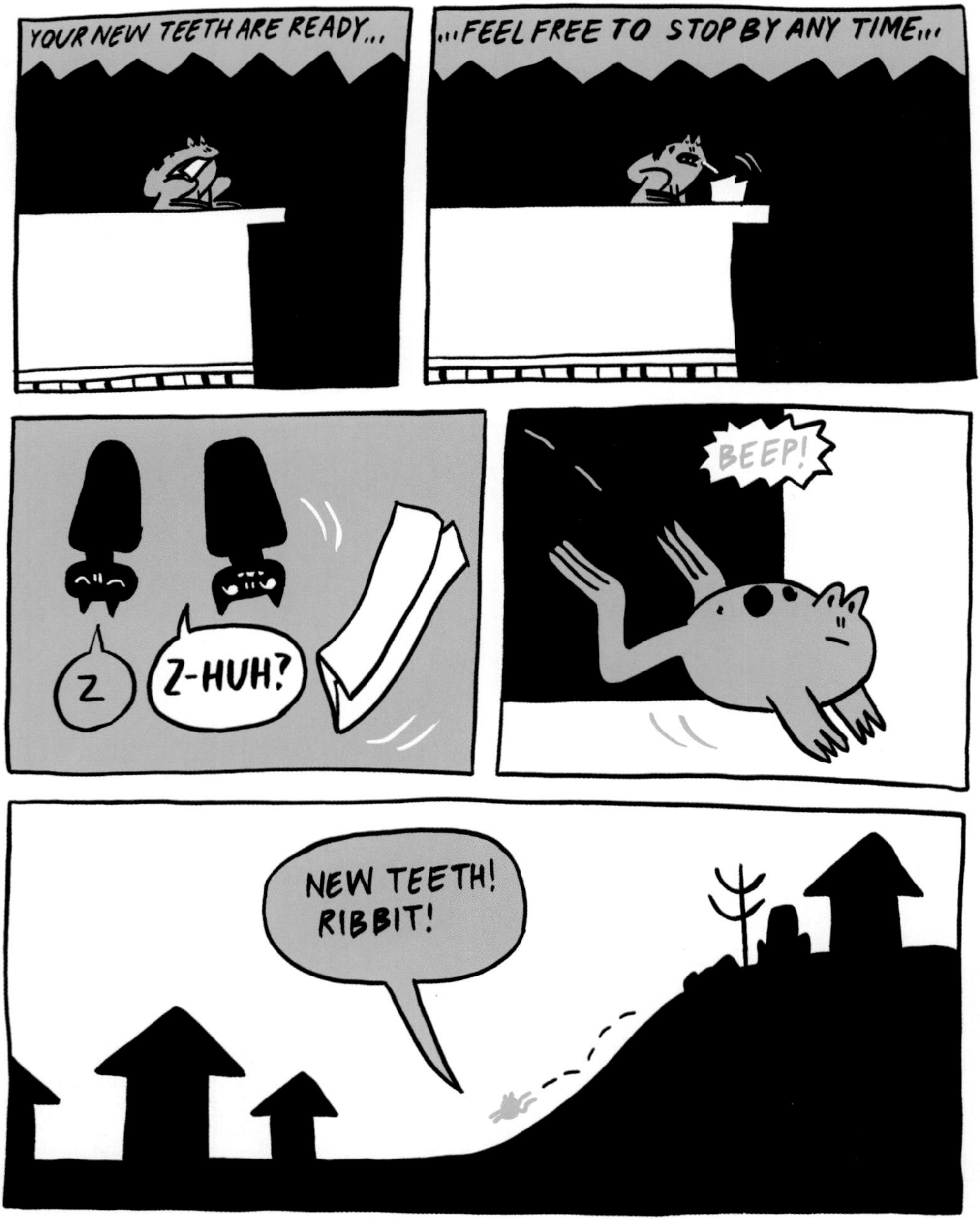
YOUR NEW TEETH ARE READY...
...FEEL FREE TO STOP BY ANY TIME...
Z
Z-HUH?
BEEP!
NEW TEETH! RIBBIT!

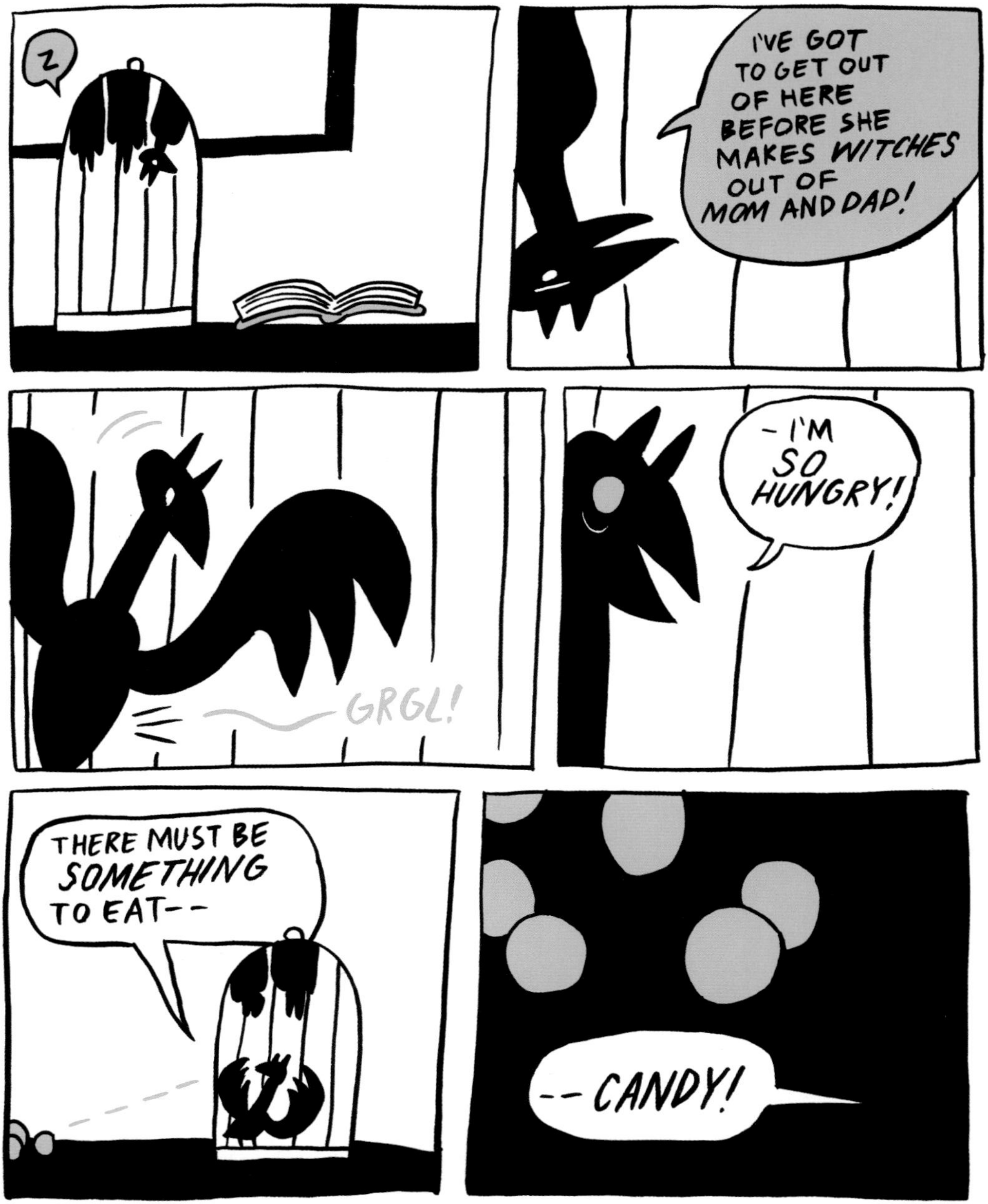
Z
I'VE GOT TO GET OUT OF HERE BEFORE SHE MAKES WITCHES OUT OF MOM AND DAD!
GRGL!
-I'M SO HUNGRY!
THERE MUST BE SOMETHING TO EAT--
--CANDY!

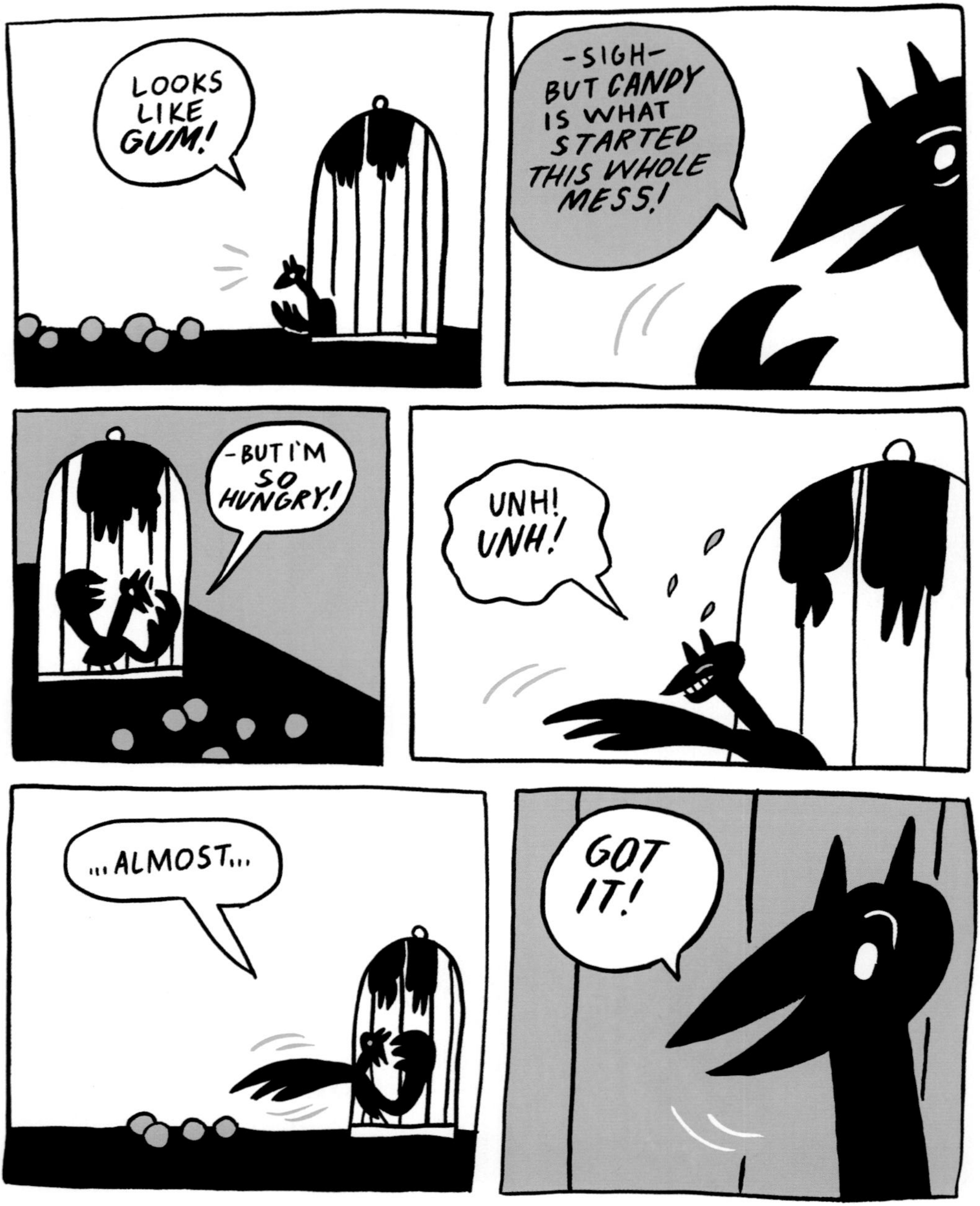
LOOKS LIKE GUM!
-SIGH- BUT CANDY IS WHAT STARTED THIS WHOLE MESS!
-BUT I'M SO HUNGRY!
UNH! UNH!
...ALMOST...
GOT IT!

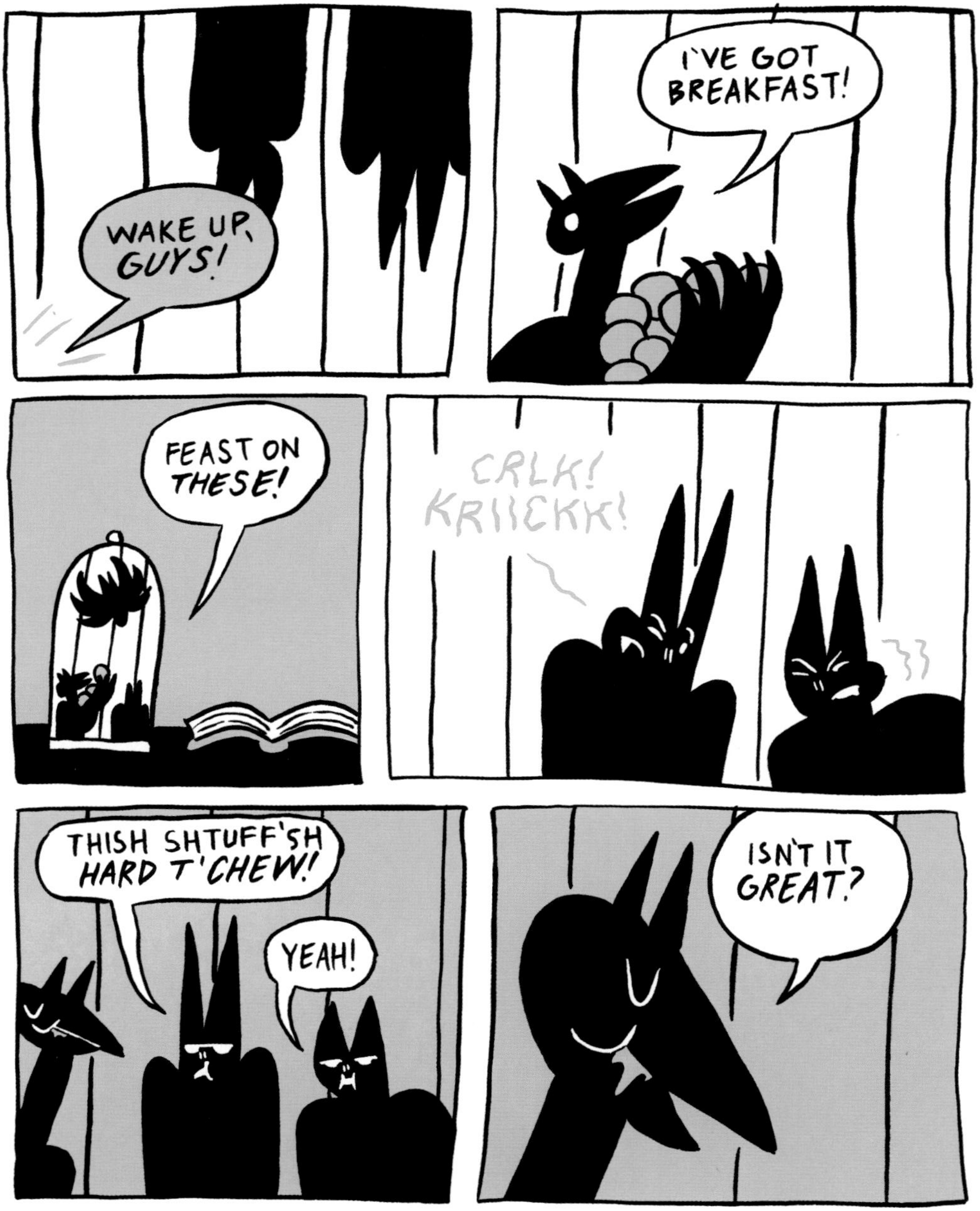
WAKE UP, GUYS!
I'VE GOT BREAKFAST!
FEAST ON THESE!
CRLK! KRIICKK!
THISH SHTUFF'SH HARD T'CHEW!
YEAH!
ISN'T IT GREAT?

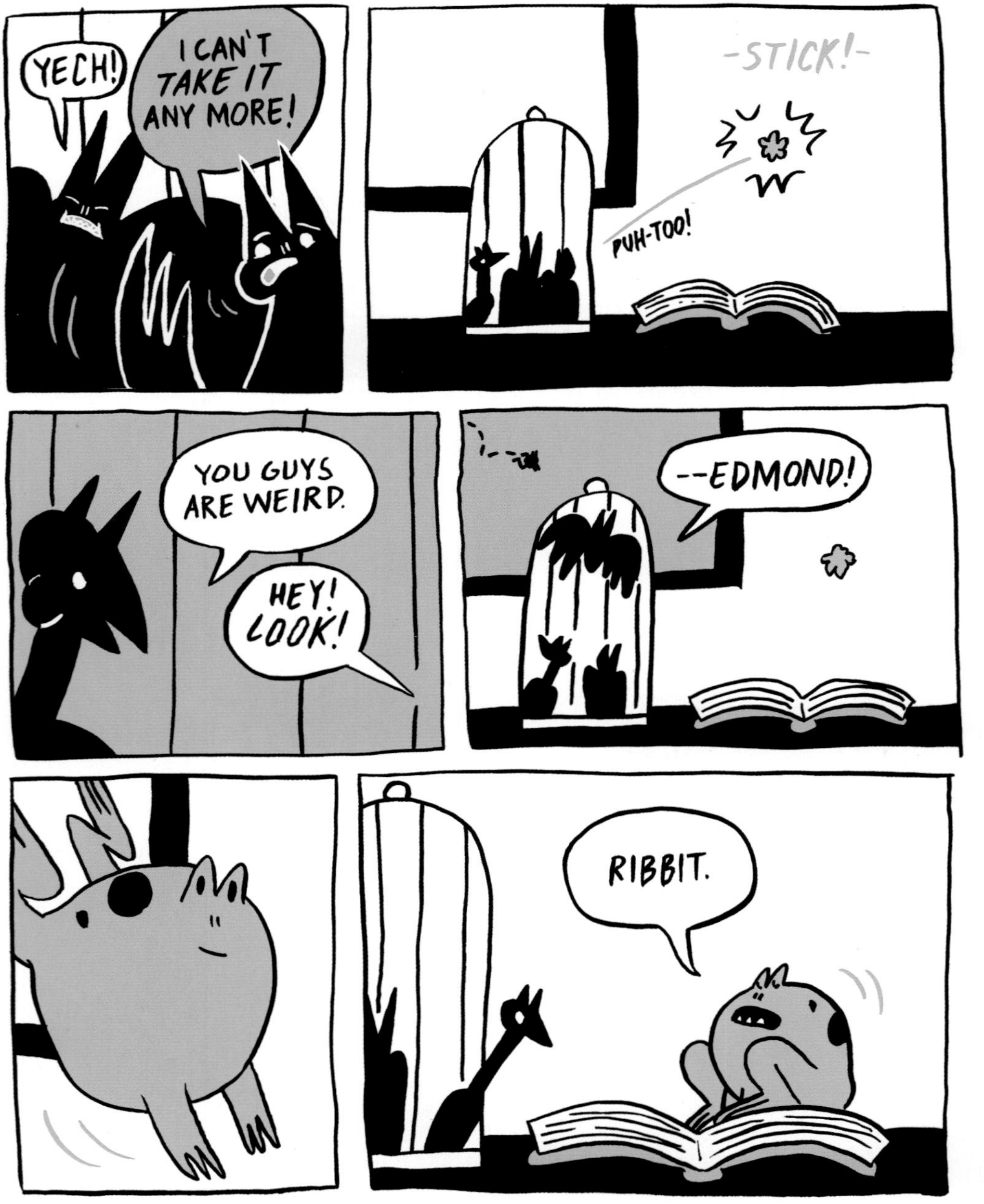
YECH!
I CAN'T TAKE IT ANY MORE!
-STICK!-
PUH-TOO!
YOU GUYS ARE WEIRD.
HEY! LOOK!
--EDMOND!
RIBBIT.

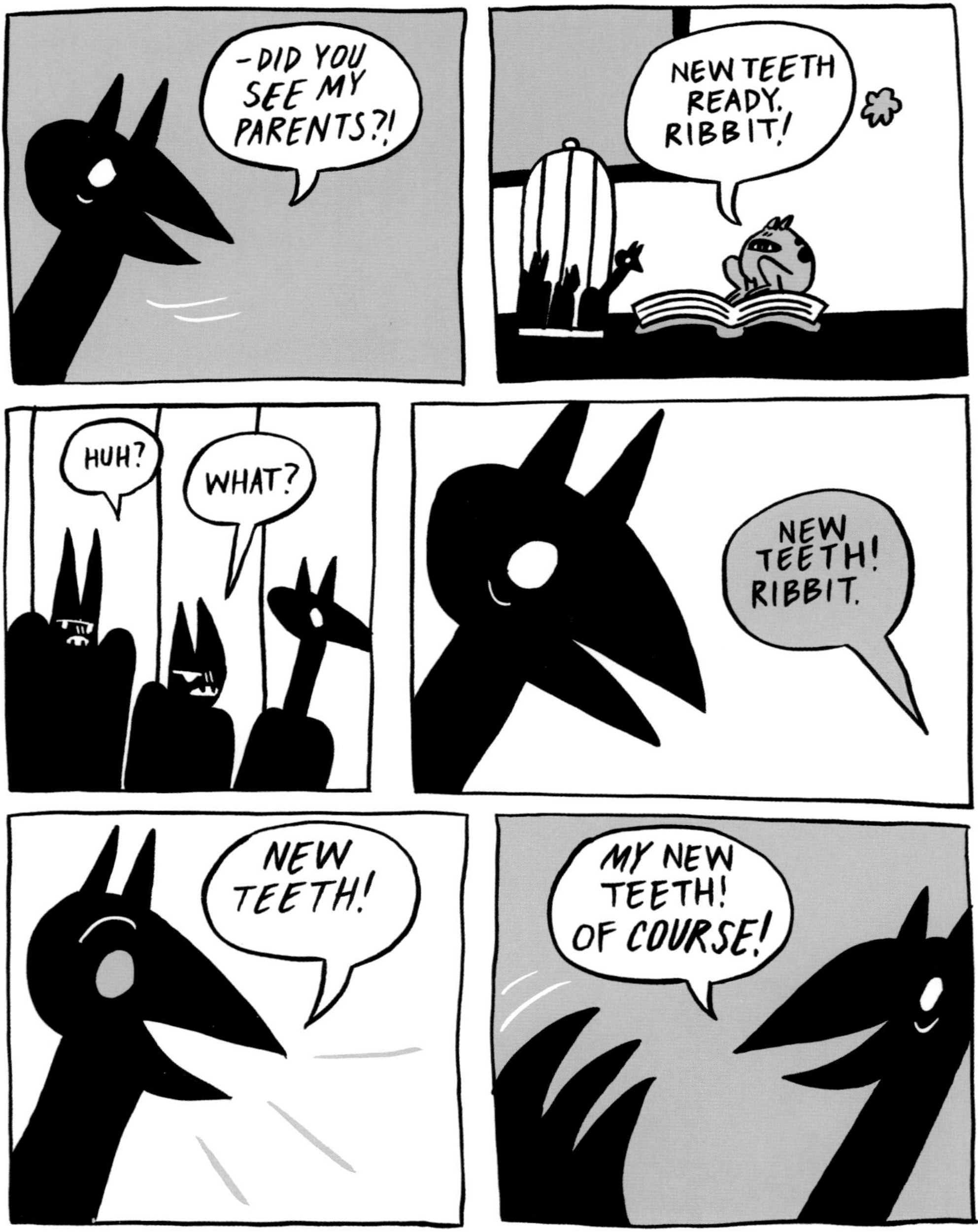
-DID YOU SEE MY PARENTS?!
NEW TEETH READY. RIBBIT!
HUH?
WHAT?
NEW TEETH! RIBBIT.
NEW TEETH!
MY NEW TEETH! OF COURSE!

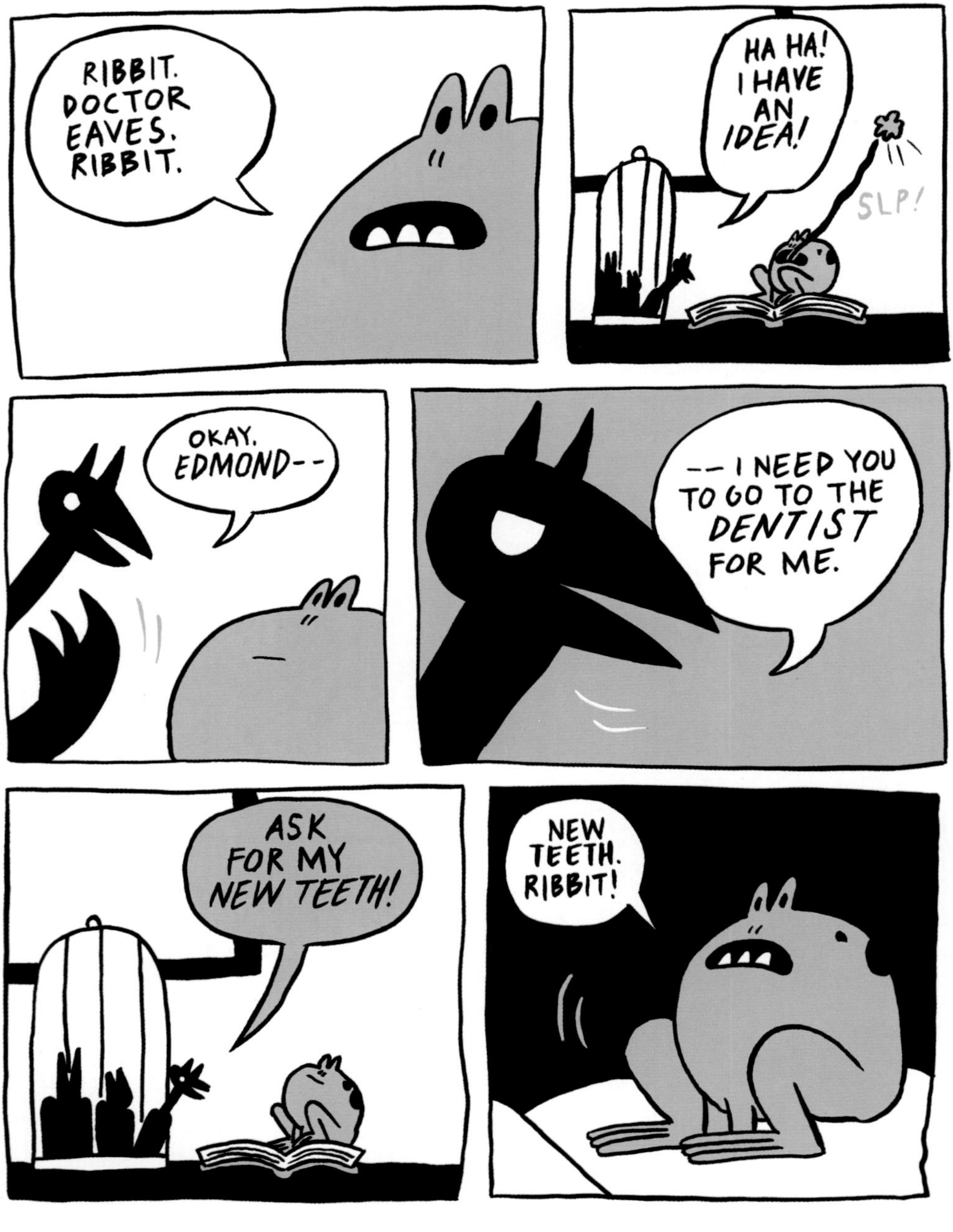
RIBBIT. DOCTOR EAVES. RIBBIT.
HA HA! I HAVE AN IDEA!
SLP!
OKAY. EDMOND--
--I NEED YOU TO GO TO THE DENTIST FOR ME.
ASK FOR MY NEW TEETH!
NEW TEETH. RIBBIT!

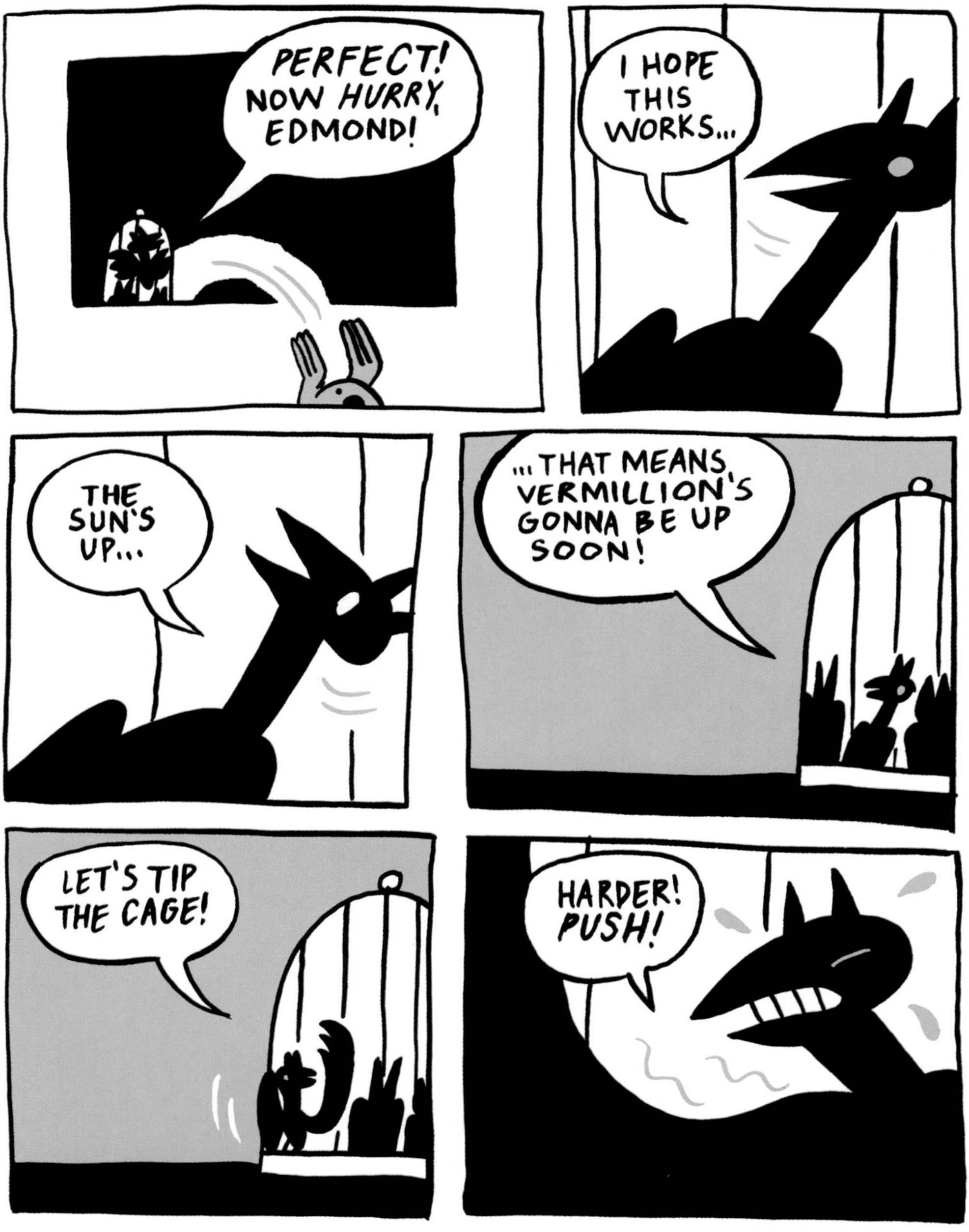
PERFECT! NOW HURRY, EDMOND!
I HOPE THIS WORKS...
THE SUN'S UP...
...THAT MEANS VERMILLION'S GONNA BE UP SOON!
LET'S TIP THE CAGE!
HARDER! PUSH!

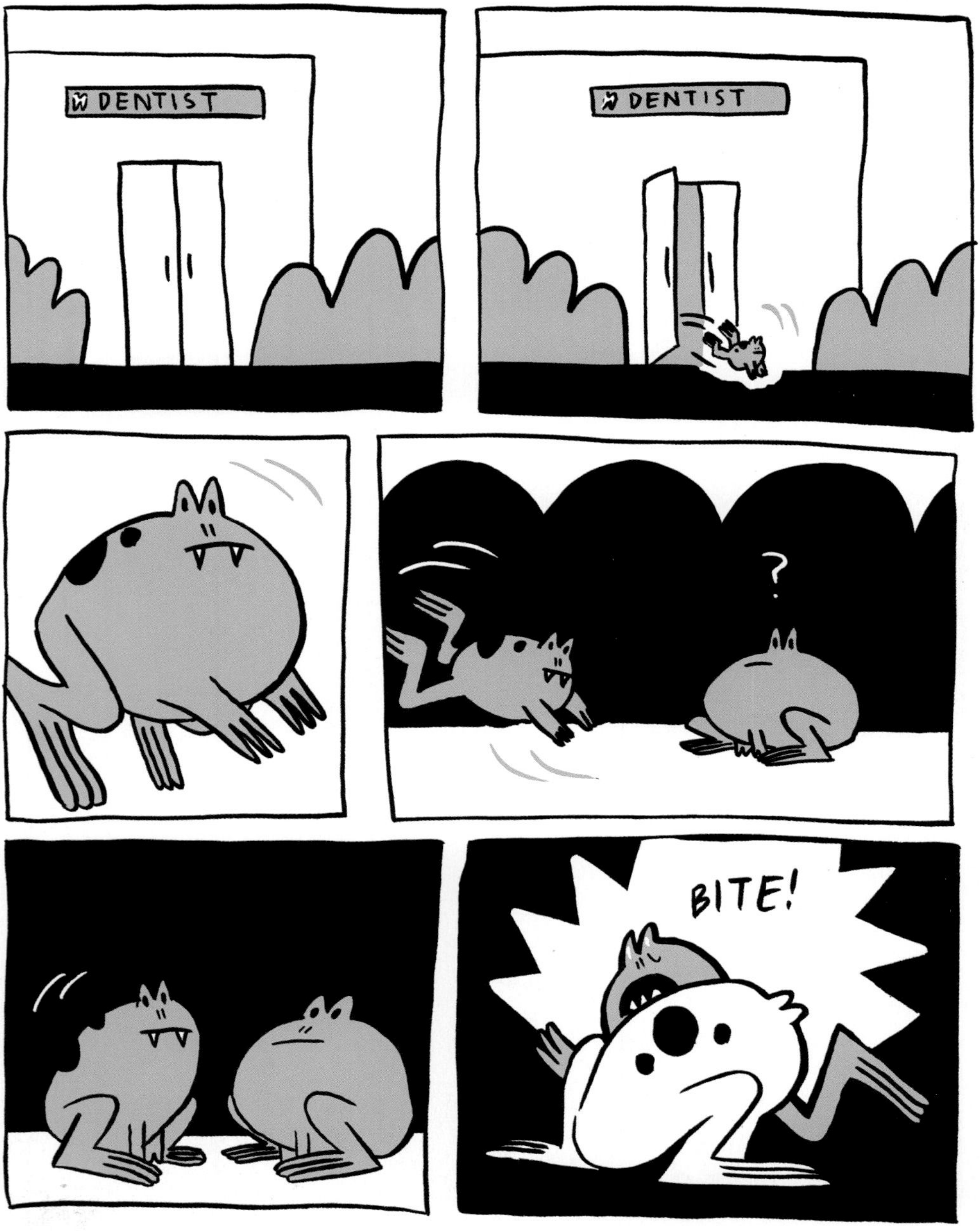
DENTIST
DENTIST
?
BITE!

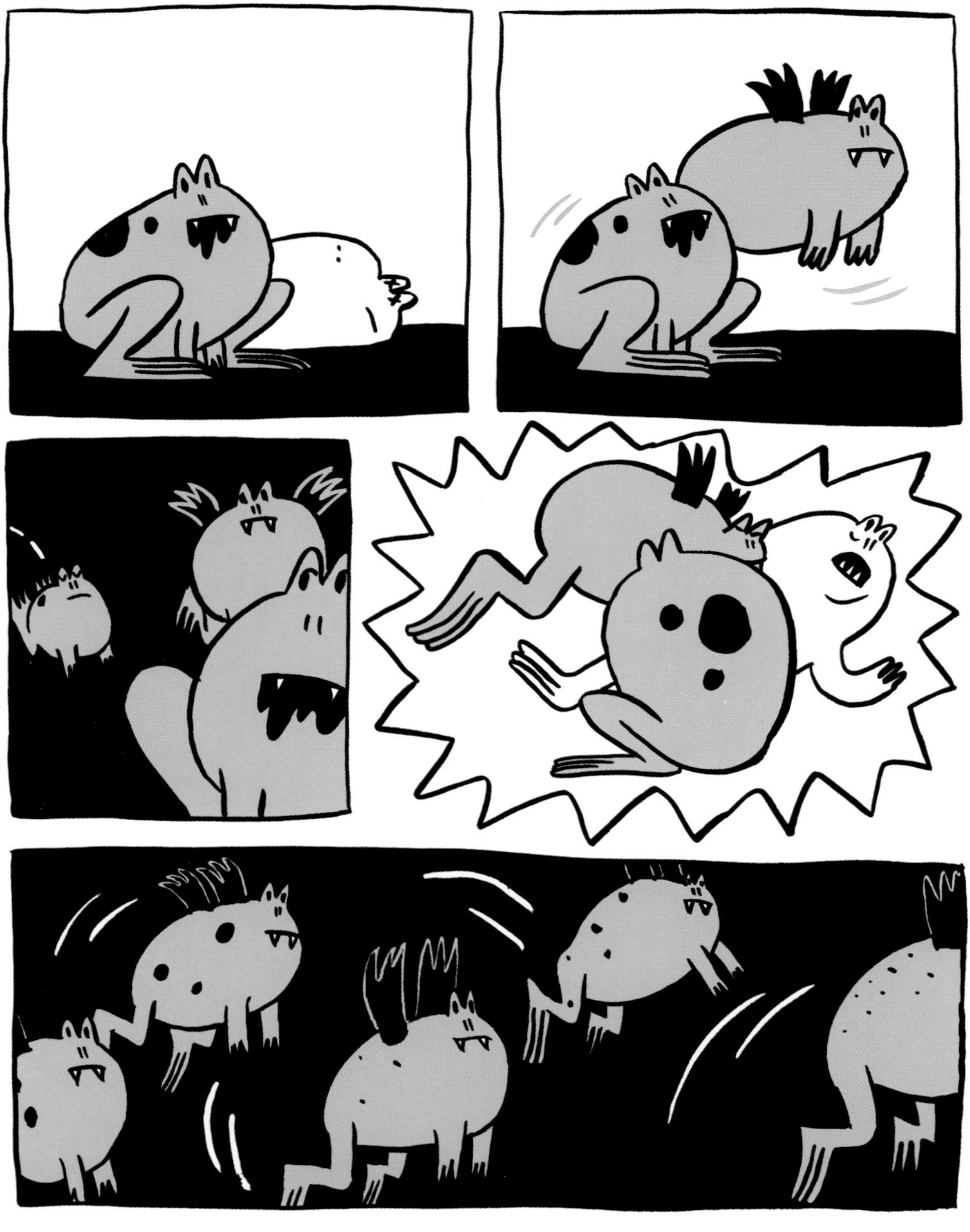

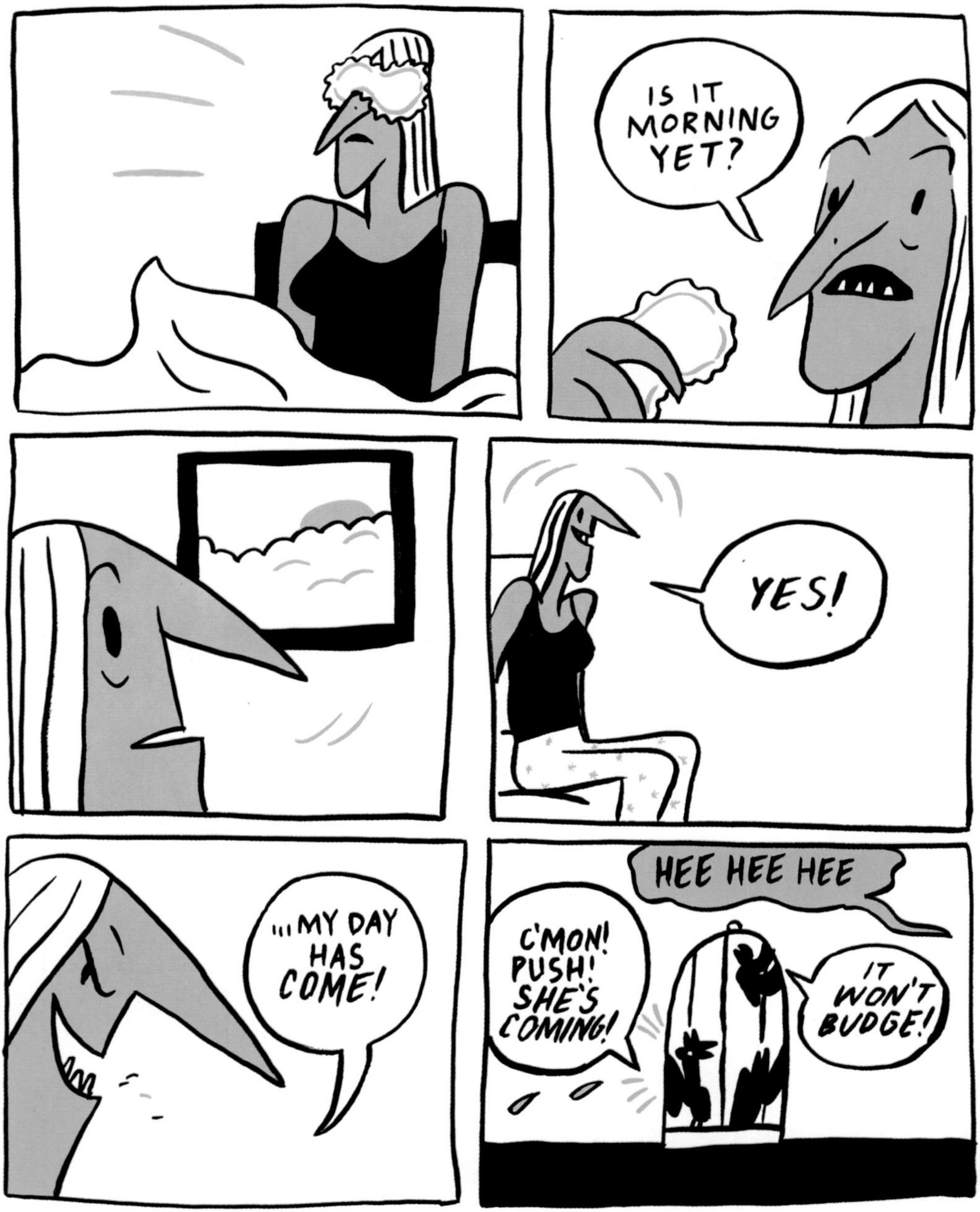
IS IT MORNING YET?
YES!
...MY DAY HAS COME!
HEE HEE HEE
C'MON! PUSH! SHE'S COMING!
IT WON'T BUDGE!

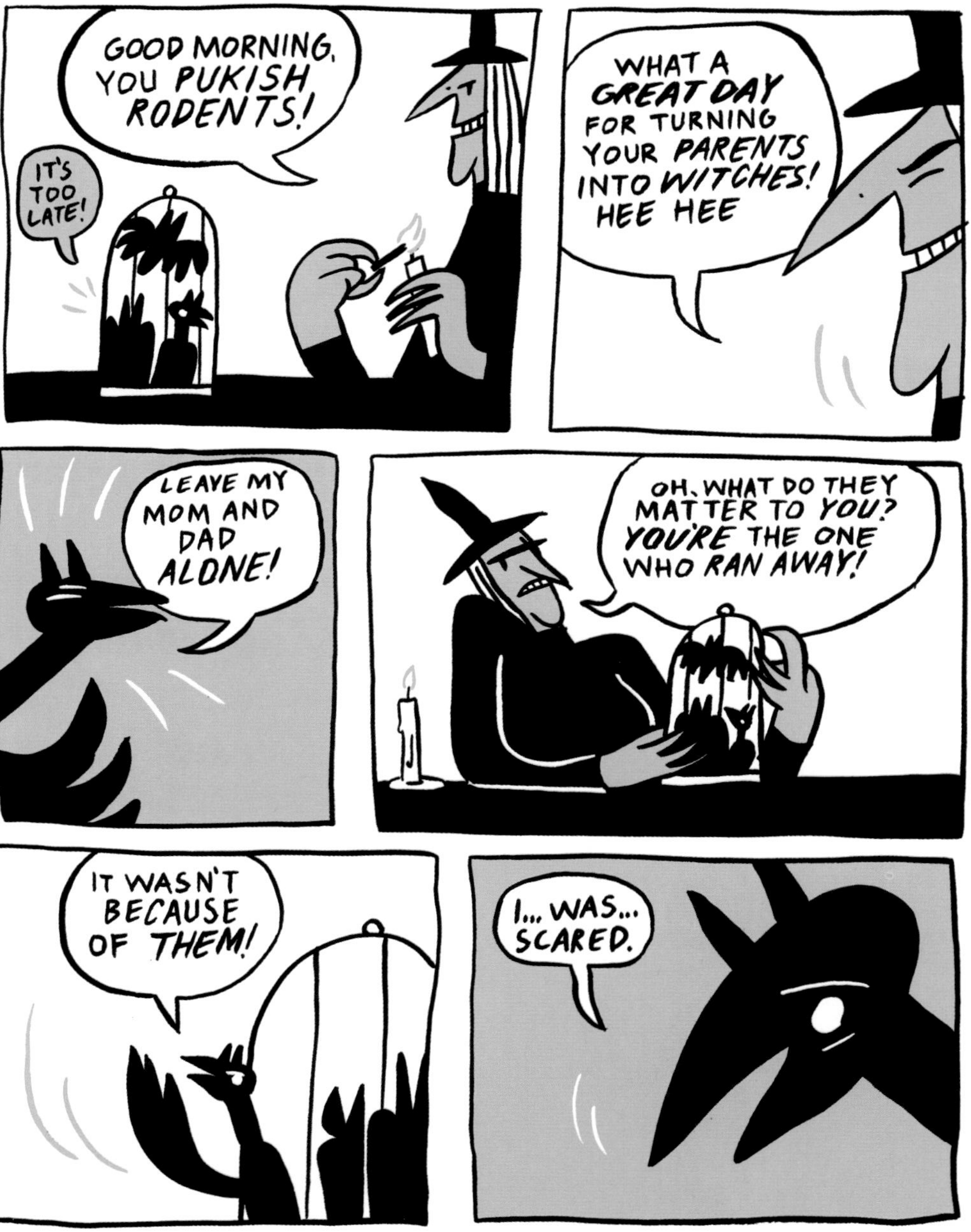
GOOD MORNING, YOU PUKISH RODENTS!
IT'S TOO LATE!
WHAT A GREAT DAY FOR TURNING YOUR PARENTS INTO WITCHES! HEE HEE
LEAVE MY MOM AND DAD ALONE!
OH, WHAT DO THEY MATTER TO YOU? YOU'RE THE ONE WHO RAN AWAY!
IT WASN'T BECAUSE OF THEM!
I... WAS... SCARED.

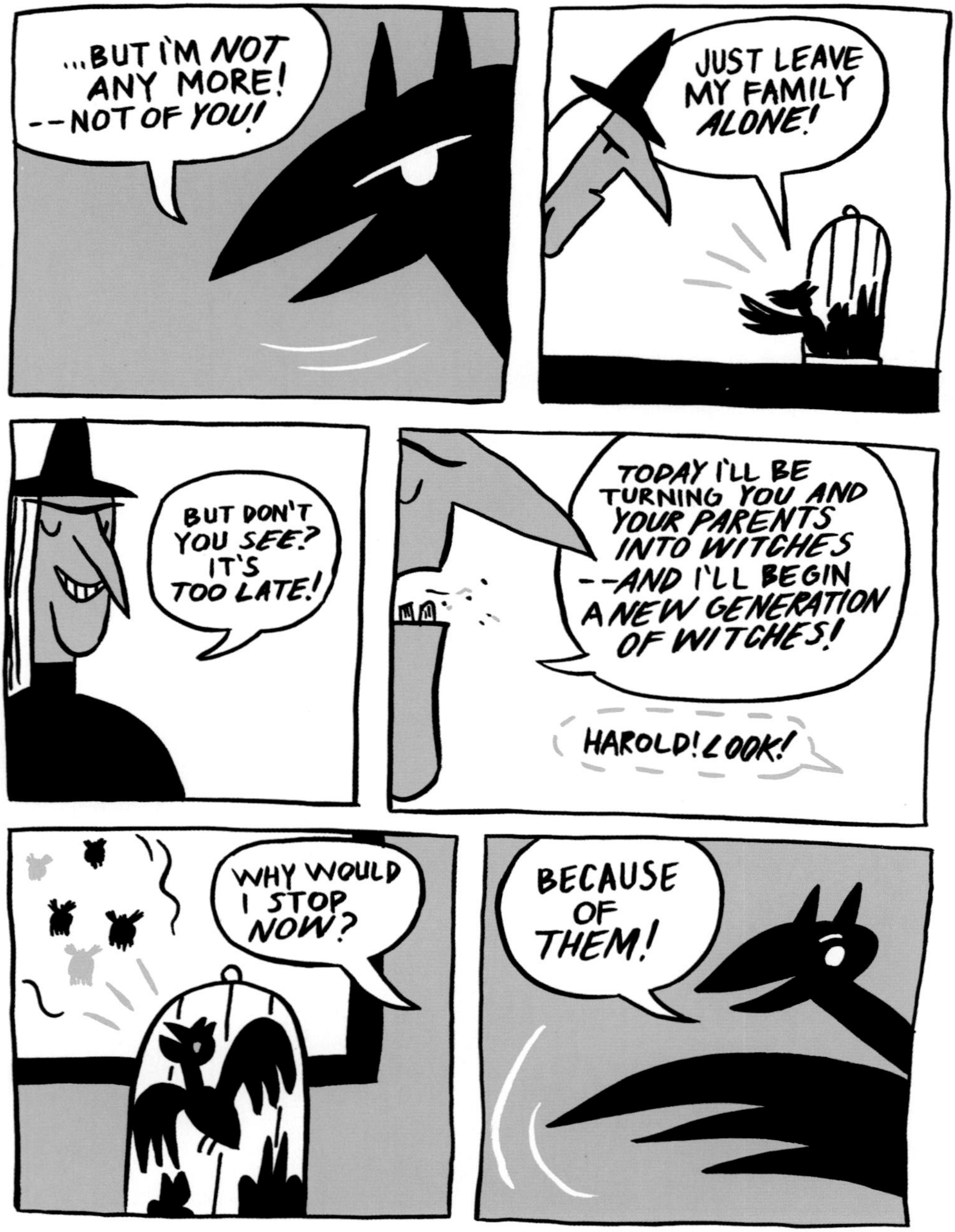
...BUT I'M NOT ANY MORE! --NOT OF YOU!
JUST LEAVE MY FAMILY ALONE!
BUT DON'T YOU SEE? IT'S TOO LATE!
TODAY I'LL BE TURNING YOU AND YOUR PARENTS INTO WITCHES --AND I'LL BEGIN A NEW GENERATION OF WITCHES!
HAROLD! LOOK!
WHY WOULD I STOP NOW?
BECAUSE OF THEM!

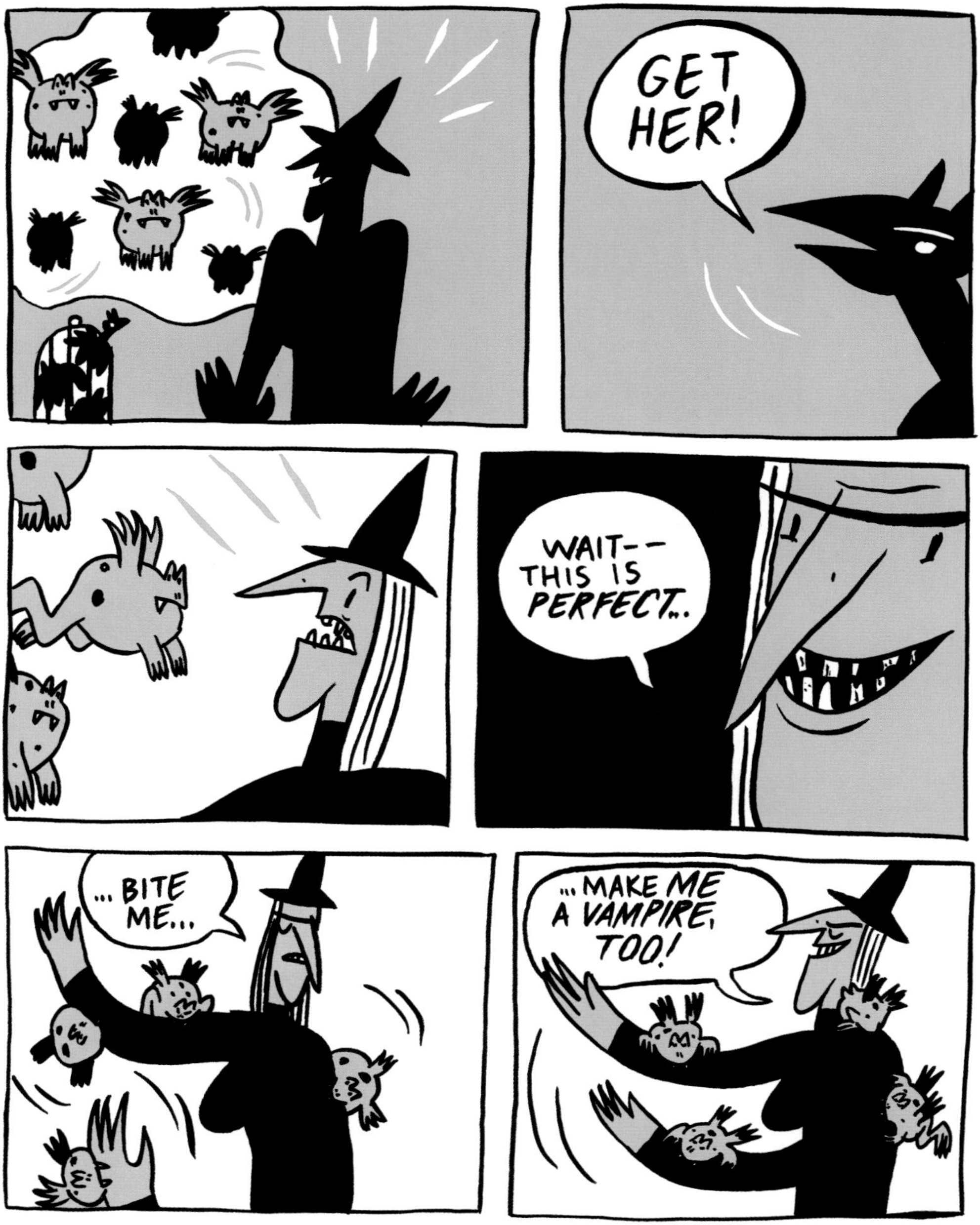
GET HER!
WAIT-- THIS IS PERFECT...
... BITE ME...
... MAKE ME A VAMPIRE, TOO!

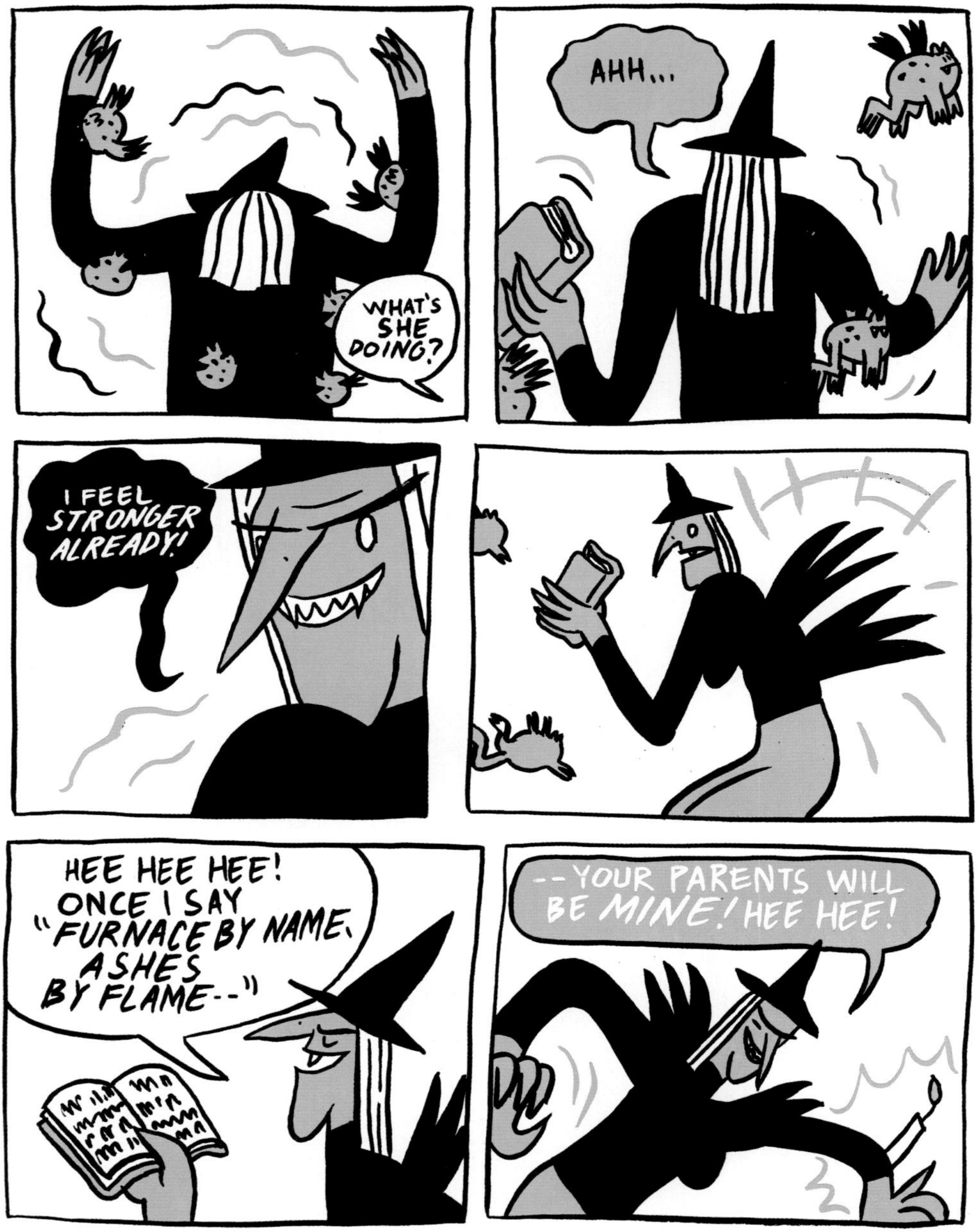
WHAT'S SHE DOING?
AHH...
I FEEL STRONGER ALREADY!
HEE HEE HEE! ONCE I SAY "FURNACE BY NAME, ASHES BY FLAME--"
--YOUR PARENTS WILL BE MINE! HEE HEE!

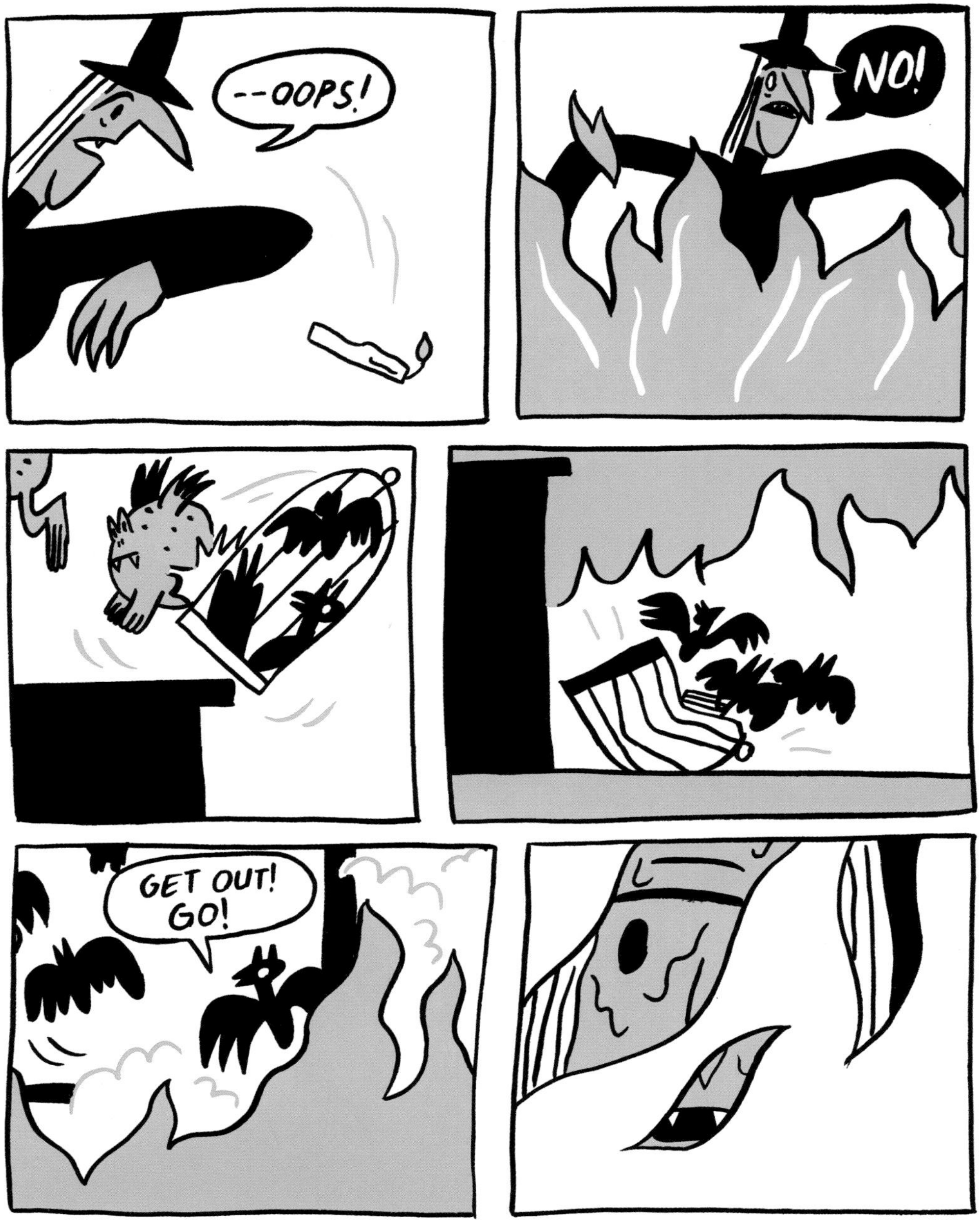
--OOPS!
NO!
GET OUT! GO!

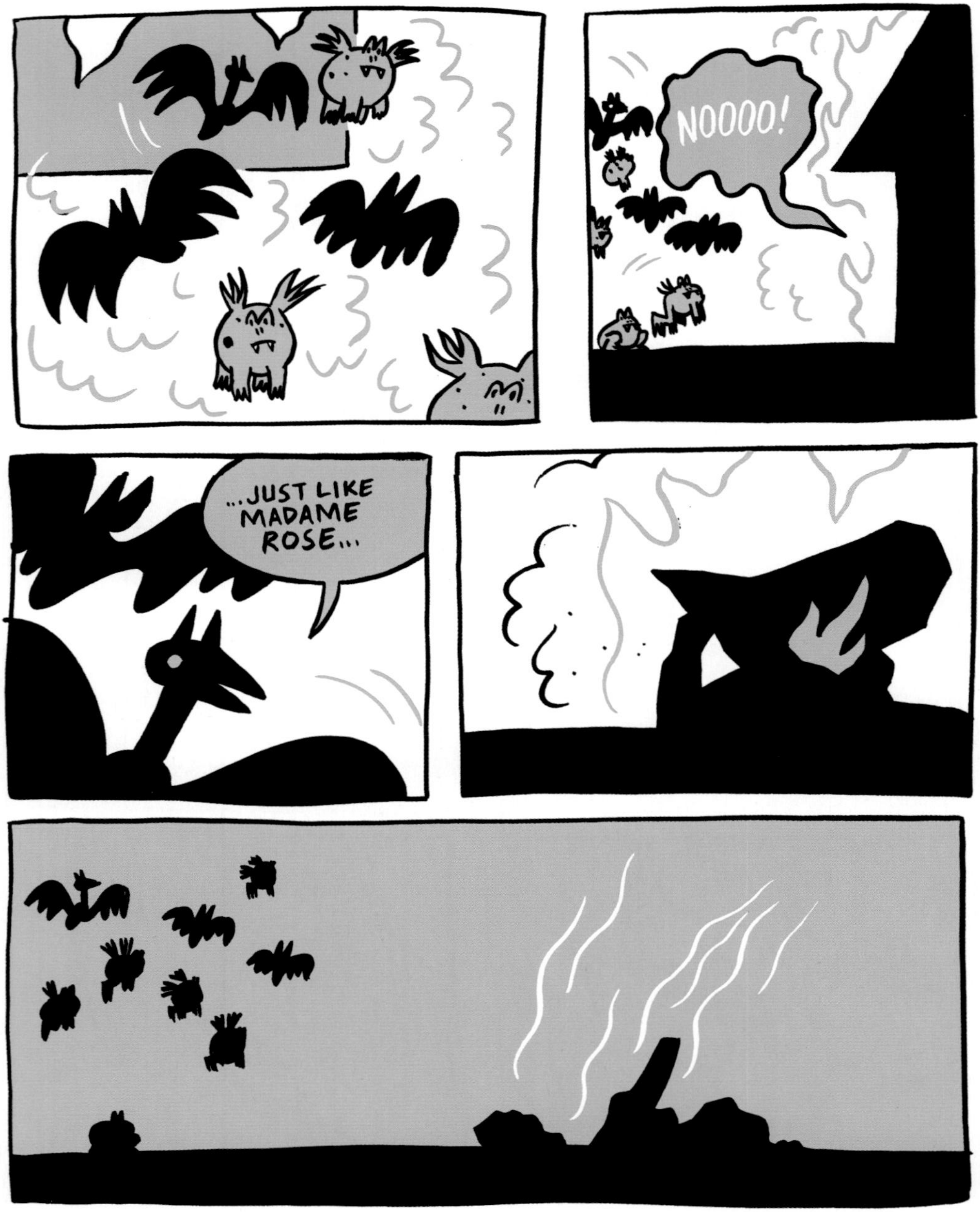
NOOOO!
...JUST LIKE MADAME ROSE...

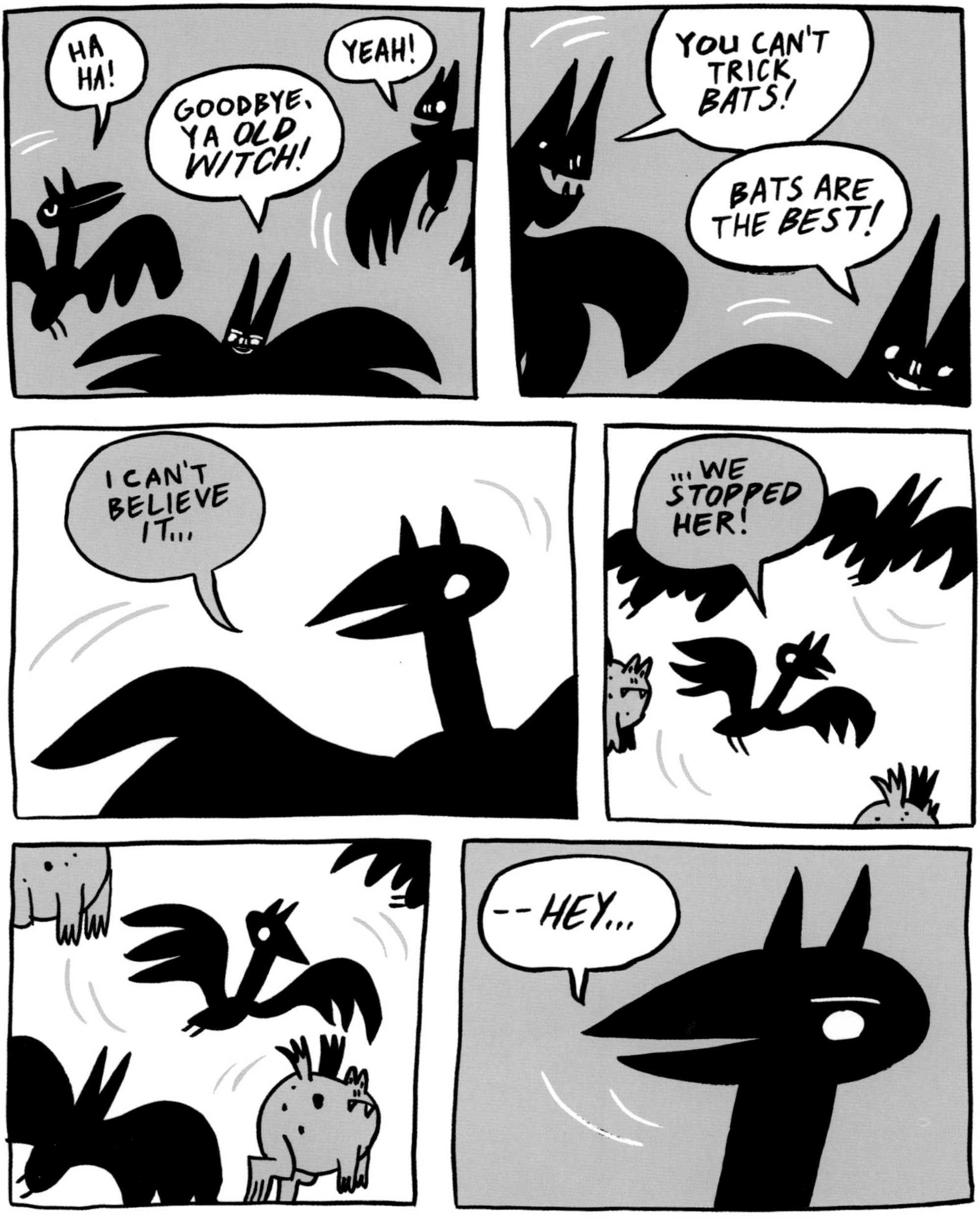
HA HA!
GOODBYE, YA OLD WITCH!
YEAH!
YOU CAN'T TRICK BATS!
BATS ARE THE BEST!
I CAN'T BELIEVE IT...
...WE STOPPED HER!
--HEY...

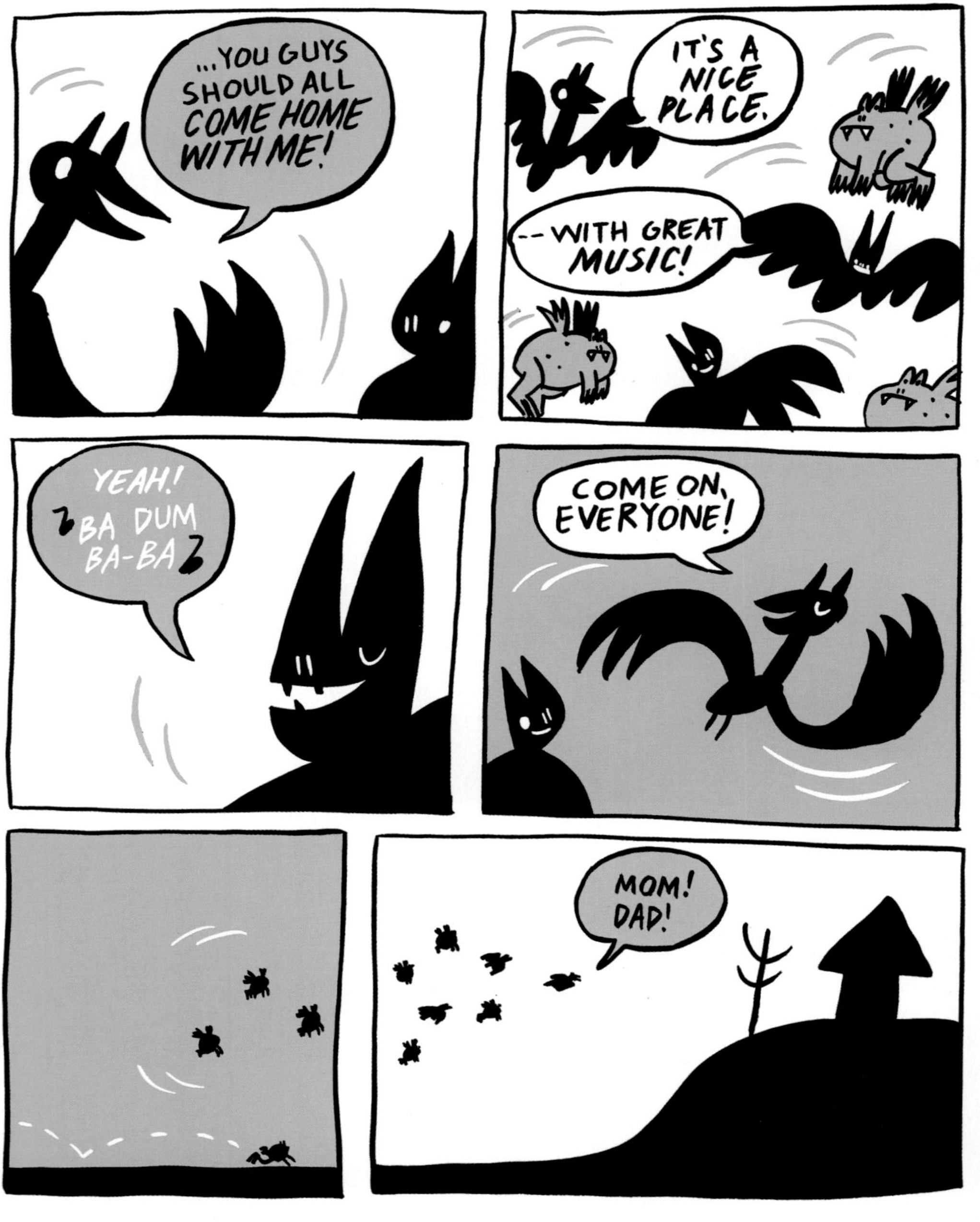
...YOU GUYS SHOULD ALL COME HOME WITH ME!
IT'S A NICE PLACE.
--WITH GREAT MUSIC!
YEAH!
BA DUM BA-BA
COME ON, EVERYONE!
MOM! DAD!

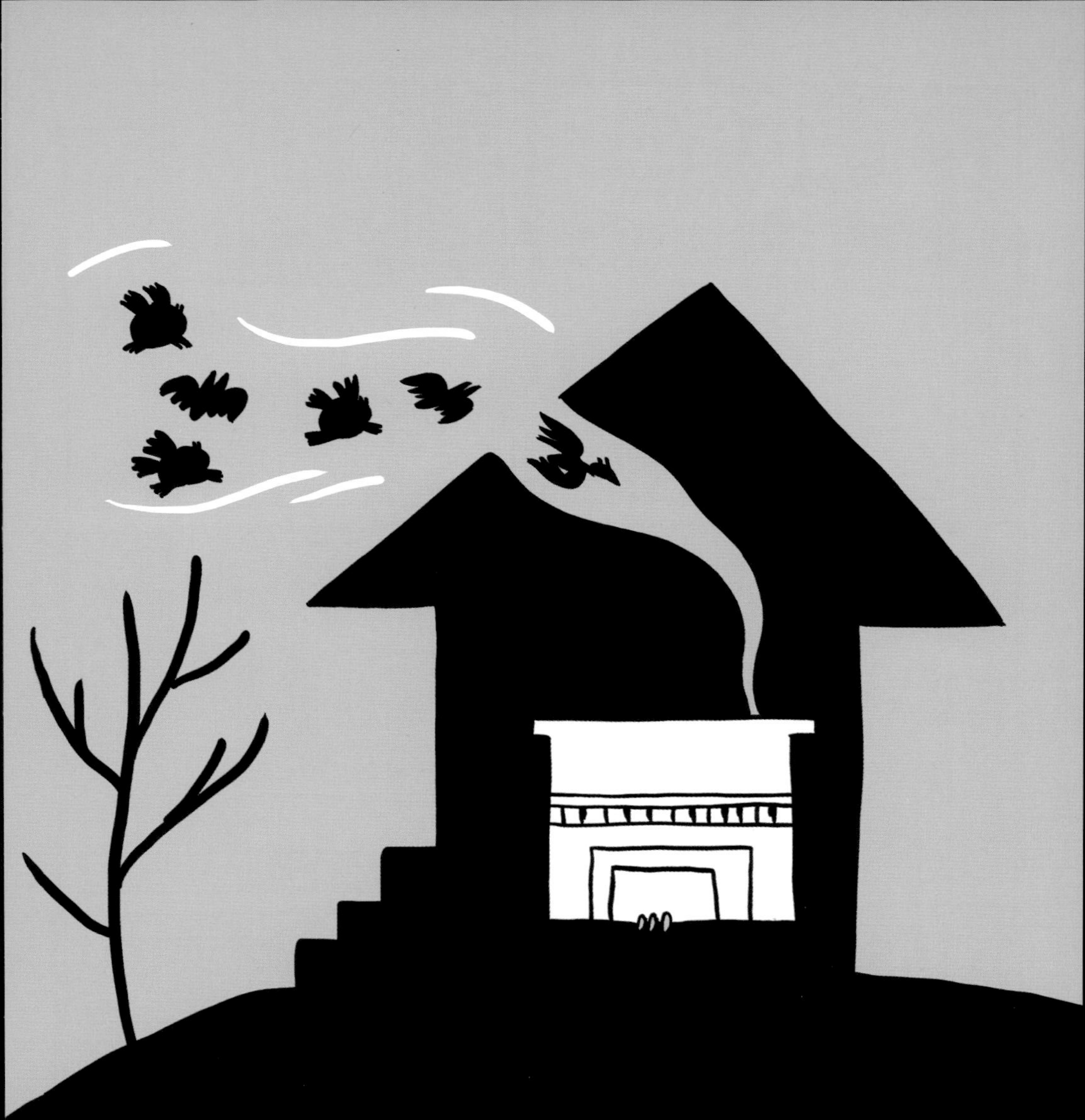

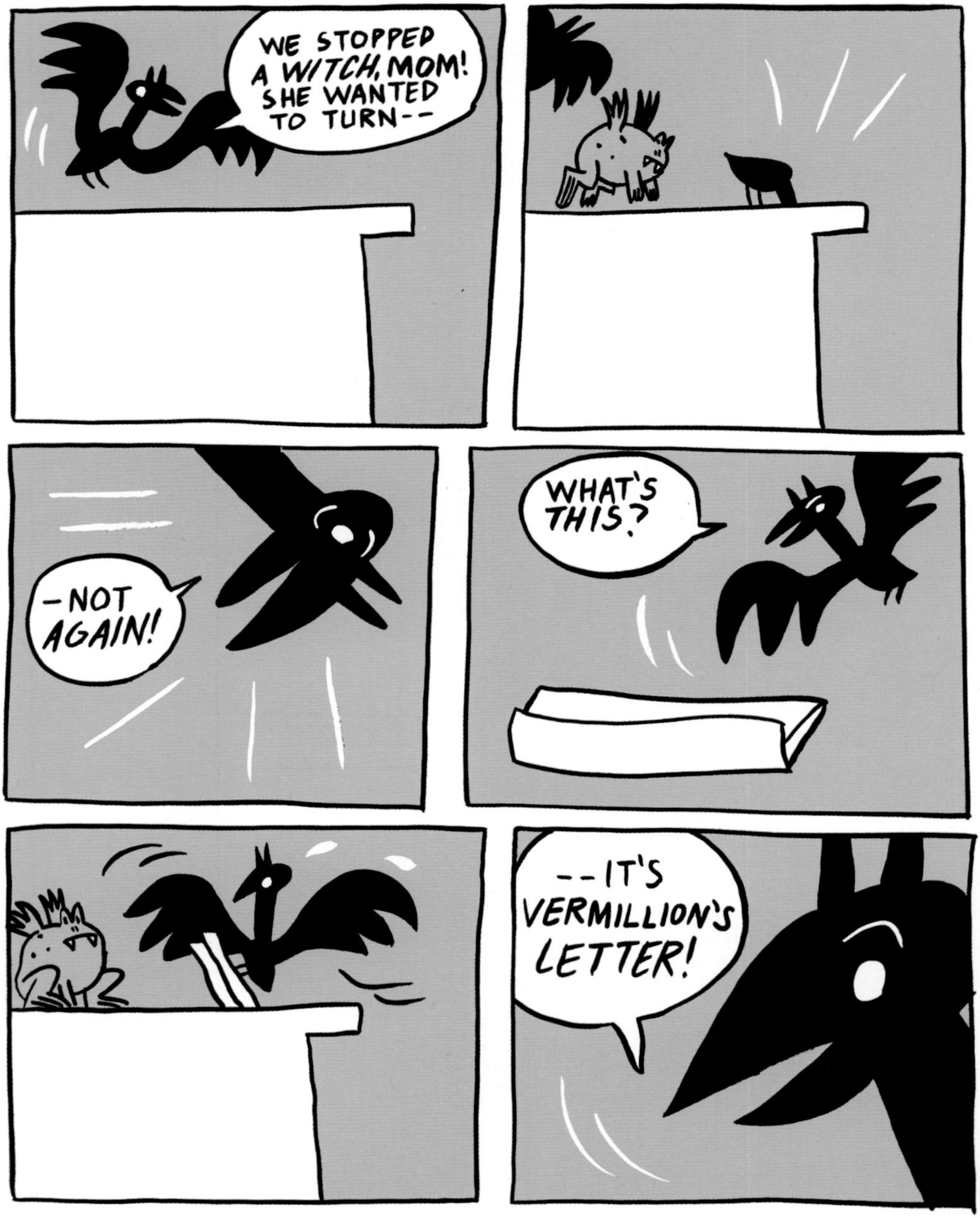
WE STOPPED A WITCH, MOM! SHE WANTED TO TURN--
-NOT AGAIN!
WHAT'S THIS?
--IT'S VERMILLION'S LETTER!

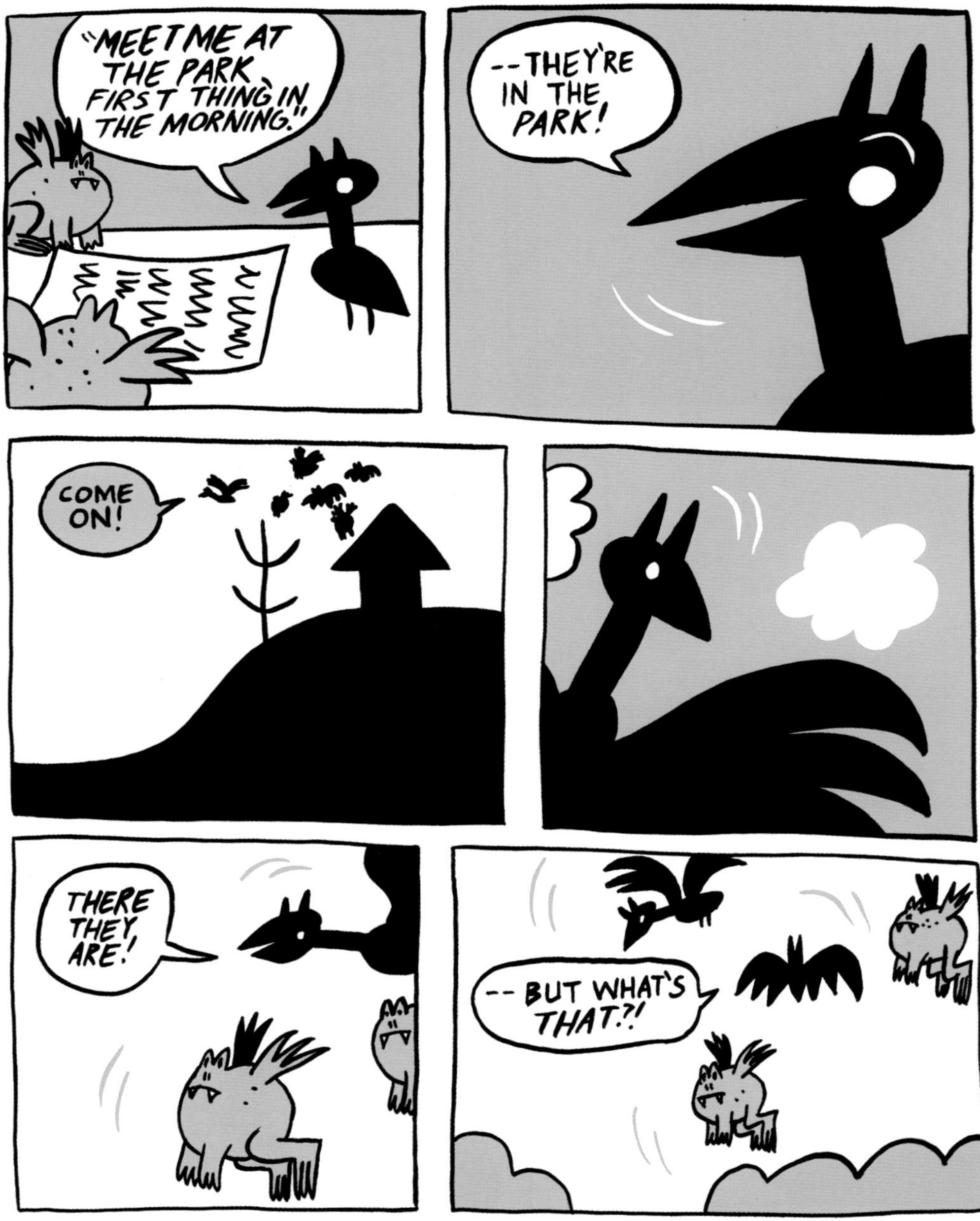
"MEET ME AT THE PARK, FIRST THING IN THE MORNING."
--THEY'RE IN THE PARK!
COME ON!
THERE THEY ARE!
--BUT WHAT'S THAT?!

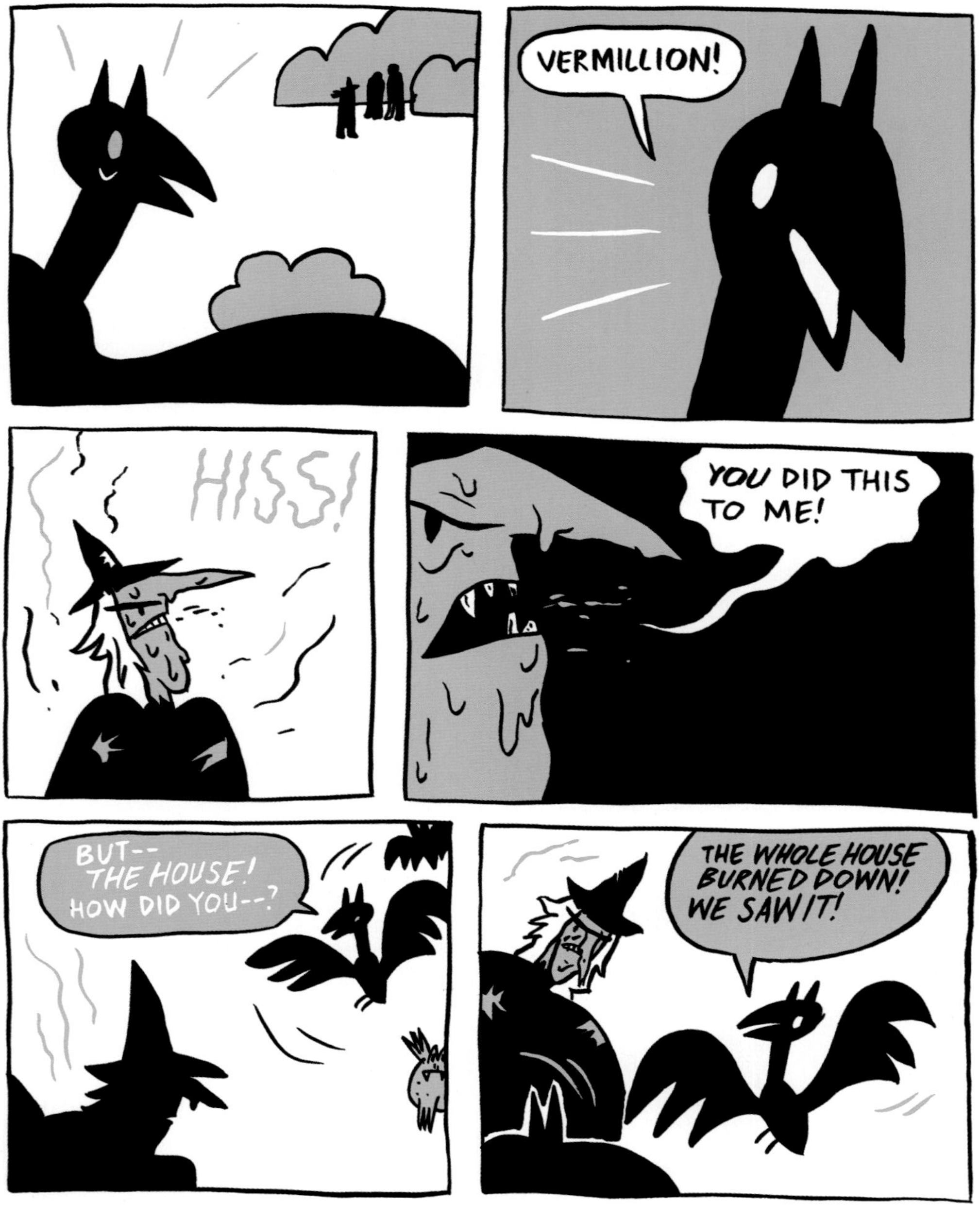
VERMILLION!
HISS!
YOU DID THIS TO ME!
BUT-- THE HOUSE! HOW DID YOU--?
THE WHOLE HOUSE BURNED DOWN! WE SAW IT!

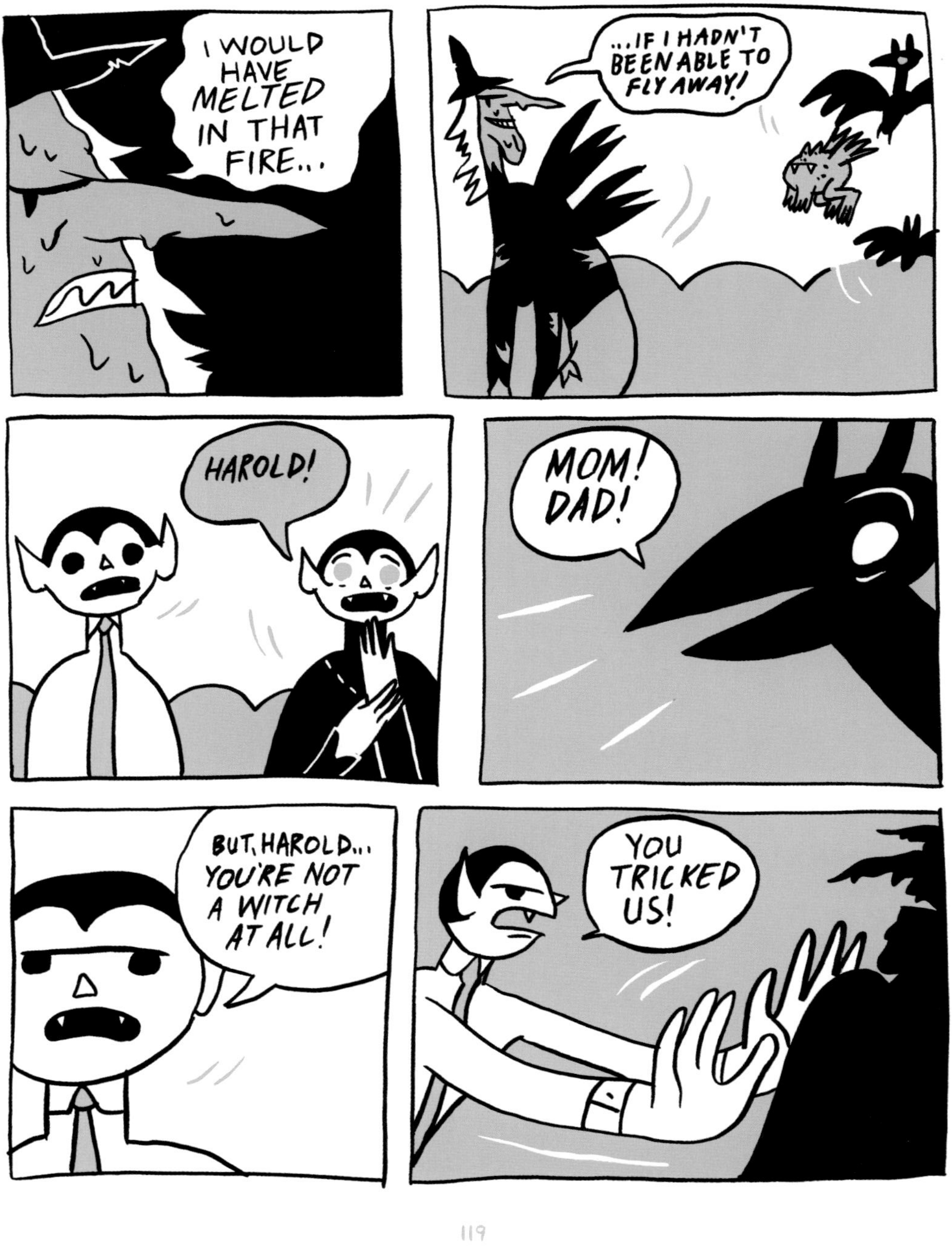

I WOULD HAVE MELTED IN THAT FIRE...
...IF I HADN'T BEEN ABLE TO FLY AWAY!
HAROLD!
MOM! DAD!
BUT, HAROLD... YOU'RE NOT A WITCH AT ALL!
YOU TRICKED US!

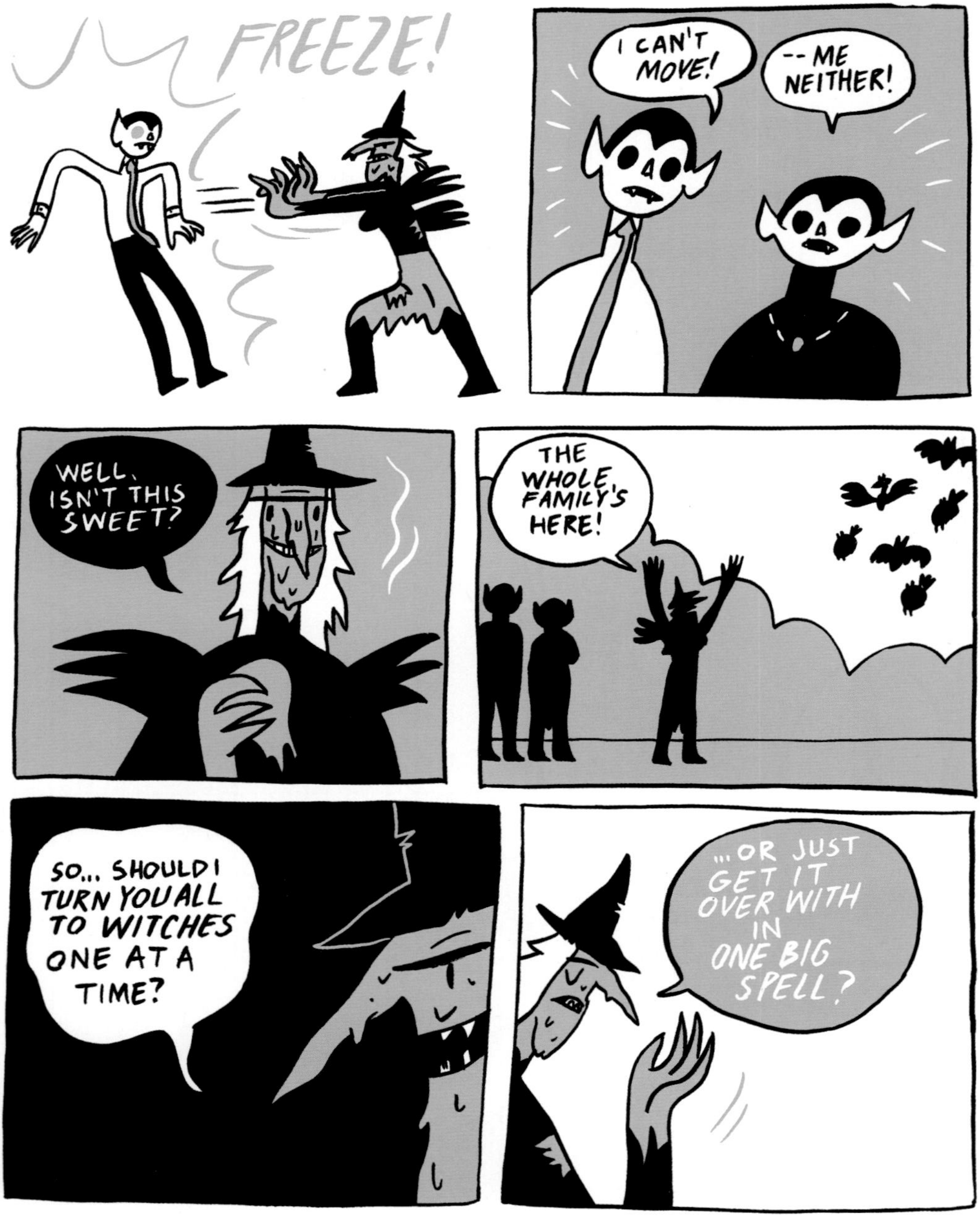
FREEZE!
I CAN'T MOVE!
--ME NEITHER!
WELL, ISN'T THIS SWEET?
THE WHOLE FAMILY'S HERE!
SO... SHOULD I TURN YOU ALL TO WITCHES ONE AT A TIME?
...OR JUST GET IT OVER WITH IN ONE BIG SPELL?

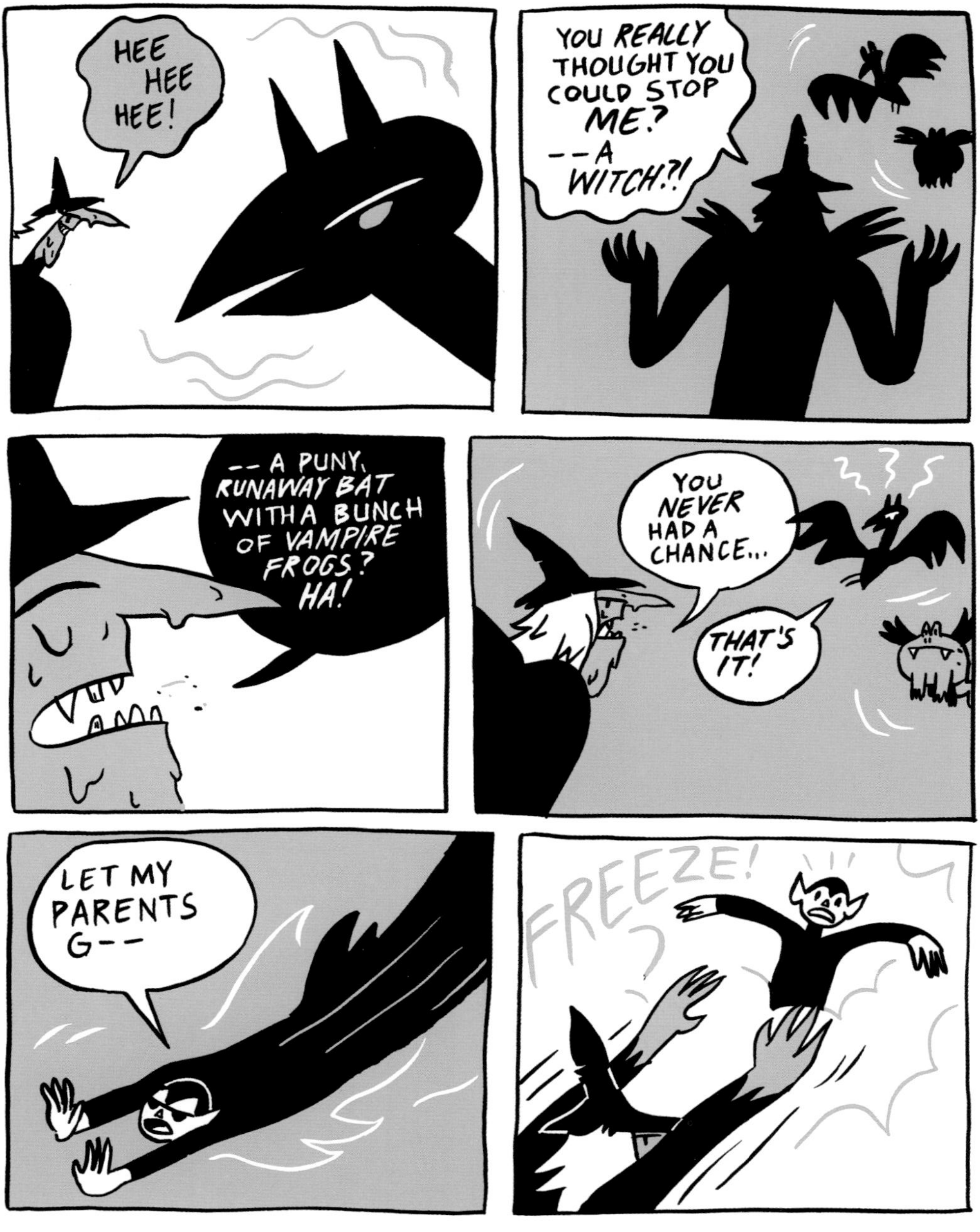
HEE HEE HEE!
YOU REALLY THOUGHT YOU COULD STOP ME? --A WITCH?!
-- A PUNY, RUNAWAY BAT WITH A BUNCH OF VAMPIRE FROGS? HA!
YOU NEVER HAD A CHANCE...
THAT'S IT!
LET MY PARENTS G--
FREEZE!

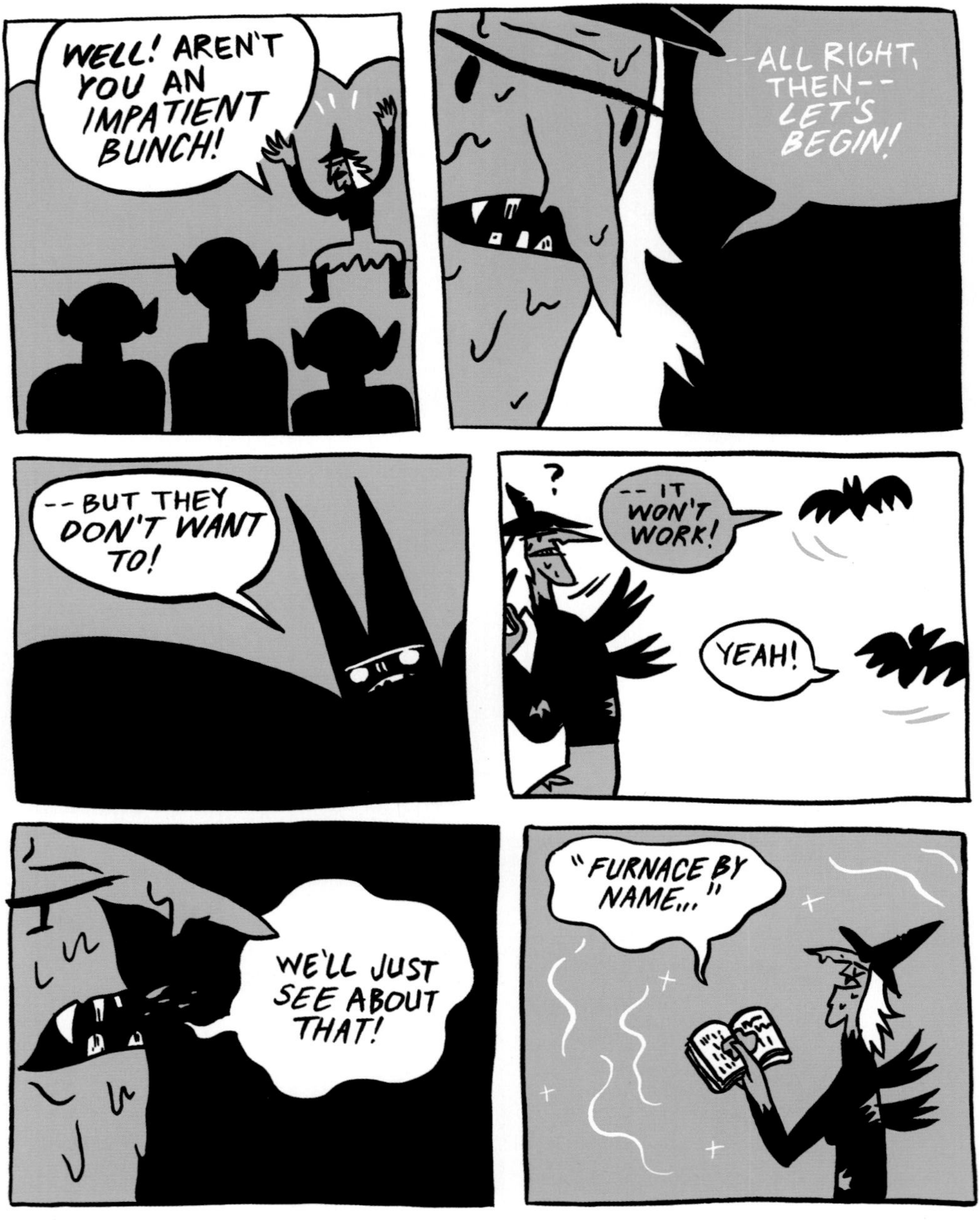
WELL! AREN'T YOU AN IMPATIENT BUNCH!
--ALL RIGHT, THEN--
LET'S BEGIN!
--BUT THEY DON'T WANT TO!
?
--IT WON'T WORK!
YEAH!
WE'LL JUST SEE ABOUT THAT!
"FURNACE BY NAME..."

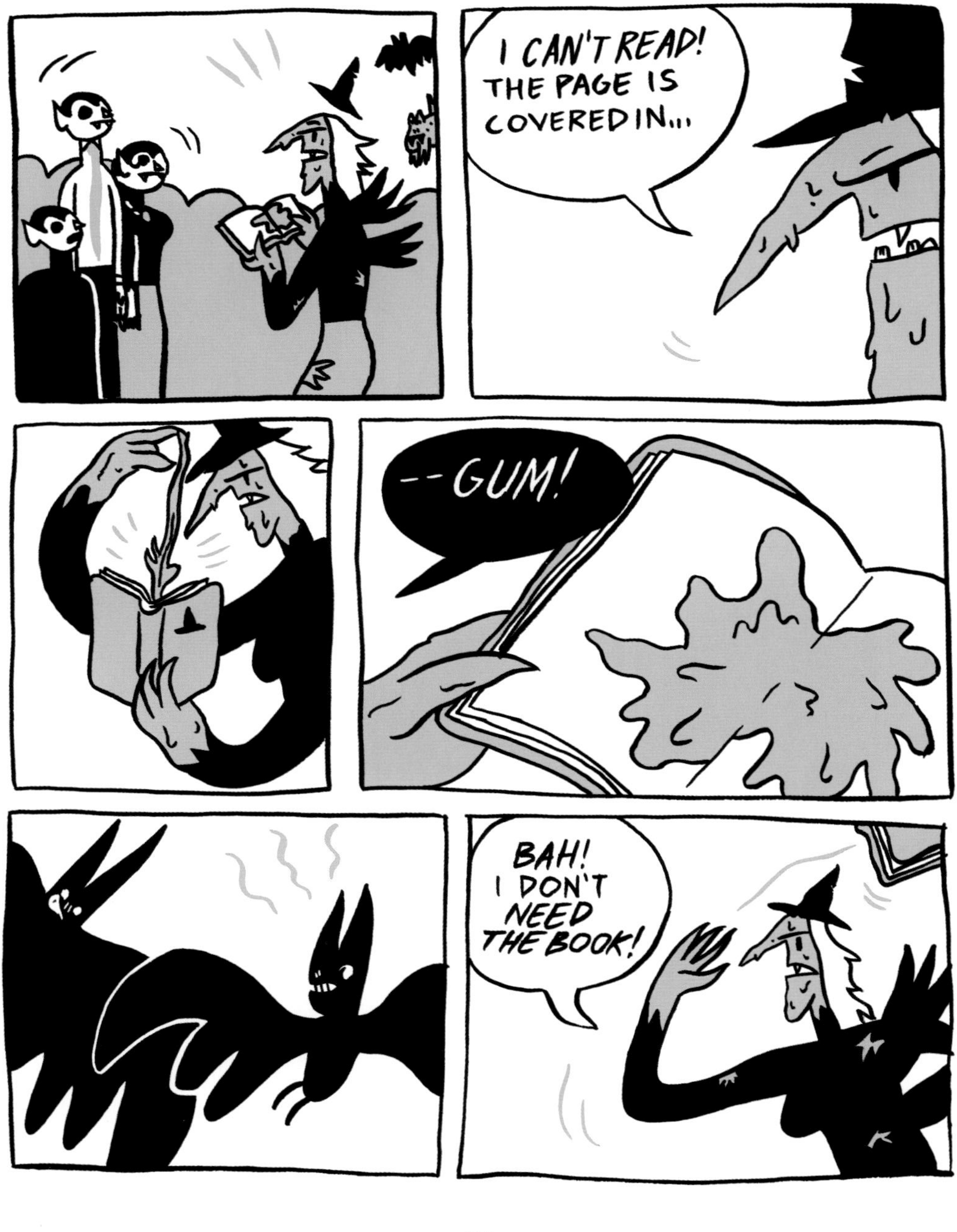
I CAN'T READ! THE PAGE IS COVERED IN...
--GUM!
BAH! I DON'T NEED THE BOOK!

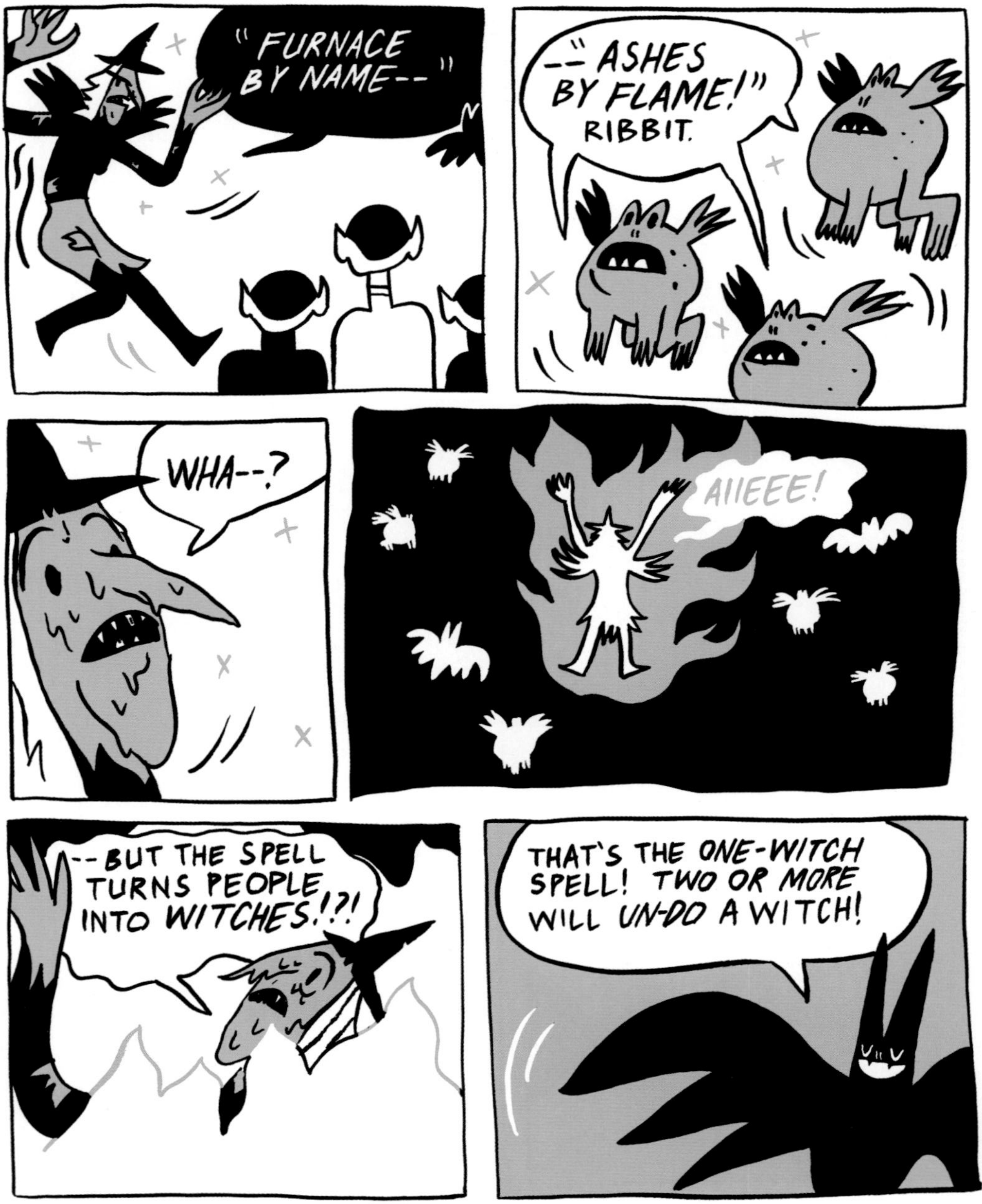
"FURNACE BY NAME--"
--"ASHES BY FLAME!"
RIBBIT.
WHA--?
AIIEEE!
--BUT THE SPELL TURNS PEOPLE INTO WITCHES!?!
THAT'S THE ONE-WITCH SPELL! TWO OR MORE WILL UN-DO A WITCH!

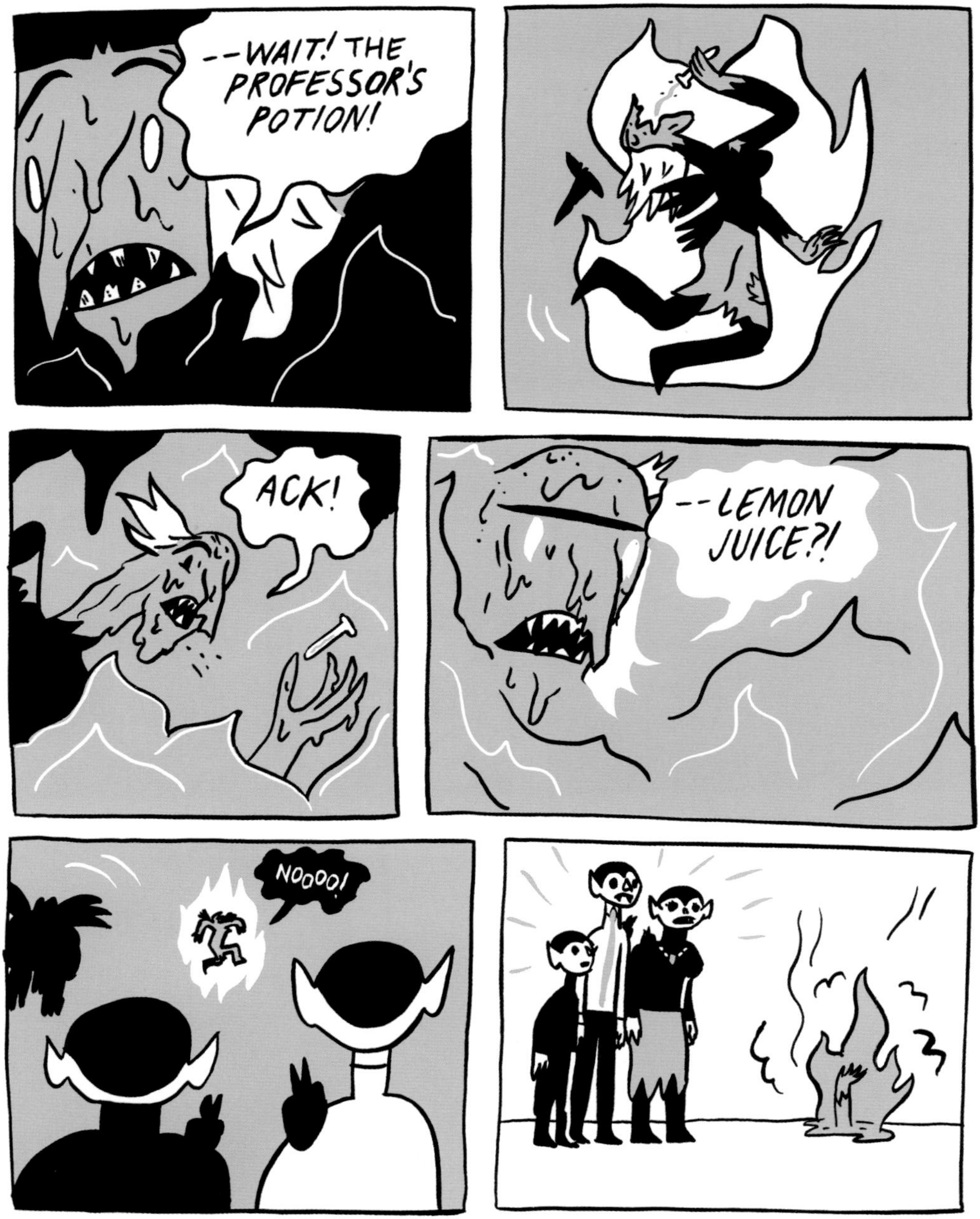
--WAIT! THE PROFESSOR'S POTION!
ACK!
--LEMON JUICE?!
NOOOO!

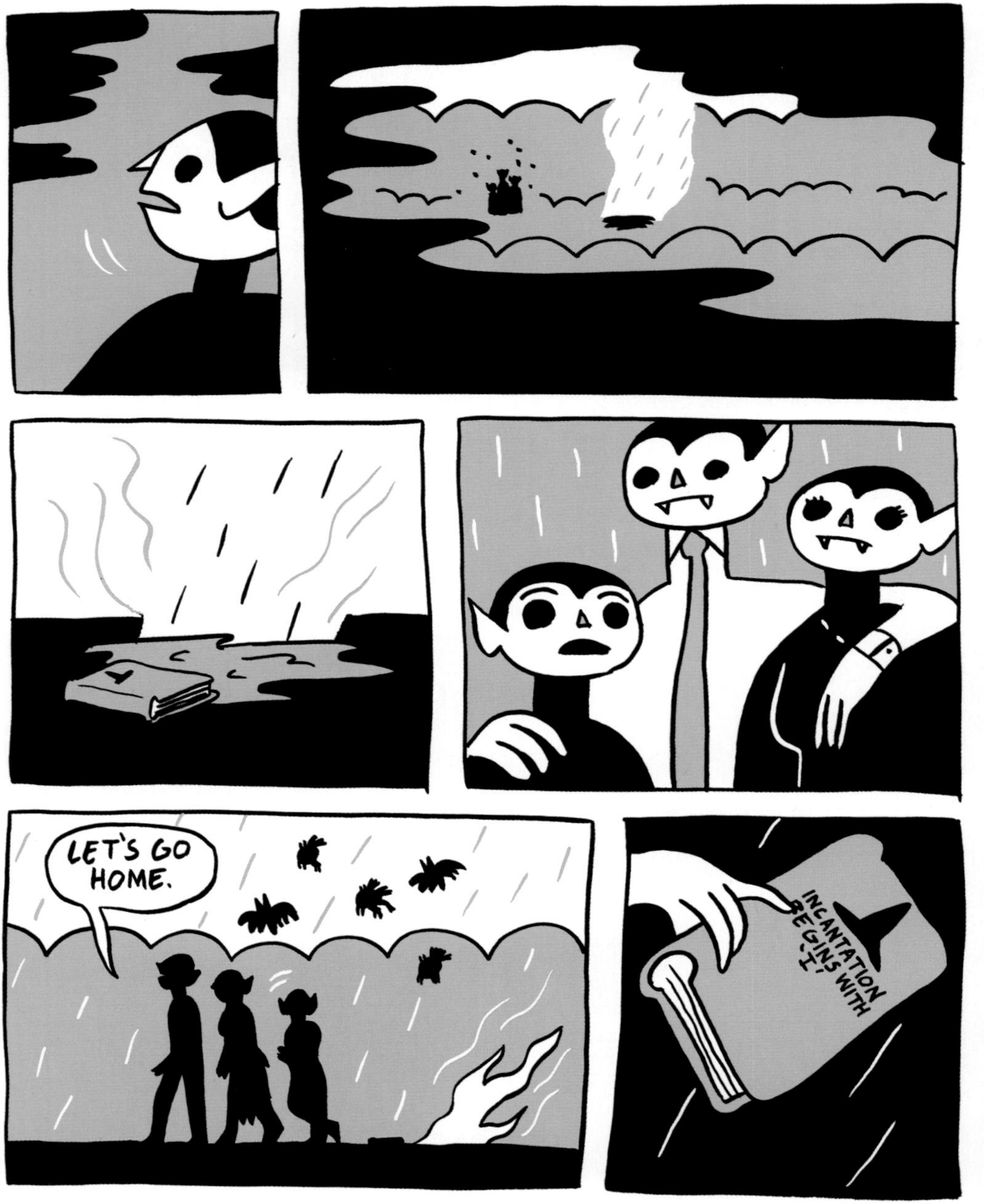
LET'S GO HOME.
INCANTATION BEGINS WITH 'I'

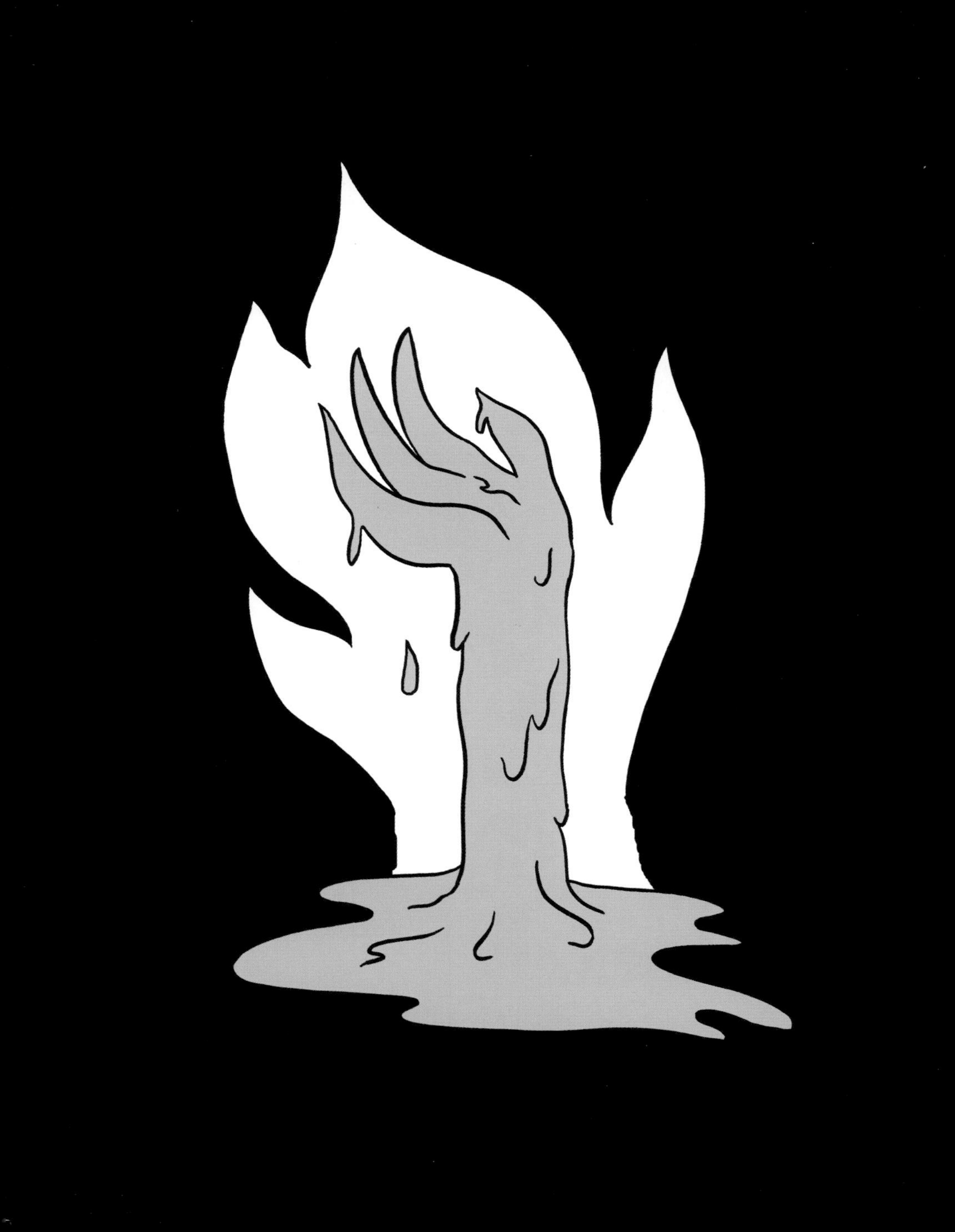

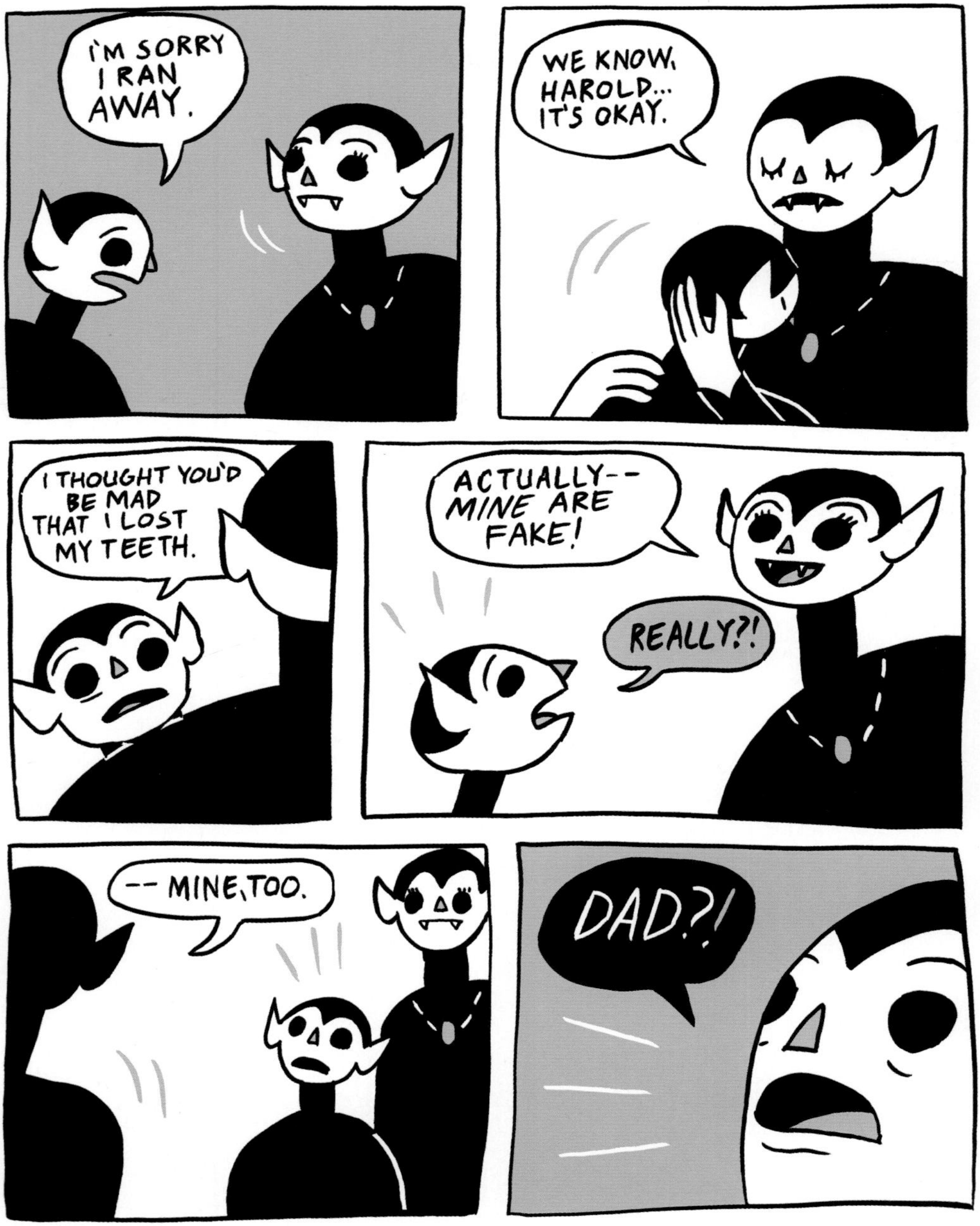
I'M SORRY I RAN AWAY.
WE KNOW, HAROLD... IT'S OKAY.
I THOUGHT YOU'D BE MAD THAT I LOST MY TEETH.
ACTUALLY-- MINE ARE FAKE!
REALLY?!
-- MINE, TOO.
DAD?!

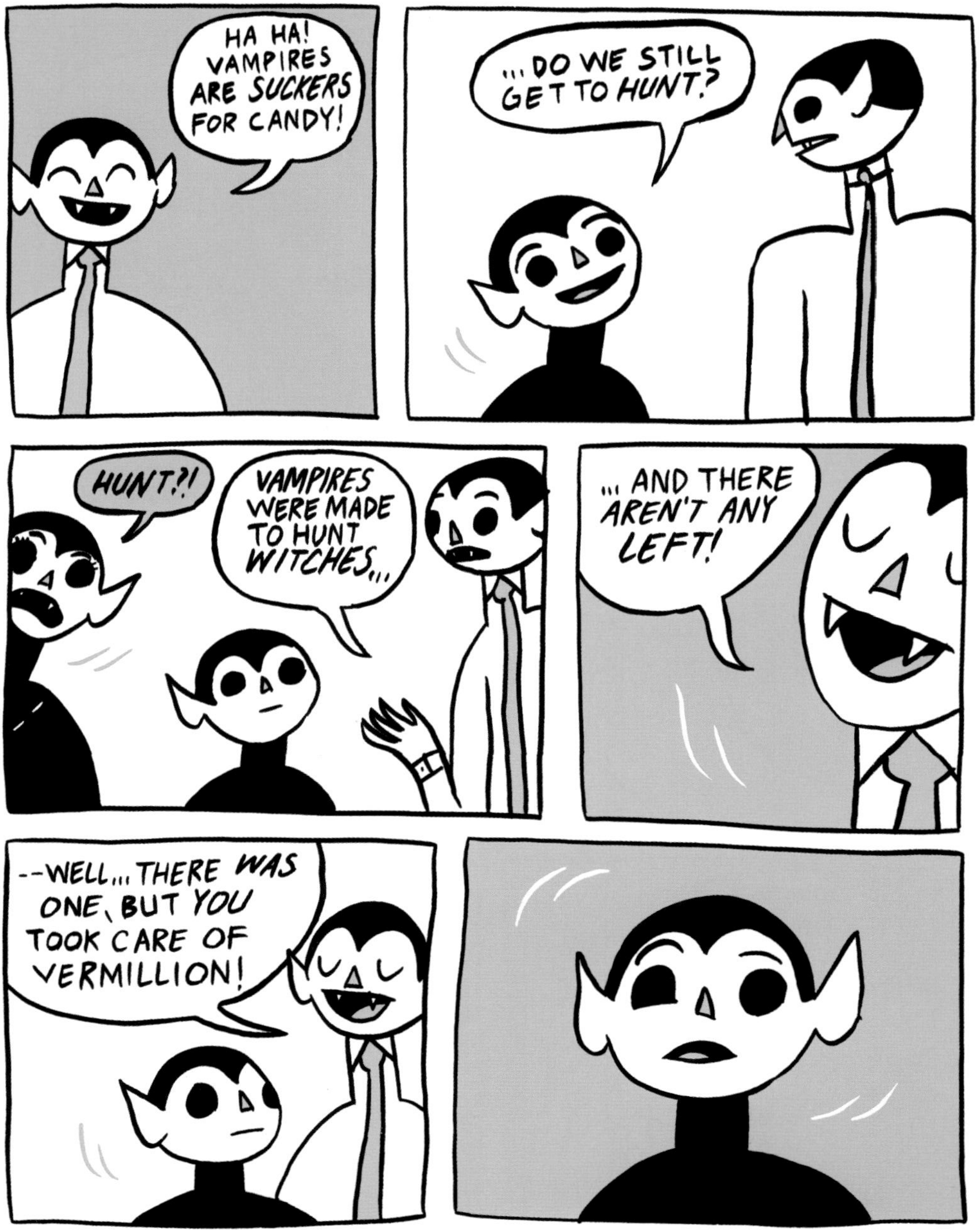
HA HA! VAMPIRES ARE SUCKERS FOR CANDY!
...DO WE STILL GET TO HUNT?
HUNT?!
VAMPIRES WERE MADE TO HUNT WITCHES...
...AND THERE AREN'T ANY LEFT!
--WELL...THERE WAS ONE, BUT YOU TOOK CARE OF VERMILLION!

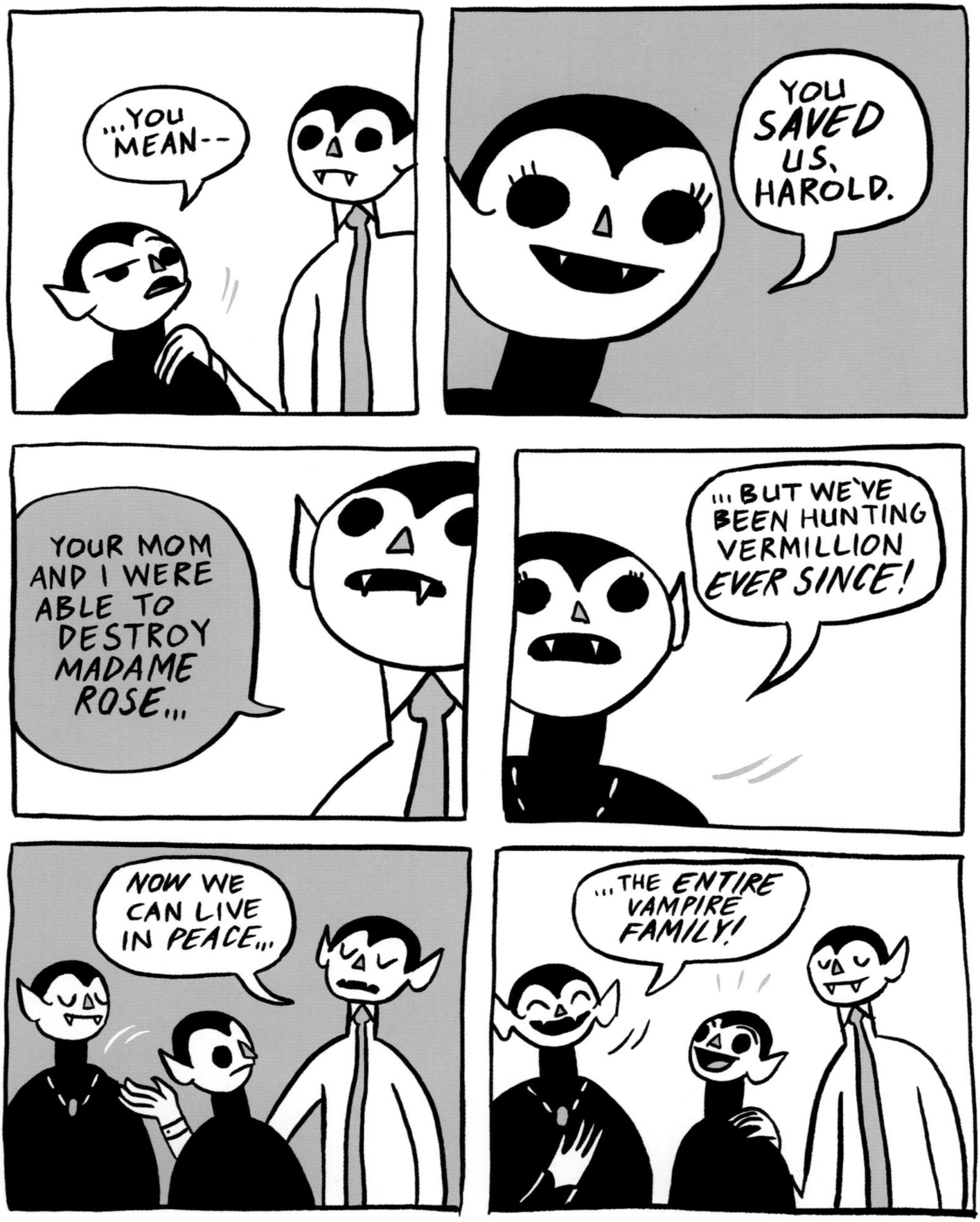
...YOU MEAN--
YOU SAVED US, HAROLD.
YOUR MOM AND I WERE ABLE TO DESTROY MADAME ROSE...
...BUT WE'VE BEEN HUNTING VERMILLION EVER SINCE!
NOW WE CAN LIVE IN PEACE...
...THE ENTIRE VAMPIRE FAMILY!

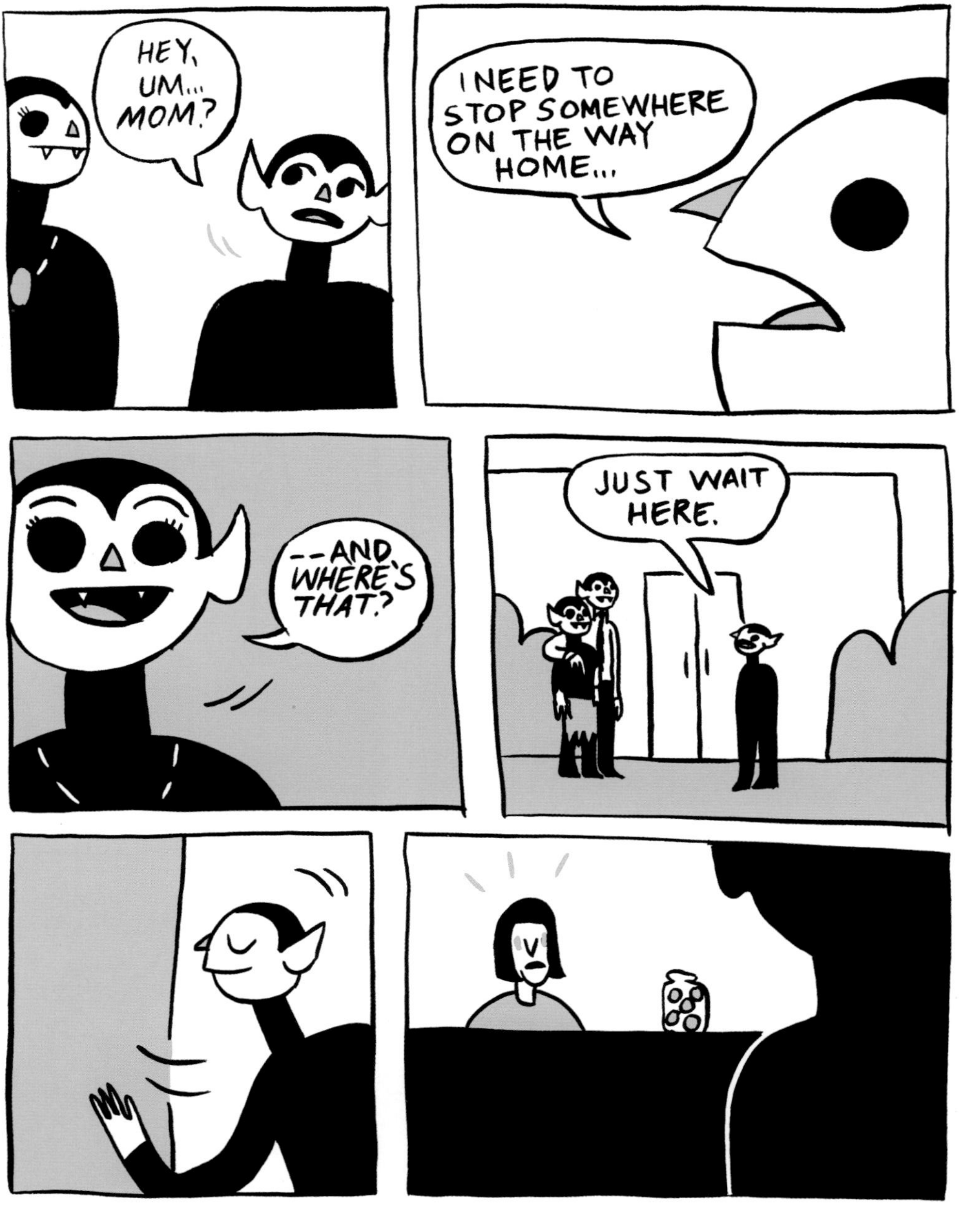
HEY, UM... MOM?
I NEED TO STOP SOMEWHERE ON THE WAY HOME...
--AND WHERE'S THAT?
JUST WAIT HERE.

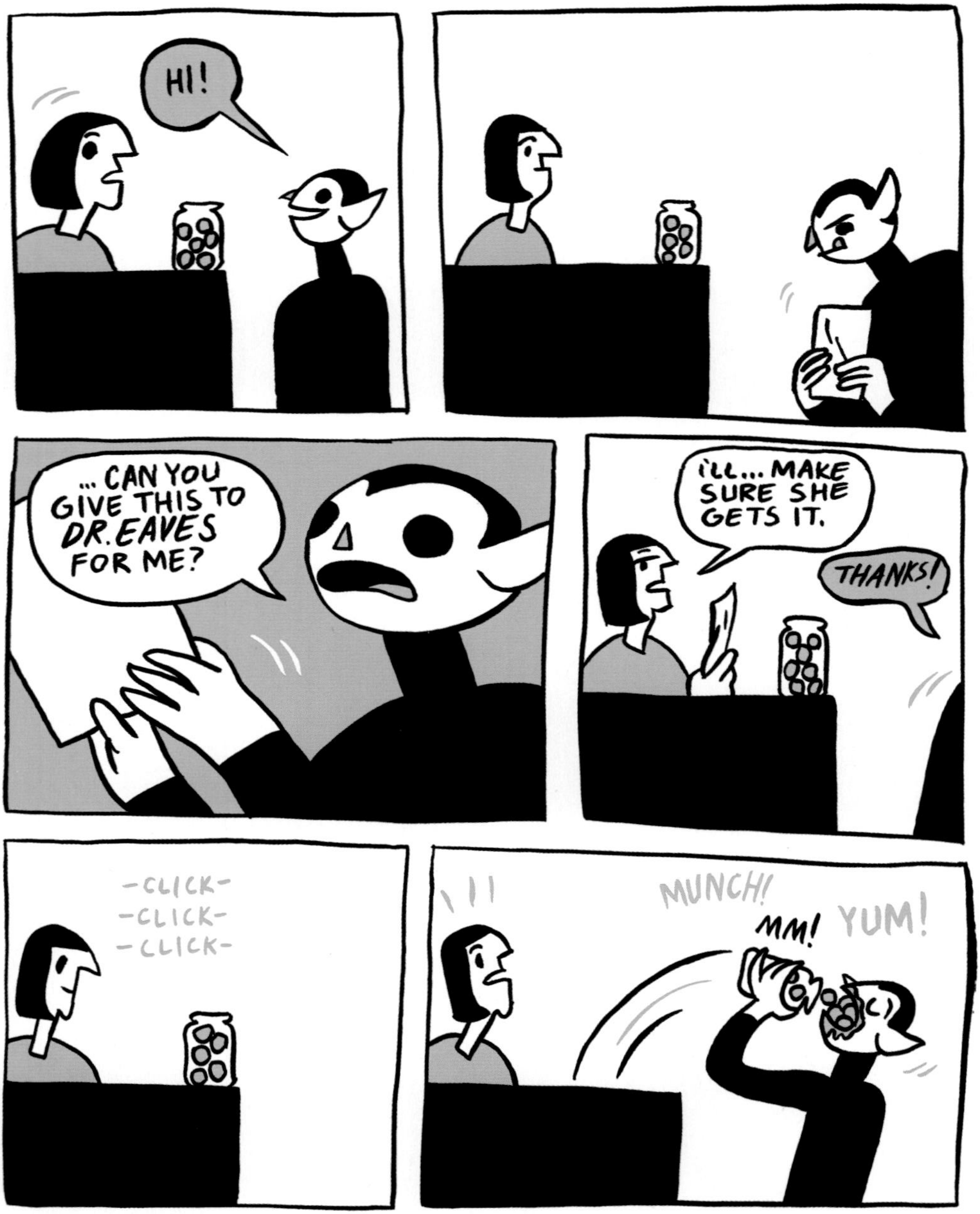
HI!
...CAN YOU GIVE THIS TO DR. EAVES FOR ME?
I'LL... MAKE SURE SHE GETS IT.
THANKS!
-CLICK-
-CLICK-
-CLICK-
MUNCH!
MM!
YUM!

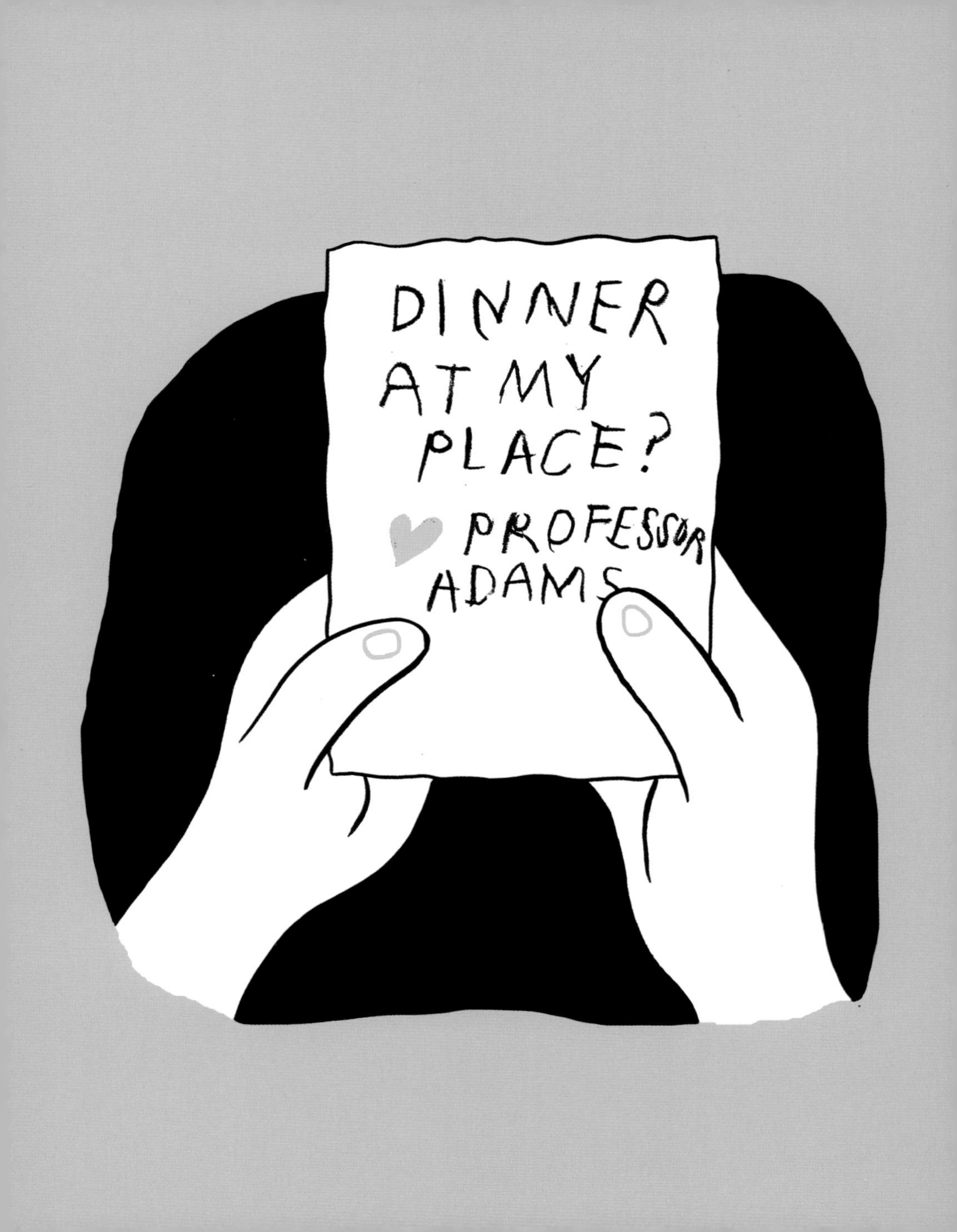
DINNER
AT MY
PLACE?
PROFESSOR
ADAMS

DING
DONG!

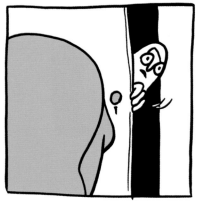

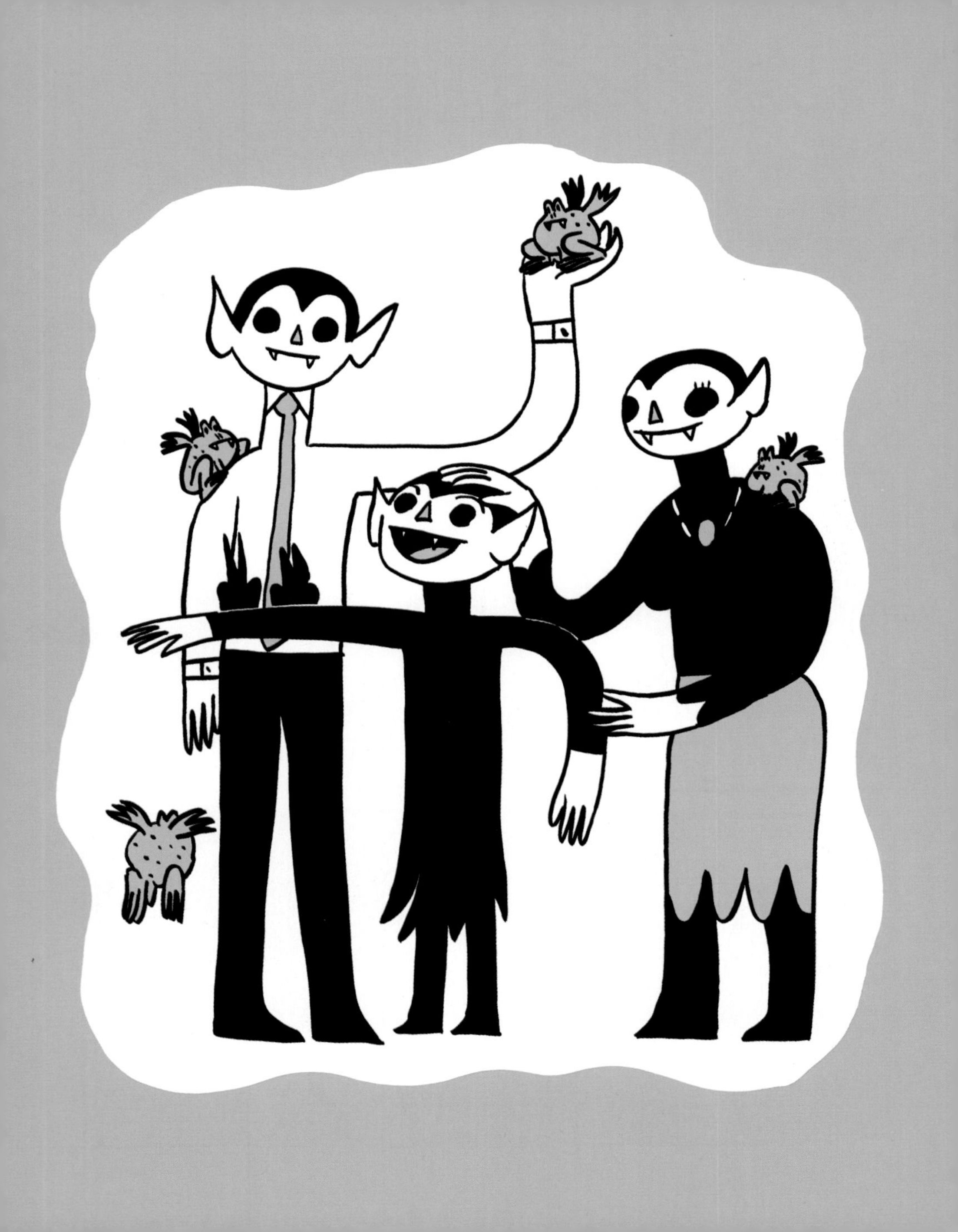

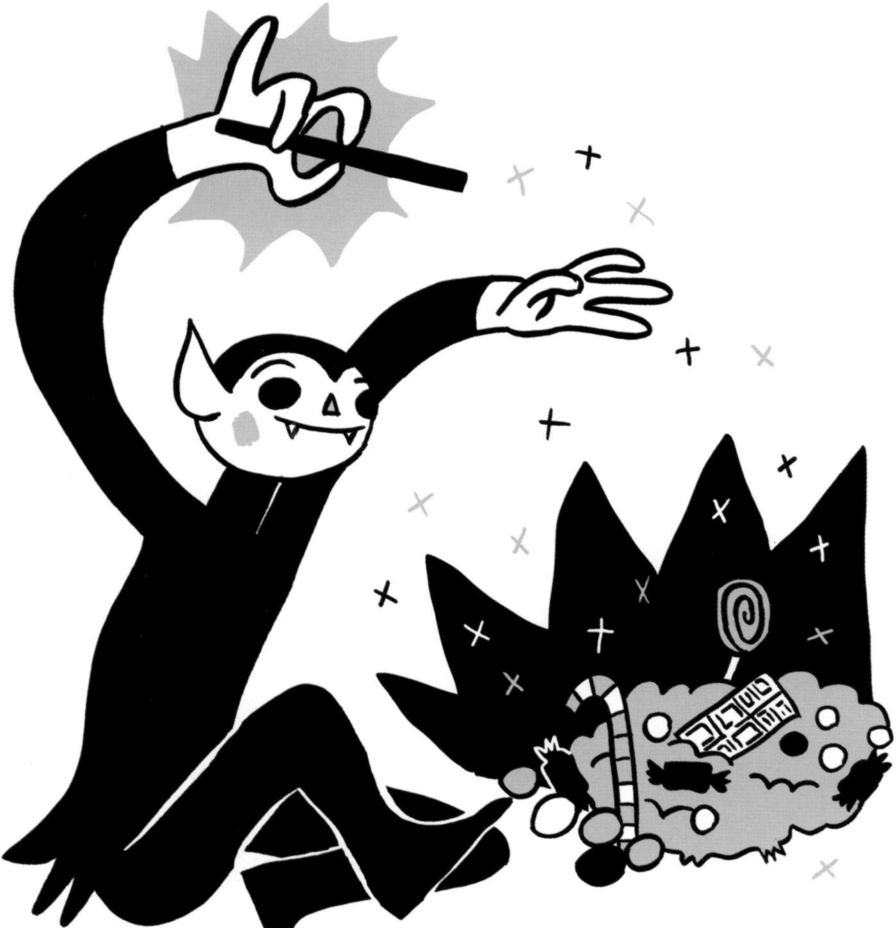

SKETCHES
for BOOK 2

*
*
*
*

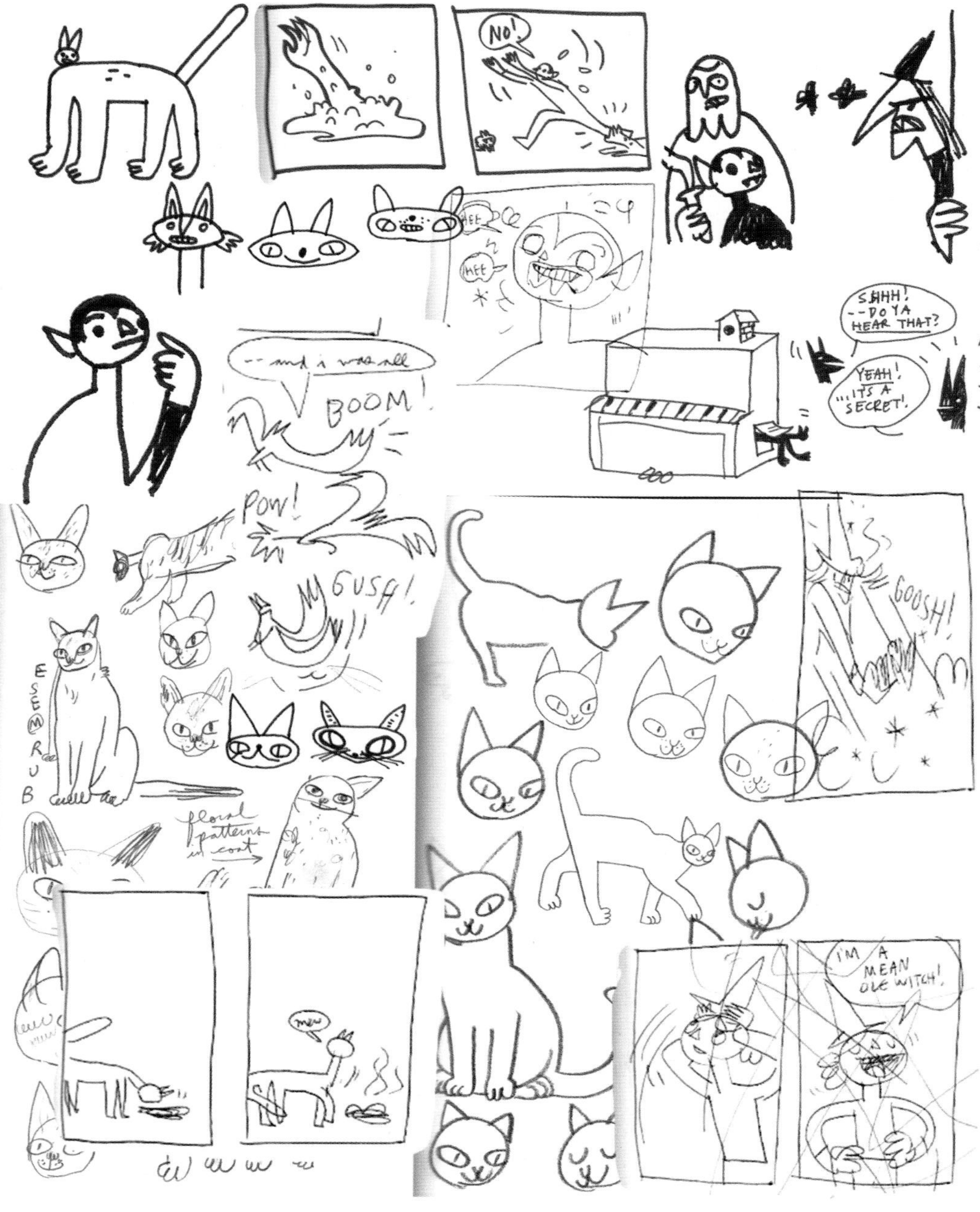
NO!
HEE
HEE
--and i was all
BOOM!
POW!
GUSH!
BURMESE
floral patterns in coat
mew
SHHH! --DO YA HEAR THAT?
YEAH! ...IT'S A SECRET!
GOOSH!
I'M A MEAN OLE WITCH!

UPSIDE DOWN
A HATFUL OF SPELLS

BY: JESS SMART SMELLY

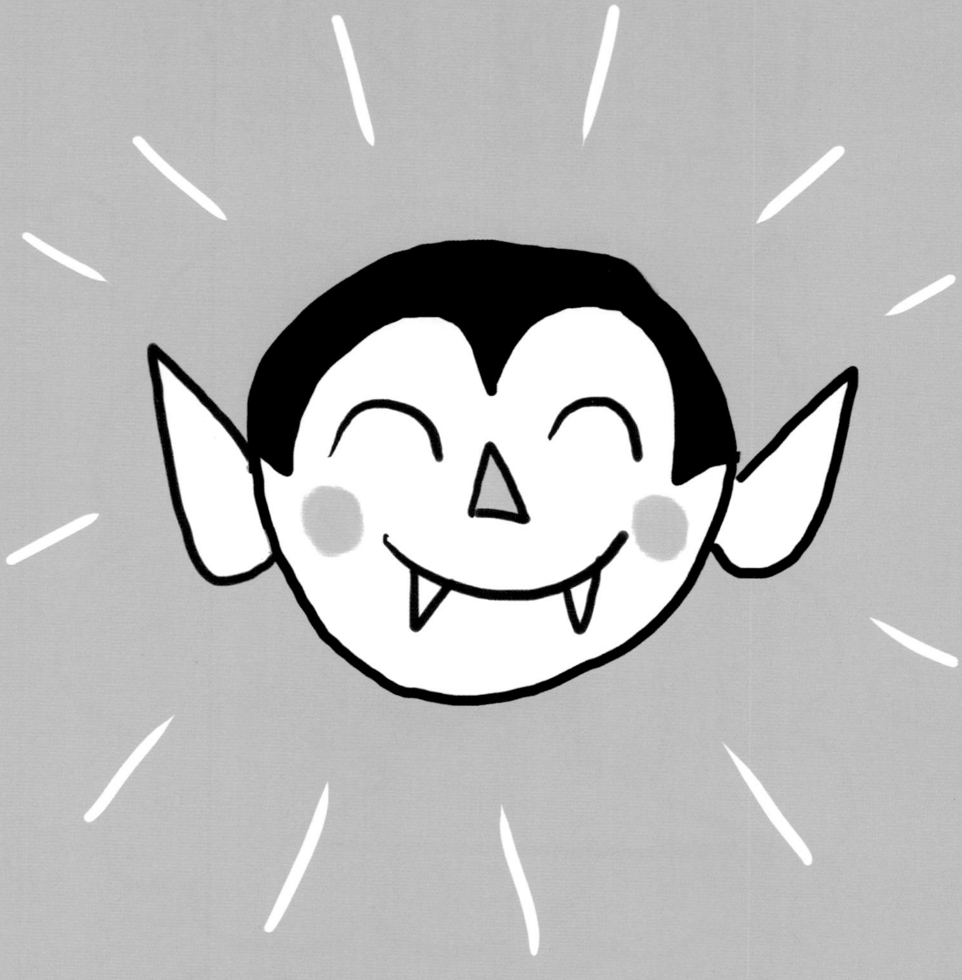

THANK YOU

* * *

MIKELLE, NOAH and EVELYN — FOR YOUR PATIENCE AND YOUR CONSTANT SUPPORT. IT'S YOU, AND IT'S ME, AND IT'S US.

CHRIS STAROS and BRETT WARNOCK — FOR TAKING A CHANCE WITH ME AND MY BOOK, AND HELPING ME LIVE OUT MY LIFELONG DREAM of WRITING and ILLUSTRATING MY OWN STORIES.

MOM, DAD, CONNIE, WAYNE, BOB and BARB — for TAKING MY DRAWINGS SERIOUSLY and for HELPING ME WHEN I'VE NEEDED IT MOST (and it's not over yet!).

THIS BOOK HAS BEEN A LONG TIME IN THE MAKING. WHILE IT ONLY TOOK A MATTER of MONTHS to WRITE, DRAW + COLOR, UPSIDE DOWN follows AN EMBARRASSINGLY LONG LIST of UNFINISHED STORIES, COMICS, and GRAPHIC NOVELS.

MY ONE and ONLY RESOLUTION for 2010 was to FINISH an ENTIRE GRAPHIC NOVEL, FROM BEGINNING to END — AND THAT'S JUST WHAT I DID.

I SET TIME ASIDE FROM FREELANCING as an ILLUSTRATOR and DESIGNER to WRITE and DRAW for UPSIDE DOWN, EVERY DAY. THE DRAWINGS WERE MADE with an AKASHIYA BRUSH PEN on STRATHMORE'S 11×14" SMOOTH BRISTOL BOARD, then SCANNED INTO the COMPUTER and COLORED in PHOTOSHOP.

I DREAMED ABOUT THE HALLOWEEN GREEN USED in THIS BOOK for MONTHS BEFORE FINDING JUST the RIGHT COLOR.